FIC 5.50

Published by
Larkspur Books
P.O. Box 31592
Phoenix, AZ 85046-1592

Library of Congress Cataloging-in-Publication Data

Evano, D.Charles (Dennis Charles), 1946-
Spirit messenger / by D. Charles Evano.
p. cm.
ISBN 0-9648507-0-2 (pbk.: alk. paper)
1. Indians of North America--Arizona--Fiction. 2. Navajo mythology--Fiction. 3. Navajo indians -- Fiction. I. Title.
PS3555. V2123S65 1995
813' .54--dc20 95-36218
CIP

Cover photograph of the Betatakin Ruins, Navajo National Monument, Arizona, by the Author, D. Charles Evano.

Although extreme care has been taken to make this novel as authentic and factual as possible, it is in no way intended to represent actual individuals, living or dead. It is a fictional work and, as such, I have taken creative license to invent all of the people and some of the places depicted in the story.

All representations in this book are made with the deepest respect for the Navajo people and their culture.

— D. Charles Evano

A note from the Author

Over the years I have traveled across the Navajo Nation, traversing it from Shiprock on its northeastern boundary in New Mexico, through Many Farms and Chinle, south to the Canyon De Chelly National Monument. Then trekking westward from Ganado over the scenic highway through Steamboat and Keams Canyon, and across the Hopi land back to Tuba City. Other times I have traveled northeast on Highway 160, visiting the Navajo National Monument, then proceeding north from Kayenta through Monument Valley to Mexican Hat, nestled in the southeast corner of Utah.

It is a land of tall sandstone buttes, red rock, vast mesas and isolated canyons, within the four sacred mountains where, according to the Navajo emergence story, the Holy People chose for The People, the Navajos, to live in harmony with nature. This is the place where The People are protected by the body of the god, Y'e'ii, who encompasses this land. While in the confines of the four sacred mountains, the Navajos believe they will be blessed with health and prosperity, averting the effects of bad spirits. Living outside of it, they believe they will run into difficulties.

While on the Navajos' sacred land, I have learned that the land and the people are one. I have never failed to be enamored by the vast beauty of its breathtaking vistas. And I have come to understand their great reverence for the Mother Earth. Among its many wonders, one can sense the essence of the land mingling with the spirit of a proud and enduring native people. It is there in the natural alcoves, within the sandstone walls of the canyons, that the ancient Anasazi made their home for centuries, then so abruptly disappeared. The Navajos have many myths and legends involving speculation on the fate of the Ancient Ones.

A great affinity for this land, and an affection for the People, whom I have come to know and respect, is clearly what has given me the inspiration to write this story. *Spirit Messenger* is the result of an arduous five year journey, involving research about the customs and religious beliefs of the Navajo people and their ancestors. It involved research about the Navajo tribal government, past and present, and the Native American Church, with the peyote ceremony that is used by its members. All of it has congealed into a unique story, painted on the pages in broad strokes, as large as the land and as great as the people that inspired it, personifying the mystical nature of the Great Southwest.

Based upon Navajo Indian folklore regarding a spirit messenger, and a cache of other myths and legends, I have creatively blended mystery, spirituality and science fiction, while evoking vivid images that are equally matched by its cast of richly imbued characters. They will lead you to an ancient Anasazi ruin, hidden deep within an alcove under the protection of a sandstone cliff in a remote canyon, where its timeless secrets have been guarded for seven hundred years. Three strangers will come together there, each of their own world, for a purpose only one of them knows. A startling secret will be revealed that will change the lives of two of them, forever!

—D. Charles Evano

CONTENTS

Daniel
A stranger who appears on the highway, he is the tall, lean hitchhiker with dark brown, graying, ruffled hair, and steeled, blue-gray eyes set into a vernal face. He is a man with a purpose, and a plan, who has traveled far to find his adversary, and the chosen who will help him. But foremost, he is a hunter! Those who meet him will never be the same again.

Zachary Thomas
A ruggedly handsome Navajo man, thirty-seven years of age, he is taller than average for a Navajo, standing nearly six feet, with a husky frame and deep set, dark eyes in a face with strong features and an impassive expression, surrounded by medium length, loosely kept, thick, lustrous black hair. Single, and considered a loner by those who know him, he is about to have his life changed, forever! He is the truck driver who gives the stranger a ride.

Jack McCloud
He is the flamboyant Tribal Council Chairman, who carries himself like a corporate C.E.O.. Impeccably groomed and self-assured, his august manner and raconteur of a good story is renowned in the tribal political arena, as well as outside the reservation, reaching national status. And the grip of his influence is felt in every corner of business and politics on the Navajo Nation. He is the boss. And he is a hunter, too! But he also has his well kept secrets. They are secrets that will bring him and the stranger into an inevitable confrontation to the death. And only his longtime friend and political ally, Police Superintendent Lemuel Redfeather, will know why!

Lemuel Redfeather
The Navajo Police Superintendent, who at age fifty-five is two years younger than his friend and political ally, Jack McCloud, whose degree in civil law, and former practice in tribal law, complemented his own accomplishments in criminal law. Together they made a powerful team, especially when Jack McCloud was running for the tribal council and Lemuel campaigned for him. Shortly after McCloud won his seat on the council, Lemuel Redfeather went from Police Sergeant to Superintendent by appointment over Captain Peter Morgan, who was favored for the promotion. A prodigious workaholic and a recovering alcoholic, the small, wiry, graying superintendent has an uncanny ability to read others as he scrutinizes them with calculating eyes. Above all, he relishes the hunt!

Captain Peter Morgan
A retired noncommissioned U.S. Army officer, he is constantly aware of the chain of command and procedure. He is Lemuel Redfeather's right hand, and he is neither bitter or arrogant about it. He is satisfied to do his job well, and

is comfortable in his niche. When he was passed over for the position of police superintendent, he accepted it gracefully, at least that's the way it appeared. And that is one of the things Lemuel Redfeather likes best about him. A quiet man, he seldom renders his opinion unless asked, and when he does, it has been well thought out. He is neat, thorough and professional, with an acute eye for details. At age forty-nine, he prides himself on his exceptional vigor and physical conditioning, getting up at dawn to run three miles every single day, regardless of the weather.

White Horse, the crystal gazer

Nearly sightless, the old sage is the one who Zachary Thomas believes can clarify the meaning of the stranger in his life, and the purpose for which he has come. In the privacy of his austere hogan, where Zachary has come to counsel, the white haired, ninety-three year old medicine man, with opaque eyes, tells the young Navajo something that startles him. He produces a gold coin similar to the one that the stranger has given Zachary. And he reveals to him the secret of the Holy Man.

Tracy Baldwin

She is a tall, slender, strikingly beautiful brunette with long chestnut tresses cascading down to the center of her back, and large, seductive, analytical dark eyes. An anthropologist and professor at Northern Arizona University, she prides herself on her knowledge of the Ancient Ones, the Anasazi, and her position among her peers. She has worked diligently since graduate school to attain status in the scientific community, and she guards her position with tenacious ardor. She guards it so well, that when Zachary Thomas tells her of the stranger and some secret knowledge he possesses regarding the Ancient Ones, she is willing to make a trek with him to the remote ruins to confront the stranger and his secret: only to be confronted with a secret of her own, one she had chosen to forget.

Sam Begay

The odious police sergeant who provokes the disdain of his superiors on a daily basis. He is short, rotund and sloppy, and he enjoys the fact that he can annoy Lemuel Redfeather and Peter Morgan at will. At fifty-seven, he appears to be a man well past his prime, and he carries himself like a man long past caring. In his mind he is a better cop than either of his superiors, although they are better educated, and he resents with bitterness their position of authority over him.

Spirit Messenger

by D. Charles Evano

A Larkspur Book
published in Phoenix, Arizona
U.S.A.

Dedicated to Mitzi,
for her unwavering loyalty
and support.
And to the loving memory
of my niece and godchild,
Julie Pullo.

Do not go where the path may lead,
Go instead where there is no path
and leave a trail.

— Emerson

Prologue

ABOUT 1200 A.D. A STRANGER APPEARED IN THE DOORWAY OF light on the canyon floor. The Ancient Ones were startled, as they viewed him from the distant safety of cover. But it was due to their spiritual beliefs and the wisdom of their counsel that they welcomed him as their Spirit Messenger from the "heavens of fire."

They guided him to their village, built into a sandstone alcove in the wall of the canyon. It was there that they gave him refuge among them in their ledge houses, and treated him as a deity. It was because these were spiritual people, that they believed his arrival was a good omen.

The stranger saw that these fine, gentle and intelligent people lived in harmony with the land. Taking only what they needed from the earth, they treated it with reverence, and they prospered in this verdant valley. They farmed the fertile bottom land, growing such crops as corn, squash and beans, storing some away in their graineries for the winter months. And they were skillful hunters, too. The stranger admired them for their ability, for he was also a hunter!

Learning their language and their customs, the stranger communicated with them, and he came to view them with affection. He saw that they were a peaceful people and he trusted them. After a time, he wished to give them a gift. He wished to share some of his knowledge with them.

Gathering the elders together in the kiva, he showed them the gateway to other worlds. He taught them how to use it. And he cautioned them not to let it fall into the wrong hands. He gave them a map to guide them, so that they could come and go as they wished.

Others came to the village from the south to trade with the Ancient Ones. They brought such things as cotton and turquoise. And they were curious about the stranger. Around the fire in the kiva at night, he shared the secrets of the stars with them. He taught them well. They bestowed him with gifts of appreciation, and considered him as one of their own.

Then the traders returned to their villages in the south, and soon more came in their place. They brought with them rumors of a prophecy regarding a strange, powerful half-man, half-god Quetzalcoatl, the fallen prince of the Toltec Nation, who was predicted to return from the east and reclaim his empire from Moctezuma, the great Aztec ruler, taking him down and re-establishing himself as Ruler of the World. When he heard this, the stranger grew concerned for the safety of the Ancient Ones. So he told them how to escape from this world, if the need arose.

Soon after, a day came when an eagle circled above the village. It passed over three times, and he interpreted this as an augury signaling his departure. Gathering with the elders for the last time to bid them farewell, he thanked them for their hospitality. He gave them a message about the future--and a warning!

The people had grown to love him. They implored him to stay. But it was time for him to leave. He embraced one and all of them that came to him on that day, wishing them all blessings of health and prosperity, until the very last of them had bid him farewell. Then the Medicine Man came to him, embracing him with tear-filled eyes, sorrowful at their parting.

Placing a gold coin in the hand of the Medicine Man, he told him it was a token of friendship, and that it also held a secret that someday men would understand.

Before his departure, he told them to watch for his return.

Chapter 1

Arrival of Suspicion

IT WAS OCTOBER.

At dawn, a chilled wind swept dust up off the high desert floor. It churned dust devils in its path. The wind moaned wicked through the red rock country, like a lonely sentinel. It was that semiarid smell that pervaded the air, the indigenous odor one encounters in such places, like that of pungent soil and tender grasses decaying and mingling their essence. It was an indication to the sentient observer that this land had a life and breath of its own.

Twilight of early morning had cast new shadows upon the land. The shadow of a tall, lean, lonely figure emerged beside a barren highway. It was a highway that shrank below the horizon in either direction, long and distant.

He traversed the wash that skirted the roadbed. Then he pulled himself up alongside the embankment, climbing, while he shuffled for footing in the loose soil. Cresting the embankment, he straightened himself. He stood solidly on the shoulder of the road. Peering around in all directions, he gauged his surroundings and his proximity to them. It was the nature of this country to appear boundless.

After a few moments of deliberation, he strode west along Highway 160. It sliced through the belly of the Navajo Nation in northeastern Arizona. It was west of Kayenta, near Marsh Pass in the Four Corners Country. Barbed wire fence stretched the length of the highway on either side. Sheep grazed on the range to the north. This land had never been verdant enough to support large herds of cattle, with the exception of some northerly climes.

While he walked, the wind blew granules of pale earth up and around his heavy boots with each step. The sun stood above the horizon to his back. It cast an orange hue on the landscape. The bright tableland reflected the early morning light. It appeared to glow like warm embers. The sky ahead of him was rapidly changing from a dim gray to a lucid blue.

A long tractor-trailer rig sped by him, creating a vacuum and a burst of icy wind that snapped in his face. He paused for a moment to look about. His large hands were tucked in the pockets of a heavy, blue denim jacket. Taking them out, he reached back over his shoulders. He pulled up the brown corduroy collar of his jacket, covering his neck. Then he straightened the black cap he wore on his head, that covered his dark brown, mottled gray hair. His hair appeared shaggy, jutting over the tops of his ears, and down on his nape over his shirt collar.

He walked at least another mile. From behind, the whir of a steadily approaching vehicle could be heard. It came nearer, then it slowed as it sounded its horn. The sound of crunching gravel and applied brakes shattered the crisp air. A dirty, faded gray, conventional Peterbilt tractor with a sleeper, pulling a full cattle trailer, ambled to a halt beside him. The diesel engine rumbled, vibrating the ground where he walked.

Stopping in his tracks, he turned reflexively to face the passenger side of the truck. Condensation on the window obscured his view of the driver. The window came down by inches, until it revealed a stoically chiseled, bronzed face with dark brown evaluating eyes, outlined by medium length, coal black hair.

"Hey, you need a ride?" A strong, dialectic voice inquired of the man.

He assessed the offer for a moment. "Sure," he answered impassively.

The Indian unlatched the door, cocking it open for the stranger. He strode the few feet to the side of the truck. The driver withdrew from the open door, leaving room for the man to get inside. Grasping the handle, he swung it full open. He came eye to eye with the Indian.

"Get in!" The Indian gestured with his right hand, while he rapidly assessed the looks of the stranger. Straight-on his face was vernal, revealing little of his age. He had a smooth, clean shaven face. The man's eyes peered back a piercing, steeled blue.

Pulling himself up with the handle above him on the outside of the cab, he got into the truck. He reached out to pull the door closed. The Indian glanced into his rear-view-mirror while he accelerated. Increasing the R.P.M.'s, the engine reverberated as he shifted gears. He eased back onto the pavement with his broad hands bracing the wheel.

"How far ya goin'?" The Indian stole a glance at him, then he double clutched. The rig lunged mildly as it pulled into the next gear.

He was hesitant. "To the next sizeable town, I guess. Wherever I can get some work! Where are *you* going?" He spoke in a distinctive tone. The stranger peered straight ahead, never diverting his attention while he talked.

"I've got these cattle to deliver. I'm takin'em to Flagstaff. It's a good size town, maybe you can find somethin' there?" The Indian suggested. His taciturn manner ebbed. "I'm Zachary, Zachary Thomas!" He said, hinting of a Christian influence. What is your name?" Producing a half-smile, the Indian offered his hand.

Sensing his friendliness, the stranger responded. "Call me Daniel," he said, with a slender smile breaking across his lips. He took the Indian's hand with a firm grip, judging the strength of the man.

"Okay, Daniel! What kind a work you lookin' for?"

"I can do most anything. Mostly I've done odd jobs, handyman work. Whatever I can get!" His eyes measured the Indian. "What tribe are you?"

"I'm Navajo!" The Indian reached for the dashboard with one hand on the wheel. He turned down the heater. "Gettin' a little warm in here!" He paused, considering the stranger. "You're not from around here?"

"Farther north," he answered flatly.

"Colorado? Utah?" The Indian asked.

"Yes, Colorado," the stranger answered, with an accent of concealment, he offered nothing more.

The Navajo pulled a pouch of Red Man chewing tobacco from the side pocket of his frayed, khaki jacket. With the pouch in his lap, he unrolled the top and spread it open with one hand. He took a pinch between his fingers and stuffed it into his mouth, behind his cheek next to his jawbone. The side of his face bulged as he rolled the tobacco in his cheek with his tongue. Then he gestured with the pouch toward the stranger, offering him some of it.

Declining, the stranger shook his head to that affect. A dog barked in a gruff, piercing tone. The sound startled him. He turned his attention to the sleeper compartment behind him. A pair of sullen eyes, embedded in a broad skull, attached to a hulk of canine flesh, stared him down from behind the partially opened curtain that separated the sleeper from the cab.

"That's *-Tsoh!* That's Navajo for big! I just call him Big!" The wet nose and golden brown muzzle receded from the opening. Big's body slumped to the bed with a thud. The Indian chuckled, his face broadened with a smile.

The sixty-six miles from Kayenta to Tuba City were long miles. They were marked by open range, cutting arroyos, buttes and distant mesas. The fences followed the terrain, cresting and dipping between sandstone buttes and over small gorges. They were quiet miles, miles that the Indian had traveled countless times alone.

"That's Cow Springs," the Navajo said, as a matter of fact. He nodded toward the north. The stranger glanced to his right.

"You're not in any trouble are you?" The Indian inquired only half-jokingly.

"No, no trouble," he replied, shaking his head slightly to confirm his denial. His voice modulated almost imperceptibly.

Hitting a pothole, the truck bounced. It jarred the cattle, causing them to shuffle about in the back of the truck. Zachary looked back in his mirror to see that everything was secure. Then he reached forward for a styrofoam coffee cup that was on the dashboard. Drawing it to his lower lip, he spat in it. "Nasty habit," he mumbled, while he placed the cup up on the dash against the windshield. The stranger peered at him curiously.

Zachary caught a glimpse of the clock on the instrument panel. "It's almost seven thirty, friend! I'm gettin' kind a hungry. How about you?"

Stroking his chin with the back of his hand, the stranger considered when he had last eaten. "Yes, I could use a bite to eat." His alert eyes glanced about measuring the landscape. "I could use some coffee, too!"

"I know a nice little truckstop! It's just outside Tuba City, about half an hour from here. They make a great Navajo taco! And the coffee's strong enough to black your tires!" The Indian smiled wide, his eyes danced with laughter. He reached for the coffee cup on the dashboard, brought it near his chin, and spat again. Then he snatched the drool from his chin.

The rig rolled into a parking lot paved with crushed reddish-brown cinders. Small pools of water, and patches of soft mud, stood where recent rains had flooded the lot. The truckstop consisted of a long, brown, corrugated metal building, with eight repair stalls facing the west at a right angle to the highway, most of it in need of repairs itself. There were several diesel fuel pumps in front of the stalls, and ample parking for as many as twenty-five or thirty rigs.

The only truckstop between Flagstaff and the New Mexico and Colorado borders, it got more than its share of business. A wealthy Navajo rancher, and businessman, owned it. He was aware that he had a monopoly on the trucking that crossed the reservation, and he saw no need to keep up appearances.

A smaller frame structure, attached to the front of it, housed the truckstop restaurant. Zachary drove the truck up to the front of the Highway Cafe. He parked it diagonally to the building, in line with several other rigs. Directly in front of them was a wall of picture windows. The windows faced the highway and the open range to the north. A mansard overhang, covered with weathered cedar shake shingles, extended around the perimeter of the roof on the three exposed sides of the cafe.

They could see through the glass that the restaurant was busy. Zachary opened his door, leaned out, then with a flick of his finger, he ejected the chew from his mouth. He let it drop to the ground.

"Come on, let's go inside," the Indian said, bounding out of the truck. He slammed his door shut.

The stranger got out. He stood beside the truck for a moment, focusing his eyes in the bright sunlight. Then he straightened his cap, pulling it down in the back with his left hand, while he adjusted the brim in the front with his right hand, his eyes scanned the section of flat, open range to the north.

While the Indian sauntered along the side of the truck, he checked the cattle. He peered through the opening between the metal slats of the trailer. One of the steers appeared to have been injured. It had a nasty gash behind its right front shoulder. He measured it with his eyes, judging it to be about five or six inches long. The blood was running down its shoulder, behind the upper portion of its leg, and dripping off of its knee.

"Must a lost his balance when we hit that pothole! Looks like he got gored by one of the other steers! Won't matter where *he's* goin'," the Navajo told the stranger. The man looked through the slats at the injured animal, catching a glimpse of its enraged eyes. It snorted plaintively.

-Tsoh barked and howled, forcing his muzzle through the partially opened window on the driver's side of the cab.

"I'd better bring'em! He can wait outside!" Zachary walked back to the cab and opened the door. The huge dog leaped from the seat of the truck to the ground, his feet grinding in the fine, loose gravel, while he wagged, anxiously waiting for Zachary.

They walked to the door together. The air outside the truckstop smelled of spent diesel fuel. "Wait here!" Zachary scolded the large, old, short haired mutt. "I'll bring you some leftovers! Just don't bother anybody!" The hulking animal slumped to the ground. Lying there, he peered up with dejected, bloodshot eyes.

Zachary pulled on the handle of the glass door with the usual labels stuck to it: those that read, We accept Master Card, Visa, and American Express. It opened to an onslaught of sounds. Stepping inside, a jukebox played country-western music. The usual truckstop breakfast noises clamored throughout the place. Laughs, talk and clanging silverware pervaded. The scent of freshly brewed coffee, crisp bacon, and toast mingled in the room.

Just inside the door to the right was a row of pay phones. They were in constant use by the drivers who called their dispatchers, or they used them just to hear a friendly voice from home. The cashier's counter, that divided the cafe from the truckstop office, stood directly ahead of them. The cashier looked up immediately to greet them.

"Hi, Zach! Who's your friend?" The cute nineteen year old, petite red head asked cheerfully. She smiled, displaying a line of freckles across her face. They converged on her nose from atop her blush cheeks. Her shoulder length hair had a heavy curl to it.

"This is Daniel! Daniel, meet Genna!"

The stranger nodded, saying nothing, he gave a brief smile, apparently self-conscious of his roadweary appearance. He removed his cap and brushed his ruffled hair back with his hand.

"We're goin' to get a table. Talk to ya later." Zachary gestured toward the dining room.

They walked into the room, then paused for a moment, spying a vacant booth. The restaurant was nearly full. Maneuvering carefully between the tables, the big Indian's presence evoked friendly gestures from some of the locals. He nodded a few times on the way to a booth in the corner, it was near the front window.

Each of them slipped in on the tacky and tattered, red vinyl seats. The morning sun peeked through the partially drawn blinds. Beams of warm light broke across the table between them. Swirls of dust particles, and cigarette smoke from an adjacent booth, hung adrift in the sunlight.

"You boys want some coffee here?" The waitress asked, with a dripping Texas accent. She was taut and shapely, and she wore her honey-blond hair pulled back from her attractive, slender face. It was in a ponytail, tied with a fashionable blue bow. Her perfume had a slightly bawdy scent.

"Yeah, sure Jeannie," Zachary responded, giving her a sidewise glance, but not an immediate smile.

"Let me wipe this table off while I'm right here!" She suggested with a pert smile.

Both men considered the woman with measuring eyes.

"My arm's been stickin' to this table since I sat down here!" The Indian quipped, while she wiped the table with a damp cloth.

"Okay, wiseguy," she retorted. "You haven't introduced me to your cute friend here! Where's your manners?"

"Left'em at home, I guess!" Zachary said. He emitted a grin, having succumbed to her exuberant warmth. This is Daniel! Daniel, meet Jeannie!"

"Pleased to meet you!" The stranger's eyes smiled at the woman. Her's smiled back at him.

"Okay, coffee comin' right up, boys!"

Jeannie turned and started across the room. Their eyes followed her for a moment. Her skintight jeans caressed her firm upper leg and buttocks, accenting her shapely thirtyish figure. She sidestepped, then gracefully moved between the tables. All the while, she moved with a well defined swaying motion that was hypnotic to the attentive male eye.

"Colorado, you say?" The Indian inquired suspiciously, focusing again on the stranger. "I haul cattle for some ranchers up that way! Maybe you've worked for somebody I know?" Whereabouts in particular?"

"Dove Creek! But I've been moving around a lot! Haven't been staying in one place for very long! I'm thinking about going to California next." The stranger averted the Indian's penetrating curiosity. He glanced away to peer out through the open window blinds.

"Here's your coffee, boys!" Jeannie uttered in a sultry tone, commanding their attention. She had done it for so long, it was more habit than intent. But she had a special eye on the stranger.

"Care to order breakfast?" She asked with her order pad in hand, and the pen poised, that she had slipped from the breast pocket of a crisp, white blouse.

"I'll have the Navajo taco! Give me a side of salsa!" The Indian spoke up, while the stranger examined the plastic coated breakfast menu. He took a sip of black coffee from the steaming mug.

"Get a life, that's all you ever have, Zach! No self respecting Indian would order that in *this* place!" She chided him with a giggle.

"It's the only thing I feel safe about ordering in this place, Jeannie!" The brawny Indian retorted in a guttural tone.

"I guess I'll have the same," Daniel said, in an agreeable voice. He casually flipped the single page, black and white menu down on the table.

"What did you do? You clone this guy, Zach?" Jeannie gave the stranger a flirtatious look and a wink. She was still laughing as she turned away.

Curling his thick hand around the warm mug, the Indian considered the stranger. *He was lying!* The Indian wasn't sure how he knew, but something deep in his sinew told him. He didn't know about what, either. His instincts just told him it was so.

It wasn't often that he picked up a stranger, in particular an Anglo stranger. His curiosity was aroused.

"Been hitchhiking all this way?" He uncurled his hand from the coffee mug. Raising it to his mouth to take a sip, he viewed the stranger's face over the top of the mug from beneath his heavy brow.

"Not all the way, I've walked across country some. Mostly though!"

Why was it that the Indian couldn't place his accent? He had listened to many travelers, from all parts of the country. Tourists, some foreign, came through by the thousands every summer. Was it that he really didn't have one? Yet, the Indian listened intently hoping to pick up a clue.

It came to him, suddenly, that the stranger's presence was unsettling to him. He peered into the quiescent, blue eyes across the table from him.

"Here's your breakfast, guys!" Jeannie balanced the plates in her hand, and on her steady forearm, while she placed them on the table. She reached for the glass coffee pot she had set down on the edge of the table behind her. She refilled their cups.

"Enjoy, fellas!" Jeannie said, withdrawing the coffee pot.

"Let's eat up! I've got to be in Flagstaff by eleven o'clock!" The Indian attacked his food with ardor. All the while he pondered what it was that was alien about the man opposite him. He searched for some stigma, some detectable difference............. something..............

Chapter 2

The Bovine Miracle

AS THEY STRODE ACROSS THE PARKING LOT TOWARD THE TRUCK, something caught the Indian's attention. The trailer shook. Then another jolt, and a sharp bang. One of the steers struck the side of the trailer, violently slamming itself against it in a rage.

Wavering in his step, the Navajo stopped a few feet from the side of the trailer. Zachary stood aghast by the agitation of the wounded, surly beast. He had dealt with a few temperamental animals in the past. And he had watched, and learned from his father about handling steers. His father had a way with them, like no one else he had ever seen. But this one, it was different. He noted it while he stared into its angry eyes. Its distended bovine nostrils secreted a heavy frothing mucus. Behind the beast's feral appearance, there was a bitter, frustrated, almost human quality that stunned Zachary.

Then he paused, reminiscently, to consider it further. He remembered that his father appeared to communicate with the animals in a way he had never been able to accomplish himself. He had been awed by the powerful gaze that his father used to control them, even some of the most aggressive bulls acquiesced to it. It was a kind of mental arm wrestling, he mused, a kind in which his father dominated.

The prospect of confronting this angry bovine creature at the stockyard, made him writhe mentally. Then he felt the eyes of the stranger at his back. They were intrusive eyes. It jarred him from a trance that seemed to be more than an inordinate daydream, but in fact was not more than fifteen or twenty seconds.

"He looks dangerous! What are you going to do with him?" The stranger inquired from behind him. The tone of his voice alluded more to a test of wills than a matter of concern. The question made the fine hairs on the Indian's neck stand rigid.

"I'll deal with it when the time comes!" The Navajo retorted. *I'll deal with it the way my father would have!* He told himself.

The sun was well up into the morning sky; it radiated its warmth profusely as it burned off the chill. Zachary removed his jacket and flung it into the cab of the truck. -*Tsoh* followed it, scrambling up into the cab and onto the bed in the sleeper.

"Let's go!" The Indian said with a ring of perturbance, feeling as though the stranger had in some way transgressed a boundary, that he had penetrated an area well guarded by the perimeters of self-sovereignty. Still, it was only a feeling!

Zachary started the truck. The diesel engine sputtered and chugged, then a billow of black smoke came out of the exhaust pipes as the motor rumbled. It spread into a cloud of gray soot that loomed over the truck. Clutching hard, with his foot on the accelerator, the Indian forced the gearshift. It jammed into gear. He cringed from the grinding noise that it made. The rig leaped forward, causing the cattle to shuffle for footing. He and the stranger were bounced in the cab as the truck rolled across the parking lot and onto the highway.

Both men were quiet, for what seemed to be the longest time since they had come together. They were traveling south-southwest on Highway 89. The sun shone through the glass onto Zachary's face. He rolled down his window. He could feel the rush of cool air over his skin. It felt good to him. Placing his elbow out through the opened window, he rested his forearm on the well worn, smooth metal edge of the window frame. He felt tranquil, while he listened to the harmonic reverberations of the diesel engine. The wind, and the roar of the motor was a symphony to his ears. They were sounds he had grown to enjoy for many years, since the first time his father had taken him to Flagstaff on this very same route.

The road had been improved, but the scenery had remained virtually the same. Nearing Gray Mountain, the terrain began to change perceptibly as the elevation increased. Humphrey's Peak, part of the San Francisco Mountains, and the highest point in Arizona, rose 12, 670 feet above sea level. From a distance, its dark silhouette could be seen spiring against the clear, placid blue sky.

Populated with large juniper, fir, and the largest stand of Ponderosa Pine in the nation, the high country of Arizona was fragrant with the sweet smell that permeated the atmosphere around it. There were deciduous trees as well.

The leaves of the aspen were already starting to turn with autumn colors. The yellow, orange and red hues looked like scattered flash fires.

Zachary was absorbed in the panorama. Suddenly startled, he became aware of those piercing, blue eyes penetrating him. It was disconcerting. He could sense that same intrusive feeling he had felt earlier.

"What are you looking at?" The Indian grumbled self-consciously.

Unlike someone who would have become disturbed or embarrassed by the rebuke, the stranger remained calm. He continued to stare. With deeply intense eyes, he met the Indian's defensive gaze, then he looked away, without a word. His demeanor never altered. It troubled the Navajo even more.

After several minutes, the stranger spoke. "Sorry! You appeared to be preoccupied with something. I was just curious as to what it was?" He paused. "So I listened!"

"But I didn't say anything!" Zachary insisted. "I was thinking about something,............but I'm sure I didn't say anything!"

The stranger nodded. His expression was rigid. He had smiled very little since they had met. "I make a study of human nature. It's not so much what a person says! Sometimes it's the unspoken word that has more meaning. Body language, the eyes, expressions, they all mean something! So I listened! You have a deep regard for the land,............ don't you? There's something about this particular area that appears to hold some special significance to you! I just picked that up."

Although the stranger was right, the Indian internalized his acknowledgment. He was unwilling to admit to a stranger, especially an Anglo stranger, that his perception was correct. His reluctance was tacit. Searching the pocket of his jacket, that lay on the seat between them, he brought out the pouch of tobacco. His eyes were trained on the road all the while. He pulled a plug from the pouch and stuffed it in his mouth.

They were about ten miles outside of Flagstaff, when the stranger spoke again. "You appear to be filled with anger and resentment, Zachary! Why? Did I say something that offended you?"

It was more than the Navajo could tolerate. He was still roiling inside from the previous assertion by this stranger, someone who he would know briefly, whose concerns or opinions interested him very little. Why was this man probing about his private thoughts, his feelings about certain things? They were none of his business!

But if he wanted to know, so be it! Zachary would tell him in words that he could understand. "You're prying into something you know nothing about! Things you wouldn't understand, ...unless you were an Indian! Of course this land is special to me! It has a spiritual significance. Something else you wouldn't understand! The Earth is mother in my culture. The People respect it, unlike the Anglos who desecrate it!"

"You're damn right I'm angry! Do you think it's easy for an Indian living in this world today? We've had to compromise some of our values and swallow much pride just to survive! My people have managed somehow to maintain many of our traditional ways. There is something in our past that makes us keep holding on to our beliefs! Sometimes I don't think it's worth it, though! It just makes life more difficult! But I can't let go of whatever it is."

He had spoken more words in those two minutes than he had said the entire time that they had been together, perhaps more than he had said to any one person in several years. And he wasn't finished!

"Just because I went to the white man's Christian school, and I speak English, it doesn't make me one! A white man, that is! I'm still Navajo! And nothing will ever change that!" He told the stranger with intense pride.

After his outburst of indignation, he spat into the styrofoam cup that he took from the dashboard. *The stranger is right again!* He thought. Now Zachary wasn't sure how to react toward him. He had vented his frustration on the man called Daniel, for prying into his personal feelings concerning an issue he had chosen to ignore, and the man had listened graciously. *Of course! What else could he do!* He told himself. The man was a captive audience, and Zachary just seized the opportunity.

Yet, he was embarrassed for his display of emotion, as reserved as it was. He wasn't sure if he just wanted to be rid of this troublesome stranger, or if he wanted to know more about him, and whether or not his inquiry came from a genuine concern, or just a meddlesome nature. Whatever it was, it was beginning to intrigue Zachary. That, and whatever was different about the man, was rousing his curiosity.

He slowed the rig, then he eased it into a clearing beside the highway. The stockyard was just ahead, about two-hundred yards off the road. Turning on the large gravel lot that fronted the fenced retention areas where the cattle were held, he swung the trailer around, skillfully backing the rig up to an unloading ramp. The rear of the trailer butted gently against the wooden posts that protruded from the ground, serving as bumpers to stop the rigs from backing into the ramp. He set the air brakes. They emitted a loud screech and released a rush of air. Then he cut the diesel engine, and it was strangely quiet in the cab for a brief moment.

"I've got to go over there...........to the yard office and give'em my voucher!" The Indian said, gesturing across the lot. He nodded in that direction with the voucher in his hand. "Then I'll be back to unload! Just wait here for me, I'll be right back," he told the stranger, swinging the door open to get out of the truck.

The stranger named Daniel lowered himself from the cab of the truck to the ground. Landing stiff-legged, he placed his hands behind his head, then he stretched from the long ride. -*Tsoh* jumped out of the open door after him, sniffing at the ground. The stranger straightened his cap, he looked about, surveying the surroundings. He walked toward the cattle pens and leaned over the wooden rail, viewing the railroad siding directly behind the stockade. There were three empty cattle cars on the siding, with the doors open on either side. He could see through the cars, and beyond to a grassy meadow. Scattered heaps of manure lie about in the pens, exuding a pungent odor that dominated his sense of smell, diluting it to other less distinctive emanations that may have been present but went undetected.

He assessed the compound. It consisted of somewhat evenly spaced vertical posts and horizontal wooden slats of dried, splintered and weather-beaten fir, with diagonal braces at the corners to stiffen them against the thrusts of massive, fearful animals that may or may not have sensed their inevitable slaughter. *Where are the hunters?* He mused, seizing on a roving thought from the past.

Recognizing the gait of the Indian as he stepped heavily on the loose gravel, he turned. "Let's get these cattle unloaded, so I can get you into town!" The Navajo told him.

Zachary climbed up the wooden ladder that was fastened to the side rail of the ramp. He let out a groan as he pulled his husky body over the top of the fence. Bounding to the floor of the ramp, he stumbled, then caught his footing. The stranger followed, pulling himself over the top rail, with agility, he vaulted over the fence.

Grasping the steel bolt that secured the heavy wooden gate on the ramp, the Indian tugged on it trying to break it loose, while the stranger, with his back to the Navajo, was preoccupied with the sensory perceptions that invaded him and captured his attention. He peered at the side rails of the chute; they were scarred and splintered from the blows struck by angry and frightened cattle. He surveyed, with intensity, the rest of the compound. He sensed an aura of anxious frenzy.

"Give me a hand over here!" The Indian shouted, breaking the stranger's trancelike fixation. Zachary was still struggling with the bolt.

"Sure," the stranger said.

They both grabbed hold of the handle. And together, they gave it a strenuous jerk, freeing the latch and the gate with the full force of their combined strength, hurling Zachary backward against the fence with the gate in tow. The gate bounced off of his rib cage, while he turned his head to avoid being struck in the face by it. "Wohw!" He exclaimed, grimacing, as he absorbed the blow. "Nobody ever fixes anything around here!" He swore in disgust.

"Are you all right?" The stranger inquired, offering his hand to help the Indian back to his feet.

"Yeah, I'm all right!" He said, straightening up. He dusted himself off. "But you'd better let me tie off this gate and open the trailer gate by myself! You'd better get on the outside of the chute!" The Navajo warned. "I've done this a thousand times before, but they're nervous! Sometimes they come out fast! You'd best be out of the way!"

While the stranger watched from a safe vantage point on the outside of the chute, where he clung to the ladder, looking over the top of the rail, Zachary placed one foot on the first rung of the trailer gate. He boosted himself up, so that he could release the top latch; as he did, one of the steers bolted against the gate jarring him backward again.

-Tsoh barked, pacing nervously beside the ramp. Zachary jumped back and regained his footing. Then he stood still, momentarily evaluating the situation. To his immediate recollection, he hadn't had more than one or two minor incidents occur in all the time he had been hauling cattle. They could be dangerous. He understood that. But he had always had a level of comfort regarding his handling of the animals. At least until today!

What is it that's different? He asked himself. *I have a wounded steer! A gate that wouldn't open! And I've been knocked off the back of the trailer! And what about this Anglo stranger?* He pondered. *He could be bad luck?* But shaking his head, he dismissed the thought. After all, he had been brought up in a generation that had put away most of the superstitions: spells, witchcraft and the like. Even though his grandfather had filled his head with such nonsense as a boy, he believed he had been disburdened of those beliefs by his Christian education.

"Can you get out of the way in time?" The stranger asked, gaining his attention.

"They're not goin' anywhere, until I release the bottom latch and open the gate!" The Navajo replied in a confident tone of voice. "They don't realize the gate is open right away! I have time to pull it open and get off to the side before they come out! Like I said, I've done it a thousand times before!" He insisted.

Saying that, he reached down to pull up the bottom gate latch. *-Tsoh* became increasingly restless, growling and barking unceasingly. The wounded, incensed steer bowled open the gate before Zachary had a chance to straighten up. He was thrust back as the animal plowed into him. Grappling the frenzied beast's neck and gripping one horn, so as not to be thrown under foot and trampled by the onslaught of the steers that followed, he could feel the warm, oozing, bloody wound as he was dragged along in the torrent of rage. He cleaved to the animal so tightly that he was forced to gaze into one hate filled eye, glazed with pain and fear, as the animal flayed him against the fence on its way down the ramp. The Indian could feel the beast's blood mixing with his own. All the torture and torment of the animal, and the anger and pain of the Navajo's thirty-seven years, was reflected in the eyes of the creature. His strength was sapped away as he clung to the beast; it flung him wildly.

The stranger hurtled the fence, and ran down the ramp behind the last steer to exit the trailer. He walked through the herd toward the wounded animal. It caught his gaze. He fixed on the animal's eyes with a hypnotic stare as he moved through the quieting herd. Then, with one final jolt, the steer tossed Zachary free. He fell to the ground with a thud. The steer stopped dead. It remained motionless as the stranger approached.

Zachary laid on the ground in agony, holding his right shoulder. It had been separated when he was dashed against the rail. The flesh of his arm was ripped open by the jagged burrs that protruded from the wood. The blood saturated his shirt sleeve.

Calmly, the stranger stood in front of the animal. Its eyes appeared to be transfixed. The Indian looked up from where he lie. He was strangely anesthetized by the transcendent communication that he witnessed between the beast and the stranger. The steer's inflamed disposition turned placid. As the Navajo watched the penetrating gaze of those halcyon blue eyes, that appeared to have a translucent quality, his own roiled fettle began to subside.

"Will you be all right?" The stranger asked, speaking in a resonant tone that was as soothing as his look.

The Indian was still dazed. "I don' know? I was really hurting a minute ago! But I feel better now! This is really strange!"

"Here, let me help you up!" The stranger extended his left hand. When the Indian reached for it, he felt a tingling sensation, like a warm electrical current, pass through him.

Rising to his feet, he said, "It's the strangest thing, I feel fine! What did you do? What is this? Is it some kind of a miracle?" The Navajo viewed the man with large, dark eyes full of amazement at what he had seen and experienced.

"Miracles are ambiguous, Zachary!" The stranger told him. "It's strictly a matter of how we wish to define an event. It can cover a broad range of interpretation! However, I just used the resources available to me."

The Navajo looked at his blood soaked and torn shirt sleeve. Although he could see the evidence of a severe injury, there was none. He felt as though he had merely been an observer in the traumatic episode. The details of it still flashed through his mind, vividly, yet he felt none of the pain. "Who are you?" He asked the stranger. The massive canine rested quietly on his haunches, peering at them from over the bottom rail of the fence, panting, with his large tongue dangling out the side of his mouth.

Just then, the yard foreman approached them. "Hey partner, what's goin' on here?" He asked with a tone of concern, but in a lighthearted manner.

"Nothing Larry, everything's fine!" Zachary told him, reluctant to divulge an event that defied an immediate explanation.

The stocky, affable fellow stood before the two men in a quandary over the condition of Zachary's clothes. He peered at them suspiciously with skeptical eyes, that were set in a full, jovial face, shaded by a large white cowboy hat with a red and black brocade band and a gray feather tucked in the side of it.

"You don't look just fine! What happened to your clothes?"

"Oh, I just fell down gettin' over the fence!" The Indian quipped, making light of the circumstances. He brushed off his clothes.

"Looks like your arm is bleeding! I have a first aid kit in the office!" Larry offered.

"It's just a scratch! But I'll come inside in a minute and wash it off!" Zachary assured him.

"Well, be more careful around here!" The yard foreman cautioned him. "We sure don't need anybody gettin' hurt!" He started to turn away, then he paused and turned back, remembering his mannerly, southern Illinois upbringing. He had been reared on a large farm, that bordered the Mississippi river basin, on a peninsula that made up Calhoun County. It lay between the Mississippi and the Illinois river, and his manner was as slow and easy as that part of the country.

"You didn't introduce me to your friend," he told the Navajo

"Larry, this is Daniel!" Zachary said, nodding in the stranger's direction.

Offering a strong right hand, the yard foreman took hold of the stranger's with a firm grip. "Pleased to meet you, Daniel!" His stout forearm bulged from beneath his rolled up shirt sleeve as he shook the man's hand. "You're not from around here are you?" He surmised, as he assessed the stranger.

"He's just passing through, I'm giving him a lift into town!" The Navajo interjected, before the stranger had a chance to answer. Politely, the stranger nodded in agreement.

Then the yard foreman's eyes strayed over the shoulder of the man, and set upon the wounded steer. "What happened to that ornery looking cuss?" He asked.

Zachary was quick to answer. "It happened on the way down here! I know he wasn't like that when I loaded them in Cahone yesterday. They got jostled some on the way down. Must a got stuck by one of the other steers! That's all I can figure."

Feeling anxious, the Indian said, "Hey! Let's go take care of our business in the office! I'll clean up, and we can be on our way!"

As they carried their conversation over to the corral gate, the yard foreman swung it open, stepping outside of the enclosure, they walked toward the yard office. The perplexed Navajo glanced over his shoulder at the stranger, who they had left standing near the gate, and who watched them intently as they walked away. His mind churned with questions. *Who is he?* He asked himself.

When he could see that the two men had entered the office, the stranger turned back to the corral gate. He opened it, then he stepped back inside. Singling out the wounded and weary steer, he approached it slowly, causing no stir as he maneuvered between the other cows. He stopped about two feet in front of the steer, reached out slowly and stroked the animals head. He then placed his large left hand, with its long tenuous fingers, against the wound, gently manipulating the flesh and muscle tissue around it as though he were shaping clay. When he had finished, the animal was completely docile. The pain had left its eyes, it had been replaced by a tranquil energy. Whatever he had done, it had returned the beast's vigor.

He stood outside the gate waiting for the Indian to return. The Navajo's huge dog lie at the stranger's feet panting and salivating, it's eyes rolled upward in its massive skull, wrinkling the loose skin on its forehead, they peered at the stranger, watchfully. Waiting with one curious ear raised, to detect what? Only the canine's keen senses knew. If he had recognized a stalking intruder, could the loyal beast flush him out to the advantage of his master?

Zachary returned looking contrite. He placed his hand on the stranger's shoulder, with a squeeze of assurance. "It occurred to me, while I was in there cleaning up, that you saved my life! If you hadn't been here, I don't know what would have happened to me? Anyway,............ I owe you my gratitude." He said in a conciliatory tone. "Whatever I can do to help you, let me know! At least let me buy you lunch in Flagstaff!" The Navajo insisted.

Letting *-Tsoh* clamber into the truck ahead of him, Zachary climbed up into the cab. He started the road worn Peterbilt. It chugged and sputtered, then belched a thick cloud of smoke as the rig pulled away from the ramp. "I'm gonna hav'ta get her checked out!" The Indian quipped. "Somethin's wrong with her!" He said, making an inference of intimacy with this inanimate machine, whose heart and soul was a large, antiquated Cummins diesel engine. Still, it was a symbol of power and dominance on the highway.

They turned onto the truck route that was 89A, it took them into Flagstaff where they caught Enterprise Drive going south across a large railroad yard, and through a light industrial area that bordered on the east end of town. It led them to Interstate 40. There was a truckstop that the Indian frequented, and where he could refuel.

"Flagstaff's a college town you know!" The Navajo said over the roar of the diesel engine, the rumble of the empty trailer on the road, and the squeal of the airbrakes as he moved along the industrial road with the slow moving noon-hour traffic. "I got a tour there once from this anthropologist lady. She comes out to the res' to study my culture. She has some kind of a grant from the government. I guided her to some of the ancient ruins in remote locations on the reservation. That was a couple of years ago! Interesting lady!" Zachary spoke casually.

Pondering the sights and sounds outside the truck, a sense of certainty possessed the stranger as he considered the events earlier in the day. In his mind, all was going according to his plan. He mused at the Indian's reference to the anthropologist.

Chapter 3

The Virgin Proselyte

HE SET THE BRAKES. THEY SQUEALED FROM METAL TO METAL friction, as the long, dusty and mud spattered truck rolled in next to the diesel fuel pumps. He killed the engine. It ran on for a few seconds, sputtering and chugging at delayed intervals, until it exhausted its combustion with a final shutter.

"I want to fuel up first! Then we can go in and get some lunch!" The Navajo told the man named Daniel. "Could you fill it for me while I go to the restroom? It'll probably take fifty gallons! That's about how much my bladder is holding right now!" He laughed, provoking a smile from the stranger. "Be back in a few minutes!"

Walking across the black asphalt pavement, it radiated the heat from the bright afternoon sun. The glare from the sun's reflection off the building's light colored facade made him squint. He reached into his shirt pocket, then he realized that he had left his sunglasses on the dash of the truck. Zachary turned back briefly, pondering the anomalous stranger. He strode the distance to the door of the truckstop. Immersed in conjecture concerning the stranger's true identity, he reached for the door. Another trucker swung the door open, causing him to step back. Then he caught hold of the door and walked inside.

Standing next to the pump, the stranger's left hand grasped the nozzle, while cold fuel flowed rapidly through it, filling the empty tank. He had watched the Indian stride toward the building, now his attention was turned inward. It was focused on his timetable and the imminent conversion of the Navajo.

The Navajo returned. "All done here?" He asked.

"Just about! I don't think it will hold much more," the stranger said.

"I'd better move the rig away from the pumps. I'll just meet you inside!" Zachary told him.

The stranger extended his hand with the Indian's sunglasses in them. Without an exchange of words, but with an exchange of knowing looks, they measured one another. "See you inside!" Daniel said.

Zachary pulled himself up into the truck and slid behind the wheel. He peered through the dirt streaked windshield at the stranger. Then he placed the sunglasses on his face. He watched the man walk away as he started the truck. The stranger's omniscience was, all at once, frightening to him. *Why the sunglasses? How did he know?* He questioned himself, as he pulled the rig in alongside some others that were parked on the lot. *Is he psychic? Could he hear what I was thinking? What is this power that he has? Is it real, or am I imagining it?*

And if it was real, than the Navajo had better take care in what he said or did while in the man's company. After all, if he indeed had such power and could do good things with it, why couldn't he do evil things as well?

The stranger was already seated at a booth. He waved the Indian over. Zachary sat down. Each of them assessed the other for a brief moment. The Navajo ran his thick fingers back through his long black hair, moving it away from his face. Then he reached into the back pocket of his jeans for a red, paisley handkerchief to wipe the perspiration from his forehead.

A young waitress approached them. The Navajo spied the menu from the corner of his eye. He took it from between the salt and pepper shakers and the catsup bottle, that sat at the back of the table against the wall. The Navajo ordered the special, liver and onions. The stranger pointed to number six on the menu. It was the chicken teriyaki. She jotted down their orders, reached across the table, replaced the menu neatly behind the catsup bottle and walked away.

"Somethin's bothering me!" The Indian said bluntly. "I don't think you're just a roustabout! You're too educated for that! Who are you really? And what are you doing around here?"

While the stranger considered his response, with one hand, he turned the water glass that rested on the table in front of him. Then he took a sip, while he gauged the Navajo with a pensive expression. "I'm a messenger," he said, stealing a quick glance at the Indian, again, for some perceptible change in his facial expression. His eyes dropped back to the glass in his hand.

"What kind of messenger?" The Indian asked, searching the man's face with deep, dark eyes of inquiry.

"The kind your people believe in! The kind your grandfather taught you about! You remember that, don't you?" The stranger asked him, jogging his memory of the past.

"Yes! But what's that got to do with you? And how would you know about my grandfather?" The Indian's expression changed from one of stoic inquiry, to that of a defensive and suspicious posture. His eyes narrowed with distrust.

"If you believed what your grandfather taught you, then you would know it is possible. Then you would know who I am!" The stranger asserted, as though he was edifying the Navajo's cultural beliefs, regarding the existence of such spiritual messengers as he implied of himself.

The waitress returned with their lunch. They ceased their conversation abruptly. But two men in an adjacent booth had overheard them. They peered at the Navajo and the stranger furtively, turning back to their own conversation when Daniel glanced over at them.

"So that's how you explain what you did earlier! That you're some kind of spiritual messenger?" The Navajo viewed the stranger with uncertainty.

Without commenting further, the stranger removed his cap and placed it on the seat beside him, revealing a shaggy crop of brown hair, salted with gray. He tasted his food, then he seasoned it with soy sauce to his liking, and proceeded to eat his lunch.

The Navajo considered him. He was not an extraordinary looking man. Actually he was fairly average looking, except for his eyes. They were unusual. *An unlikely Spirit Messenger though,* the Indian thought as he mulled over his food.

He had witnessed what he thought to be something of a phenomenon. Yet, he had doubts as to the actuality of it. He felt as though he had been on the periphery of the event, rather than a participant in it. It had all happened so quickly, that it was vague in his mind as to what really took place. The only evidence of it was the torn, blood stained shirt sleeve, and a scratch on his arm that he had washed and bandaged at the stockyard office. Perhaps it had not been as cataclysmic an occurrence as it seemed at the time? He wondered.

And what was it that the stranger really did? Had he imagined this mysterious force that he thought he saw this stranger exhibit? Or was it because of a disoriented state of mind that he had attributed some power to this man? It was all very unclear to him. He pondered these questions silently, while he dissected his lunch. He hoped that the stranger couldn't read his mind, as he had appeared to do earlier in regard to the sunglasses, while he considered the best way to deal with this situation.

Zachary broke the silence. "How's your lunch?"

"It's really very good! You're right, the food is good here!" The stranger remarked.

"My mother was a good cook............when she was alive," the Indian mused. "She died shortly after my father." Unwittingly, the Navajo had opened a line of dialogue that the stranger would use to his advantage. He had revealed his vulnerability. And like a skillful *hunter*, the stranger would attack his apparent weakness.

"Do you have other family, Zachary?" The stranger queried.

"Yes, my brother Marvin. He's the oldest. He lives on the reservation with his wife and two kids. I love those kids like they're my own!" The Indian said, with a thoughtful expression.

"Aren't you married?"

"No, I just never got around to it! And after dad died, mom needed someone around to look after her. There just wasn't time! Besides, I'm kind a set in my ways now," Zachary quipped. "I don't think any woman's going to put up with me!" Exhausting a deep breath, he smiled. He emitted a mild laugh. "I like living alone anyway!"

Then his expression changed to one of serious concern. "Where will you stay? I mean, if I leave you here in Flagstaff?" The Navajo inquired in earnest. "Do you have any money?"

"A little!" The stranger admitted. "I'm not sure where I'll stay. But I'll manage!" He insisted.

"Look! I've got plenty of room at my place. You could stay there until you find work! I could do that much for you!" Zachary offered.

Peering at the Indian with measuring eyes, the stranger considered the sincerity of the offer. "You sure it wouldn't be any trouble? It would sure make things easier for me!"

"No, no trouble at all! It would be nice to have some company for a while!" The Navajo acknowledged. "We should be going! I've got some things to do around home before dark. I can show you around a little, too! Let me pay the bill and we'll get out of here! You can leave the tip if you want!"

"Sure," the stranger replied.

The stranger reached for his cap, lying on the seat next to him, he placed it on his head. Then he got out of the booth and snatched up his jacket, taking three coins from his pocket to place on the table. He followed Zachary to the cashier.

Walking by the table shortly after them, the waitress scooped the coins into her hand. She stopped for a moment, held the coins with her palm open and admired them. They all appeared to be new, and of uniform size, and they were all bright gold! She noticed an inscription on the coins. It appeared to her to be in Latin.

One of the men sitting in the adjacent booth, who had overheard the conversation between the Navajo and the stranger, reached out and grabbed the girl's hand as she walked by. He jerked her back. She looked at him, startled! "Let's see those coins, honey!" He said, holding tightly onto her wrist.

"Why should I?" She retorted.

He squeezed her wrist more tightly, until she opened her hand. He was dazzled by the coins. So was the man with him.

"Get your hands off me!" The girl screeched. He released his grip immediately. She backed away from him with an angry scowl on her face, clenched the coins tightly in her fist and rushed away.

"I'd like to get my hands on some of those coins!" The man remarked to his companion.

"So would I! Maybe we should follow those guys?" His companion hinted. "It shouldn't be too tough!"

They pulled away from the truck stop and headed north, back to Highway 89. The stranger sank back into the seat with his shoulder against the door. He pulled his cap down over his eyes and fell asleep. The Navajo was left with unanswered questions, and thoughts that buzzed around in his head like a swarm of bees. He switched on the CB radio for company, listening in on the local chatter to help drown out his thoughts.

Later, when they were near Kayenta, the stranger awoke. He straightened up and looked around. "Are we almost there?" He asked.

"Yes! How was your nap?" Zachary inquired.

"Good. It felt good to get some rest! I haven't slept in a while," the stranger replied.

"Well, it won't be long now. Then you can get more sleep!" The Indian assured him. "I have to turn left at Highway 163 and go north about ten miles. We should be there in about fifteen minutes."

As his eyes captured the surroundings so familiar to him, he pondered the stark beauty of the desolate land he had been born to. "You know, ...I believe the Anglos thought they were giving us back a worthless piece of real estate." He said this in a reflective tone. "But now I think we got the best end of the bargain!" His voice filled with irony. "You've heard the old saying, *What goes around, comes around!* Haven't you?"

"No. I can't say that I have! But I can understand the philosophy connected with it! What you do to someone else will come back to you, eventually!" The stranger asserted.

The Indian nodded, acknowledging his understanding. "Yes! And now they're buying mineral rights from us! And they're comin' in their station wagons and R.V.'s to see all these natural wonders, and to learn about our culture. And they're payin' us for the privilege besides! They even want to learn about our medicine!"

Then he continued with a note of sarcastic humor. "And to top it off, they buy all that stuff we sell in our gift shops to take back to the city for souvenirs!" Zachary chuckled, heartily.

His eyes filled with retrospect, the stranger peered at the road ahead. "There is a certain irony to it all, isn't there! But you know Zachary, it isn't just you and them, there is more involved here!"

"Meaning?" The Navajo queried.

"Meaning, soon your kind will be forced to recognize your dependency on one another, rather than your differences! And accept the responsibility for all of your actions!" He hesitated. "Like your adage implies!"

Suddenly, all of those questions, Zachary had put aside, were back! And they began nagging at him incessantly. "So, ...if you're a messenger, does that have something to do with the message?"

"That's part of it! Assuming I'm really a messenger, that is!" The stranger said with a sardonic smile.

He had been so distracted by the conversation, that the Navajo had failed to see his turn coming up. It was the first time, in all the time that he had lived on the reservation, that he had ever missed that turn. "I should've been paying closer attention!" He conceded. "I'll turn around up here!"

Reaching an area where the shoulder of the road widened on both sides, he slowed the rig and left the pavement. He turned the trailer around in a wide radius, that incorporated the shoulder on the opposite side. He brought the truck around to a hundred and eighty degrees and back onto the pavement. They were now going south toward the turn off.

"You see all these little houses spread out around here?" The Navajo said, pointing to the right. "They were provided by the government! Mine is just at the end of this gravel drive." He turned the truck onto it. "When my parents first moved into it, there wasn't any electricity or water out here. We had to carry our water in! Now we're on a well!"

"Here it is!" Zachary announced. Straight ahead of them was a small, frame house with white shiplap siding. It had faded blue shutters on the front windows. The little house appeared marginally maintained. He pulled the truck up to the south side of it, where there was a broadened parking area of gravel to accommodate the rig. They stopped about fifty feet from a metal outbuilding, like those used on farms to store feed and equipment. The sliding door was open and the tailgate of a late model, maroon pickup truck was visible.

They got out of the truck, straightening up after the long ride. Moving toward the front of the truck, they stretched their legs. The old dog climbed down from the truck. Yawning, he stiffened his legs while he stretched out his long torso, causing his rib cage to protrude from beneath the tautness of his toughened skin, and short, coarse hair. Then shaking the stiffness from his joints, he walked slowly toward the Indian. Zachary reached down and patted him on the head, then he stroked him behind the ear. *-Tsoh* barked, letting out a restive growl when the stranger approached them.

"Okay, that's enough!" He scolded the uneasy canine. "He won't bite.

He's just a cranky old boy! I've had him since he was a pup."

Daniel extended his left hand, slowly, reaching for the dogs head. He stroked it gently.

"Looks like you have a way with animals!" The Indian noted.

"Let me show you around my place," he offered. "I just have an acre, but it's enough for me!" He paused. "I have all that too!" He said, pointing toward the open range and the distant mesas to the west.

They walked around the north side of the metal storage building to the rear yard, where a wood frame chicken coupe stood on posts, a few feet above the ground, surrounded by a chicken wire fence. Alongside the storage building sat a stripped down, decaying, four door sedan with the hood up and the windows broken out. In the opposite corner of the yard stood a pile of rusted, miscellaneous car parts and old appliance cadavers.

"I have my own fresh eggs, almost everyday," the Navajo remarked, as the two men stood before the chicken coupe, facing the west. "When *-Tsoh* was younger, he use to get in and kill a chicken once in a while. Dad was still alive then. He wanted to shoot'em! But I promised I would keep him out! It's taken fourteen years, but he doesn't bother them anymore!" The Indian chuckled.

Standing side by side, the two men contemplated the horizon. The sun stood low. It appeared to be balanced atop a red mesa. The undersides of low, scattered clouds absorbed its ocher rays, emitting yellow and orange hues.

"I never get tired of the scenery out here!" The Navajo said, bending to pick up a small white plastic bucket to fill with feed. "To me, the earth contains the power of God. I can see it! And I can feel it!"

In silence, the stranger meditated on the view. He imagined that this is what the evening sky must have been like where he was from. That the evening star would have been as splendid.

"I'd better feed these chickens!" Zachary told him. "Why don't you come with me into the storage shed, I'll show you where everything's at!"

He led the stranger into the metal building. Zachary reached for the switch on the inside of the door to the right, turning on the overhead light to see in the midst of the failing daylight. They walked beside the late model pickup truck. It was parked in the open bay of the storage building, covered in dust. "This is my pride and joy!" The Navajo commented as they stopped next to the truck. "It's a one ton! I don't drive it very often, only when I need to pick up some feed or supplies."

Turning to the storage bins on the adjacent wall, he scooped up a bucket full of feed. "My father and I bought that rig! It's been a good business! And it's made a good living for me!" He mused. "It's helped make us independent. That's the aim of the tribal council, for the Navajos to be financially independent of the federal government. We want to be self-sufficient!"

He turned from the bins, gesturing toward the opposite side of the building. "You see that work bench over there, that's where I keep all my tools! I have just about anything you'd need to do a job. A lot of them belonged to my father. I've just added to them over the years." The Navajo looked with reminiscent eyes, and a solemn expression. "We'd better feed those chickens before it gets dark!"

They walked back to the yard. -*Tsoh* followed close behind them. Zachary scattered the feed through the fence, while the stranger named Daniel watched. The massive dog laid down on the cool ground next to him, pressing his bulk against the stranger's leg. The stranger stooped to stroke the dog's head with a strong, reassuring hand.

In the half-light of the evening sky, there appeared the white crescent of the waxing moon. "What would it be like at this time of day where you come from?" The Indian asked casually. He hoped that the stranger would, heedlessly, make a significant disclosure as to what part of the country he was from.

The stranger pondered the rapidly encroaching darkness of the night sky. It slowly revealed the myriad, brilliant celestial bodies of the firmament. "Similar in some ways, ...so I'm told. There were many bright stars visible in the night sky,............much like this!" The man's eyes appeared to be looking into a distant place in the heavens, that the Indian couldn't see for himself. "We had seven moons! Although not all of them were visible at one time, four could be seen in various stages." He ruminated. "It is said that the winds would always come at night! They brought the black rain!"

Now the Navajo was puzzled. Nowhere on earth could seven moons be seen! And black rain? *Where is there black rain?* He asked himself. Except for acid rain originating in the industrialized areas of the upper midwest and northeast, that was now known to be contaminating remote wilderness lakes and streams as far west as the rocky mountains, and killing forests on the slopes of the mountains in the southeast and the west, there was nothing that could be considered as black rain. *But it's close enough!* He told himself. *Then maybe he's from the midwest? Or even Canada? But the seven moons, what is that all about?*

"Black rain?" The Indian asked in a perplexed tone. "Where on earth is there black rain?"

"It wasn't always!" The stranger said, regretfully. "It's what we *did* that made it that way!"

"Who?" Zachary asked him, stooping to set the pail on the ground next to the chicken coupe. He cast a curious eye in the stranger's direction.

"My people!" He answered simply. "We did what yours are doing now! But that was a long time ago!" He had said enough to whet the Navajo's appetite.

"It's getting dark, we'd better get inside! Maybe you can tell me more about where you're from, later?"

"Perhaps." The stranger said, sounding weary.

Zachary walked toward the wood pile next to the back door of the house. The stranger followed him. "It's going to be cold tonight, I'd better bring in some wood for the stove," the Indian said. He bent over and stacked four split juniper logs in the crook of his right arm. Then he stepped up onto the porch and opened the screen door with his left hand. The stranger held the screen door for him, while Zachary pushed open the unlocked interior door.

Stepping inside, he switched on the light. They stood in a modest kitchen with a knotty pine table, and four chairs that had printed fabric cushions on the seats. A small, shaded light fixture hung over the table by a frayed electrical cord. The kitchen was open to the adjoining living room, allowing a clear view of it and the tattered furnishings it contained.

The Navajo walked through the kitchen to the cast iron wood stove against the inside center wall. He set the wood down on the raised sandstone hearth that surrounded the stove. *-Tsoh* scrambled across the room and vaulted onto a threadbare, overstuffed sofa. He growled, then he placed himself strategically, planting his haunches against the back of the sofa, with his large front paws dangling over the edge of the cushion and his head sunk down between his legs. His sharp but sullen eyes scanned the room with minimal effort, monitoring any movement that might be seen through the slits in his tired and wrinkled eyelids.

Closing the door behind him, the stranger stepped a few feet into the room, then paused. "Your door was unlocked. Aren't you afraid someone will come in while you're away?"

From where he knelt next to the stove, the Navajo appeared amused at the inquiry, as though he had never thought it a serious matter of concern, he answered, "No, that door's never been locked! Navajos generally don't steal from each other anyway! I know everyone around here, and they have as much as I have, maybe a little more! What would they take? Besides, we have our own law! And our own system of justice on the Nation!" He mused aloud. "Why don't you just come in and have a seat while I start the fire! There's an empty coat hook on the wall next to the door, right behind you, if you want to hang up your jacket!"

Slipping out of his jacket and hat, he put them on the hook. Then he walked into the living room, where Zachary wadded newspaper to stuff into the wood stove. He sat down on a well worn recliner and, leaning forward to watch the Indian, he rested his elbows on his knees with his hands folded beneath his chin. In a corner of the room devoid of significant light, his eye sockets appeared as hollowed black voids in the recesses of his high cheek bones. The slouching, massive quadruped viewed him with a diligent eye from where he laid.

Adding kindling and stacking a few juniper logs on top of it, Zachary struck a wooden match and held it to the wadded paper. The amber flame from the match glowed in the room immersed in a quiet, limbo like dusk, that was barely illuminated by the dim light of the ceiling fixture in the kitchen. The puny light made a frail attempt to infringe on the sanctity of the surroundings, that were cast in an aura of secrecy.

The Indian closed the blackened, cast iron door on the wood stove. It concealed the rising flames. Then he slid the damper open for more draft. The light of the flame that flickered through the elongated slots, sent shimmering pillars of light dancing, that distorted the shadows on the wall across the room from them. He stood, dispatching a cramp from his leg. Then he walked over to the sofa. Easing down into it, he sat back. The cushions swelled with the force of his weight as he settled into them.

And as he did so, he considered the questions whose answers would cause him to act with the conviction of a virgin proselyte, before the night converged on the dawn again!

Peering at him in the eerie light, from the opposite side of the room, the Navajo asked, “The black rain, ...how did it happen?”

Chapter 4

Mescal, Hot Chili and the Compact

ALTHOUGH THE STRANGER'S EXPRESSION WAS VAGUE, ZACHARY could discern a sense of urgency in his voice when he said, "They say we used up most of our fossil fuel, clouding our atmosphere with trillions upon trillions of tons of acidic and toxic debris! Until its poisons were brought down to the ground in the violent and unpredictable storms that brought the black rain!" He fell quiet for a brief moment. Pockets of sap in the dry juniper popped in the fury of the flames that eagerly consumed it, exploding like muffled gun shots in the bowels of the cast iron stove. It overtook the silence.

"So, where is this place?" The Indian ventured to inquire. "In the east?" He asked, still presuming that it was a place within the confines of the world he knew.

"Very far!" The stranger mused aloud. "So far away, that I will never return to see it!" He asserted with conviction.

"What is it like now? Has it changed? Are the people different?" Zachary asked a barrage of questions, with the hope of getting one answer that would specify the origin of this traveler.

He was met with a response that was totally unexpected. "I don't know. I've never been there!" The stranger said.

"What do you mean you've never been there? It's where you're from!" The Navajo blurted in a tone of amazement, still unable to comprehend the idea of a tangible world that existed beyond the boundaries of the one where *he* was extant.

"It's been many generations since anyone has been there! Although I've never seen it, I sometimes long for it." He paused in a thoughtful repose.

Zachary pondered his words, while a glass encased pendulum clock, with its brightly polished brass movement, clacked in an appreciable tone atop an antique hutch, stealing away the seconds, and then the minutes.

"Stellar travel takes generations, Zachary. I've been away from home for a long time! I know of it, only what I've been told!" The man, who had said that his name was Daniel, told him this in earnest.

Hearing this, the Navajo could only wonder if he had befriended a poor, sick, deluded soul, who believed he had some extraterrestrial origin: who needed to be humored, fed, and allowed a good nights rest, and to be sent on his way in the morning.

"Why don't I make us something to eat!" Zachary offered, preferring to change the subject, rather than waiting for the man to expostulate at length on his delusory fantasy. "You can take a shower if you like! The bathroom is down the hall, first door on the right! You can't miss it!" He quipped.

"That sounds like a good idea! Thanks!" The stranger said, rising from the recliner. He walked toward the darkened hallway.

"There's a light..............." Before Zachary could finish what he was saying, the stranger reached out in the dark for the light switch, as though he had done so a thousand times before. "There are clean towels on the shelf, just to the right of the door," the Indian told him, as he disappeared into the hallway.

Zachary got up from the sofa and went to the kitchen. -*Tsoh* bounded from the sofa after him. He opened a lower cupboard and pulled out a large bag of dried dog food. Scooping it out, he filled the bowl on the floor. The dog's nose hung over it in anxious anticipation. While-*Tsoh* crunched the hard nuggets, Zachary went to the sink to fill the dog's water bowl.

He couldn't help but think about what the man had told him. However outrageous his story sounded, he couldn't dismiss from his mind the earlier events of the day. *How did he know?* He asked himself. *He just switched on the light like he had been here before! Coincidence? It had to be! Just like all the other things that happened.* But the Navajo was not totally assured that there was no validity to any of them. Indeed, there existed a glimmer of doubt that gnawed at him.

What if all of this was real? What *if* this person was telling him the truth? He could be the first to know things that no one else has ever known before! He felt a twinge of excitement. Zachary placed the water dish on the floor next to the dog. Then he walked over to the refrigerator, opened it, and brought out an aluminum kettle filled with chili. He took it to the stove and set it on a burner to warm.

But as he stood there, he thought, *I'd look like a fool, if he turned out to be a fake, an escaped lunatic! There has to be some way to find out for sure?* He reached into the cupboard and took out two bowls. Zachary set the table. Then he returned to the cupboard for two small glasses, that he set on the edge of the table. The stranger entered the room looking refreshed. His hair still damp, he stood near the table buttoning his gray flannel shirt.

"Feeling better?" The Indian asked.

"Much! Thank you!" He replied.

"Good! The chili will be hot soon! Have a seat. I'll pour you a drink!" Zachary said in a cheerful manner, displaying the more exuberant side of his nature.

Going back to the cupboard, he opened it and brought out a plain brown jug, about a half gallon in size. "I have somethin' here that will warm you inside! I make it special! It's called mescal!"

He walked back to the table and uncorked the bottle, allowing the scent of the aromatic liquor to escape. He filled each of the small glasses. Then he set the jug on the table. Raising his glass, he said, "Here's to a new friend!" They both sipped on the pungent liquid.

"What's this made from, Zachary?" The stranger asked, noting its acrid taste. He breathed deeply in an effort to cool his throat.

"Cactus! And it's not hard to come by in this part of the country! Of course, it might be where *you're* from?" The Navajo hinted in a wily manner.

Taking another sip, the stranger's face took on a contorted look. "It's bitter!"

"After a while, you won't notice!" Zachary set his glass down on the table. "I'd better check the chili! We wouldn't want to burn it. It's too damn good to waste!" He walked back to the stove and lowered the flame on the burner.

"You take crackers or bread with your chili?" The Indian inquired, opening the pot to the escaping steam and the tangy odor that broached his nostrils as he leaned over it.

"Whatever you have will be fine!" The stranger said agreeably.

"I like crackers, myself," Zachary said, standing in front of the stove, pondering, as he looked down at the gurgling chili. He stirred it slowly with a wooden spoon.

Anticipating Zachary's inescapable questioning, the stranger sat with his arms resting on the table, and the empty glass in his left hand. He tipped it, peering at it thoughtfully.

"So this message you have, ...it has to do with the fact that our kind........meaning we humans.........don't get along very well with one another! Is there more?" The Navajo asked. He turned off the stove and reached for a potholder that hung on a hook on the wall above. Then he opened a drawer next to the stove and withdrew a ladle.

"There's much to be considered, Zachary!" The stranger said, still looking thoughtfully. "It isn't just a matter of your kind anymore. I wish it was that simple, ...but there's much more at stake now!"

"Sounds pretty serious!" The Indian retorted.

"It is!" The stranger replied.

He grabbed the handle that was hanging down to the side of the kettle, and raised it with the potholder, to bring the pot of chili to the table. "Here you go! It's the best damn chili in the Four Corners!" He used the ladle to scoop the chili from the kettle into the bowls on the table. "It's very hot, so you'd better wait a few minutes before taking a bite!" He warned the stranger.

"I'll get those crackers!" Zachary returned to the stove. Setting the pot of chili down upon it, he reached into the cupboard for a box of saltines. "Would you like a glass of water?"

"Yes, please," he responded. "You're a good host, Zachary!"

"Thanks! I don't get company out here very often." He returned to the table with two glasses of water in hand, and a package of saltines tucked under his arm. Pulling out the chair across the table from his enigmatic guest, he sat down. "We all lived here together at one time! Me and my family, that is!" As he said that, his eyes flashed reflectively about the room. "My father and my brother and myself, we built this house." He paused momentarily. "Actually, we helped my father!" He admitted. "Marvin was ten years old, and I was seven. I remember some of the tribal members coming out and lending a hand, too! My mother was all excited about it, because we'd been living in a mobile home, but she wanted a real home, one built on the ground!"

"There's a lot of memories here for me," Zachary said, thoughtfully considering the past. "My mother made many trips between this table and that stove, when we were all here together."

"It sounds like you miss them, Zachary," Daniel said. Taking a spoon full of chili from his bowl, he held it close to his lips, then he sampled it.

"Yeah, it's too quiet around here for me sometimes! It's nice to have some company," the Indian intimated. "Maybe you'll be staying around for a while?" He crumbled some crackers into his chili.

The stranger gave him a pensive look. "Maybe. Maybe you can help me," he suggested. He bit a cracker, then he took a bite of the hot chili, followed by a sip of water. "This is good! But hot!"

Eyeing him inquisitively, the wary Navajo asked, "How can I help you?"

Deliberating for a moment, the stranger asked, "Who is the most influential person that you know well?"

"The chairman of the tribal council, I guess! Jack McCloud. He's kind a like our business manager, C.E.O., and chief, all rolled into one!" Zachary told him.

"Then he's a very important man, right?"

"Yes, very important! He knows all of the influential people in the tribe, and many outside of it, too!"

"That's what I need from you! I need you to introduce me to him!" The stranger stated with great emphasis. "I *must* meet him!"

He had placed such import on it, that it troubled the Indian. *What could be so important that he needs to meet Jack McCloud?* He asked himself. He put aside an immediate response. Zachary reached for the open package of crackers in the center of the table. "How's your chili?" He asked.

"Fine," the stranger responded, mulling over it.

"It's really good, once you get use to the heat! Would you like more?" The Navajo inquired politely.

"No, thank you. Did you make this yourself?"

"Hell no! There's a woman down the road that cooks stuff, and brings it over for me once in a while! It gives her an excuse to come over'n visit me. Her man left her with five kids! Anyway, I think she's taken a liking to me! She's a good woman! But I'm just not interested. Besides, she's just too big for me!" The Indian expressed it, gesturing with his outreached arms as if he was encompassing her girth.

Then he looked at the stranger mindfully. "So you want me to introduce you to the tribal chairman? Why?" Zachary asked flatly, his dark eyes peered intently at the stranger across the table from him.

"I have a message for him. I have to give it to him, soon!" The stranger indicated with the same sense of urgency that the Navajo had detected earlier.

"You didn't even know who he was, until I told you about him a few minutes ago! How could you have a personal message for him?" The Indian inquired in a tone of distrust.

"That doesn't matter." He said in a voice filled with calm resignation. "Trust me! I have to meet him!"

Zachary looked up from his bowl, with his spoon still immersed in the chili and broken crackers. "What if I don't?" He asked boldly. "Then what happens?"

"Are you asking me if I'm going to do something to you?" The stranger viewed him with an expression of inquiry, and his head slightly askew, holding his hand beneath his chin.

The Indian's question had resounded with all that it implied. He could feel beads of sweat forming over his brow. Was it the chili? Or the intensity of the moment? "I've seen you do things! At least, I think I have?" He hesitated. "I'm not sure! I 'm not sure *who* you are, or if you're telling me the truth!" As he glared at the stranger, he could feel the perspiration running down his hair line, over his left temple. And then on the right side.

"That's for *you* to decide, Zachary!" The stranger named Daniel said, in an unyielding tone. "But you needn't worry, I'm not here to harm you!" He paused. "However, a lot can happen to you indirectly, and to your people if you decide not to help me!"

"Like what?" Zachary asked, taking his kerchief from his back pocket, he wiped the sweat from his face. "Damn chili's hot," he muttered as he did so.

"Like life as you know it could change radically," the stranger told him. "It's already started."

He had kindled the inherent interest the Navajo had in the welfare of his people. "That sounds pretty ominous! You mean my help is that important to you?"

The stranger gave him a look of certainty that confirmed his answer.

"I'm not sure about you. But there's something deep inside of me, that's telling me to give you the benefit of the doubt! I don't know if it's the things my grandfather taught me? Or if it's just my own curiosity? Whatever it is, I'm willing to listen!"

Zachary shook his head, displaying his perplexity. Then he slid his chair back on the grooveworn linoleum. He got up and reached for the stranger's bowl. "You sure you don't want more?"

"No, thank you, Zachary! But give my compliments to the chef!"

Somehow, he felt relieved. His tension had dispatched. "You can do it yourself,............if you stick around long enough!" Zachary commented, donning a mischievous smile.

He took the bowls to the sink. Then he glanced at the electric clock on the wall above him, noting the time. It was ten minutes after nine. Zachary turned to face the man named Daniel, who sat at the table across the room from him: who he had only known for less than a day, and who now asked him for his trust and his confidence. "I would feel better about all of this, if you could tell me more," he said.

"Yes, I could tell you more. But remember, whatever I tell you is going to change your life,...........forever!" Daniel assured him. "Once you have knowledge, you can never turn your back on it!" He said this in distinct, resonant tones that affirmed his conviction.

Turning away, Zachary averted the stranger's riveting gaze. "Let's go sit in the living room. We'll be more comfortable in there. You can tell me more." He walked by the table, grabbed the jug of mescal, picked up his glass, and started for the living room. Daniel picked up his glass and followed him.

-Tsoh was already asleep on the sofa. Zachary waited for Daniel to sit down on the recliner, then he took his glass. "Let's have another drink while you fill me in on the details!" He poured the stranger's glass full. Then he filled his own and placed the jug on the lamp table next to him. With his glass in hand, he extended it toward the stranger, gesturing a toast, then he tipped his head back and shot the wild extract into his mouth, taking it down with one gulp. His eyes watered noticeably.

The stranger sipped his slowly, giving the Indian a look of assessment, while Zachary strode wearily to the stove. Picking up a steel poker, he used the tip of it to open the latch on the door of the wood-burning stove. He prodded the fire until its luminosity increased, then he added two more logs. Hot sparks flitted from the open door as the flames licked the cold fuel, causing the wood to pop. Closing the door with the poker, he leaned it against the wall next to the stove.

Then he went to the sofa, and with a hint of annoyance, he attempted to move the mass of canine flesh sprawled out over it. He gave the dog a firm shove, while he settled in beside it. *-Tsoh* lithed, then conceded some space with a brief growl and a snort, falling back to sleep.

In the dimness of the flickering light from the fire, Zachary asked, "What is it that you want from me? Who are you?" The very questions that he asked, confirmed his subconscious belief that meeting this stranger was no accident, that he was more than just a transient handyman on his way to find a better job. He had a sense of reckoning with an obscure past, one he did not fully comprehend.

"It's as I have told you, I just want you to help me! And in doing so, you'll be helping yourself, and your people as well. As for the other, you have the beliefs of your ancestors to reckon with! If you believe the way of the Ancients, then you will see me that way! But if you do not, then you will see me otherwise!" He paused for a brief moment. "We can only be imprisoned by what we believe, without doubt, to be the truth! And the truth is in continual metamorphosis, and is different for every man!" Daniel told him.

The Indian pondered his words, considering how his ancestors would have viewed the stranger. "Then if I believe you're my Spirit Messenger, I'm correct. And if I believe the things that I think I've seen you do, then you have done them." He mused aloud. "Is that my truth?" Zachary asked him, earnestly pondering the question.

"Is it?" Daniel retorted.

"I'm not sure," Zachary said. He stared at the specter of what, his eyes told him, was an ordinary flesh and blood man. He was unwilling to bolster myths or legends that had no proven basis in his own reality. Coming face to face with an unresolved conflict, it was one for which he had no immediate resolution. But he was now certain that he was set on a course that would take him to that answer. However he chose to view him, he already felt he had obligated himself to help this man.

"What is this message you have for Jack McCloud?" The Navajo asked.

"It's more of a challenge than a message! Among my own, I was bred to be a hunter! It is my purpose! My job!" Daniel hesitated. "*It is* what I am bound to do!"

"Why Jack McCloud?" Zachary asked nervously. "What do you want from him?"

"Nothing. I don't want anything from him." Daniel said flatly. "It is for him to prove where he stands! There are opposing forces at work, regardless of how you believe! I wish merely to test him, to see what side he is on!"

There was something about the way the stranger spoke that provoked Zachary's interest. The prospect of proving a man's worthiness as a warrior, his manhood, had been an innate part of ancient cultures, and most civilizations from the beginning of history. A mere test seemed harmless enough. "But how will this help my people?" He asked.

"If he is a good leader, then he will pass the test! If he is not, he will fail and a better leader will emerge!" The stranger answered convincingly. "It is really that simple!"

Considering what Daniel had just said to him, Zachary replied in defense of Jack McCloud, "I've known him for years, ever since I was a boy! He's a good man! He and my father were very good friends. He knew my grandfather as well."

"Jack wasn't on the council then." Zachary continued. "He had gone away from the reservation to go to law school. I was only about ten years old when he came back. I remember him coming out to our house for dinner. He, my dad, and my grandfather would talk for hours about the tribe. I used to listen! I was so impressed by him, being educated and a lawyer and all. He told my grandfather how he was going to help the Navajos move into the twentieth century. He talked about how we were going to be more independent and self-sufficient. I listened, and I wanted to be just like him when I grew up! He had big dreams for the tribe!"

The Navajo paused for a moment, with a ponderous expression. An aberrant thought had crossed his mind. "Something happened though! After a while, he changed. He started getting into tribal politics, then he stopped coming around. Jack didn't even come to my father's funeral. I guess it was all the power, ...and being seen with the right people. I suppose we just weren't the right people anymore!" He said it with a hint of regret in his voice.

"Anyway, I stopped wanting to be like him. I had a chance to go to college. I could've gone to N.A.U. on a scholarship. But I saw what happened to Jack! Sometimes I don't think he's a Navajo anymore!"

The stranger had been silently attentive. It was as though he had already anticipated the outcome of the conversation.

It was a vagrant apparition of doubt that had persuaded Zachary, not the stranger. At least he thought not. "I'll call Jack McCloud's office in the morning for an appointment! I'll tell him it's important! He'll believe me." He hesitated. "But what will you say to him?" The Indian asked, curiously. He peered at the form in the chair across from him, in the duskiness of the living room, awaiting a response. The fire in the stove flickered with failing intensity.

"I'll know what to say, when I meet him!" The stranger spoke confidently.

The brass clock on the hutch struck eleven. "I think we'd better get some sleep!" Zachary yawned wide. "Let me show you to your room!"

Lying in his bed, the Navajo couldn't help but wonder if he had made a compact with the devil, the Evil One he had learned about in his Christian religious studies. Or, if this was some phenomenon, a Spirit Messenger, sent by his ancestors to guide him, as his native religious beliefs implied. He thought the stranger too coherent to be deranged. There was only *one* other possibility, and to him, it was the most absurd.

He slept restlessly.

Chapter 5

The Chairman, the Hunter and the Challenge

JACK, IT'S ZACHARY THOMAS! HOW ARE YOU THIS MORNING? GOOD. I was wondering if you're going to be in your office today? You are. I'd like you to meet with a friend a mine. No, you don't know him, he's from...........Colorado. Well,...........it is important! He's come a long way, and I promised I'd introduce him to you! What does he do. Well...........

The Navajo heard the stranger's distinct footsteps on the kitchen floor as it flexed under his feet, creaking, and the soles of his heavy boots that squeaked against the linoleum with each deliberate step. Until he could feel his looming presence at his back. He turned to face the man named Daniel, as he stood at the phone on the wall beside the cupboards. "I study human cultures," the stranger said, noting the bewildered expression on the Indian's face. He answered the question forthright.

And Zachary translated that into his response. *He's an anthropologist! He studies native cultures. Ten-thirty would be fine. His name? It's Daniel. Just Daniel! That's all I know. Okay, see you then. Thanks. Bye.*

Hanging up the receiver, the Navajo's eyes lifted to meet the encroaching stare of the obtrusive visitor. It was a controlling gaze that thwarted him at that moment, causing him to feel a foreboding chill. The steeled, blue eyes in the too smooth face of the stranger, drilled him with inquiry, possessively.

"He'll see us at ten-thirty," Zachary said, swallowing hard afterward. He endeavored to match the mettle in the stranger's eyes with his own. "He's

So we have about an hour drive. We'll take the pickup
"

s eyelids hadn't blinked in several minutes. It made Zachary omfortable. He relinquished this contest of wills, retreating f other thoughts. "I'll put on some coffee! Then I'm gonna ak ! I'll be dressed and ready to go in about twenty minutes." The Navajo to him, while pressing by the stranger. He had been standing between Zachary and the way out of the kitchen.

Halting at the edge of the carpet, briefly, the Navajo turned to give a slanted look from over his shoulder. "Help yourself to the coffee. The cups are in the cabinet directly above the pot!"

-Tsoh slumped beneath the kitchen table, watching the stranger with indecisive eyes as he took a cup from the cupboard.

Returning to the kitchen, prepared to leave, Zachary grabbed a mug and poured coffee for himself. Taking several small sips, he set it down on the kitchen countertop nearest the door. Then he stuffed a bag of Red Man chewing tobacco into the pocket of his jacket. "We'd better go! Jack's a busy man. We don't want to be late." He snatched up his keys and his coffee mug and bolted out the door, with the dog slipping out between the screen door after him. The stranger pulled the door closed behind him and followed.

It was another cool, bright morning, typical of mid-October on the intermediate steppes of the mesas and high plains in northeastern Arizona. Zachary backed the pickup truck out of the shed. It idled roughly, burning out the residuals of disuse. "I don't use it enough!" The Navajo commented, as he turned to the stranger who was entering on the passenger side.

Barking plaintively, the persistent mongrel sat on the ground outside of the truck, staring at Zachary with a look of abandonment. "Oh, so you want to go too?" He quizzed the animal in a tone of reprehension, as if the too large, surly beast had the faculties to express his disapproval at the prospect of being left behind.

Zachary got out and lowered the tailgate, so that *-Tsoh* could climb up in the back of the truck. The huge dog dove for the tailgate, landing on his belly with his hind quarters dangling over the edge, kicking and shuffling. The Indian gave him a shove and *-Tosh* scrambled into the truckbed. Then he returned to the driver's seat, taking the pouch of Red Man in hand from beside him. He uncurled the top of it, and broached the foil bag with his thumb and forefinger, taking a pinch of the sticky, dark brown and black, tobacco and molasses chew between them. He stuffed it into his mouth, packing his jowls with it.

Wheeling the truck around in the driveway, he sped off toward the main highway, to what might prove to be a hapless meeting with a man whom he had given scant consideration for many years. Spitting into a cup, he drew the back of his hand across his chin. "I haven't had much to do with Jack for a long time! Don't know how much help that's gonna be to ya? I'm surprised he agreed to meet you!" Zachary told the stranger, lacking the sense of enthusiasm he had the night before, after the two glasses of mescal, for a trial of Jack McCloud's integrity. Although he had considered it well founded, he wondered if he and this stranger should be the ones to conduct it, if it wouldn't be best to leave it to fate and the political process? He wrestled with that, as he measured the dull headache that he had since he had gotten up, which he also attributed to the mescal.

And then he considered the stranger, who had said very little to him since before they had left his house. Zachary wondered when he had found time to shave? *He must've gotten up before me!* He told himself. But he hadn't heard the water running. Why did such a thing bother him, he wondered? He sped westward on Highway 160, with the sun trailing in the morning sky to their backs. And through his partially open window, the wind whistled like a tea kettle coming to a boil. He rolled it down farther to eliminate the shrill sound.

Quiet, the stranger appeared to be contemplating the scenery, with his attentive eyes scanning the plateau to the north in the area where Zachary had picked him up the morning prior. It was near the Navajo National Monument, comprised of the Tsegi Canyon system, where the Kayenta Anasazi had flourished for centuries, from as early as 950 A.D. until about 1300 A.D., when they abandoned their cliff dwellings and disappeared, leaving many questions about their existence unanswered.

What about his clothes? Zachary asked himself. *They're everyday clothes that anybody would wear! They're worn and dirty! And yet, he expects me to believe he is something more!* But that is what perplexed Zachary the most. He didn't expect it.

Zachary thought aloud. "If you were a spirit messenger, wouldn't you look different?" He posed this question to the stranger as abruptly as it had entered his mind. "Why would you be dressed the way you are dressed? If you wanted me to believe you are a messenger, wouldn't it have been easier to appear some other way? I mean, you don't look all that different!" He wasn't sure what he meant. His head was throbbing. And his thoughts were scattered. He wasn't even sure why he was saying these things. Or why he was actually taking this stranger to meet with Jack McCloud.

Although the stranger's eyes were fixed on the surroundings, he had listened attentively. He had heard every word that Zachary had said. And when he turned to face Zachary, to respond, it was with the calm intensity that seemed to exude from the man. If, that is what he could be called.

"Your mind's eye sees me the way that you want to! The way that you are capable of seeing me. I'm a mirror of what you perceive to be reality!" The stranger named Daniel told him.

For a brief moment, Zachary pondered what he had said. "Then why don't I see you as a Navajo? Wouldn't that be more comfortable for me?" The Indian asked him, displaying an exceptional wit.

Amused by his quickness, the stranger gave up a rare smile, that was exceedingly difficult for Zachary to ignore when he glanced over at the man, after he had posed his question. It had a disarming effect that took the edge off the moment.

"And suppose I did?" Daniel asked him. "Suppose I looked like one of your people? Wouldn't you find it even more difficult to accept anything that I've told you?"

"Yes, I suppose so!" The Navajo answered, needing little time for deliberation about it. "If an Indian told me some of the things that you have, I'd probably think he was drunk or on drugs, maybe even eating a little too much peyote!"

"There you have it! You see what you are willing to accept as credible!" The stranger asserted.

"So, how do you really look?" Zachary asked with a flippant expression.

"Not so different." The stranger responded flatly. He gazed about with a preoccupation.

Finding the banter entertaining, the Navajo could not resist the next question. "But your clothes. Where did you get them? Don't you have some kind of special uniform or something? You know, something kind a flashy with zippers all over and chrome boots or something! Something more................" He hesitated to continue. What he was about to say struck him as odd. It had an implication that made him uneasy.

Looking reflectively, the stranger glanced at Zachary and said, "I'm not trying to draw attention to myself,..............and I have no need to wear them. The clothes I'm wearing are very easy to acquire, as you know!"

Zachary felt the stranger's demeanor become cool and distant. He pulled off the road into the parking lot of the tribal council offices. They were already ten minutes late for their appointment. "I don't know what his agenda is like, but we'd better hurry if you want time enough for him to hear everything you have to say!"

He swung the door open and ejected the tobacco chew from his mouth, then he got out of the pickup truck. The Navajo walked to the back of it to check on *-Tsoh*. "You stay right here boy!" He cautioned the dog, who laid flat in the truckbed with his sullen eyes addressing his master's request. "And don't bother anybody!"

They walked into the lobby of the council offices. Zachary approached the receptionist's desk. "We're here to see Jack!" He told the attractive young Navajo woman.

She was demure in manner and responded succinctly. "Your name sir?"

"Zachary! Zachary Thomas!" He told her.

"Please have a seat Mister Thomas, I'll be right back."

The young woman got up from behind her desk, and walked down the corridor until she was out of sight. Zachary and the stranger, Daniel, took a seat across from her desk, next to the entry. From his position, Zachary leaned forward to peer through the glass door at *-Tsoh*. The dog rested his muzzle over the side of the truck, with his eyes peering around the corner, looking as though he awaited a summons to join them.

"Zachary! How are you?" He heard a familiar voice, and turned his head to see Jack McCloud approaching them. He stood. "It's been too long!" Jack declared, extending his hand to Zachary, while his eyes briefly measured the stranger, then quickly returned to an old friend.

He was a well groomed man in his early fifties; his hair was cut close and graying at the temples. He wore a silver bolla with a large turquoise stone inlay, over a western style, blue and white plaid shirt that was neatly pressed. And he moved decisively, with the stride of a confident corporate executive. But there was no mistaking his Navajo heritage. His strong native features dominated his earnest expression.

"So this is your friend," Jack McCloud said, taking a step back to look up at the man. Jack was an average sized Navajo of about five feet eight inches, somewhat shorter than Zachary Thomas, who was taller than average. He was nearly six feet, and the stranger, who towered over both men, was about six feet two inches tall.

"Yes, this is Daniel." Zachary replied, introducing the two men. "Daniel this is Jack McCloud, the council chairman."

"Good to meet you!" Jack said, reaching for the stranger's hand. He took a firm grip. "Let's go back to my office and talk," he said, releasing his hand. Then he turned and started toward the corridor, pausing briefly to speak to the receptionist who had resumed her place behind the desk. "Hold my calls, Anita!"

As he led them through the door of his office, Jack McCloud said, "Come in and sit down gentlemen." He gestured toward the two high back, padded black leather chairs set immediately in front of his large, ornate, ostentatious oak desk. Jack stepped with agility, around the corner of it, taking his place behind the desk in a chair that was every bit as stately, with scrolled wooden arms matching the adornment on the desk. It enveloped him in privileged comfort as he eased into it. It also enhanced his powerful image, and he didn't appear to be shy of it.

He sat at the desk, set diagonally in the room, in front of a corner window that afforded a view of the stark tableau in which he was a dominant figure. There was mahogany paneling on the walls surrounding him, and to the right of his desk was a large bookcase filled with volumes on U.S. Government Indian Treaties, dating back to the late 1800's. There were also volumes on tribal and civil law. And on the wall behind them was a large glass case. It contained awards and gifts bestowed upon the tribe by civic and historical organizations. To their left was a long, oak credenza with a bronze casting of an Indian on a horse.

But there was more than affluent luxury that surrounded Jack McCloud. On the wall above the credenza there was the head of a large black bear, with its jaws frozen open and its fangs displayed prominently beneath a ceaseless, angry snarl. There were less intimidating animal heads displayed on the walls too. The head of a mature, big horn sheep was displayed on the wall to the right of Jack McCloud, over his shoulder, and on the adjacent wall was the head of a ten point buck, white tail deer, and that of a large antelope.

Jack McCloud was something more than the leader of the Navajo Nation and the spokesman for, as they refer to themselves, The People. He was more than a statesman and politician, and an organizer and businessman. He was a *hunter!*

The stranger removed his cap and placed it on his lap, he held onto the brim and moved it between the fingers of both hands, while he looked ponderously at the images that he saw around the room. Then he peered at the sturdy Navajo sitting across from him, and he noted his strong, intelligent, and recalcitrant dark eyes.

"Zachary tells me that there's something important you wanted to speak to me about! He tells me that you're an anthropologist. Of course, we're always interested in assisting the scientists who study our culture!" Jack McCloud stated graciously. He leaned farther back into his chair, with his strong hands grasping the carved wooden arms.

"I'm here to help you protect future generations of your people from extinction, Mister McCloud!" The stranger told him with a bold expression that took him by surprise.

Jack looked puzzled. "The Navajo people are protected by federal law. We protect ourselves, too! What's the basis for your remark?" He leaned forward with a guarded expression, planting his stout forearms firmly on the glass top that covered his desk. Then he peered at the stranger with an incredulous look.

The stranger was unyielding in his pursuit. "There are no laws that will protect your people from the kind of extinction of which I am speaking!" He said in a tone of assurance. "Your protection is in your ability to implement change!"

"What is this guy talking about, Zachary?" He said, addressing the Navajo sitting beside the stranger, who looked as stunned as he.

"I'm not sure, but I think you'd better listen!" Was Zachary's reply.

"What has this got to do with anthropology? And what has it got to do with me?" Jack McCloud demanded of the Anglo. He displayed his obvious disdain at the presumption of the stranger.

Assessing Jack McCloud with a calloused look, the stranger said, "The preservation of a race has always been a concern of anthropology!" He paused, detecting the chairman's impatience. "I'll make this as brief as possible Mister McCloud," he said drawing a ready breath. "There are forces at work. Call them Good and Evil, or the Dark One and He Who Walks In The Light! Whatever your interpretation of this duality, it exists. They have always been in opposition," he said as a matter of fact. "And now they have reached a critical moment." He hesitated. "I've been there before, on other worlds where the same thing has occurred! Over, and over again! It is always the same! *He* uses the resources of that world against its people, pitting them against one another! I know, it happened on my own world!"

Strained by the audacity of the stranger, Jack McCloud was indignant. "Who are you, anyway!"

"I'm a hunter!" He said with a sigh of resignation. "It is what I do. It is what I have been bred to do! I've hunted *Him* on world after world! And now I am here!"

Somewhat embarrassed, yet mesmerized by what this peculiar man was saying, Zachary suggested nervously, "Maybe we'd better go!"

"No! I don't think he is finished yet, and I've heard this much!" Jack McCloud was insistent. "Who is *he,* this one that you hunt? And what is it he's doing to put my people in jeopardy? Please explain this to me!" He asked sarcastically, taking an amused posture. Zachary sank deeper into his chair in silent retreat.

Appearing to be undisturbed by the hostility in Jack McCloud's voice, he measured the man calmly with cold, unrelenting eyes that bordered on an emotionless, icy blue. "You call him by many names! But he is many, with only one name! He is the Dark One! I know him well,...............we have been adversaries for longer than I care to remember!"

His voice carried an apocalyptic overtone, that was inwardly disturbing to Jack McCloud, although his expression remained rigid and unyielding, as the stranger said, "You appear to be an educated man, and well read I presume! You've read about oil spills in the newspaper, or heard about them on the news: the cutting and burning off of the Earth's rainforests, the pollution of your fresh water supplies, the contamination of your agricultural lands by the overuse of chemical pesticides and herbicides, and the pollution of your air by hydrocarbon emissions, radioactive wastes in your water and on your land, toxic waste materials ineffectively handled or misused, acid rain poisoning your lakes and rivers, and destroying your forests, all extracted as the cost of doing business!" He gave a calculated pause. "That's how!"

"It's like I said, *He* uses the resources of each world against its people!" The stranger reiterated. "Their greed and apathy are *His* weapons!"

"What's your point? What has this got to do with me?" Jack McCloud asked bluntly.

"You do business, don't you?" The stranger asked knowingly.

"Yes, I do business for the Tribe! Myself and the council, that is!"

"But you're a powerful man, and you've been doing business for yourself too!" He told Jack McCloud.

"What's he saying here, Jack? What's he mean about you doing business for yourself?" Zachary inquired with stern eyes, and a tone of distrust.

It was a staggering insinuation, one that the chairman was in no way ready or willing to sit upon. He stood up and walked around the corner of his desk. "Zachary, can I talk to you outside for a minute?" He said as he stepped quickly toward the door. The Navajo got up from his chair and followed Jack McCloud out into the corridor.

"Pull that door closed behind you, Zachary!" He glowered angrily at the man who was, perhaps, part of what was the nearest thing to family he had known. "We've known each other for years, that's the only reason I agreed to see you and your friend today!" He said in a gristly whisper, and one gulp of breath, with consternation in his voice. "Who is this guy?"

"I found him hitchhiking yesterday morning along 160, a few miles west of here! I offered him a ride and he's been with me ever since. He didn't have anywhere to go, so I let him stay over at my place last night!" Zachary explained, while Jack McCloud stood eye to eye with him. "Why did he say that to you? Is there something to what he's saying?" Zachary was persistent.

"Of course not! I have no idea what he's talking about!" Jack McCloud replied defensively. "You know me, I've always had the welfare of the Tribe at heart! What could he possibly be talking about?" Jack shook his head in vehement denial.

"I know some of what he's saying sounds strange, Jack! But I can't help but feel that there's something to what he's been telling me! I just don't know how it all comes together yet! But this feeling I've got, it's overwhelming!" Zachary was adamant.

"Then you're as crazy as he is! And I'm not going to sit around and listen to this crap! I've got too many more important things to do than listen to some lunatic rattle off about the environment, and make accusations about the way I handle tribal business!" Jack McCloud said.

Zachary measured him intently. "I don't think that's what he was telling you, Jack! And I don't think he's crazy! Anyway, I've seen him do things." The Navajo spoke softly. "He saved my life yesterday in Flagstaff. One of the steers was injured, it drug me down the chute and almost trampled me! He came out and stopped the animal. He has this power! I don't know what it is, but it's there!"

"I've never known you to be a liar, Zachary, but this is going a little too far!" Jack said impatiently. "I don't know what this guy is doing to you, but you'd better get rid of him before he gets you into some real trouble! That's my advice to you as a friend!" He huffed. "Let's go back inside, and you can take him with you. I just don't have anymore time for this today!"

Zachary caught his arm as he turned toward the door, pulling Jack

McCloud back around to face him. "One more thing, Jack! There's something I forgot to tell you! I think he can read your mind, he probably knows everything we've talked about!"

Bursting into laughter as he reached for the door, Jack McCloud said, "Well, I guess I won't have to tell him to leave then, will I!"

He sat quietly, staring out the window behind Jack's desk. He appeared captivated by the view of the buttes in the distance. But his mind's eye was looking much farther, far beyond the present. Zachary patted him on the shoulder as he sat down next to him. He felt it again when he touched him. It was that energy. His attention was brought back into the room, to Jack McCloud's glaring eyes, and his expression of annoyance.

"Look here," Jack said, bluntly, "I empathize with your concerns, but I'm sure that everyone is doing whatever they can to make things better! And I don't have anymore time today to talk about this! But I assure you I will do everything that I can to make my people aware!"

"Will you?" The stranger queried. "Or will you continue to serve your own interests?"

Anita knocked softly on the door. She opened it part way and said, "Mister McCloud, your next appointment is waiting."

"Thank you, Anita! Gentlemen................"

The stranger stood up with his cap in his hand, holding it by the brim in front of him. "That's all right Mister McCloud, you won't have to ask me to leave, as you suggested earlier!"

"I didn't!"

"Yes you did! Think about it! And think about what I've told you, I'll be around for a while. I think you'll know where to find me!" He placed the black cap on his head.

"Sure," Jack said, reluctantly reaching across his desk for the stranger's hand. He felt a cool, metal object cross his palm. When the stranger released his grip, the chairman was compelled to clench the object in his hand. He viewed the stranger curiously. He held it momentarily, then he quickly slipped it into his pants pocket.

"Take care, Zachary," Jack McCloud said as he took his hand. "Don't be a stranger!"

Jack stood behind his desk watching the two men leave the room. "Leave the door open please, Zachary!"

On their way out through the lobby, they passed the two men that were Jack McCloud's next appointment. Anita was showing them the way back to his office. The man named Daniel recognized them. One was thin. The skin on his pockmarked face was taut, it gave his large, narrow set eyes, and almost black, small irises a bug eyed appearance. He had a scar over his right eye, russet brown skin like an Indian — but he was not — and black hair pulled back tightly in a short ponytail, held in a gold ring.

The other man was taller and heavier, with a muscular frame, and he had strong hands with grease laden and jagged fingernails. He had long, stringy blond hair that buffeted the top of his shirt collar, and a thick mustache, with several days growth on his robust face. He was edgy, and his light brown eyes were cold and dishonest.

They were the two men from the restaurant in Flagstaff.

Chapter 6

The Intrusion

STANDING ON THE SIDEWALK OUTSIDE OF THE COUNCIL OFFICES, the stranger was occupied with thought regarding the two men who had just entered Jack McCloud's office. He turned to Zachary with a ponderous expression, and wary eyes filled with suspicion. He asked, "Do you know those two men?"

"No, I've never seen them before. Why do you ask?" The Indian inquired curiously.

"They were at the restaurant yesterday. I saw them. There's something about them. I don't know what it is, but I have a feeling about them," the stranger insisted.

But the Navajo already viewed the stranger with unnatural trepidation. He was hesitant to give further credence to the man's shrewd insinuations. And he saw the stranger's suggestion that there was something sinister about the two men, who went into Jack McCloud's office, as a ploy to distract him from his thoughts concerning the exchange that had taken place between himself and Jack McCloud. If there was something that the man knew about Jack, about his dealings, he wanted to know it, and his attention would not be averted.

He looked back at *-Tsoh,* who had awakened from his nap and greeted them with a growl and a couple of breathy barks. Then they got into truck and left.

"I told you never to come to my office!" Jack McCloud berated the tw
men with an obvious tone of perturbance in his voice. They sat before him
in front of his desk, in the two chairs the stranger and the Navajo had occupie
earlier. This time the door was closed securely and Anita had been excuse
for an early lunch break.

"We thought, maybe, we can do somethin' fer you, Jack! Seein' ho
you've done so much fer us!" The dark, thin man said. The blond man sa
quietly, listening. "We seen those two guys, that just left here, in a restaurar
in Flagstaff yesterday. We seen the tall one give the waitress some gold coins
I thought you'd be interested in knowing about it!" The dark man hintec
with a grossly evil expression crossing his face. "You know'em Jack?"

Jack McCloud gave them both a furtive look, while he considered wha
the dark man had told him, before he responded. "The Navajo is Zachar
Thomas. I've known him for years. His father and I were good friends." H
paused. "The other man is someone he picked up on his way down fror
Kayenta yesterday. At least, that's what they told me." He had slipped hi
hand into his pocket while they were talking. Jack McCloud felt the shape o
the metal object with his fingers.

"Do you know something more about him?" Jack McCloud asked th
two men, addressing both of them with his intensely dominant dark eyes.

"No. But I know what I saw! Those coins. I got a good look at'em!
never seen anything like'em!" The dark man said excitedly. "These was brigh
gold! And they had some kind of an engraving. I tried ta get one, but the bab
wasn't cooperatin'! Anyhow, I'm sure there's more where those come from!

"So, what are you suggesting?" Jack McCloud asked.

"That we'd like ta hang around fer a while, an' watch this dude! Ther
could be a lot more fer all of us, if we was ta find out where he's keepin'em.
The dark man told him. The blond man simply nodded agreeably, with
larcenous smile.

Jack's fingers were moist from pressing them against the object in hi
pocket. He had not taken time to look at it, but he knew now what it was an
was anxious to see it! But not in the company of these two men, whom h
loathed but, with whom he had deemed it necessary to have an association

"Fine, I'd be interested to know more." Jack McCloud agreed, givin
them his permission, but with a word of caution. "Remember, stay out o
trouble! And let me know as soon as you find anything out about this guy!
He warned them adamantly.

After the two men left, he pulled the object from his pocket. It was
gold coin that matched the description the dark man had given him. H
swiveled around in his chair to hold it up to the daylight, that shone throug
the window behind him. The brilliance of it stirred a passion within him.
was an acquisitive lust that he felt. Then he examined it more closely. It wa

different from any coin he had ever seen. The inscription on the border of the coin was foreign. On the face of the coin was what appeared to be seven stars surrounding a planet, with four smaller spheres encompassing it. When he turned it over, he saw several mathematical equations engraved on the coin.

He mused over it, and the man who had given it to him. Jack McCloud hadn't the slightest notion who this man was, but to his estimation the stranger could be the benefactor of enormous wealth, or the harbinger of his ill fate. He was determined to find out what this one had come for!

Zachary was contemplative for a long time, while he drove. Then he asked, "What is it that you were accusing Jack of? I think that you've known something about him all along. And you used me to get to him! Why?" The Navajo's demeanor indicated neither anger, or acceptance of the circumstances. But his tone was insistent on a credible answer.

"Are you a hunter, Zachary?" The stranger inquired of him.

"Yes, but what has that got to do with Jack McCloud?" The Indian was perplexed.

"Don't you study the habits of the prey that you hunt? So you'll know how they think and where to find them?" The stranger measured the Navajo for a response.

"Of course! But what's that..............." Then he realized what the stranger had said earlier about the Dark One. "Is that what you think? That Jack is your adversary?" Zachary wasn't sure whether he should be shocked or amused. But he sensed that the stranger was serious. And he wondered where that put him in the scheme of things?

"I told you, he uses people! And the resources available to him! I'm not certain. But we'll find out who Jack McCloud really is! I promise you that!" The stranger vowed.

There was something else on Zachary's mind. It was something that he believed could reveal the stranger's true identity. And if indeed there was something to this concept of a spiritual messenger that visited the living, then that would possibly be revealed as well. It was part of a belief system he had never relied upon before. At least not since his grandfather had passed away, and he had been inundated with a Christian education. But even his Christian beliefs allowed for the presence of holy messengers sent by God, to His chosen for a specific purpose. In either case, it was generally accepted that a spiritual being, or an angel in the case of Christian scriptures, was the bearer of some revelation to an individual.

And as Zachary understood it, that is why Native Americans were able to assimilate Christianity into their cultures more as another facet of their beliefs, rather than a substitute for them, and still cling to their native religions. Because, other than in pedantics, their mythology was not so far removed from that of the Anglos.

"I'd like to take you to a place I used to go when I was a boy." The Navajo told the stranger named Daniel. "My grandfather took me there many times! It was a special place for me, a spiritual place! There are legends surrounding the people who once lived there. I'll tell you about them when we get there! I guess when you were talking to Jack, it made me think of this place. In fact, I used to camp there over night under the stars, and I would look up and wonder what was out there!" He glanced over at the stranger in the passenger seat, awaiting a response.

"I'd like to see your place. It sounds interesting!"

"Then we'd better have some lunch. And I'll prepare some provisions for our trip," Zachary said.

They turned off the road onto the long driveway that led to the house. When they pulled up in front of the shed, *-Tsoh* jumped out of the truck. He ran to within a few feet of the back door, stopped sharply, and started to bark incessantly.

"I wonder what his problem is?" Zachary commented as he stepped down from the truck. His boots hit the loose gravel, grinding it under his mass as he moved cautiously in that direction. "He usually doesn't act that way, unless there's a stranger around!" He told Daniel.

They approached the back door together. *-Tsoh* was now standing with his front paws on the first step, growling at the open door. "What's the matter boy?" Zachary patted the dog's side. Then he stepped past him, and climbed up the four wooden steps to the door. The screen door was cocked slightly ajar. And the interior door was wide open. "Looks like we've had company," he said, as he entered the kitchen.

Standing a few feet inside the room, his keen eyes swept about while he took stock of it. And his sharp ears listened for audible signs of the intruder's presence. The large, old, protective canine darted into the center of the living room from behind him. He continued to bark and growl as if someone was there. Zachary could see from where he was standing that someone had either been, or was still in the house.

"Who the *hell* is in here?" Zachary shouted, as he scanned the overturned furniture and the cushions tossed about in the living room.

The stranger walked up behind him. "There's no one here now, Zachary."

"How do you know?" The Navajo retorted with anger in his voice. Someone had violated his space. They had invaded the intimacies of his past. He felt attacked.

"They're gone!" The stranger reiterated.

Zachary walked slowly down the hall toward the bedrooms. The stranger followed closely. When he reached the door of the bedroom, where Daniel had slept the night before, he found that the drawers of the dresser had been pulled out and tossed to the floor. The rest of the room had been ransacked.

"A Navajo didn't do this!" Zachary proclaimed. "It was done by others!"

The stranger stood behind him, to the Indian's right, peering over his shoulder in silence. He could sense the man's intense rage spewing from his essence. He stepped back as the Navajo turned with a stoic expression, and walked across the hall to his own room. His mattress was overturned, his closet door was open, and boxes had been pulled off of the shelves and ripped open. His personal belongings had been strewn everywhere.

"*Why* would someone do this? What the hell were they looking for?" He uttered, shaking his head in dismay. "It doesn't look like anything was taken! And I don't have any enemies, at least that I know of, that would vandalize my place like this!"

"I'm not sure, Zachary, but I have a suspicion." Daniel said. "Remember the two men we saw going into Jack McCloud's office this morning? The two that I had seen at the restaurant. I think they may have been looking for something."

"What?" The Navajo asked in earnest.

The stranger reached into his pants pocket. "They may have been looking for some of these." He handed Zachary one of the coins.

"And I thought you were broke!" The Indian exclaimed. "A poor drifter! This looks like real gold!"

"It is! I guess it was careless of me to give any of these away yesterday. But it's all that I had with me!" He confessed to the Navajo.

"Who did you give them to? I didn't see you hand any of them out!"

"The girl at the restaurant! You asked me to leave a tip. Remember?" The stranger reminded him. "This was all that I had, so I left three of them on the table."

Zachary examined the coin as he walked back into the living room. He tossed a cushion back onto the couch, then dropped down onto it, apparently exhausted from the emotional trauma. Sitting there, he mused. "If those guys were still there, they must have seen the coins. I can see why they might be after them! How much are these worth?"

Daniel uprighted the recliner, and sat down. "I don't know what value they would have here. Where I'm from they are merely tokens."

"How much do they weigh," the Navajo queried.

"It would be equivalent to one and one-fourth ounces." The man named Daniel calculated.

"Jeez! You gave that girl enough to put her halfway through college!" Zachary exclaimed. His humor had surfaced again. "Do you have anymore of these?"

"Yes, I have a few more. I brought them as a symbol of friendship."

"Well, so far they haven't cultivated too many friends! You'd best keep them to yourself!" He arose from where he sat and approached the stranger to hand it back.

"Why don't you keep that one as a gift!" He told Zachary.

"Thanks," the Navajo said, putting the coin in his pocket. "How about helping me put this place back together after we've had some lunch? At least the kitchen is still intact!" He quipped.

"Sure, Zachary!" The stranger responded.

The Navajo pondered. *What kind of spirit messenger would carry gold coins?*

"Hey, Jeannie!" The dark man called to the attractive, slender, blond waitress, getting her attention. He gestured to her, calling her over to the table where the two men sat.

"Do you remember seein' an Indian by the name of Zachary in here yesterday? He was with this tall, white dude. And he had a black cap on. You remember, hon?" He quizzed her.

Keeping at arms length from the malignant grasp of the dark, impudent young man, she replied, "Yes, they were in here yesterday morning. I waited on them. What do you want to know for?" She asked, with an intense frown, bordering on a scowl, that was foreign to her otherwise pleasant face.

"Did the tall dude give you anything special?" The dark man inquired further.

"I wish he would, but that's none of your business!" Jeannie retorted sardonically.

"I'm talkin' about some coins, sugar!" The dark man gave her a vulgar smile.

"But how about you and me gettin' together! How 'bout it, babe!" He leered at her with penetrating, lustful eyes, as he measured her sensual form.

The blond man with the mustache put his arm around her waist. He drew her near to him with the grasp of his powerful arm, clenching her waist with his rude hand. She squirmed from his hold, forcing herself away from him, with her hand pressing against his massive shoulder, while she still faced the dark, thin man. "Don't sugar me, you slime ball! And you, you big dumb ox!" She said, looking down at him, repulsed. "Get your slimy hand off me right now!" Jeannie protested. "Before I call Cal out here from the kitchen to kick your ass! I don't, for the life of me, know why they ever let you guys out!" She cursed them, breaking loose of the blond man's grip.

"Okay, okay! We ain't lookin' fer trouble, hon!" The dark man assured her, gesticulating, as he placed his hands out in front of him, with his palms toward her, to avert her wrath. His crude eyes backed down from her impetuous manner, and he laughed.

"Good! Just place your order!" Jeannie told him.

"If they come back in, you'll let me know, right?" The dark man asked sheepishly, displaying a coy expression.

As Jeannie turned her back on the two of them to walk away, she muttered a reply, "It'll be a cold day in hell, asshole!"

She wondered what the two of them wanted with somebody like the stranger, Daniel. *He doesn't seem like the type to be running with their kind!* She thought. *What kind of coins was he talking about? I hope he's not in some kind of trouble?*

Zachary placed an ice chest on the kitchen table. He took some frozen ears of corn from the freezer and placed them inside of it. Then he took two large potatoes, and two white onions from the pantry and placed them in a sack.

"I'd like to get out there before sunset," he told Daniel. "I have two sleeping bags in the hall closet. How about getting them down?" Then he went back to preparing the pack that they would take with them. He threw in some kitchen matches.

Daniel walked in with a sleeping bag clutched in each hand. He held them by the nylon ties that kept them bound in a tight roll. He walked over and dropped them on the floor near the back door. "What else can I help you with?" He inquired of Zachary.

"Just take the camp set, and the sleeping bags out to the truck. I'll have the rest of it ready in a few minutes. You like venison?" He asked.

"Actually, I've never had it!" The stranger admitted. "What is it?"

"It's deer meat!" The Navajo responded. "Trust me, you'll like it the way I fix it!" Zachary placed two steaks in the ice chest, along with a six pack of cold beer and some ice. "We're ready now my friend," he said as he tossed some spices and miscellaneous Navajo condiments into the sack on the table.

Daniel stood in the doorway. He held the door, while Zachary placed the sack atop the ice chest and carried it out. "Perhaps we should lock it this time, Zachary?"

"No. Just close it! They didn't find anything. I don't think they'll be back! Besides, I haven't had the key for that door in years." The Indian told him.

Sitting at the rear of the truck, -*Tsoh* waited impatiently for Zachary to open the tailgate. "No." The Navajo told the dog. "You stay here tonight! Be a watchdog, earn your keep!"

Daniel tucked the sleeping bags against the cab in the bed of the truck, then he got inside. Zachary slipped in behind the wheel, and as he drove away from the house, he could see -*Tsoh* in his rearview mirror. He chased the truck to the end of the driveway. "I think that's all the exercise that old dog gets anymore!" Zachary chuckled. They turned onto the main road and headed north.

As the late afternoon sun retreated toward evening, it cast long, phantom shadows across the desert landscape. They appeared as cool, shaded specters settling behind the buttes and high mesas. The horizon was a medley of darkened shapes.

"It's about twenty miles cross country," Zachary commented. "It should take us about forty-five minutes, if the road isn't washed out anywhere. We've had a lot of rain lately. It gets pretty rough about ten miles up. There's just a trail from there on!"

"This place we're going, is it a place of spiritual significance to your people?" The stranger asked.

"The place we are going is sacred, but it's alright if we go there! It was told to me by my grandfather, that the Ancients held ceremonies there under the stone arch." Zachary said.

The road narrowed to a one lane trail, with an occasional wash intersecting it. Some were deep, carved out by flash floods during the heavy rains. Though no water ran in them now, Zachary had to maneuver the truck carefully around boulders and through the soft soil. He had been caught in a wash before and he was determined to forgo the experience a second time.

"It's about five more miles. See that butte on the left!" The Navajo pointed in that direction as he was speaking. "And the nose of that large mesa with the overhanging cliff! We'll pass right between them. It's just on the other side of the mesa."

They were traveling northwest, and began to climb. The ground was now hardpacked under the tires of the truck, and the trail became easier to travel. But the sun was low and the daylight becoming increasingly scarce.

"Look, straight ahead, it's the arch," Zachary declared when they were in sight of it. "We'll camp right underneath it, just like the Ancients did! The Great Spirit carved this place out for us! He caused the wind and the rain to carve that hole in the rock. You see the sun is setting in the center of it!" The Navajo spoke as though he had made a transition from one world to another, that had been lost to him.

The golden-yellow tint that the fading sun radiated on the interior walls of the sandstone arch, made it appear as a gateway to another world, a doorway to the empyrean heavens, the "Heavens of Fire." It was no wonder that the Ancient Ones chose this place to worship their god. Even the stranger, who had seen many such places, was in awe of it.

"It is a beautiful place, Zachary!" Daniel said. He appeared genuinely affected by the magnificence of it.

"This is only part of it!" The Indian exclaimed. "There is much more to be seen from the arch! But we should stop right here and pick up some juniper brush for our fire."

Zachary stopped the truck in the canyon below the arch, next to a clump of dead, gnarled, dry juniper. They got out of the truck and gathered some deadfall from the ground, and tossed it into the back of the truck in a heap. The Indian climbed the side of the hill next to the truck. Breaking loose some dry branches, he carried them down cradled in his arms. "We'd better get enough, so we'll have some for our morning fire too!"

When they had picked up all that they thought they would need, Zachary drove up the other side of the canyon and parked below the arch. "We can carry everything up from here!" He told the stranger. "Let's go set up our camp! There's steps carved into the side of the rock, going all the way up. Just follow me!"

Lowering the tailgate, the Navajo took a bundle of branches in his arm. The man named Daniel dragged the camp set from the back of the truck. It was a wooden box with an assortment of cookware. He put it up on his shoulder, then he grabbed a sleeping bag in the other hand and followed Zachary up the steps. When they reached the top, there was a flat area about the size of a football field directly under the arch. It appeared to have been leveled. A few boulders were scattered about. In the center, there was a large fire pit built out of small boulders, that had been set in a circle about ten feet in diameter. Walking over to it, Zachary let the bundle of firewood fall to the ground from his arms. Daniel set the sleeping bag and camp set on the ground nearby.

"Let's go to the edge! I want to show you something!" The Navajo told him. They walked the thirty feet to the west rim of the leveled ground. Below the rim was a sheer drop of approximately fifteen-hundred feet to the canyon floor. The irregular walls of the canyon were laced with bluffs and pinnacles. It opened into a vast array of mesas and gorges that appeared to go on forever. The day's last light pulled the copper hues from the sandstone walls. Zachary and the stranger stood at the edge, taking in the spectacular panorama that engulfed them.

"Look below, over on the canyon wall to the north!" Zachary said, turning his head with an inclination, he raised his hand to gesture in that direction. "See the ruins of the cliff dwellings?" They appeared draped in the shadows of antiquity that moved over the canyon. "They were inhabited by an ancient people, the Anasazi, over seven hundred years ago. They disappeared. No one knows why! And they left very little behind to trace them."

Zachary turned to face the stranger, whose eyes were transfixed with visions of an ancient past. "It is told that they held great ceremonies under this stone arch! And that they were in contact with the spirit world! That they could come and go from one world to another as they wished. At least, that is the legend!" The Indian mused. "Anyway, we best get the rest of our gear and set up camp! It will be getting dark soon!"

They unloaded the truck and brought up the remainder of the firewood. Zachary built a fire in the pit, while Daniel opened the camp set and set out some cookware. He sat on a boulder next to the pit. His discerning eyes studied the immediate surroundings. For him, this place had a haunting familiarity to it. As he looked about, he recalled somewhere in the clouded past, that another place was starkly similar. But he had been so many places and traveled for so long.

"The boulders, Zachary? They don't appear to be native to this area?" The stranger queried.

"From the lower canyon, maybe! I've wondered about that myself!" The Navajo admitted. "But this place has many secrets!" He told the stranger as he stooped near the fire. It illuminated his face with a yellowish light, giving it a tawny look.

The night had taken over. Zachary picked up a stick. He scraped out two small holes in the soft earth on the edge of the fire, that was now consuming the wood with a gluttonous fury. The smoke and heat that spired upward, carried glowing sparks aloft. He buried the potatoes, then he reached into the ice chest and brought out the two ears of corn. The husks were still on them, and they were wet.

"These are perfect," he commented. Then he placed the corn on smooth oval stones that were set at the base of the fire. "They'll roast well here!"

The fire cast shadows on the walls of the stone arch. Their own shadows rippled in the dancing light and the ascending heat. It was as though ancient spirit dancers had come out to join them.

Chapter 7

Zachary's Dream

THE DARKNESS HAD ISOLATED THEM FROM TIME. THE PAST FUSED with the present. They sat next to the fire in the center of a place that had known many such fires. Centuries were as days to this place.

"See those stars! My grandfather and I would lay here while our fire died down, looking at them. Wondering! Until we fell asleep!" The Navajo told the stranger, looking up from where he knelt by the fire. He melted some grease in a skillet, slowly, at the edge of the flames.

"They seemed so remote," he mused. "But now they don't seem as far away for some reason. Something is different."

The stranger pondered the stars with a far off look about him. "That group of stars, it is the Pleiades. It is also known as the Seven Sisters in the constellation of Taurus. You see, it is on the coin that I've given you." He jolted Zachary's memory. "It reappears in precisely the same position every fifty-two years. The Maya Indians of Mexico used it as the basis for their solar calendar. The cycle represents fifty-two Haab years, and is known as the Calendar Round. But the Maya had another name for the star group! *Tzek'eb!* It means the rattlesnake's rattle! They believe today, as their ancestors did, that they belong to these stars."

The stranger had spoken with a fluent comprehension that stirred the Indian's fears even more. *If he is a spirit messenger, he could know this!* Zachary told himself. *But what is his concern with the Maya? And what of the coin?* This confused him.

Silently, the Navajo stooped by the fire with one knee on the ground. He supported his forearm on the other, while he sauteed the onion he had sliced into the cast iron skillet. The grease spattered from the skillet as it became hotter. He wondered. He wondered what he should believe? What he should believe about the stranger? What he should believe about Jack McCloud? What he should believe about the past and what his grandfather had taught him? He wondered if what he thought, or did, would make a difference? He wondered aloud. "Does it matter? I mean,...........I wish I knew!" He said, drawing a tired breath. "What's going to happen? And is it going to make a difference?" Zachary asked as though an unspoken portent had been understood.

Sitting on the ground next to the fire, with his back against the large, cold boulder, the stranger named Daniel peered into the fire. "I don't have the answer! I wish I did, but I don't. But I do believe that all of the actions you take, and all of the words you speak, will continue on throughout the fabric of the universe, like ripples in a tide pool."

"But will it change anything?" The Navajo inquired earnestly.

"Maybe. Maybe not. But you will have fulfilled your destiny, and I will have fulfilled mine! And maybe that's all that really matters!" The stranger said.

Zachary's face bore a solemn expression. He placed the venison steaks into the skillet. They seared in the hot grease. The sound cleaved the silence of the night. It sealed that moment forever. It was an uncomfortable silence, born of the openness of feeling that had been expressed between them, between two men who for all practical purposes were strangers, except for an indeterminable bond that the Navajo was beginning to recognize.

"The steaks will be ready soon." The Indian reached into the sack. He pulled out some special, Navajo herbs. "A little of this, and we'll be ready to eat." He handed the man a plate with a steak on it. It was smothered in sauteed onions and herbs. "Try this!" Zachary said. "I'm sure you've never tasted anything like it,...........anywhere!"

He set the tin plate on his lap. He picked up a fork with his left hand and held the venison with it, while he cut through the tender, succulent meat. The redish-brown juices flowed from the slash, and in the center it was lean and slightly pink. He put a piece to his mouth and savored the taste. It was good.

"I shot this deer myself, last year!" The Navajo exclaimed with some pride, and perhaps an equal amount of reverence. "It will be time to hunt again soon," he mused. Zachary set his plate upon a rock next to him, and picked the potatoes out of the fire with a stick. He drew a sharp hunting knife from its sheath on his beaded belt and slit the potatoes. They burst, releasing a puff of steam. Then he prepared the potatoes with condiments. Stabbing one, he passed it to the stranger on the blade of his knife.

"There are many kinds of hunters, and hunted, on many worlds!" The stranger named Daniel assured Zachary. "Sometimes, the hunters become the hunted!"

"Why do you say this?" The Navajo asked.

Looking up from his food, Daniel addressed him with a thought-filled expression, and a certainty in his eyes. "I was thinking of Jack McCloud, and the two men who visited his office. I think they are hunters! But not for food!"

"What than?"

"They hunt for personal gain! They are the kind that often become the hunted! We need only bait the trap!" Daniel told Zachary.

"You suspect Jack of having dealings with those two, don't you!"

"I sense there is a connection. But we will set the bait, and then sit back, and we will wait for them to come to us!" The stranger said.

"You're a smart hunter! You would make a good Indian!" He smiled. The Navajo's eyes glistened mischievously from the light of the fire.

"Perhaps you will teach me," the stranger said. He was amused.

An understanding was growing between them. They sat quietly, and consumed the remainder of their meal. Off in the distance a coyote howled with a mournful resound. The smoke from the fire rose languorously into the dark and the stone ceiling above. It disappeared.

Zachary gathered up the cookware, while Daniel cleared a place for the sleeping bags. He untied the laces that bound them into a roll, and allowed them to fall open on the ground.

"You said this place has many secrets, Zachary! What are they?"

"It has been told that there is an opening here, a way to get on the Other Side! Into other worlds! Legend has it that the Anasazi escaped from their enemies by going through the opening," the Navajo told him.

"Where is this opening located?" Daniel asked.

Kneeling on the ground, Zachary smoothed the wrinkles from his sleeping bag, stretching it flat. "Some say it is right here! On this spot where we are now! Others say it is in the canyon below! No one is really sure, but people and things have been known to disappear out here!"

As he stooped near the fire to gather some warmth, he placed more branches on it. It flared vigorously. A chilling night breeze had settled in upon them, it carried some ghostly sounds up from the canyon floor. "They say the spirits still wander about the canyon at night. That they cross between this world and the next, just as they did in the past!" The Navajo told the stranger.

Daniel sat atop his sleeping bag, his legs crossed, and his arms outstretched behind him. He peered at the fire, mesmerized. He was fascinated by the idea, the notion that the Navajo had about traveling between worlds in a physical or spiritual form. He reflected. *They were wise to keep the technique a secret. The others weren't ready! It could have been a disaster! There are none ready still!* He thought.

Yawning wearily, Zachary said, "I think it's time to turn in! It's getting pretty cold out here, and I'm ready for a good night's sleep!" He zipped down his sleeping bag, and laid the top cover over to one side. Then he sat on it while he pulled off his boots, placing them upright to keep out unexpected guests, and within reach in case he needed to find them in the night. He settled down, and pulled the cover over him.

A few feet away from the Indian, the stranger lay awake in his sleeping bag, watching the fire die out, listening to the feral sounds that emanated from the canyon.

Zachary snorted. He squirmed in his bed. Then he rolled over to his side, putting his back to the fire. His sleep deepened, and he began to dream. He dreamed of the spirits of the past. They came and stood around him in his sleep, in their colorful ceremonial robes, beckoning him to follow them to the Other Side. He pleaded with them to leave him alone, that he was not ready to go beyond. He told them that he had something important to do. His people needed him to help save the future of the tribe. But they would not leave him alone! They taunted him with images of his father and mother, calling to him!

Then an image of his grandfather appeared and spoke to him. *You are right to choose to stay! Do not listen to them. It is not your time. You must help protect our people from the ones who would destroy our world.*

Many Navajos have passed to the other side on this land. It is sacred. The womb of life is in danger, it must not be allowed to die! You must do as the One of Many Faces tells you to do! As he spoke, the images of the Ancients faded away into the darkness.

Taking Zachary's hand, his grandfather led him to the ledge overlooking the canyon. While he stood there, the image changed form before his eyes. It turned into an eagle. He watched it glide over the canyon. It flew over the ruins and circled three times, then it disappeared.

He stood there in a dreamy state, looking out over the canyon. Although Zachary believed he was dreaming, it all seemed lucid and tangible to him. Then a bright, blue-white, luminous ball arose from the canyon floor. It turned into an oscillating spire of light as it moved toward him. As it came closer, it appeared as an opening outlined with a blue aura. Zachary became frightened. He started to back away, then he stumbled and fell to the ground. He laid there on his side with his arm shielding his face, watching, while the ball of light traveled over him and came to rest next to Daniel. The image quivered like a mirage in the heat. Then the stranger awoke and sat up. He looked over at Zachary, smiled, and stood up, then he walked into the light. It enveloped him, then it began to shrink away. It drifted out over the canyon again, and slowly contracted to a very brilliant point of light. Then it vanished.

It was daybreak. Zachary awoke abruptly. His heart was racing as he cleared the sleep from his eyes. He peered through the breach in his sleep laden eyelids, at the sleeping bag where the stranger had lain. He was gone!

A bolt of panic sent tremors through his body. *How could this be? It was just a dream!* Zachary thought. His mind was still hazy. He sat up trying to make sense of it all, trying to pull it all together into a neat, orderly pattern that he could readily comprehend. *Daniel got up early! He took a walk! He must be down by the truck! Sure, that's it, he's at the truck!*

He reached for his boots. A scorpion darted from under one of them. Zachary snatched up some dirt in his hand, and he threw in the direction of the venomous arachnid as it scampered away. He shook his boots to be certain there weren't any others. Then he pulled them over his feet and stood up. He walked briskly over to where he could view the truck. The stranger wasn't to be seen. The Navajo stood pondering. He shook his head in bewilderment. *Why would he leave the camp?*

He turned and strode back to where the sleeping bags lay. The fire was smoldering. There was a knot in his stomach. He scanned the area for some signs of the stranger's movement. Of course, there were some footprints, but there were many from the night before. He stood over the open sleeping bag, studying the immediate area for evidence. *He may have been taken by force?* Zachary considered it. He searched for signs of a struggle. There were none. But he thought it ridiculous anyway, no one could have come near without him hearing them.

Another sudden thought possessed him. *The ruins! He may have tried to go to the ruins!*

Zachary trod swiftly to the edge overlooking the canyon. He cupped his hand to his forehead, over his eyes, attempting to focus on the ruins. Then he thoroughly scoured the canyon below, looking for any sign of movement. The sun was to his back and climbing steadily over the top of the mesa. It illuminated the canyon floor. He turned his attention again to the ruins. The primary light of day cut across the ruins like a laser beam, leaving the lower portion still in the shadows. If Daniel was climbing up from the canyon, chances are that the Indian wouldn't be able to see him anyway. *But why would he go there alone?* Zachary asked himself. *And he couldn't have gone before daylight, there's just no way?*

Just then, something else caught his attention, something more ominous. Above the ruins there circled an eagle. It looked just like the one in his dream. Perhaps it wasn't a dream after all?

Perplexed, he strode with a languid step toward the camp. While he gathered up the campset and sleeping bags, he began to think assuredly regarding the stranger named Daniel. He had arrived here by himself; he had to be quite capable of taking care of himself. If he had to leave, he must of had a good reason. *But why now?* He asked himself. They were just getting started. He felt that they had begun to develop an understanding, that he was beginning to know what it was that this stranger wanted from him.

Maybe he'll come back to the house! Zachary told himself. He loaded the truck, got into it, then he sat there having second thoughts. He grasped the steering wheel, squeezing it tightly with both hands, then he let his head drop forward, placing his forehead against the wheel. The palms of his hands became sweaty. His whole body felt damp and clammy. The morning air was cold. Still, beads of perspiration broke out on his forehead and face as he recalled the dream.

He considered, for a moment, searching for the stranger. But to what avail? If he had wanted to stay, he would have been there when Zachary awoke. The Navajo cursed. *Why me? Why did he single me out? What do I need with all of this anyway? Two damn days with this guy, and my life is becoming complicated! Maybe he won't come back at all! Maybe this was all just a bad dream, and it'll go away!* He wanted to believe this, but the churning in his gut told him differently.

On his way home, his mind was shaded with apparitions of his dream. The more he tried to block them out, the more persistent they became. Until he arrived at his house, and drove into the yard where he stopped the truck a few feet from the entrance of the storage shed. *-Tsoh* didn't come out to greet him. It puzzled him. His mongrel companion always dashed out of the shed to meet him. Even before he could get out of the truck, on most occasions, the dog was up on the door, with his cold, wet nose pressed into the window. But not today.

For what seemed to be an inordinate amount of time, he sat there behind the wheel, pondering. At last, he mustered the courage to reach for the door handle. He pushed the door open with a sense of foreboding. *-Tsoh* still did not appear. He lowered himself from the truck, left the door open, and strode cautiously from the sunshine into the large, shaded opening that was the entrance to the shed.

There he stood, with his right hand on the edge of the metal door. He peered around the corner of it, looking down at the spot where the dog usually laid. Then he ventured slowly forward on the dirt and gravel floor of the building, until he stood in the center of it. He looked about at the storage bins. The feed sacks had been slit and the feed poured onto the ground. Metal bins had been dumped over, and nuts, bolts, nails and other hardware lie scattered all around. Then he turned, and he looked underneath the workbench. Something in the back corner, behind it, caught his attention. He knew what it was instantly. He moved closer, with fearful steps, to confirm it. *-Tsoh's* lifeless body lay against the back wall of the building, under the workbench. Zachary stooped down next to it. He reached out to touch the bloody, matted fur, around what appeared to be a bullet wound. It was behind the left front shoulder blade, and high enough to pierce the lungs or the heart.

He had to crawl here to die! He shook his head in disbelief, with a mournful expression. *Why would anyone do this?* The Navajo asked himself. Putting his hand to his face, he wiped the moisture from the corners of his eyes. He was enraged. The tears still welled, as he brought himself to a standing position. He had to check the house.

When he reached it, the doors were closed. There were no immediate indications of anyone's presence. Yet, he had to be cautious. Whoever it was, had a gun. They had already shot the dog, and he doubted that they would have second thoughts about shooting him as well.

Before he reached the door, with fear and anger combined, he slipped his hand onto the bone handle of the nine-inch hunting knife that he carried on his belt. Then he realized it was no match for a bullet, and he stepped back from the door. He slipped the knife back into its sheath. Then he turned toward the truck, and the deer rifle that was latched to the rack in its rear window. Whoever these people were, they had no consideration for him or his property. They meant business. And now, so did he!

His attention had been diverted from the stranger's disappearance to his immediate concerns. He pulled the rifle from its mount. He cocked the bolt as he brought it out of the truck. Turning with it, he walked with a deliberate stride toward the house, with the rifle tucked under his right arm, and ready. With his brow contorted, and his facial muscles tensed, he flung open the door and entered. The curtains were drawn in the living room, leaving the room immersed in a cool darkness. He stepped slowly in the direction of the wall that divided the kitchen and the living room. The rifle was up and ready to fire, as he turned the corner with a step backward and out into the room.

Nothing appeared to have been disturbed in the living room, this time. Then he focused his attention on the hallway directly ahead of him. Daylight from the bedroom window cut through the doorway, illuminating the hall. His sharp eyes scanned for shadows of movement from the bedroom doorways. He saw none, nor did he hear any sounds. As he entered the hallway, he stopped at the first door on his right. The bathroom door was slightly ajar. His heart pounded inside his chest as he pushed the door open with his foot. It had occurred to him that someone could hide around the corner, inside of the shower stall. With one quick step, he swung into the doorway with the rifle raised to fire. Then he reached for the light switch. Nothing!

Exhaling deeply, Zachary backed out of the doorway into the hall. He turned with discretion, then he moved forward toward the bedroom doors. He stopped. He couldn't cover them both at once. Whichever one he chose, he would be vulnerable. His rage overtook his fear, as he lunged forward into the room where Daniel had slept the night before. He checked on the floor beside the bed, there was no one there. Then he turned without hesitation to face the entrance to his own room. Fearlessly, he stepped through the door to confront whatever lie in wait for him. Again, there was nothing!

With his strength sapped, he felt his knees become lithe. The rigid tension that had been supporting his body abandoned him. Zachary stumbled toward the bed and dropped down onto it. He sat there for a moment, then he fell to his back letting the rifle fall onto the bed beside him. He drew a deep breath and sighed with exasperation. He lay motionless for a time, while the tension dissipated from his body.

His life was coming apart at the seams, and he was determined to get some answers. But first he had to take care of *-Tsoh.* He peeled himself up from the bed, picked up the rifle, and went out to the storage shed. From now on, the gun was going to be loaded and nearby at all times, until this thing was settled.

If it *was* the two men from the restaurant, and Jack McCloud's office, he believed they were looking for more gold coins. He stood over the debris, left from their search in the shed. Zachary brought forth the gold coin from his pocket. He held it in his palm and examined it, wondering if that was all this was about? Gold. If that was the only reason *-Tsoh* was dead, and his house had been invaded. Because of greed? He tucked the coin back into his pocket and leaned the rifle against a post.

-Tsoh needed to be buried. Zachary snatched the pick and shovel from the corner next to the door. He strode out to the rear of his property to select a suitable spot for a grave. With a sharp swing of the pick, he began to hammer at the brittle soil, angrily.

While he worked, he thought. *Jack appeared to be acquainted with those two men!* From what Daniel had told him, they had gotten the smell of money and weren't about to let go! Where did that leave Jack McCloud, he wondered? If he was to find them, he would need to talk to Jack. He was the obvious one; after all, if anyone could help, it would be him, someone who he thought he knew well. Of course, he could go to the police. But before he did, he was inclined to try settling this matter on his own.

He broke the crust loose from the topsoil with steady blows from the pick, and he considered the best way to approach Jack McCloud while he did it. Should he tell him about the coins? Or should he just tell him about the break-ins? As far as he knew, Jack knew nothing about the coins. Then why tell him. He could just say he noticed the two men following them around.

The Navajo thought about it for a moment. *But what about the stranger? What if he asks about him?* He reminded himself. *Should I tell him that Daniel disappeared?* Then he would have to tell Jack that he was out at the stone arch. He'd want to know why? Zachary didn't think that Jack McCloud believed in any of the legends. The Indian knew he was going to have to come up with a story.

Clearing the loose dirt from the hole with the shovel, he thought. *I'm not sure I can trust Jack!* He dropped the shovel onto the ground. Then he slipped his jacket off of his shoulders, and laid it on the ground beside him. He rolled the sleeves of his shirt up on his husky forearms, took up the shovel again, and dug the rest of the hole with it.

Then, with a bit of reluctance in his step, he walked back to the storage shed. He dragged *-Tsoh* out from behind the workbench. *It had to have happened sometime early the night before,* he told himself. The dog's body was stiff and cold. He wondered if he and Daniel had been there too, if all three of them would be dead now? Cradling the dog in his arms, he carried it out to the shallow grave. He laid the body in it. Then he covered it over with the loose soil. Afterward, he piled some rocks on top of the grave to keep out the vultures, and the other carrion-eating scavengers from digging it up.

On his way back to the storage shed with the pick and shovel, he felt a pang. He looked up to note that the sun was near midheaven, and he knew it was late morning. He was hungry for food, but that could wait. At the moment he felt more of a need to satisfy his appetite for justice, even if he had to dispense it himself!

It was 11:20 a.m. according to the clock in the living room. Zachary passed it on his way to the bathroom to wash his hands. He knew if he didn't call Jack McCloud soon, he would leave for lunch and he might not be able to catch him the rest of the day.

Jack, it's Zachary. I need to see you today. No, it's not about the stranger. It has to do with some trouble out at my place. Yes, it's serious. Someone's broken into my house! And they shot my dog last night! I guess they were looking for something. -Tsoh must have gotten in their way. I don't know what! I don't want to call the police! Not yet anyway! I think you might be acquainted with the men that did this! Of course not! I don't think you had anything to do with it! I saw these two guys going into your office yesterday. I think they've been following me around. Yes, two o'clock is fine. I'll see you then!

He had time to shower and change clothes before he set out for Tuba City. And he had plenty of time to think! He thought about the stranger, Daniel. Where did he go? And why? More importantly, why didn't he say he was going to leave,..............if he knew? One thing was certain, he wasn't taken against his will. There were no signs of a struggle, no other footprints but their own around the camp.

Sitting on the end of his bed, Zachary put on a pair of clean socks while he thought further. *What about the dream? Was it an invitation to the Other Side, to another world? Did Daniel take it? Why would the Ancient Ones be interested in him? Or did they already know him?* He pondered all of this.

Poking his feet through the legs of a fresh pair of blue jeans, he stood to pull them up. *The light?* He had never seen anything like it before. *If it wasn't a dream, then perhaps it's the way to the Other World? The opening the legend speaks of!* He had heard of a vortex existing in the area. He had attributed the idea to the over active imaginations of some New Age disciples. Yet, his native beliefs were steeped with legends regarding the Ancients and their ability to pass between worlds at will.

He tucked in his shirt tail, and laced his belt through the loops on his jeans. He sat back down on the bed to pull on his boots. It was time to go see Jack McCloud.

Reaching over the steering wheel, he grabbed his sunglasses from the dash. *If the Ancients could pass between two worlds, why not three? Why not more?* The Navajo asked himself. And, after meeting this stranger, and witnessing, at least, what he thought he had, could he allow himself to think that there were any limitations at all?

Chapter 8

Baiting the Trap

THE NAVAJO WONDERED IF THE STRANGER WOULD RETURN TO the same place, where he had disappeared. He considered whether or not he should go back and wait. *I don't think he would have expected me to wait for him, not knowing if he would return!* Zachary told himself.

Passing the place on Highway 160 where he had found the stranger walking alone a few days earlier, he thought about how much everything had changed. That the stranger was right, it appeared as though nothing would ever be the same again. But he told himself, he, Zachary Thomas, was still the same man as before. And he had a score to settle, and *nothing* was going to get in his way. The question was how? How would he settle it?

As he drove this familiar stretch of highway, even *it* appeared to have been changed in some way. Or was it his perspective? Were his eyes now seeing things differently than they had in the past?

His broad hands hugged the steering wheel of the pickup truck. His dark eyes were filled with contempt for two men, whom he more than suspected of the attack on his home. These two men he had chosen to face alone. *But what if they try to kill me when I find them?* The Navajo asked himself. *Then what? Then anything I did would be self-defense, wouldn't it? Or, I could wait for them to return to my house again, then I could deal with them on my terms. But why would they return? Unless they thought Daniel would be there? With Daniel there, the odds would be better. But the decision would be better made after talking to Jack McCloud!* He had convinced himself.

He slowed the pickup truck, and eased off the road into the Council parking lot. Then he pulled in alongside Jack McCloud's four-wheel-drive truck. When he stepped out of his truck, he took notice of the tires on the four-by. They were caked with mud, and the sides of the truck as well. He turned and looked at his own. There was a distinct shade to the soil near the ruins, different from anywhere else on the reservation. Zachary recognized it. If Jack had not been out to the ruins, he had been somewhere near them recently.

Zachary walked into the lobby. He removed his cap as he approached Anita's desk. Although he had seen her only a few times before, and he had talked to her on the phone, he had never really thought about how very attractive she was, until now. She couldn't have been more than twenty-eight or twenty-nine years old. He knew that she had been away at college for a couple of years, then she had returned to the reservation, and had worked for the Navajo Tribal Council ever since. Anita was bright and sophisticated, and she intimidated most of her young male suitors.

She intimidated Zachary as well but, at the moment, he couldn't stop thinking about how attractive she was. He cleared his throat, and she looked up from her desk with large, soft brown, expectant eyes. "Can I help you Mister Thomas?" She inquired in a distinctly pert voice. Then she smiled.

He felt uncomfortable, and he sensed that she knew it. She noticed that he was fidgeting with the brim of his cap. "I'm here to see Jack!" Zachary told her. His tone was tense.

"Alright Mister Thomas."

"Call me Zachary," he said.

"Alright Zachary, come right this way," she said as she stood up.

She led him back to Jack McCloud's office. He noticed her black mid-heels, and, the light gray, tailored wool suit that fit her tastefully. The door was partially open. Anita entered and announced him. Jack hung up the phone when Zachary stepped into his office.

Jack McCloud greeted him as he was midway across the room. "Hello, Zachary! Come on in and sit down!" He said in an affable voice. He appeared to have gotten over the strained conversation of the day before.

Walking over to one of the chairs in front of Jack's desk, Zachary turned to glance at Anita as she exited the room.

"Fine girl, Zachary! You ever think about getting married?" Jack McCloud quipped.

"Yeah! I've thought about it!" Zachary responded. "But I think I'm too set in my ways!" He pulled up a chair and sat down.

Jack McCloud laughed. "A good woman would straighten you right out! Take my word for it! Look at my Tessa. I wouldn't be where I am today without her."

But the burly Navajo had more pressing matters on his mind. "Look Jack, I've had some trouble on my place! And I don't like it! I think I know who's doing it, and I want to put a stop to it!"

"That's what you said on the phone." Jack McCloud fingered the ballpoint pen that lie on the desk near his right hand. "I'm sorry to hear about it! And about your dog! Who do you think it was?" He said, expressing himself sympathetically.

"I think they're the same two men that were in your office yesterday morning," Zachary said. "Someone broke into the house yesterday, while we were here talking to you. They returned last night while me and Daniel were away."

"Did they take anything?" Jack McCloud asked.

"That's the odd part," Zachary paused. "They didn't take anything at all."

Jack rolled the pen between his fingers. He looked at it, then he looked up to catch Zachary's gaze. "Maybe it's that weird friend of yours, you know, the one you had here yesterday,...........that Daniel. Are you sure he doesn't have some of his buddies casing your place? Where is he, anyway?"

"I left him at the house, just in case those guys come back," Zachary insisted. "I don't think these are friends of his."

"Why don't you call the police and file a report? Maybe they can keep an eye on your place for a while. I know someone at the Kayenta District, if you want me to call and ask?" Jack set the pen down in the center of a yellow legal pad on his desk. He leaned back in his chair.

Zachary leaned forward, his face donning a resolute expression. "No. I don't want to call the police. If you can just tell me who those two guys were that visited here yesterday, I'll deal with it myself!"

"How do you know they're the one's that broke into your place? Did you see them around there?" Jack asked, attempting to cast doubt on Zachary's conviction. He placed his hand on his right pants pocket; he was consciously concealing more than just the coin.

The Navajo retorted, defensively, in a gristly tone. "No. But we saw them in Flagstaff the day before yesterday! And it seems kind a strange that they showed up here!"

Jack McCloud became conciliatory. "That's hardly enough to go on Zachary. You know you can't just go around accusing someone because you think they look suspicious. The police wouldn't question anyone on that kind of evidence."

"Do you know them?" Zachary asked flatly.

"I've never seen them before," Jack McCloud swore. They said that they were from up around Page. They told me that they were looking for work,............you know, odd jobs and the like! I just told them I didn't know of anyone who was looking to hire. I don't know why they came to me?

Except, they might have thought I had an idea of what was going on in the area."

He gave Zachary a heavy look of discouragement. "I think you're barking up the wrong tree with those two, Zachary! You'd best forget about them! You said nothing was taken, and you can't go after someone because you think they killed your dog. If I were you, I think I'd just forget the whole thing! You may just bring more trouble onto yourself by pursuing it!" Jack McCloud warned him.

Zachary raised up, boldly, from where he sat. He stood in front of Jack McCloud, peering down with deeply determined eyes. "Thanks for the advice, Jack! But I'd appreciate it if you'd let me know, if you see those two again. I think they're still around here somewhere!"

The Chairman stood and reached out for Zachary's hand. "Good luck!" He told him. "You'd best be careful!" He gave him a final word of caution.

"I will!" The Navajo replied. "You can depend on it!" He moved the chair back, and turned toward the door. He broke stride halfway across the room, looked back over his shoulder at the imposing figure standing behind the weighty oak desk, that appeared to be symbolic of his station, then he nodded and said, "See ya Jack!" He left the door open on his way out.

After Zachary was out of view, Jack sat down in his chair with a calculating expression. He reached for his glasses to the right on the desk. He put them on. He ruminated for a brief moment, then he picked up the phone and began dialing.

"Bye Anita. By the way, that's a very nice outfit you're wearing," Zachary told her as he walked by her desk.

She smiled, politely. "Thank you, Zachary! Take care now!"

"I will Anita. I will!" he said on his way out the door.

He was thinking that sometime he would ask her to dinner. *Why not?* He told himself. But he was hungry right now. And he knew just the place to go while he was in town, the Highway Cafe, for food and perhaps some information as well. *Jeannie knows everyone and everything that's goin' on around here. She hardly misses a thing! Maybe she knows something about those two shady characters?*

On his way over to the cafe, he pondered the conversation with Jack McCloud. *Was he hiding something? He said he didn't know the two men, but he's not in the habit of seeing just anyone who asks. Unless he had a good reason?*

When he pulled into the parking lot of the Highway Cafe, he sat there. He thought further. *Anita announced them. She said Mister McCloud, your next appointment is here.* Zachary remembered that clearly. *Why would Jack lie? The mud. The dried mud on his four-by-four? When was he out at the ruins? Should I have asked? It had to have been since the last rain.*

Business was slow in the cafe at this time of day. Only three other cars were parked in front of it. It was too late for lunch and too early for dinner, but Zachary's stomach didn't care. He went inside. Tina, the cashier, the effervescent, petite nineteen year old redhead was counting receipts and balancing out to end her shift.

"Hi Zach! I thought you only came in for breakfast," she quipped. "Kind of late for that, isn't it?" She giggled.

"No. Not if you haven't eaten all day!" He retorted.

Jeannie sat at the counter sipping a coke and talking to the day cook, Cal, who stood behind the counter looming over her. They both looked up when Zachary walked into the dinning room.

"Hey fella, what's goin' on?" Cal blurted in his deep, raspy voice. A two-hundred and eighty pound ex-pro-wrestler, at forty-seven, now a chain smoker and heavy drinker, he could still hold his own in a bar brawl. And he did! He and the sheriff's deputies had come to an agreement a few years back. They wouldn't go in any bar in the county that he was in at night. Therefore, they could avoid the unpleasant task of having to arrest him for drunk and disorderly. But when he was sober, the man had a heart of gold.

"Hi, Cal! Hello, Jeannie!" Zachary said. He sauntered over to the counter to sit down next to Jeannie. "How about making me some breakfast!" He chuckled.

"You're not going ta make us work now, are ya?" Jeannie responded with a warm smile. "Where's your good lookin' friend?" She asked.

His expression turned more somber. "I left him home to guard the place. I've been havin' a little trouble out there the last couple days. Someone broke into my place while I was away."

Cal stood behind the counter towering over both of them. He scowled as though he had been victimized himself. "Did you catch'em?"

"No." Zachary shook his head confirming his response. "But I have an idea who they are! They're two guys hanging around town. I haven't seen them around here before."

"You need some help, you let me know!" Cal growled.

Lifting the glass of coke to her mouth, Jeannie took a sip. She had been listening attentively. Then she turned to Zachary and placed her hand gently on his forearm. "What do these guys look like?"

Zachary thought about it for a moment. "One's about average height. He's thin, with long black hair pulled back into a knot on the back of his head. His face is dark, but he's not an Indian. Hispanic maybe? He's got a scar above his right eye. His friend is taller and heavier, with long blond hair. He wears a beard."

She moved her hand away from his forearm. Then Jeannie slipped a cigarette from the pack that Cal had laying on the counter. "What makes you think they're the one's that broke into your place?" Jeannie put the cigarette to her lips. Cal reached across the counter with his lighter.

The Navajo assessed her soft, contemplative, blue eyes. "We've seen them twice in the last few days. Once in Flag' at the truckstop, and again in Jack McCloud's office. Daniel recognized them."

Zachary brought out the token he carried in his pocket. "I think they are after some of these! Daniel gave me this. It's a kind of token he says, but it could be valuable."

Cal reached out for the coin. "Let me have a look at it!" He snatched the shiny gold coin out of Zachary's hand. Raising it to the light, he examined it curiously. "Sure looks like real gold to me! A fella could buy at least one round with this!" He announced excitedly, then he passed the coin back to Zachary.

Jeannie extended her hand, viewing the coin with an anxious expression. "Can I have a look at it?" The Navajo placed the coin in the palm of her hand. "You say Daniel gave you this? This is very unusual. I've never seen anything like it. What do all these markings mean?" She asked, returning the coin.

He hesitated. "Well,............Daniel says it's a token of friendship. He says it carries a kind of message. I'm not sure what that means." He slipped the coin back into his pocket. Suddenly he felt uncomfortable about showing it.

"Hey, it's almost four o'clock! How about feeding me!" Zachary groused jokingly. The three of them laughed.

"What'll ya have!" Cal blurted.

"What's the special, Cal?"

"I still have some roast beef back there. How 'bout an open faced sandwich with some mashed potatoes and gravy? I'll bring ya a cup a mixed vegetables too!"

Zachary nodded. "Sure, sounds good Cal! Of course, anything would sound good right now!"

"Comin' right up!" Cal gestured exuberantly with a stout arm raised in the air, then he turned and rambled off toward the kitchen.

Turning to Zachary again, this time with a grave look of concern, Jeannie said, "I know who those guys are. They were in here yesterday. The dark one, his name is Jake. He asked if I had seen you and Daniel, if he had given me anything special. I didn't know what he meant at the time, but I think I do now! They're a couple of bad characters, Zachary. It wouldn't surprise me if they had broken into your place. But how did they know about the coins?"

"Daniel left some on the table for the waitress at the truckstop in Flag', they must have gotten a look at'em then." Zachary told her. "I'm sure they must've followed us home, then waited to search the house after we were gone."

An impish thought entered Jeannie's mind, and it was expressed outwardly by a spontaneous smile, accented by mischievous eyes. “I knew there was something about that guy that I liked, other than his body that is!” She laughed. “I wish he would give *me* some of those, I’d retire!” Then she turned pensive. “Where did he get those anyway? And where is he from?”

Giving her a quick, sidewise glance, Zachary averted her expectant look. He peered straightaway when he said, “I’m not sure. Besides, you wouldn’t believe me if I told you where I thought he was from. Anyway, he’s not from around here!”

“I gathered that! But could you be more specific, Zachary?” Jeannie insisted.

“When he gets back, maybe I should get him to explain it.” The Navajo muttered. Then he realized he had said something he hadn’t intended. But it was written all over his face, and he could only anticipate Jeannie’s next question.

She stared at him suspiciously. “I thought you said that he was out at your place?”

He looked around the room, furtively, to be certain that no one could overhear what he was about to say, not even Cal. The dinning room was still vacant of customers. He turned to Jeannie with an earnest expression. “He’s a lot different than you ’n me. I don’t know if I can explain it, but he doesn’t belong here.” He hesitated. “He’s from very far away!”

Now she looked puzzled. “How far away?”

He squirmed apprehensively. “How about another world. Would you buy that?”

“Not really. Try again?” Jeannie said in a bantering tone. She laughed, thinking that he was joking. But Zachary didn’t laugh. He didn’t join in her amusement.

His expression became more grave, and his tone more weighty. “He disappeared last night, Jeannie. I don’t know where he’s at! That’s why I can’t call the police in on the trouble out at my house. They’d ask all kinds of questions. They’d want to know what I thought these guys were looking for. I’d have to come up with some answers,.............and they’d be like the one I just gave you! Then they’d want to know where Daniel is. They might even suspect me of doin’ him in! And then what?” He said with a dreadful look.

“Alright, just relax.” Jeannie placed her hand on Zachary’s shoulder. She looked at him compassionately. She could sense his anxiety. “Do you have *any* idea where he might have gone?”

“We were camping out near the ruins last night, under the stone arch.” He admitted. “He disappeared from there! I’m going back out there tonight to see if he shows up again! That’s all I can think of to do right now.”

“The two guys you asked about, Jake and Carl, if they were after those coins, maybe they kidnapped him?” Jeannie speculated.

Zachary shook his head. “No. I don’t think so, Jeannie. There was no evidence of a struggle. The only footprints were the ones we made ourselves the night before. And he didn't walk away from there! At least I couldn't find any tracks to prove it!"

Cal came back from the kitchen with Zachary's food. The conversation halted abruptly.

"Here ya go fella! Watch that plate, it's hot!" Cal warned him.

"Thanks Cal!" Zachary carefully positioned the plate in front of him, while he wondered about what Jeannie was thinking. "Can I have some coffee to wash this down?" He asked. Then he began to devour the first meal he had all day. Cal reached around for the coffee pot on the counter behind him, and poured Zachary's cup full.

Leaning across the counter toward Jeannie, Cal said, "It's about time for ya ta go home doll!

"I know!" She responded, sighing wearily. "It's been a long day. But I'll wait a few more minutes, until Sue comes in. Tina's already gone! I don't want to leave you by your lonesome! There might be a rush of business!" She laughed.

Cal chuckled in his gristly tone. He straightened up, arching his back to get the kinks out, and causing his belly to protrude from under his apron. His spine popped audibly, letting out a series of crunches as he contorted his back. "Too many years in the ring!" He mused aloud. "Or being tossed out of it!" He quipped. Then he reached inside of his apron, into his shirt pocket, to retrieve a pack of cigarettes.

"Looks like Zachary's goin' for seconds!" He commented with a broad grin. Then he placed a cigarette on his thick lower lip.

"I guess so!" Jeannie replied.

Shaking another cigarette loose from the pack, Cal extended it to Jeannie. She slipped it out, and Cal lit it for her. Then he lit his own. "Say! Doesn't Sue go with one a those fellers you was talkin' about?"

Zachary dropped his fork onto the edge of his plate. He washed down the bite of food with a sip of coffee.

Taking a drag from her cigarette, Jeannie exhaled. With a thought-filled expression, she replied. "That's right Cal, she goes with Carl, the blond one with the beard."

"Then she would know where to find him, and his friend!" Zachary said. He was encouraged by the possibility.

"You're right, Zachary!" Jeannie told him. "But let me find out for you! I don't think it would be wise for you to ask her yourself. You don't want to tip your hand!"

The Navajo conceded. "I don't want them to be expecting me."

Cal took a hit on his cigarette and let the smoke roll out of his mouth. "I've run up agin' those fellers a time or two myself! They's trouble from the word go! They's both been in 'n out a the joint a few times. Drugs n' what hav'ya! Ya best be careful, they's the sneaky sort!" Cal warned him.

"How 'bout another plate a food?" He asked.

"Sure Cal," Zachary nodded.

He picked up the empty plate and headed for the kitchen. Jeannie turned to Zachary, intent on resuming their previous conversation regarding the stranger, Daniel. "Would you like me to go out there with you tonight? I'd like to help if I can," she offered.

But Zachary tactfully declined. "I appreciate the offer, Jeannie, but I don't think that's a good idea. It might get dangerous out there! Besides, I don't think it would look real good if someone saw us together." He also knew that he didn't want to attract unnecessary attention to himself, and that could happen very easily with a blond, blue eyed Anglo woman in his company. "You can help me a great deal by finding out what you can about those two men! Leave the rest to me!" He told her.

Jeannie blushed demurely. "I'm concerned about your friend, he seems like a nice guy! It sounds like he might be in some kind of trouble. I wouldn't want anything to happen to either one of you. Just be careful! I'll find out whatever I can about Carl and Jake for you tomorrow."

"But let me contact you!" Zachary told her, placing great emphasis upon it. "I wouldn't want you to get involved in this. You could get hurt!"

"You'll let me know when you find him?" Jeannie asked.

"Sure! I'll bring him back here so you can see him again!" He told her.

She smiled. "Here comes Sue. I've got to go! Talk to you later, hon!" Jeannie got up from the stool. She slipped on her jacket, turned, and greeted Sue who was halfway across the dinning room. "Hi Sweetie! Kay is coming in to help you tonight. It's going to be getting real busy here in a short while! See ya!"

Zachary watched her leave. He believed she was someone he could count upon to be discrete, regarding what he had told her. Cal came back with his second helping of food. He set the hot plate of food down, its steamy aroma rising, on the counter in front of the distracted Navajo.

"She's a special lil' lady, that Jeannie!" Cal exclaimed.

"Yes," Zachary agreed.

He lingered over his food, while dinner customers began to spill into the restaurant. It was 4:25 p.m. according to the clock on the wall behind the counter. Sue came over with the coffee pot. She offered him a refill.

"Half a cup is all I have time for!" He told her, gesturing with his hand for her to stop. "Thanks Sue!"

He was sorely tempted to make inquiries of her. But he thought better of it. *Jeannie's right!* He told himself. His anger was waning and he was thinking more logically. Depending upon how much she knew about what they were doing, Sue could tip them off. He wasn't about to risk it. He had to devise a plan, a way to trip up the two intruders, to get them to show their hand first.

Of one thing he was certain, the two of them would be watching, and waiting, for him to lead them right to the stranger, Daniel. And the gold coins too, if there were anymore? Perhaps he could lead them into a trap instead?

Getting up, he reached for the check. He placed a tip on the counter next to his plate: a dollar bill and some loose change that he dug from his pocket. When Zachary turned to leave, his eyes combed the room for Jake and Carl. With Sue on duty, it occurred to him that they may have come in after her. There were only a few locals in the dinning room. They were people he knew only in passing, acquaintances. *No close friends here,* he told himself.

As he passed by a table at the front of the dinning room, an elderly Navajo couple stopped him for a moment. The old woman asked how he was. The old man asked if he was still living in the same house. They reminded him of his parents; they would have been about the same age. Zachary wished them well, then he went to the cashier, paid his bill and left.

If he was going to make it to the stone arch before dark, he knew he had better be on his way. He had nearly a two hour drive ahead, and he was anxious to get home. There were some preparations to make, before he drove out to the stone arch and the site of the ruins. He wheeled his truck across the gravel parking lot and onto the highway. He sped east. There was no more time to waste!

He began to watch the backroad through his rearview mirror. He glanced at the sideroads, too. If someone was following, or waiting for him, the Navajo wanted to be aware of it. Then he spotted a red pickup truck in his rearview mirror. It was gaining on him.

Chapter 9

Into the Sea of Darkness

THE SUN WAS BEHIND HIM, SETTLING ON THE WESTERN HORIZON. The glare from it obscured his vision, so that he had difficulty seeing the approaching vehicle. Until it overtook him and passed. It was a Navajo family. Three children were in the bed of the truck, sitting against the back of the cab. They smiled and waved. The anxiousness that had invaded him retreated, as he watched the red pickup truck shrink away into the distance.

There was still plenty of daylight left, enough that he could get to the stone arch before sunset. His mind wandered restlessly. *If Daniel doesn't return to the stone arch tonight, then I'll have to go out to the ruins in the morning!* Zachary told himself.

He mused over the past few days. The events had somehow managed to engulf his life. All at once, and with sudden clarity, he became overwhelmed by the significance of it. It was the violation of his home, the loss of his dog, his daily companion,-*Tsoh,* and then his preoccupation with the two men and their fervor in pursuing the gold coins, that had clouded his perception. The latent reality that he had been host to an extraterrestrial visitor had come home to him.

It was a sense of curiosity and anticipation that had been evoked by the Navajo's contact with the stranger, more than fear. He realized it at this moment. Whatever its basis, a bond had been established between them, inadvertently, or perhaps by design. He wasn't sure which?

A semi-tractor-trailer rig pulled up close behind him, preparing to pass. It reminded him that he still had other responsibilities. He had promised to transport cattle for several ranchers around Page. He couldn't afford to lose the work. Winter was coming and he would have plenty of time off. But he was going to have to find a way to delay the hauling for a few days, at least while he searched for the stranger, Daniel.

Zachary stopped at his home long enough to gather up provisions for the night, and the following day. There was no evidence of further intrusion, his nemesis had not returned. He kept a box of .3006 shells in the cupboard next the back door. He took them. Although he could think of no reason for the two men, Carl and Jake, to search his house further, he couldn't help but feel that they weren't far away.

His arms full of supplies, he pushed the back door open with the force of his body and bounded down the back steps. Then he paused briefly. It was long enough to catch a glimpse of the grave he had dug. The aberration of it, that the old dog's little annoyances, his persistent begging to come along, would be no more, that even the very everyday things that he had taken for granted had been altered so, left a hollow spot deep inside of him.

He moved swiftly toward the pickup truck, dropped the supplies into the truckbed, behind the cab, shoved them in place, and slipped in behind the wheel. Zachary reached back to touch the rifle, unconsciously, as if grasping for some assurance.

With a flick of the key the engine roared. He trounced the accelerator once, then he put the truck in gear and sped away. He wanted to make time in order to get to the arch before nightfall. And, he wanted to be aware of any company he might acquire along the way. This was no country to be driving in after dark. There were too many unseen hazards at night in this ruggedly defiant land. Each perhaps natures way of insuring its autonomous existence. It was a land that retaliated, it refused to be tamed. It was much like the People themselves.

The legends of witchcraft, and ceremonies that took place on the mesa above the stone arch, had always been of concern to the Navajo. The fear of witchcraft induced illnesses had encouraged many of their curative ceremonies. Zachary was well aware of the folklore that had evolved about the area, although he had never had a personal experience with any of it, nor a desire to get involved with it. However, it came to mind as he drove. It was never clear to him whether the Ancients practiced it. But if they did, could it still exist in the form of evil spirits that dwelled around the mesa? He began to wonder.

He spat in the styrofoam cup that he kept on the dashboard. Then he checked the pocket of his jacket for an extra pouch of chewing tobacco, he thought he had placed it there earlier. The Navajo felt satisfied that he had remembered. *The dream could have been caused by a spell placed upon me, if such a thing is possible?* He thought. *But what about Daniel's disappearance into the light? Was that part of my dream? Or was it reality?* He couldn't be sure, and only Daniel would be able to tell him.

Cold air from the open window assailed him, it had a sobering effect. He began again to watch for signs of surveillance. If anyone was following him, he wanted to be aware of their distance at all times. He needed an edge, it could be his only one!

Passing an older, shabby, dust laden, dark green pickup truck that was parked on the shoulder of the road, and on the same side of the highway, he took notice to see if it was occupied. It didn't appear so. The Indian peered into his rearview mirror until he was a good half mile away. It pulled onto the highway. *If only I knew what kind of truck or car those guys drove? Why didn't I ask Jeannie, she might've known?* He chided himself. The other truck stayed back about a quarter of a mile. It was an older vehicle and Zachary wasn't concerned about outrunning it if he had to!

He viewed the road ahead, and scanned the sides of the highway as well. *It could be a trap! They could be in more than one vehicle!* The Navajo considered the possibility.

The low sun in the westerly sky reflected in his rear and sideview mirrors. His seeing became more difficult. Time was his greatest concern at this moment, he had to be sure that he was in place before the sun set. He couldn't shake the feeling that he was being led by something. And he didn't like it! If it was so, what control did he have over any of this? He wondered. The answer was too disconcerting to dwell upon.

Still behind him, the green pickup truck maintained the same distance. A semi and two cars had passed them both in the last fifteen minutes. Both cars had out of state license plates, he wasn't concerned about them. An Arizona Highway Patrol car passed westbound.

In ten more miles he would be off of the paved road, and the next twenty miles would be desert terrain. The old, dusty, green pickup truck lingered in the distance.

Damn, I left the carton of shells in the back of the truck! He swore to himself, as he turned northwest toward Skeleton Mesa and the butte that he used to gauge his distance. *But the clip is full!* He told himself with assurance.

Rolling his side window up to block out the increasingly cold wind, Zachary peered out through the dust obscured windshield at the heavy clouds gathering on the horizon. They absorbed the ochre rays of the setting sun, diffusing the light in a spectrum of yellow to red-orange, with a tinge of green. They were tall, thick, thunderheads with dark bottoms, like those that preceded a winter snow storm. He noticed a small herd of cattle on the range to the east. In mid-October, the cold nights warned of the approaching winter. The cattle ranchers and sheep herders were preparing to bring their stock into winter feeding grounds on the lower elevations, where water and vegetation were still accessible.

The Navajo was certain there would be more rain soon, though it looked to him to be several hours away. He hoped that there was enough time to find Daniel and get back out before the washes flooded.

Glancing in the rearview mirror, it confirmed what he had suspected. He had been off of the main road for twenty minutes, and the dark green pickup truck had followed him onto the dirt trail. Zachary slowed, testing the other driver. When the driver realized he was gaining, he backed off. It was what the Navajo had anticipated. Now he was certain, he was being followed!

The dirt road turned into a vague and seldom traveled trail over the next ten miles. He could see the noselike protrusion of the otherwise flat topped mesa, and the butte that he used as a landmark to chart the location of the stone arch and the ruins. The sun was gradually disappearing behind them, with the lower portion of its increasingly yellow-orange convexity submersed in a black shadow, and the tops of the rock formations cast amorphous shadows, like prehistoric shapes, upon the incessantly stark landscape.

Zachary's mind was on the truck that followed. It fell back farther. He caught a flicker of sunlight that reflected from its windshield as it traversed the coarse terrain. And he could see the dust rise behind it.

Pressing on over the dry washes, he could feel every uneven ridge, stone, and ripple in the earth beneath the truck's heavy tires, coursing up through the steering wheel into his hands. The other truck had now disappeared behind the obliquity of the landscape. A cloud of dust was the only indication of its presence.

If they intended to go unnoticed, they haven't done well! He thought. And he was far enough ahead to make it to the stone arch well before them. From there he could see anyone who approached. Unless they came around the north side of the mesa, or over the top of it, where they could easily spot him. He had considered that, too.

The Navajo pondered these questions. *Do they know how to get up there?* Few people did, except for some of the tribal guides like himself, and maybe a few archeologists. *But they aren't from around here! They came down from Page. There's no good reason for them to be out here. No drug deals, or..............? What about Jack McCloud's four-by-four? The mud? Carl and Jake, ... and their visit to his office? There could be a connection! But what?*

He was climbing steadily. The truck's engine strained. He shifted to a lower gear for additional power. *Another advantage!* He thought. Their truck was older, less capable of wending the upgrade of the terrain. Zachary had more time to prepare for them. As he neared the canyon there would be more protection. There was only one way in, and one way out! *Except!* He thought further. *If they were to block me in, there would be no escape in the truck.* He thought too, if they got close enough, once he had taken his position under the arch, he would not be able to get back to the truck. As Daniel had put it, *was he the hunter, or the hunted? Or both?*

When he drove through the mouth of the canyon, he went on to where he and Daniel had stopped the night before. Zachary left the truck running, while he got out to hastily gather some firewood. He remembered that there had been some remaining from the previous night. He moved quickly. Returning to the pickup truck, he drove to within a hundred feet of the steps leading to the stone arch.

As he got out of the truck, he scanned the area above him hoping to see some sign of Daniel. There was nothing to be seen. Zachary snatched the camping gear out from the back of the truck and proceeded up the crude, stone steps that had been carved into the side of the sandstone cliff.

Daylight was failing rapidly, he would have to set up quickly. When he reached the top with his gear, Zachary turned to look out over the canyon. He had lost sight of the pickup truck that was trailing behind him. *They could be waiting just outside the mouth of the canyon until dark!* He told himself. *Or they have gone another way, perhaps around the north side of the mesa?* Whatever the case, he had time to ready himself.

The Navajo placed his equipment near the firepit, then he went back down for more wood and his rifle. When he got down to the truck, he looked about, it was quiet. *Too quiet!* He thought. He took the rifle from its rack over the rear window. With the door still open, he leaned the rifle up against the front seat. Then he walked around the back of the truck to get the firewood. Something moved in the brush about ten yards away. He turned sharply. It was a ground squirrel. His heart fell back into his chest, followed by a few deep breaths. He swallowed hard, then he collected the wood from the back of the truck into the crook of his left arm. Walking briskly over to where the rifle stood near the open door, he set the lock, reached for the rifle with his right hand, and slammed the door shut with a vigorous shove from his broad right shoulder and massive forearm.

Back on top, Zachary went about building a fire. He kept the rifle nearby, and within in easy reach, against a boulder while he worked. He wouldn't be able to see out over the canyon at all but, because of the fire, someone could distinguish him quite easily if he moved about indiscriminately. There was no doubt in his mind that those who followed him would know exactly where he was. But the same was true of Daniel, the fire would serve as a beacon for him, if he was still out there somewhere?

Bending on one knee next to the firepit, the Navajo struck a match. While the fire began to swell into a blaze, he sat down behind the boulder next to his rifle. He gazed into the rising flames, mindfully pondering his strategy regarding the two men whom he believed to be stalking him. He wasn't concerned about the steep side of the cliff that bordered the western edge of the stone arch. It would be impossible for anyone but a skilled climber to undertake, even in the daylight. Zachary was convinced that they would have to come up the same way that he had — if they were bold enough to try it! But he perceived them as being more likely to skulk in the shadows, rather than show themselves. The only other possibility was the cliff that jutted from the top of the mesa, where they could observe him if he was out in the open. His back was to them, but well protected by the boulder where he rested.

It was beyond dusk. An attenuated line of dim light lingered over the western horizon. The moon would be obscured by cloud cover, plunging the night into an abysmal darkness that would shroud the Navajo in an otherworldly aura. He reached for his pack, pulled it over the ground toward himself, opened it, and removed a sandwich from it. Then he tore open the wrapper and took a bite. With sudden anxiety, he swallowed hard. *Why were they waiting for me? How did they know where I was going?* He asked himself. *They were at least ten miles east of my place! They already knew! Who told them? Was it Jeannie? She's the only one who knew that I was coming back out here! She's the only one that I told! Cal was in the kitchen, he couldn't have overheard!* His mind raced with conjecture, but Zachary convinced himself that there had to be another explanation. He doubted that Jeannie Parsons could be involved.

The fire popped loudly. Zachary's attention turned to it, then back to the sandwich he held in his hand. It was dry in his mouth and hard to swallow. So he reached for a can of soda from his pack, pulled the tab, and drank from it. He gazed into the fire, transfixed by it, and immersed in thought. A cold wind swept through the canyon, buffeted the interior walls of the stone arch, and changed directions several times, thrashing the flames, then it subsided. All he could do was wait.

Taking the last bite of the sandwich, he washed it down with the few remaining drops of soda. The rain would be coming sooner than he had first thought. The Navajo could smell it in the moisture laden air. He stuffed the empty soda can and sandwich wrapper into the backpack. His eyes began to feel heavy with sleep. He fought it. Except for the wind, the night was otherwise quiet and eerie. It came and went, and the flames of the fire were tossed about haphazardly. He relaxed back against the boulder, placing the rifle across his lap.

There were no bright stars to be seen in the heavens, only a vast enveloping darkness. Zachary stared out into it. He wondered about the stranger. He wondered if he hadn't brought bad luck onto himself and his home by befriending this one, this foreigner, from a place he wasn't even certain existed.

The Navajos were a superstitious people, they believed in witchcraft and spells. Their legends were laced with stories of the supernatural. They believed that there were some among them who were witches, although they would not readily admit to the practice of it. As a boy, Zachary had heard many such stories told by his grandfather and the old crystal gazer, White Horse. He wasn't sure if he believed any of it.

Finally, his head fell forward, the power of sleep overtook him. The cold, intrusive wind rushed through the cavern, formed by the sandstone arch, like a pack of hungry jackals. It caused the fire to burn itself low quickly. Until only a glimmer of light emanated from it.

The Navajo began to dream. He dreamt that he heard voices, they came from above, atop the mesa. The voices became louder, and there was arguing. He saw three men in his dream — although it wasn't clear who they were — one of the men pulled a revolver from his belt. He held it on the other two. There were more angry words. Then the gun went off. He heard screams in the night air. Then they were drown in a sea of darkness.

Awaking suddenly, anxiously, he looked around in the black of night. Zachary could see nothing. It was quiet again, except for the sound of rain falling around him. He leaned the rifle against the boulder, then he reached for his bedroll. The cold, and dampness of the night air, penetrated his sinew. He spread the sleeping bag onto the ground next to him, while he avoided leaving the cover of the large boulder. Then he slipped inside of it, with the rifle at hand.

Zachary slept soundly through the night. When he awoke it was dawn. The rain had stopped. The early light revealed scattered dun clouds to the east.

"There is no more time to waste!" He muttered to himself. "If I'm going to find Daniel, I have to go now!" The Navajo sprang from his sleeping bag, making haste to collect his gear. While he did so, he watched for signs of the intruders. He folded the sleeping bag over once lengthwise, then rolled it tightly and bound it with laces.

Then he rose with the rifle in hand, and walked over to the edge of the stone steps. Zachary looked out over the narrow canyon to the east. His eyes studied it for movement. There was none. There was no sign of the truck that had followed him the night before. *If they've been here at all, the rain's washed away their tracks,* he told himself. He could only trust that he was alone, that no one would follow him to the ruins.

He strode back to where the sleeping bag and the backpack lie on the ground, set the rifle down, and tied the bedroll to the pack. Then with a brisk motion, he picked it up from the ground and swung it around behind him. Zachary cinched the straps that held it over his shoulders. He bent down to retrieve the rifle.

Bounding down the steps, he started his descent into the canyon. He thought that it would take about an hour and a half to get to the ruins, that is if the arroyo wasn't running deep and he could cross it with ease. The Navajo began to traverse the switchback.

It had been several years since Zachary had been to these particular ruins. It was a favorite place when he was a boy. His grandfather had taken him there many times in the past. He would tell Zachary stories of the Ancient Ones, who lived in the canyon hundreds of years before the Navajos came to this place. These cliff dwellers were given the name Anasazi by the Navajos, because they had not known what these people had called themselves. They were hunters and gatherers first, then they settled in the Tsegi Canyons and took up farming and successfully raised crops in the fertile bottom lands along the arroyos. They were thought to have acquired these skills from other Indians who came from farther south, and with whom they had traded, the Mayans it was believed. The Hopi, the Navajos neighbors, whose reservation rests in the center of the Navajo Nation, although a much smaller population, were thought to be direct descendants of the Ancient Ones.

The food that Zachary carried in his backpack would be enough to last a man two days, if eaten conservatively. And there was fresh water from the natural springs that seeped through the layers of sandstone, enough that a man with acute powers of observation could spot readily. The Navajo thought this in regard to the stranger as well as himself. *If he is a hunter, he knows how to survive!*

Following the trail that descended into the canyon, he searched the sandy soil for evidence of recent passage. As he looked about, he considered that any footprints would have been washed away by the storm. Though there were no tangible traces of the stranger, the Indian was compelled to go on. He felt the same urge. It was drawing him again, as if he was being led to the ruins. Besides, it was the only logical place that Daniel could be, if he had remained in the canyon.

His mind wandered as he moved adroitly along the trail. His thoughts shifted sporadically between Daniel and the Ancient Ones. While he descended farther into a sparse stand of Ponderosa pine, the Navajo considered how the Anasazi had lived well from what nature had most generously provided in this fruitful valley, at least for a time, until they had disappeared from the area. There was a wide variety of trees and plants, not all of which were exclusively indigenous to this altitude or location, that were beneficial medicinally or as a source of food. The Round Leaf Buffalo Berry was used in making a salve for sheeps' eyes and perhaps in the treatment of other ailments, and the Pinion pine, its nuts a favorite food of the southwestern Indians, was also plentiful.

Moving ahead, Zachary took stock of the resources available to a man should he have to survive out here. There was Utah Juniper, used in the construction of hogans, and a plentiful source of firewood. The clusters of Douglas fir that eked nutrients out of scant topsoil to flourish, where used for roof poles and ladders on the lodges of the cliff dwellings. Much of it remained intact. *And game is abundant, too,* he thought. *If a man had to survive here he could,* the Navajo told himself, thinking again of Daniel.

The altitude was deceiving. Zachary pressed on, although his breathing was labored as it had been since he started down from the seventy-two hundred foot elevation. His descent would be no more than a thousand feet before he started to climb again.

He came into a clearing with wild grass. There was a patch of Broad Leaf Yucca alongside the trail. It was in shallow topsoil that had collected between the rocks. Zachary stopped to rest there. He sat down on a rock ledge next to the trail. The sun had risen above the mesa. It illuminated the foliage below him in the lower canyon. He gazed upon it. The beads of dew that had collected on the leaves, glistened in the sunlight like a billion tiny prisms.

Zachary surveyed the surroundings. He had lost sight of the ruins. So well were they concealed by the dense forest, that they would not be visible again until he was within several hundred yards of them.

The Anasazi were aware of all aspects of their environment. The cliff dwellings were located in such a way that they received the direct sun only during the winter months, but were sheltered from it during most of the summer. The location was also ideal for observing intruders who might happen upon the valley. They would be seen long before they knew that they were being watched.

Has he already seen me? The Navajo asked himself. *And what about the others? What if they've figured out that Daniel could be hiding in the ruins? Maybe they're waiting for me?*

Abruptly rising to his feet, and with his senses sharply attentive, the Indian choked up on the rifle with one hand. He stood wary.

Chapter 10

Prophecy of the Chosen

WITH DISCRETION IN HIS STEP, THE NAVAJO MOVED FORWARD. He confronted the trail ahead with a keen eye, watching for anything out of the ordinary. Spotting some deer tracks in the damp soil, where several deer had recently crossed the trail, he paused briefly. Then he continued, looking about for signs of human movement.

The scattered aspen and pin oak, as well as the cottonwood trees, had begun to turn fall colors. The canyon was a fire of yellow, red and orange flame. It proved a momentary diversion for Zachary's thoughts, as his eyes engulfed the splendor of this Eden.

Trekking into densely overgrown foliage, he saw that the trail had been partially reclaimed. If someone was hiding in wait, he thought while he pressed through the brush, he wouldn't know it until they were upon him. Then the Navajo heard the sound of roiled water flowing ahead of him. He was nearing the arroyo. And the sound of the racing water became louder, and more distinct, as he came closer to it. The water ran fast and deep after a storm. When he had been here last, it was in the summer. It had been dry, and the stream was low and easy to cross. But in the years that had passed, the torrents had cut a deeper ravine making it difficult to forge.

Zachary pushed the brush aside until the turbid water of the arroyo was in view. He walked to the edge of it. The water ran as swift and deep as the sound of it had indicated. The floor of the canyon, where he stood, was now some eight to ten feet above its tumultuous surface. And the banks were steep and loose. He laid his gun aside, and dropped his pack in the clearing. Standing close to the edge, he scanned both sides of the arroyo in either direction for as far as he could see. The Indian was searching for a better place to cross. Up stream about two-hundred yards he spotted a fir tree that had fallen across the banks. It was partially submerged at the far side, acting as a dam; it caught branches and debris that floated downstream and collected behind it in a tangled, treacherous mass.

Dropping to one knee, he took a canteen from the side of his pack. The Navajo put it to his mouth, and his head fell back as he gulped the tepid water it contained. He wiped his mouth with the back of his hand. Then he twisted the cap back onto the canteen. While he knelt there, he listened to the water rush through the arroyo. He thoughtfully considered his next course of action.

The ravine is some thirty feet across, he told himself. *If I'm lucky, that tree is wedged into the other side of the bank! I'll have to take the pack and the rifle along with me, but I'll need both hands free! There's no shoulder strap on this rifle, so I'm going to have to make one!*

He pulled a short piece of rope from his pack. *It will do!* He thought. Zachary tied it to the metal ring on the underside of the gun stock. He tied the other end of the rope around the narrow part of the shoulder stock, just behind the trigger guard. It made an adequate sling. He could use it to carry the rifle across the stream on his back.

Sitting back into the low, wild grass in the clearing, he considered that it was already taking him longer to reach the ruins than he had first anticipated. He had no wristwatch to tell the time but, he knew from the position of the sun, it appeared to be about nine o'clock in the morning. He was hungry, but there was no time for a meal. Zachary remembered that he had placed some jerky in his backpack. He pulled a plastic bag from the pack, removed the tie, and exposed a piece of cured venison. He tore a bite loose with his teeth, and chewed it. It was hard and too salty, but it would do.

He put the remainder of the jerky back inside of the pack, cinched it up, and slung the pack behind him. Standing up with the rifle in hand, he slipped the rope sling over his shoulder and strode in the direction of the fallen tree. While he walked the Navajo monitored the pale wind, he probed it with his sharp senses, searching out the presence of other human kind. *If someone was nearby it is likely I would hear 'em!* He told himself. *And if they were up wind, I'd hear 'em for sure!* He reassured himself that he hadn't been followed.

It just seems strange that those two in the pickup truck just disappeared like that! He thought maybe it hadn't been the two men that he had suspected after all.

Coming upon the place where the fallen tree lie across the ravine, it looked more risky than he had surmised from a distance. The Indian wasn't as fit as he once was, and he realized it. But this was something he had to do.

He surveyed the condition of the tree, also the limbs and the debris that surrounded it. Floating rubbish had built up behind the tree. It was pressed up against it by the powerful current. The force of the water flowing over and around the tree caused the debris to heave and bob about. *If a man wasn't careful he could slip through that stuff and get caught up under it, or be swept down stream before he knew what happened!* He concluded. Zachary guessed the base of the tree trunk to be some twenty inches in diameter. It narrowed to less than twelve inches before in disappeared under the water. But from where the tree was submerged to the opposite bank, there was another ten feet of open water moving rapidly. *What's under there is anyone's guess,* he told himself.

He moved to the end of the trunk where the soil encrusted, gnarled roots were exposed. They jutted out like tentacles. He grabbed hold of a thick root and pulled himself up on the trunk of the fallen tree. The rotted bark was loose, and damp from the rain. The Indian straddled the trunk with his legs, and gripping it with his hands, he slithered down slowly, carefully. Chunks of bark broke away as he moved toward the midway point, where the water rushed under the tree. He paused to catch his balance. His feet dangled over the surface of the turbulent water. He couldn't see into the water below him, it was clouded with soil that was endlessly washed away.

At that moment, he wondered why he hadn't thought to take off his boots and secure them to his backpack before starting across. Now he was in too precarious a position to manage it, and getting into the water was unavoidable. The Navajo shook his head in resignation, and laughed to himself, "If I'm goin' across, I'm gonna get wet!" He thought too, he'd have to walk in soggy boots the rest of the way to the ruins. It wasn't a pleasant thought!

Zachary worked his way down into the water, close to the place where the tree went under. He could feel his boots fill with water around his ankles, and they became heavy. He continued to move down into it gradually, until he was waist deep in the water. It was slippery, and he nearly lost his grip. The tree had been in the water long enough to turn the bark to mush. He hugged the tree tightly, trying to decide how he would impel himself the remainder of the distance across the arroyo. The current cut forcefully around his thick body as he slipped down farther into the water. There was very little time to consider the options.

The Navajo had never been a great swimmer. And this was no time to test his skills, especially in this current. He probed for more footing. His foot slipped on the submerged tree. Its bark had been stripped away by the current. The only thing he could think of to do was to lunge forward toward the bank, hoping he could grab something near it, a rock, or an exposed root, anything to keep himself from being washed away.

Just as quickly as he had considered it, he did it. He plunged into the water. The current hurled him. It spun him around and sucked him under. Zachary could feel himself being tossed and bounced, until he landed with his back against a solid object, all the while totally immersed. He clawed at it until he felt his hands above the water. Then he dragged himself up, pulling his head above the surface. He gasped for air, taking several deep breaths that seemed deficient. Then he took several more, until his lungs felt satiated and the burning stopped.

The object was a large boulder protruding from the bank. He crawled up onto it. Zachary laid face down on the rock for several minutes, while he collected his strength. Then he sat up in the full sunlight and took stock of himself and his gear. The pack was still on his back, the bedroll too, but it was waterlogged. He reached around behind him for the rifle. Amazingly, it was still there. He placed it out in front of him, flat atop the rock, to inspect it.

Clambering up the side of the large rock formation, Zachary carried his rifle by the rope sling he had tied to it. When he was almost eye level with the canyon floor, he paused to look around, to be certain no one was waiting for him to ascend. When his keen senses where satisfied that he was alone, he pulled himself up over the edge of a jagged rock and onto the even ground on the other side of it.

He began to strip down, removing the pack and bedroll from his back and laying them on the ground beside him. Everything would have to be drained of water, and dried, before he continued his journey. He spread the sleeping bag out in the sun over a large, semi-flat boulder that was nearby. Then he emptied the backpack, and took inventory, removing the items and laying them out. Fortunately those items that weren't in cans were in plastic bags and there was no damage to his provisions.

Seating himself on a low rock next to the boulder, where he had laid down his pack, the Navajo leaned against it pulling off his boots one at a time. Water gushed from them as he turned them upside down. He shook them out vigorously, grumbling to himself as he did so. Then he laid them down to dry. Removing his socks, he wrung them out and stretched them flat over the rock. Barefoot, he stood up. He took several quick glances around, self-consciously, before he began to strip down to his boxer shorts. Then he laid the rest of his clothes out in the sun, with the medley of belongings that were strewn over the rocks. They served as a blatant signal marking his location, even to the unschooled observer. Zachary slumped down with his back against the boulder, feeling ridiculously vulnerable. He took a pinch of chewing tobacco from its foil pouch and placed it in his mouth, rolling it back into his cheek with his tongue. Then he seized his rifle and clutched it tightly across his lap in an attempt to compensate for his near nakedness.

As he sat there impatiently waiting for the sun to evaporate at least some of the water from the sleeping bag and his clothing, he pondered the remaining distance to the ruins. He thought it to be no more than a mile. And he considered leaving the sleeping bag and backpack to dry, while he continued his trek to the ruins, he could reclaim them later.

Checking his rifle for damage, he removed the clip, shook some water from it, then blew into the chamber to disperse beads of water that had collected on the mechanical parts. Zachary wiped the gun with the tail of his shirt and replaced the clip. He squeezed a few more drops of water from his pants, then he stood and pulled them on. They were cold against the flesh of his legs, and caused him to shiver in the crisp air. He wrung out his socks once more, sat, brushed the dirt from the bottom of his feet and put them on, trying not to stretch them too badly. His boots were cold and wet, and they emitted the slightly repugnant odor of wet leather. It made his nostrils twitch momentarily, then he struggled to pull them up over his socks.

He stood, while he put on his shirt. It was nearly dry and helped to retain the warmth of the sun against his skin. Then he grasped the rifle and put his arm through the makeshift shoulder strap. Zachary walked briskly in the direction of the trail. It was about two-hundred yards west of where he stood, and fifty yards or so from the fallen tree. He made a mental note of it for his return.

Advancing along the trail to a clearing, the top row of ledge houses could be seen. Zachary's eyes combed what he could see ahead. He spotted a tenuous line of light gray smoke rising from the center of the ruins, below the upper ledge houses. It appeared that someone was there, or had been recently.

Now he proceeded cautiously. Stepping quietly, he looked about for more signs. He wended his way through the brush that overshadowed the trail. Ten more minutes and he would be at the cliffs below the ruins. And then he would know if it was Daniel, or the two men whom he thought had followed him.

The Navajo stepped out from behind the foliage that concealed the trail, in clear view of the ruins, and stopped. The sun caught the westernmost portion of the gallery of ledge houses, perched atop vertical slabs of Navajo sandstone. It made them appear almost white, like alabaster monuments guarding some ancient secret. They were accented like props on a stage, prepared to accommodate the actions of ancient players. Zachary peered at them, feeling at any moment they could come to life.

If a man could travel in time, he mused, *then I have traveled seven-hundred years into the past!* He stood in awe of this ancient masterpiece, and of those who once dwelt here. A sense of communion fell upon him as he viewed the crumbling remains of perhaps as many as twenty-five or thirty apartments, some two and three stories high, built of sandstone blocks and earthen mortar.

THEN HE HEARD HIS NAME CALLED OUT! Startled, he listened.

"Zachary! Zachary! I am here! Look up here!"

The voice echoed in the grotto, distorting the sound and, causing him confusion. His eyes searched frantically for the source of the voice that addressed him.

It spoke again. "Zachary! Look up here to your left!"

He turned quickly and looked up. There in the shadow of the uppermost apartment, to the east of it, stood a figure clothed in white robes. A tall, stately figure with his left hand raised to greet Zachary.

At first bewildered, Zachary stood silent. *Is this the spirit of an Ancient One guarding the ruins?* He asked himself. *Is he the one who has led me here? Does he know of Daniel?*

The figure spoke again. "Zachary! It is I, Daniel!" He stepped out of the shadows into plain view. "Come, meet me down below near the kiva!" The robed apparition climbed down a ladder adjacent the building on which he had been standing. He hurried along the central walkway that connected the village from end to end.

As he approached, Zachary could see that it was indeed his friend, Daniel. "I knew you'd be here!" He shouted. Taking a deep breath, he added excitedly, "Where have you been?" His voice was first resonant with his obvious relief, and then with his delight at seeing the stranger, Daniel, once again. He became aware of his own excitement, and it caused him momentary embarrassment. Then in an effort to quickly reach Daniel, he began to scale the ledges and toe holes leading to the lower portion of the ruins.

They met outside the kiva, a room that had been used for religious ceremonies. Daniel reached for Zachary to embrace him. Although he was not comfortable with the gesture, Zachary accommodated him.

"I have a lot of questions that need answers!" The Indian told him, pointedly.

"You won't need your weapon here!" Daniel told him, referring to the rifle that he carried over his shoulder. "Come inside and sit down! I'll try to answer all of your questions!"

Daniel stooped under the low doorway, making his way into the room where a fire still smoldered. Zachary followed him inside. He mindfully lowered the rifle from his shoulder and set it to rest against the stone wall just inside the doorway. The smoke filtered upward through a hole in the ceiling, part of which had been caved in by a rock fall. The interior walls were blackened from many fires, centuries earlier.

The Navajo's imagination conjured up the vision of a group of Ancient Ones sitting around the fire, conducting a religious ceremony in this room, as he sat down on a stone bench across from Daniel. Then he spoke. "When I saw you standing up there, I thought you might be the spirit of one who was guarding the ruins!" Then he viewed the stranger curiously. "Why are you dressed like that?"

"These are ceremonial robes," Daniel told him. "They are the kind that I wear in the presence of my leader. I have traveled far, and returned, since we have last seen each other, Zachary. And I must go again! But there is much you can do in my absence."

Zachary pondered the stranger's face. Somehow he appeared different, perhaps transformed in some way. His hair appeared lighter in color than Zachary had remembered. *More gray?* He thought. The man's eyes seemed to him cool and distant. *There are no lines on his face,* he told himself musingly, while he decided what question he would ask next. He thought it to be the white of the robe, and the sunlight that beamed through the hole in the roof. It illuminated his face. *Ageless,* Zachary thought.

Speaking sternly, the Navajo told him, "There's been trouble since you left! Where did you go?"

"I went to the *one* who sent me! I do not act alone, Zachary. I answer to one with higher authority than myself." The stranger answered him candidly.

Zachary was guardedly suspicious. "You told me a few things about this place you're supposedly from,............and somethin' about your purpose for being here,............but you've never said whether there was any others like you here? Where are they anyway? Am I gonna see more like you?"

Amused, the stranger smiled reassuringly. "No Zachary, I am the messenger! I come alone, but I am given power to act by *he* who has sent me!"

"I thought I was dreamin'! The night you disappeared I had a vision. I saw some Ancient Ones circlin' me in my sleep. They were tryin' to get me to go with'em! I refused. I told'em I had somethin' to do. Somethin' important! Then my grandfather appeared, he told me I was right not to go. He said it wasn't my time yet!" The Navajo paused, he waited for Daniel's reaction, wondering if he had already known about the dream.

"I can only tell you that you were correct not to go with them. It is not your time. You have much to do!" The stranger said, never indicating whether he knew anything about the dream, leaving the Navajo with uncertainty regarding it.

Zachary confronted Daniel. "But I saw you disappear into the light that came up from the canyon floor! Was that a dream?"

There was silence between them for a moment. Zachary waited for Daniel's reply. He broke contact with the stranger's eyes to rest his own. The Navajo looked down at the dirt floor, wondering what the stranger's answer would be. Then he looked up again to catch the steady, penetrating gaze from the eyes that addressed him with a look of acknowledgment, and a placid face that was wrought with assurance.

"No, you weren't dreaming. You did see me go into the light."

"Than the other wasn't a dream? I mean the Ancients? All that was real? My grandfather?" The Navajo posed with a muddled expression.

"It was real in that it served a purpose for you, Zachary! It is for you to interpret its meaning!" Daniel told him this with a distinct tone of conviction.

Zachary's mind was ripe with speculation. "We Navajos, we believe in the spirit world," he told the wraith figure sitting on the stone bench across from him. He said it as though he was affirming an unspoken belief, something hidden away in his subconscious mind, unsettled. We believe that a spirit messenger is sent from God to tell the individual what He expects from him! Are you that kind of messenger? Are you *"ba' alilii"*, the one who has supernatural power? My grandfather said, *listen to the One of Many Faces!*

Is that you?"

The stranger chose his words carefully, so as not to mislead the Indian, but to retain his confidence. "I am the one that the Ancient Ones believed to be the Spirit Messenger. I am also the one that others referred to as *"ba' alilii"*. It is I that your grandfather spoke of."

Zachary eyed him fervently. "Then you're my spirit messenger?"

"Yes,...........I am. I am a messenger. I am a messenger for your kind." He told him flatly. There was an almost imperceptible hesitation to his answer. It was one of which he was fully aware, but the Navajo was too preoccupied to note it.

"And the purpose of the dream?" Zachary inquired, intent on resolving the meaning of his vision.

Daniel reached across to put his hand on Zachary's forearm. He said solemnly, "To confirm your beliefs!"

Looking down at the stranger's hand the Navajo asked, "If you're a spirit, how come you feel alive?"

He pulled his hand away abruptly. "What you consider a spirit, Zachary, is an entity that exists simply in another time and space. I am alive! Do you remember what I told you? *Your minds eye sees me the way that you want to see me, the way that you are capable of seeing me!* It's what you're comfortable with at this time. These surroundings have a spiritual significance for you, so your thought patterns picture me within them in a particular way."

The Navajo was in a quandary. He struggled to grasp the complexity of what the stranger had implied. Daniel knew it. He also knew that sometime in the not too distant future that Zachary would be able to understand it all.

"So than how should I call you?" The Indian asked, resigning to his uncertainty.

"The same as always, Zachary! And don't be concerned for reverence to me, that is reserved for your own spirit!" Daniel told him.

Scratching his head in an awkward gesture, Zachary said "I brought some supplies I thought you might need, but when I crossed the arroyo I went into the water and I had to lay everything out to dry. I can go for it and bring it back to you. It's only enough food for two days, though, no longer."

"I'll be fine Zachary! I appreciate your concern, but there is much to do and you must be on your way soon!"

"The two men!" The Navajo blurted with a sudden urgency in his voice. "They came back to my place! They killed -*Tsoh,* and they searched the storage barn this time. They're lookin' for those gold coins, I'm sure of it! And they're not stoppin' at anything 'til they get some! I think they're lookin' for you. A pickup truck followed me out here last night. I'm pretty sure it was them! They followed me to the mouth of the canyon, then disappeared. I thought they went up on the mesa, but I never saw'em again!"

"I know!" The stranger said with a profound certainty. "But don't be concerned with them. They will no longer be a problem to you. There is another of whom you should be wary! He is greedy! He will try to trap you to serve his own purpose. Even as we speak, he sets his plan into effect!"

Suddenly, a horrifying series of flashbacks pervaded his thoughts, in explicit mental pictures, of the dream that he had experienced the night before. Zachary viewed the stranger with alarm. "How do you know this? How do you know that the two men will no longer be a problem?"

"It is my purpose to know! I have come to be instrumental in the fulfillment of a prophecy! And nothing can be allowed to interfere!" The stranger told him candidly. "But there are other forces! They will try to work against me! They are harbingers of the one I hunt! You must assist me in routing them out! You have been chosen!" He was adamant.

"Chosen? What do you mean, chosen?" Zachary said with terrified amazement. "Who chose me?" He started to get up.

Daniel took hold of his arm gently, and sat him down. "You must listen to me! The dream, your grandfather and the Ancient Ones, it's all part of the prophecy! You have been chosen by them, and by *he* who has sent me!"

"I thought you were some kind a alien! Now I find out that you know the Ancient Ones, these spirits! And this *he* that you talk about, who is he?" Zachary retorted.

The stranger hastened to soothe his concern. "I am able to travel in time, between worlds, even universes! The Ancient Ones were taught some of these techniques long ago, but they were lost. My kind have been coming into your world, and leaving it at will, for eons. There have been messengers before me! You mustn't be alarmed. No harm is going to come to you. I promise you that."

Still bewildered, Zachary listened intently while Daniel continued. "You must trust me. In three days you must bring the anthropologist, the one from the university that you told me about. Don't tell anyone else that I am here!"

"But what if she won't come?" The Navajo insisted. What am I supposed to tell her?"

Speaking in a tone of assurance, Daniel said, "She will come! You told me that she is interested in Indian cultures. Tell her you know someone who has made a great discovery about the Ancient Ones. Her curiosity will bring her here. Remember, three days!"

"Why three days?" Zachary asked.

"It is the time I need to prepare! I must provide some evidence that will convince your anthropologist friend." Daniel told him.

"Convince her of what?"

"Convince her of the connection she has long suspected to exist, Zachary!"

"You mean your kind's connection with the Ancient Ones? If you have evidence of that kind, I'm sure she will be interested. I'm interested too! Maybe that's what keeps me comin' back!" The Indian sighed, shaking his head in exasperation.

The stranger stood up. He gestured with his hand for Zachary to follow him outside. Exiting the kiva, Zachary stood face to face with him.

"Do you want me to leave you the rifle? You may need it if anyone suspects you're out here!"

Giving Zachary a look of certainty, Daniel told him, "No, I won't need it! We've had no use for weapons like that in more than a millennium. I have other ways of dealing with my adversaries. Besides, no one will find me out here!"

He took the Navajo's hand. "You must go now! There will be someone waiting for you when you return to your vehicle. Remember, tell no one where I am!" Daniel reminded him.

Zachary felt that same rush of energy pass through him. He wondered if it was how the stranger kept control over him. Daniel smiled and released the Indian's hand.

"What about the supplies? Do you want me to bring'em back to you?" Zachary asked again.

"Don't worry, I'll get them myself! Please go now!" The stranger urged him.

Putting his arm through the sling on his rifle, the Navajo slipped it over his shoulder. Then he started to turn away. He hesitated, and turned back for a moment. "We're different kinds of hunters, you and me! I still need this weapon!"

"Adaa aholya!" He said, with a tone of sincerity in his voice. "It means take care of yourself!"

"And you as well my friend," Daniel said as they parted.

Chapter 11

The Anonymous Phone Call

CASTING ABBREVIATED SHADOWS, THE MIDDAY, AUTUMN SUN warmed the mild wind that rendered dry the remnants of the early morning storm, and the canyon soil that now showed little evidence of it.

While making his way back to the stone arch, using a branch that he had cut from a bushy juniper alongside the trail, Zachary stopped several times to brush out his tracks in the sandy soil. He continued on until he reached the area where he had crossed the arroyo. Its flow had diminished. More of the fallen tree was exposed to the shore. He crossed it again, with less difficulty.

Several times the Navajo strayed from the trail. He walked across some flat rock formations, and through some tall grass to avoid leaving indications of his route. He had thought to take whatever precautions were possible. Daniel's words were etched in his mind, *Tell no one where I am!* To Zachary, that meant in his actions as well as his words. He was determined not to leave a trace of his course of travel.

When the stone arch was in view, Zachary recalled Daniel's words regarding someone who would be waiting for him. He mulled it over in his mind while he climbed steadily, arduously. He asked himself, *Who will it be? The two men who've been following me? But he said I didn't have to worry about them anymore? Jack McCloud? What reason would he have to come looking for me? Jeannie? No! Who than?* He wondered as he climbed the final leg of the switchback. *The one who is greedy? Who is that?*

He lowered the rifle from his shoulder to his hands. Zachary remembered that Daniel had told him he wouldn't need it. But how would he know that? *What does he know of the kinds of people a man encounters? Especially a hunter!* He told himself. *He's not even from this world!* He mused, now convinced.

Approaching near the south end of the stone arch, he would have to ascend a ridge before going down to where his truck was parked. He considered that it would be easy enough for him to spot anyone waiting for him from the top of the ridge. The Navajo kept the rifle in a ready position while he mounted the hill. He was only a few feet from the top when he heard a voice call out, "FREEZE! And drop the rifle!" It came from behind and to his right. Zachary halted, then turned slowly. "DROP IT NOW!" The voice called out again. This time it was with a menacing reproval. It gave the Indian a nauseous feeling that made him swallow hard. He could sense cold steel at his back.

Zachary let the rifle fall from his hands to the ground. Not knowing who had the drop on him, and thinking it could be one of the men who had followed him there the night before, a sense of panic racked his body.

"Lock your hands behind your head!" The voice resounded. It came from directly behind him this time. "Turn around slowly!"

It was definitely a voice that he didn't know. He turned to confront his captor. A clean-shaven, young Navajo Police deputy in dark glasses and a neat, buff colored uniform, stood poised holding a shotgun directed at his midsection.

"What's this all about?" Zachary asked in a perplexed tone. His voice cracked from the anxiety that constricted his vocal cords.

"Are you Zachary Thomas?" The deputy inquired in earnest.

"Yes." He answered sullenly, and regretting it was so at that moment.

"Back away from the gun! Move back some more!!!" The deputy retorted.

The handheld radio he carried on his belt, crackled. A voice came over it. "Come in Dean!"

The deputy held the shotgun under his right arm, it was still aimed at Zachary's stomach. He reached for the radio with his left hand. Then he pulled it from his belt and put it to his mouth, pressing the transmitter button with his thumb. "I've got'em!" He shouted confidently into the radio. "I'm up here on the ridge to the south of his pickup truck!"

A reply came over the radio. "Hold him right there, we'll be right up!"

Zachary stood with his hands behind his head. He peered at the deputy and the shotgun aimed at his belly. His eyes squinted from the bright sun.

Two more deputies crested the ridge, one shouted, "Good work Dean!"

Meanwhile, Zachary's mind scrambled for an explanation. *Things aren't getting better, they're getting a lot worse!* He told himself. *Don't worry he said! What the hell's he talking about? Why are these guys after me anyway?*

They should be after those two thieves and killers, Jake and Carl!

"Okay pal, keep your hands behind your head!" One of the other deputies walked up behind him from the opposite side of the hill. He grabbed one wrist, then the other, snapping the handcuffs tightly closed around them. Then he pulled the hunting knife from the sheath on Zachary's belt. He slipped it into his own belt. He patted Zachary down, frisking him for other weapons. When the deputy was satisfied that Zachary was unarmed, he nodded to the others.

"Turn around and start walking!" He commanded Zachary. The deputy grasped his shoulder and spun Zachary around to face him. Coming eye to eye with the burly Navajo, he gave him a challenging look. Then he gave him a shove forward, bending to pick up Zachary's rifle.

The third deputy remained at the top of the ridge, standing with a bullhorn in his hand. He raised it to his mouth when he saw Zachary and the other two deputies moving toward him. "We're coming down, Captain!" He shouted. His voice echoed throughout the canyon. Waiting for Zachary to walk up beside him, he joined the others and started down the hill. The deputy with the shotgun walked behind Zachary. He held the gun at an angle, directed away from the Navajo's back, but ready to turn it on him if necessary. The other two walked parallel with him, one on either side.

To Zachary's amazement, there were three Navajo Police squad cars parked behind his truck. A police helicopter, with its rotor blades turning slowly, sat perched in a clearing a few hundred yards away. "Kayenta District!" He said to himself, under his breath, as he descended toward the waiting squad cars.

Three more men stood waiting next to his truck. There was one in uniform like the deputies, the other two appeared to be detectives. The shoulder holsters obtruded from their chests. They were dressed in dark pants and white shirts with neckties. All of them were wearing sunglasses. One of them held a radio transmitter, he had the sleeves of his shirt rolled up on his forearms.

"What did I do to deserve all this attention?" Zachary asked sarcastically, turning to the deputy on his right. The deputy peered at him with a grave expression, saying nothing.

When he reached the bottom of the hill, Zachary stumbled over a rock. Then he caught his balance. The deputy on his left, the one with the bullhorn, reached for his arm to keep him from falling.

As he moved forward, Zachary recognized one of the men in plain clothes. It was the police superintendent, Lemuel Redfeather. His memory regressed rapidly as he recalled that the Superintendent and Jack McCloud went back a long way. They had been political comrades at one time. Then Zachary remembered where he had last seen him. It was at a tribal meeting two years ago, where he spoke regarding the enforcement of tribal law against the use of peyote on the reservation. *The man has a silver tongue!* The Navajo told himself.

He stopped toe to toe in front of Lemuel Redfeather. "Zachary Thomas, you're under arrest! Suspicion of murder!" The Police Superintendent said, clearly, articulately.

"What are you talkin' about? I haven't killed anyone!" Zachary swore.

The Superintendent took a cigarette from his mouth, then he exhaled while his astute eyes studied the husky Navajo. He flicked a long ash from the cigarette with his finger. Then he said, "We found two dead bodies right here, below the mesa, this morning." He spoke in a calculating tone. "As far as we can tell, you're the only one that's been out here since last night."

Zachary knew at once who the two men where that he was talking about. He knew it instinctively, as though he had been expecting it. His presence was incriminating, he knew that too. Still, he had to ask, if for no other reason than to confirm his premonition. "Who are you talking about?"

Taking another drag from his cigarette, Lemuel Redfeather let it drop to the ground. He crushed it with his foot, under the sole of a neatly polished, black boot. Then he removed the reflective sunglasses from his face and placed them in the case that protruded from his shirt pocket. "Two men, one dark with a scar above his right eye..........a thin fellow. The other is a blond man with long hair and a mustache...........stocky! You know them?" He asked with an annealed expression, while his assessing, dark eyes measured those of the big Indian standing before him. He measured the man for the slightest twitch, or a scant degree of nervous reaction.

Inwardly, Zachary struggled to maintain a calm, stoic expression as he addressed the Police Superintendent's suspicious query. He knew that if he lied, Lemuel Redfeather was sure to ask around, and the truth was bound to come out. He deemed it better not to deny it. He peered intently into the Superintendent's dominating eyes, noting the crows feet at the outside corners of them. And the puffy eyelids that surrounded them, hinting of too little sleep — and perhaps too hard of a life.

He swallowed hard. "Sounds like the two fellas that've been hangin' around Tuba City. How'd it happen?"

Lemuel Redfeather nodded. The deputies stepped back from around Zachary. They stood at ease while Lemuel moved from in front of him, turning to face the mesa. Then he placed one foot upon the edge of the front bumper of Zachary's pickup truck, leaning forward with his elbow resting on his knee. He placed his forefinger into his mouth, making a sucking sound as he picked a food particle from between his teeth.

He pondered the rugged tailings at the base of the mesa. Then he said, "That's what I thought *you* could tell me, Zachary! We found'em right down there! Both of'em shot at close range. I think they were shot on top of the mesa, then somebody threw their bodies off of it!" He paused to glance over at Zachary.

"That's a pretty good fall," he mused. "Those bodies are broken up real bad!" Lemuel Redfeather expelled a heavy breath. "You own a handgun, Zachary?"

The deputy who had cuffed and frisked him, stepped between Zachary and Lemuel. "He didn't have one on him, sir, but he's probably hid it somewhere!" Then the deputy stepped back.

Lemuel Redfeather turned his full attention on Zachary Thomas. He spoke tersely. "How about it, Zachary? Did you waste these guys? Come on! It'll go a lot easier on ya if you cooperate!" He focused on Zachary with intensity, awaiting a reply.

Standing motionless, with his hands cuffed behind him, Zachary turned his head to glare at Lemuel Redfeather. "No! I told you I didn't kill anybody!" He answered defensively, with a note of ire in his voice.

He reached into his pocket for the sunglasses he had placed there earlier. Taking them out of the case, Lemuel unfolded them, adjusted them, and put them on his face. When he turned toward Zachary, the gold rims of the mirrored sunglasses flashed in the intense sunlight. He straightened up, dropped his foot back to the ground, then he stepped toward Zachary Thomas again.

Coming to rest close to the large Indian's face — closer than any man should be when confronting another — he said something that Zachary Thomas didn't expect. "I don't think you did it either, son! But you're the only suspect we have right now. So I'm going to have to take you into the district station for questioning."

He took a stick of gum from his pocket, then he motioned toward Zachary with it, gesturing an offer of it. The captive Navajo shook his head, declining. The Police Superintendent unwrapped the stick of gum, popping it into his mouth, while he considered the inquisitive expression on the young man's face.

"How'd you know something happened out here?" Zachary Thomas asked.

"I got an anonymous phone call around ten this morning. Whoever it was, they knew you were out here!" He paused thoughtfully for a moment. "He knew these other fellas were out here too! I tried to trace the call, but I didn't have enough time." He paced slowly, deliberately, in front of Zachary. "You're not the only suspect, son! The man that made that call is in the running too!"

Lemuel motioned to the Police Captain, the other man in plain clothes who was still on the radio beside one of the squad cars. He was the one with his shirt sleeves rolled up. He came over to where they stood. When the man approached, Superintendent Redfeather commanded him abruptly, as though addressing a sudden annoyance, "Morgan! Get that state 'copter out a here! He's been here too long already! Let them know we don't need'em! Tell'em we've got our man! Otherwise, they'll be all over this place like stink on shit trying to tell us how to do our job!" The Captain strode back to the nearest squad car. He used the radio to notify the state police, calling in the helicopter that sat waiting a few hundred yards away.

Motioning for the deputies to take Zachary Thomas in one of the squad cars, the Superintendent ordered forcefully, "Let's get out a here! Take him over to the station. I'll meet you there!"

Two of the deputies escorted their prisoner to an awaiting car. One of them opened the rear door, the other forced him down into the back seat. He closed the door and walked around the back of the car to the other side. Getting in next to Zachary, he glowered zealously at the subdued Navajo, one of his own people, as if he had transcended some former inferiority by donning a police uniform. Then the other deputy, Dean, the one who had caught him, got in behind the wheel and drove off.

Zachary turned with a look of resignation to question the young deputy sitting next to him. "What about my truck? You're not going to leave it out there?"

"Relax fella! There's a flatbed on its way to pick it up! It'll be impounded!" The deputy told him with a degree of ambivalence.

"When can I get it back?"

The deputy chuckled. "After the criminal investigators go over it, if there's anything left, you can have it! Than again, maybe never!" He laughed maliciously.

Turning his attention away from the deputy's glib humor, Zachary stared straight ahead. *Who's the greedy one?* He wondered. *Is it Redfeather? Maybe Jack McCloud? It could be either one! After all, they have the same appetite for power and success!* He told himself. He had to consider Lemuel Redfeather in the scheme of things, based on his knowledge of both men and their relationship with one another — personally and politically.

Lemuel Redfeather shared his early childhood in common with Jack McCloud. They were both products of the boarding school era in Navajo education. Both were educated outside of the reservation. Each of them attended the same school only two years apart, Intermountain School in Utah. Lemuel Redfeather being the younger of the two, it would have made him fifty years old. Both of them were high school and college graduates. And each of them had gone to law school. Lemuel majored in criminal law, while Jack had a penchant for civil law. Jack McCloud's first time out for council chairman, Lemuel worked vigorously on his campaign. It was never forgotten. Jack McCloud *always* rewarded loyalties. Shortly after Jack was elected, Lemuel, who was a police sergeant, was promoted to his current position as police superintendent. He bypassed Captain Peter Morgan, who was considered the leading candidate for the position.

They had a history, there was no denying that fact! It was not a well kept secret. Jack McCloud and Lemuel Redfeather were known to be powerful allies. As Zachary Thomas considered them, he told himself, *If someone is putting their plan into effect, like Daniel said, these murders and my arrest must be part of it!*

It was 4:05 p.m.. The ride to the police station in Kayenta was seemingly brief. The car came to a halt next to a sidewalk that led to the rear entrance of the station. It housed the Kayenta District Court and the office of the prosecutor. The deputy sitting beside him gave Zachary a nudge, jarring him from his distracted thoughts. "Don't try to get out until I open your door! Watch him, Dean!"

A detention cell awaited Zachary Thomas.

§ § §

Lemuel Redfeather walked through the front door of the Tribal Council offices in Tuba City. "Anita, is Jack still here?" He asked with a weighty look about him. "I need to see him!"

"Yes, sir. Right this way." The young woman answered, acknowledging him with a brief glance, as she stood up and stepped from behind her desk.

§ § §

He sat on the bunk in his cell wondering how he would get out of this. Zachary had requested a DNA attorney to represent him, a legal assistance program provided under the auspice of the Navajo Tribal Council. He was told his counselor would be there soon.

There were footsteps in the corridor adjacent the cell. He got up from the bunk to look. It was a deputy with a tray of food in hand. "Dinner time!" The deputy shouted as he approached the cell. "You'll have to eat alone tonight! You're the only one in the lockup!" He laughed. He slid the tray through the slot in the steel bars. Zachary took it from him. "I hope you like corned beef and cabbage? I had it myself! It's not bad!"

The deputy watched as Zachary walked back with the tray to a small tabletop, suspended from the wall by two chains that were anchored securely to it. He placed the tray on it, then he pulled out a steel folding chair and sat down. The deputy walked away, after he was certain that the man in the cell wasn't going to get violent and toss the tray. At least not while he was present.

He sat there pondering. *How am I going to get back there in three days?* He asked himself, while he mulled over the food on his plate. *The anthropologist, Tracy Baldwin, how am I going to get in touch with her in time? If she finds out that I'm in jail, arrested on suspicion of murder, she's not going to go out there with me anyway! If Daniel knew so much, why'd he allow me to get into this mess? What good am I going to do anybody in here?"*

Zachary picked at the food. Then he heard more footsteps in the corridor. This time there was more than one person. One set was heavy, like those of the deputy, the others were lighter, like those of a woman. He turned in his chair when he heard them approach.

"Your attorney is here," the deputy announced.

A plain looking Caucasian woman of average height, with light brown hair, bobbed just above her shoulders, in beige slacks, and a navy blue and white, floral blouse, stood next to him, not the stature of jurisprudence he had anticipated.

"I'm from DNA, Mister Thomas," she told him as the deputy unlocked the cell door with one hand on his unlatched holster, exposing an imposing view of the full butt of his revolver.

Zachary started to get up when the door swung open. "Stay seated mister!" The deputy reproached him with a scowl. He clutched the butt of his revolver until the Navajo eased down into the chair. "Do you want me to stay miss?"

"No. I think I'll be fine." She carried her briefcase over to the bunk and laid it down. "Give us about fifteen or twenty minutes, please!"

"I'll be right out here if you need me, ma'am! I'll check on you every five minutes or so!" The deputy assured her, as he stepped out of the cell and latched the door behind him.

"Thank you, officer!" She said in a soft, almost fragile voice.

The woman stood about five feet from Zachary. "I'm Rita Collins, Mister Thomas," she said with a faint tremor. "I work for the DNA," she repeated. "They told me that you requested counsel. "I'm here to help you in any way that I can," she stated timidly.

Zachary studied her from where he sat. "I guess I was expecting someone else!" He said carelessly.

As her face reddened with indignation, impulsively, her voice became hardened with confidence. "Look Mister Thomas, I may not be what you expected, I'm not a man, that is, but I do know the law! Do you want me to represent you?!"

Flush with embarrassment, Zachary said, "I'm sorry. Please sit down. Would you like the chair instead?" He offered.

"No, no! I'll sit right here Mister Thomas, on the edge of the cot." She exhaled deeply as she sat, her tension subsiding.

"Please call me Zachary, Misses Collins."

She smiled, with an amicable warmth returning to her face. "It's Ms. Collins,............but you can call me Rita! I've already talked to Mister Redfeather about the charges against you, Zachary." She continued in the same breath. "Frankly, as far as I can tell, they really have nothing with which to detain you!" Feeling it necessary to qualify her remark, she said, "I mean they don't have any real evidence. The fact that you happened to be near the scene of a crime isn't enough for them to hold you, let alone convict you!" She laughed mildly while considering it. "If they don't come up with some real evidence, Zachary, they will have to release you within forty-eight hours!"

Feeling a glimmer of relief, Zachary smiled briefly. "You mean they have to let me go?"

"That's the way it looks right now! But if something else comes up, if they find any evidence to substantiate the charges, you'll be held pending an arraignment." She cautioned him. "I have to ask you some questions, Zachary, and I want you to answer me honestly! I'm going to record your statements. This is all confidential. It's called attorney, client privilege, so you need not worry that anything you tell me will be used to incriminate you. It's strictly for me to determine how to build your defense, should it become necessary."

The deputy walked up to the cell and peered in, then turned and walked away. Zachary nodded apprehensively. *How much should I tell her about Daniel, if anything?* He asked himself.

"Did you kill those two men, Zachary?" She inquired bluntly.

Flustered at the thought of being accused, Zachary stammered. "I, I, didn't kill anybody!"

"Did you know them?" Rita Collins asked sharply.

Regaining his composure, Zachary answered straightaway. "I knew who they
were, I had seen'em around, if that's what you mean?"

"Were you doing any kind of business with them, Zachary?" She asked pointedly.

"No! But I believe they broke into my house! Twice! And I wanted them to know that I knew it was them, and to stay away!"

"So did you go looking for them? Did you follow them out to the mesa, Zachary?"

"No, it wasn't like that! I went out to the stone arch to, to,............get away an' think for a while. I noticed that they followed *me* out there! But I never saw them last night,...........not at all!"

"Did you see them break into your house?"

"No."

"Do you have a witness that saw them?"

"No."

"Did you file a police report, Zachary?"

He responded nervously. "No! I just didn't want the police involved!"

"If you didn't see them break in, Zachary! And you don't have any witnesses! How do you know it was them?"

Zachary tensed up in the chair, he breathed deeply, exuding his frustration at the questioning. "Because I know it was them! That's it!! I just know it!!"

Rita switched off the recorder. She cautioned him sternly. "I have to ask you these questions, Zachary! They're going to question you tomorrow! And they are going to try to establish a motive! I need to know exactly where we stand! So you had better tell me everything you know!" Rita switched on the recorder.

He writhed mentally over the subject of Daniel, while he acquiesced to further questioning. "I had a witness who could back me up!" He admitted. "He saw those two, Jake and Carl, hangin' around. As a matter of fact, I think they were after somethin' he had!" He paused, guardedly. "They followed us from Flagstaff the other day. We saw them in town."

"Who is this witness, Zachary? Where is he now?"

"I don't know where he is! He disappeared!"

"Is this a friend of yours?" Rita asked suspiciously, probing for a more revealing disclosure.

"I met'em earlier this week. He was hitchhiking on 160. I picked him up and gave'em a ride to Flagstaff. He didn't have any place to stay, so I asked him to stay with me for a few days."

"So he's a stranger, and you just picked him up and brought him home! What's his name?"

"Daniel. His name is Daniel." The Indian said nervously.

"Does this Daniel have a last name?" Rita Collins asked with one eyebrow raised.

"I don't know?" Zachary told her, knowing it was not a good answer. It was not what she wanted to hear.

She questioned him poignantly "Are you always in the habit of picking up strangers? And bringing them into your home, Zachary?" Then hesitating with a thought-filled expression, she said, "It sounds like this man could have more of a motive than you! Was he with you last night?"

The deputy returned again. He grasped the bars of the cell door and peered inside. "How much longer ma'am?"

Rita turned to address him. "Just five more minutes, officer."

"Okay ma'am! Five more minutes!" He took his right hand from the cell door, returning it to his side. He brushed it across his holster as he walked away.

"Well Zachary! Was he with you?" She repeated sternly.

"No, he wasn't with me last night!"

"Than where is he?"

"I, I don't know!" He swore. "You're questioning me like you think I'm lying or somethin'!" Zachary retorted defensively.

Rita responded in earnest. "No, I don't think you're lying, Zachary. But if you're not telling me the whole truth, it could jeopardize my strategy! And if you think I'm being hard on you, just wait until tomorrow when the police investigators, and Redfeather, get a hold of you! I think you'd better tell them about this fellow named Daniel! It will help you out immensely!"

"Do you think they're going to let me go?" The Navajo asked.

She switched off the recorder, then snapped her briefcase shut. "I'm very confident that they will have to release you. But that doesn't mean that they can't pick you up again later! I want to make sure that we keep you out of jail, Zachary, so I suggest that you tell them all that you know about this stranger. He may have been connected with these two men in some way."

Zachary, being moved by the young woman's zeal, said, "You're somethin' else! I mean,...........I didn't expect............."

"You didn't expect what Mister Thomas?" She interjected sharply. "You didn't expect me to know what I am doing because I'm a woman?"

He flushed with embarrassment once more. "I guess I just didn't think you would be as tough as you are! I'm impressed!" He said, trying to vindicate his assumption.

Amused, Rita smiled. "Okay big fella! I'll forgive you this time, but don't let it happen again!"

Returning, the deputy looked in at them, glanced at his watch, then he gestured that their time was up. Rita got up from the edge of the cot. She snatched up the briefcase in her right hand and stepped over to Zachary. Placing her hand reassuringly on his shoulder, she looked down at him, smiled, then winked. "Don't worry, everything will be just fine! I'll be present tomorrow morning during your questioning."

The deputy turned the key in the lock, and the door swung open. Rita turned to the door and strode toward it with her head back, and her posture erect, exuding a self-confidence she had not displayed upon her arrival. What Zachary didn't know was that his was Rita Collins' first criminal case.

Chapter 12

Allegations of Conspiracy

THURSDAY MORNING AT 9:25 A.M., ZACHARY SAT ON THE COT IN his cell reading a magazine, given to him by the deputy who brought him his breakfast. He hadn't slept well the night before. He had lain awake, staring at the faint light that infringed upon the darkness and the linear shadows that it produced on the ceiling of the cell, exceedingly aware of his predicament. And sorely reminded of it from every angle of vision that night.

The soles of the deputy's shoes squeaked on the tile floor as he approached the cell. Another set of footsteps followed closely behind him. Zachary looked up from the magazine in the direction of the corridor, to encounter the deputies who stood at the cell door with telling expressions. It was time.

"There's some people waiting to talk to you!" One of them said as he turned the key in the lock. He opened the door and stepped inside, while the other deputy remained standing outside the cell.

"Stand up and turn around! Place your hands behind you!" The deputy commanded. Zachary slipped the magazine from his lap onto the cot. He stood reluctantly, conforming to the deputy's command.

Cuffing him, the deputy took hold of his arm and guided him toward the open door. "Come along mister!" The waiting deputy grasped the upper portion of his other arm. They led him down the corridor, stopping at a pair of steel doors with wire reinforced glass windows. They appeared to have been freshly painted, with a glossy, dark brown enamel over a previous coat that had chipped and flaked. It left blistered patches under the new paint. The deputy on Zachary's right released his grip to raise his key to the lock, while the fettered Navajo peered through the obscured glass at yet another corridor beyond. Unlocking it, the deputy pushed the waist high bar that released the latch and opened the door. The man on Zachary's left escorted him through the door. Then the door was locked behind him.

Continuing down the corridor past several offices, occupied by the prosecutor and his staff, with the doors open and a flurry of activity inside each room, they came to a halt in front of a closed door with a sign on it that read, Knock Before Entering. Zachary could hear familiar voices coming from behind it. The deputy holding his right arm rapped sharply on the door.

"Come on in!" A voice shouted from within the room. The deputy reached for the door knob, he turned it, then pushed the door open into the room. Lemuel Redfeather sat behind a large table facing the door, with his back to the windows lining the outside wall of the room. He leaned back in the chair, yawning with an already-taxed expression, and his arms stretched out behind him above his head. "Come in and join us, Zachary," he said sardonically.

Escorting him into the room, the deputies entered behind Zachary. The last one stood at the doorway with his hands at his waist. "Remove those cuffs!" Lemuel Redfeather said, as he eased his chair back to the floor, with his arms resting on the table once again. The deputy did as he requested. Zachary brought his hands out in front of him and massaged his wrists. Rita Collins stood up next to her chair. She smiled warmly at Zachary. "You can sit right here, next to me," she said, gesturing at a chair adjacent to hers.

"Wait outside boys!" Lemuel told the deputies, raising his head slightly to initiate his request. They closed the door behind them.

"Have a seat, Zachary! We have a lot to talk about, son!" Redfeather said equivocally.

A short, markedly overweight man stood at the far end of the table. He peered at Zachary Thomas from the corner of the room. His face was pockmarked, and his expression was somber. His eyes sat deep into his swollen face. The buttons on his shirt strained at his midsection.

"I'm Detective Sam Begay," he growled, breathing deeply and exhaling as he said so. His brocade belt on his navy blue slacks indented his middle, concealing half of its large silver buckle.

Zachary took his place next to Rita Collins. Detective Begay lumbered between the empty chair and the wall at his end of the table. He squeezed past Rita Collins, causing her to move forward against the table's edge. Then he stopped between Rita and Zachary. He glowered at the suspect Navajo in an obvious manner: in an attempt to intimidate him.

Rita reached for Zachary's arm to distract him from the looming presence over his right shoulder. "I'm here to make sure that you're not coerced in any way, Zachary! If there's any question you feel is misleading, or may cause you to incriminate yourself, I'll be here to advise you!"

Lemuel Redfeather cleared his throat. "Look, we're not here to accuse you, Zachary," he said in a conciliatory tone, being cognizant of the young man's counsel. "We just want you to tell us the truth about everything that you know! If you tell us everything, we can clear all of this up a lot faster! I had investigators out yesterday until dark. They've been back out to the mesa since early this morning! We're not going to leave a stone unturned! I mean that literally," he emphasized with conviction. "There's a murder weapon out there somewhere, and we're going to find it!"

Sam Begay placed his heavy hand on Zachary's right shoulder, he squeezed, applying moderate pressure. Turning his head to look up at the sagging jowls of the portly caricature, Zachary's eyes were met by a morose expression. "So where is it, son?" The Navajo's eyes shifted to Rita Collins who stared at Detective Begay with disdain. Then he looked again at Begay whose sullen eyes still grilled him.

"Where is *what?*" He asked sarcastically, fixing his eyes on the chubby hand that clutched his shoulder.

A reprehensive glance from Lemuel Redfeather told Sam Begay to remove his hand promptly. But with a pugnacious manner, he persisted. "The handgun, boy! The handgun!" He bellowed.

"I don't own a handgun! I've never had a handgun!" Zachary swore adamantly, as his eyes settled upon the unmoved, stolid expression inhabiting Lemuel Redfeather's face at that moment. It was an indifferent look, that made him appear oblivious to the proceedings at hand.

Redfeather leaned forward in his chair, with his right arm across a notepad lying on the table in front of him. "Did you know the two men who were killed?"

Zachary took a moment to respond. He swallowed hard. "I didn't know them personally. I saw them in Flagstaff once! And then again in Tuba City!"

"When did you see them? I mean what day?" Lemuel retorted.

At once, Zachary felt distressed. He had said something that could lead to questions regarding Daniel. He had suddenly realized that it had not been him who saw the two men, Carl and Jake, in Flagstaff.

Sweat broke out on his forehead. Lemuel noticed. "Well Zachary?"

"I,...........I was in a restaurant in Flagstaff on Monday. I was with a friend. My friend noticed them. Then I saw them at Jack McCloud's office the next day!"

Lemuel sensed the ambiguity in his story. "Who's this friend of yours, Zachary?"

Zachary scanned Rita's face, searching for a glint of assurance. She sat poised anticipating his disclosure. He turned again to Lemuel Redfeather. "It's,...........he's just a friend. A guy I met on Monday............on the road!"

Sam Begay pressed by, behind Zachary's chair, nudging him forward.

He stopped on Zachary's left. Then he pulled an empty chair around. Sam placed it at the corner of the table and flipped it around with the back against the table's edge. He sat down, straddling the chair, then leaned forward with his arms crossed over the back of it, positioning himself obtrusively in Zachary's face.

"A guy you met on Monday,............and he's already your friend? Did you know this guy before Monday?" Sam Begay inquired breathily.

Hesitant to acknowledge his questioning, Zachary's eyes remained straight forward, averting the threatening gaze of Sam Begay, he stared out the window beyond Lemuel Redfeather. After a brief moment, he said, "No! I didn't know him before Monday. And yes, I do consider him my friend! What's wrong with that?!"

Lemuel cleared his throat loudly to get Zachary's full attention. "Was this friend out there with you...........night before last? What's his name?"

Zachary turned sharply to Rita Collins.

"She can't answer that for you, son!" Lemuel advised him.

"You best answer it yourself, boy!" Sam Begay added abruptly.

"I think you should tell them about this man, Zachary. I believe it would be in your best interest." Rita told him, urging his response.

"His name is Daniel," the burly Navajo answered reluctantly. "He was hitching a ride out on 160 just west a here. I picked him up. He seemed like a nice guy. We got to talkin', and he said he had no place to stay. He was passing through on his way to California where he had a job,............at least that's what he told me! I felt sorry for'em, so I offered him my place for a few days! He left Wednesday morning for California. I haven't seen him since!" He hesitated for a moment. "So you see, he couldn't have been with me!"

Redfeather was encouraged by Zachary's revelation concerning the stranger. He pursued the stranger's identity further. "What's this fella look like? Can you give me an accurate description? What was he wearing when he left here?" He tossed the notepad across the table at Sam Begay. It landed aslant in front of him. "Write his description down, Sam!"

He was not in the habit of lying, and Zachary was already displeased with himself for having to fabricate a story to protect his friend: a friend whose identity of which even he was not fully certain. He struggled with the idea of further deception, turning toward Sam Begay who viewed him with eyes of unrelenting inquiry.

"He's,............he's tall! Maybe six two, six three! Kind a lean! Weighs maybe one-eighty or ninety. He's got brown hair and blue eyes!" Zachary said.

"How old's this guy?" Sam Begay inquired hoarsely.

"Mid-forties, maybe! I never asked him." Zachary answered, intending to be as vague as possible and still tell the truth.

"Any other distinguishing features? Scars or anything?"

"Never noticed any scars!"

"He tell ya anything about himself? Where he's from? Anything like that?" Begay probed as scrupulously as he was able.

"Just said he was from back east somewhere. Never said where! He didn't talk much about himself." Zachary told Sam Begay straightfaced.

"What was he wearin'?"

Zachary's hands were folded out in front of him, resting on the table. He looked down in an attempt to avoid Lemuel Redfeather's scrutiny. Rita Collins was engaged in note taking of her own. She pushed her glasses up on the bridge of her nose, while she jotted down the details of Daniel's description for her file.

"He had on a pair of well worn jeans, a flannel shirt, and a pair of dark brown boots."

Sam Begay ceased writing abruptly. "Were these cowboy boots? Or were these regular boots? Were they new ones? Or were they old ones?"

Suddenly amused, Zachary looked up at Sam Begay, he laughed. Lemuel Redfeather, seeing the humor in Begay's pedantics, laughed too. Rita Collins looked up from her notes, aware she had missed something, and smiled naively.

"Jist answer the question!" Sam Begay groused, irritated as well as embarrassed by the outburst of laughter at his method of interrogation.

"They were plain brown boots! Not cowboy boots!" Zachary retorted, sensing Begay's irascibility.

"This Daniel, did he give you his last name?" Lemuel Redfeather inquired of Zachary. He asked it with a tone of empathy in his voice, hoping to solicit Zachary's confidence.

"No. He never mentioned his last name. It never occurred to me to ask." Zachary responded, while considering the lack of necessity for Daniel to have a formal last name, knowing it was of no significance to Daniel or himself.

Lemuel Redfeather, taking note of his momentary introspection, looked over at Sam Begay. He raised his hand to signal a pause in the questioning. Rita Collins observed them curiously, wondering what prompted their motion to stop. She studied Zachary for a moment, then took notice of his far off gaze.

"So, is there something more we should know about this Daniel? Something that just came to mind perhaps?" Lemuel asked, hoping to catch Zachary off guard, and capitalize on his thoughts.

"No, not really." Zachary replied, bringing his attention back to the immediate.

The Police Superintendent confronted Zachary Thomas bluntly. "I don't believe you're telling me everything you know! I talked to Jack McCloud yesterday! He told me about the visit to his office, on Tuesday, with your friend Daniel. He told me you came back on Wednesday morning too! With accusations about the two men you thought had burglarized your house,...........and killed your dog. He said you were enraged over the alleged break-in. And you threatened to take matters into your own hands! He said that you insisted he knew these two men and their whereabouts! He told me he asked you to call the police. But you declined, saying you would deal with the matter on your own terms! Mister McCloud also told me about your friend! He said that this fellow rambled on about some strange message of some sort! He said both of you rambled on about it, as if you were in some sort of drug induced delusory state! McCloud told me he thought this fellow was some kind of a cult member. That he acted strangely, and he appeared to be dangerous!"

He turned his attention to his counsel, Rita Collins, to whom he realized he had not given the full details of his association with Daniel. She appeared disconcerted. *If his relationship with this Daniel proves to be more than that of a mere acquaintance, a passing stranger whom he offered a place to stay, then Zachary is in more trouble than I had anticipated.* She told herself. *He could be an accessory!* And then she thought further. *It will be more difficult to divert the suspicion from Zachary to the stranger!* Zachary read the concern on Rita's face.

"What about it, Zachary?" Lemuel Redfeather persisted. "I see your counsel is as eager to hear the truth as I am!" Seldom did he miss an opportunity to isolate the perpetrator from his safety net. "Is all of this true?"

He turned away from Rita Collins. The pit of his stomach felt hollow and on fire. He focused again on Lemuel Redfeather, who scrutinized him relentlessly. "No. Not all of it is true!" He answered apprehensively, while trying to anticipate Redfeather's next query.

"You planned the murder of these two men, Jake Garcia and Carl Simmons, with this man, Daniel! Didn't you? Well? Didn't you?!" Redfeather hammered away at Zachary incessantly.

"Come on! Out with it!" Sam Begay grabbed his shirt collar, pulling Zachary into his face.

"Enough, is enough!" Rita Collins screeched as she bolted out of her chair. "You get your damn hands off of my client, or I'll have you up on charges so fast your head will spin!"

The room fell quiet. The only sounds to be heard were Sam Begay's labored breathing, and Zachary's groan of relief at being released from his clutches.

Rita trembled as she dropped back into her chair. She was obviously distraught over the aggressive behavior that Redfeather and Begay had just displayed.

Zachary took a deep breath. "We,............I didn't plan anything with anybody! We,...........me and Daniel, that is, saw these two men go into Jack McCloud's office on Tuesday. We were on our way out! We suspected that Jack had somethin' to do with'em! That's why I went back the next day to question him about'em. I thought he could tell me who they were, and what they were doin' around here!" He continued with a breath of exasperation. "I just wanted to tell them to stay off my place! That's all!"

"So where was this friend of yours, while you were with Jack McCloud? What was he doing?" Redfeather retorted strongly. He tried to dredge up more information about the stranger. "How can you be sure he wasn't tracking down these two men? Planning to murder them? What do you know about this guy anyway?" He posed to Zachary in an effort to dissuade him from his loyalty to Daniel. "He could be a psychopathic killer for all you know!" All of this Lemuel Redfeather said with the skillfulness of a surgeon, cutting away at the stranger's credibility.

Zachary, still believing to the contrary, answered defensively. "He's not a killer! In fact, I believe he's far from it! He's different in some way, more like a spirit messenger,...........or a prophet!" The Navajo admitted candidly, evoking a snicker from Sam Begay and a puzzled expression from Rita Collins.

He eyed Sam Begay contemptuously, then he continued. "Anyway.........," he said, taking a long breath of consideration, "He was at my place while I was with Jack McCloud!" Zachary swore. "And he couldn't have left there, he would have been on foot! He had no means of transportation, I had my truck!" The Navajo said convincingly.

"A spirit messenger or a *prophet?*" Lemuel Redfeather scoffed. "Zachary! Are you sure that the two of you haven't been eating peyote together?" Redfeather said laughingly, impugning Zachary's judgement. "Jack McCloud told me about a message that your friend, this Daniel, has to deliver from God knows where! Something about saving the world, or the planet and our people,...........or some damn thing! What is this save the world stuff all about anyway? It sure sounds like some kind of cult thing to me!" He laughed openly, condescendingly, making Zachary out to be a fool.

Sam Begay joined in, laughing heartily, with a grating coarseness to his voice. He coughed, then cleared his throat. "I can't believe this fella'd leave town without telling you where he was goin'? I mean, if you're both members of the same cult or something, wouldn't you want to keep in touch? Did he leave his mailing address to forward donations? Or a phone number maybe?" Begay said with a pompous humor, wanting of originality.

She had been taking notes feverishly, since her outburst of indignation over Sam Begay's method of questioning. Suddenly, looking up over the top of her glasses that had slid halfway down her nose, Rita Collins tossed her pen down, sending it bouncing across the table. She eyed Redfeather and Begay with despisal. "Now that I have your attention, *gentlemen!* And I use that word loosely, facetiously! It may not have occurred to you by now,............and I'm sure it hasn't! That my client has been used by this stranger, to fabricate his own alibi! It's apparent! At least to me! Don't you see what's happened here?" She viewed them both scornfully. "He's put up a smoke screen, and you fell for it! Your murderer may be out of the country by now! My client's only mistake is being in the wrong place at the wrong time!" Rita shook her head in reprehension. "What a fine piece of police work this is!"

"We don't need your advice on how to do our job, lady!" Sam Begay bellowed.

Feeling flush with anger at her assertion, Lemuel Redfeather struggled to keep his composure. "Miss Collins! May I suggest that you save your rhetoric for the courtroom! Trust me, when I say it will be of no significance here!"

Zachary stared at Rita Collins, as she acquiesced to Lemuel Redfeather's rebuke. She would stop at nothing to divert the suspicion from him. He was grateful that she was on his side. He knew she would do whatever it took to defend him. *But what about Daniel?* He asked himself. *Where will all of this suspicion over his involvement lead to?* He couldn't help but wonder about it. But he was sure of one thing! They would not stop until they found the stranger.

The clock on the wall above Rita Collins caught Zachary's attention. He had never been so preoccupied with time. It was nearly 1:00 p.m.. In two days he had to be back at the ruins with Tracy Baldwin. He had to have enough time in which to contact her, and make arrangements to meet her. And, he had to convince her that she had good reason to return to the ruins with him.

He focused again on Rita Collins. *She has to get me out of here! But how?* Zachary asked himself. A feeling of desperation overwhelmed him.

She caught the sense of urgency on his face. "Mister Redfeather, can I have a little time alone with my client? I want to make sure he understands all of the implications!"

Lemuel Redfeather looked up at the clock, then he gestured to Sam Begay indicating time out. He stretched his arms in the air and stood up. "We'll take a short break. Would you like a sandwich Miss Collins? How about you Zachary? Sam here will take your orders!" He lifted an empty, paper coffee cup from the table, next to where he had been sitting, peered into it momentarily, with a prepossession, as if he were searching for an answer in it, then he carried it to the wastebasket next to the door and dropped it in on his way out of the room. A deputy, standing outside the door, reached inside and closed the door behind him.

Sam Begay unstraddled his chair and took their orders for sandwiches and sodas. "I'll be back in about twenty minutes! Don't think about goin' anywhere, there'll be two guards right outside this door!" He warned, addressing Zachary Thomas with sneering eyes. Sam lumbered toward the door. He placed his hand on the door knob.

"I have to use the restroom! How am I supposed to get there?" Zachary inquired of Sam Begay.

Sam stopped with his hand suspended on the door. "Knock on this door three times and one of the guards will escort you. Or you could have Miss Collins there, go with you! I'm sure you'd be in good hands!" He burst into laughter. His own vulgarity amused him. Then he left the room.

"That has to be one of the foulest men I have ever met!" Rita Collins exclaimed. She was disgusted by Sam Begay's apparent lack of class. They both took the opportunity to leave the room, then returned a while later.

"Rita, you've got to get me out of here! I have somethin' very important that I have to do! There's someone dependin' on me!" Zachary pleaded with her.

She peered at Zachary with a look of reproval. "Does this have something to do with your visits to Jack McCloud's office? And your friend, Daniel? You should have told me about all of this yesterday! I certainly don't need these surprises! I told you to be totally honest with me, Zachary!" She admonished him. "You didn't lie, but you didn't tell me everything either. Jack McCloud's opinion carries a great deal of clout around here! Whether there is substance to it or not!" She added. "His inference that your friend, Daniel, is somewhat off balance has already implicated him. Although he would appear to be the stronger suspect, the fact that you were with him makes you look like an accomplice!"

Rita Collins' face softened. "Zachary, is there any truth to this accusation about your friend. I mean, about him being part of a cult? Or on drugs?"

He looked at Rita intently. "Are you asking me if I'm a cult member? Or if I'm on drugs?"

"Yes." She answered with frankness, and without hesitation. "That's what I'm asking you as well! I have to know!"

"The answer is *no* on both accounts. And that goes for my friend, Daniel, too!" Zachary told her with a forthright expression. "Nothing could be farther from the truth. I swear to God he's no murderer! And I'm not either! I don't know what happened to those two men?" He vowed. "I told you the truth about that! Now, can you get me out of here?"

Addressing him confidently, she said, "Yes, I do believe that they will have to let you go. As far as I can see, they have no conclusive evidence with which to hold you! Redfeather will present his case to the prosecutor tomorrow. I'm almost certain he will throw it out."

Zachary appeared perplexed. "What do you mean, *almost certain?*

"Unless, of course, the investigators find the murder weapon near the scene of the crime! Or perhaps in your house! Or some kind of evidence in your truck! In which case you would be held over for arraignment. I hope your judgement regarding your friend is correct, or you could find yourself facing charges for a crime that someone else committed!" Rita Collins cautioned him strongly.

The Navajo spoke in an ingenuous tone. "I believe he is someone very special, Rita!"

Sam Begay burst into the room carrying a large, white paper bag. "Here's lunch folks!" He set the sack on the corner of the table. "We've got a ham and cheese on rye! We've got a tuna salad on whole wheat! That's yours, right Miss Collins?" He asked, holding the tuna salad sandwich out to her. He slid two cans of soda across the table toward Zachary. Then he took a place at the table, commencing to wolf down a sandwich that he held half unwrapped. He popped the tab on a soda can with his free hand, while he continued to gluttonously consume the sandwich in the other.

Chapter 13

Suspects, and the Missing Gold Coin

THROUGH THE DOOR DIRECTLY BEHIND HIM, ZACHARY COULD hear fragments of a conversation in the hallway. The words were vague and the voices muffled. He strained to hear. He heard his name mentioned at least one time. Then he recognized Lemuel Redfeather's voice. But the other voice was indistinguishable. Yet it had a familiarity to it that was disturbing to Zachary.

The door latch clicked abruptly and the door swung open into the room, revealing the close of the conversation as Lemuel Redfeather said, "Second door on the left! Captain Morgan will take your statement, ma'am."

Zachary could hear the other voice more distinctly, it was a female voice. *Jeannie?* He asked himself. But the hallway echoed with footsteps and chatter as Lemuel Redfeather entered the room, closing the door behind him. Female, yes! But he couldn't be certain it was Jeannie Parsons.

He stood behind Zachary Thomas for a moment. He peered around the room: first at Rita Collins, then at Sam Begay. He turned, and walked around the end of the table behind Sam, who lowered the soda can from his mouth and placed it on the table in front of him. He stepped authoritatively, with an expression of control upon his face, and deep set, dark eyes filled with determination: determined to get at the truth.

"Okay, let's get back to business!" Lemuel Redfeather looked about, addressing everyone present. Then he pulled out his chair and took his place at the table. He trained his resolve on Zachary Thomas. "This fellow, Zachary! This Daniel! You think he could still be in the area?"

It crossed Zachary's mind that he may have asked that question again because of the conversation in the hall with the woman. "I told you he said he was goin' to California! That's all I know!"

"I've got someone who says that *isn't* all you know!" Redfeather replied sharply. "I got someone who says you were out at the stone arch, trying to find this guy, night before last! You told me he left Wednesday morning. Why were you out trying to find him that night, if he was on his way to California? What about it?" Lemuel relaxed into his chair, awaiting Zachary's reply.

Looking up from the table, where he had been contemplatively turning the empty aluminum soda can with one hand, Zachary stopped. "I don't know what you're talking about! Your information is incorrect! Who's your source, anyway?"

Rita Collins turned her attention from her legal pad to Lemuel Redfeather, anticipating his answer. She lifted her glasses from her face and placed them on the table in front of her, while she peered expectantly in his direction. "Yes, who is this person that has information about my client's intentions that night? I certainly want to talk to them!"

"No reason you shouldn't know. No reason at all!" Redfeather smirked. He said it, knowing he couldn't deny her access to this witness. Yet, he was beginning to regret the fact that he had pressed the issue so soon. It was his only real lead connecting Zachary Thomas together with the stranger, Daniel, out near Skeleton Mesa that night.

"Sue Boggs! She works at the Highway Cafe. She's a waitress there. She says Zachary was in the restaurant earlier that evening! That he was talkin' around about how he had to find this friend of his! And how they were going to find Carl and Jake, the victims, and settle the score with them! Isn't that true, Zachary?" Lemuel Redfeather asserted strongly in a confident tone.

Rita glanced at Zachary who sat silent, then she turned back to her notations, positioning her glasses on her face.

"Well, what about it?" Redfeather persisted.

"That's not the way I remember it!" Zachary offered defensively. "I just stopped in for dinner. I talked to some people I know. She wasn't one of'em! She didn't arrive until I was almost ready to leave. I didn't talk to her at all!" He swore.

"So, who did you talk to? Give me some names, so that I can clarify what it was that you told them!" Lemuel Redfeather continued to prod Zachary carefully.

Something was very wrong. As Zachary recalled it, his memory served him well regarding the conversation he had with Jeannie late that afternoon.

Cal and Jeannie were the only ones that he had talked to about the break-ins. *If Sue Boggs knew details of the conversation, she knew them because they were told to her, either intentionally or inadvertently*, he thought. *And they had both seen the coin,* he remembered. Yet there was no mention of it.

"Cal and Jeannie! I talked to them a little. But I never said where I was going! And I didn't say anything about settling a score with Carl and Jake!" Zachary swore adamantly, trusting blindly that they would not divulge all that he had spoken. And maybe Redfeather was baiting him? *He must know that Sue was Carl's girlfriend! He could be guessing?* Zachary told himself. Whatever his reason, there was no doubt in Zachary's mind that Lemuel Redfeather knew how to fill in the blanks.

Lemuel Redfeather stood up, drawing the attention of Rita Collins away from her note pad, and that of Sam Begay who had lost interest in the discussion shortly after lunch. He had been daydreaming, with his head tipped back and his arms folded over his stomach.

"We're done for the day, but I'm sure I'll have more questions later!" Redfeather made his comment in the direction of Rita Collins, who eyed him, and Sam Begay, with vehemence.

She stood. "You boys have had your fun! Now it's my turn!" Zachary could only anticipate what she was about to say, but he knew that *I'm going to put you in your place* tone of voice. He had experienced it for himself a day earlier.

"You and I both know, Mister Redfeather, that you have no conclusive evidence linking my client to the murders! Or to Jake Garcia and Carl Simmons, the deceased. You're grasping at straws, sir! Frankly, you and your gorilla, Mister Begay, are quite scary!" She said, openly expressing her disdain for the detective. "It appears you try to make a case out of anything. The prosecutor could never make a case out of what you have! You know it as well as I do! You're going to have to release my client, and I'll be here tomorrow to see that you do!"

Now everyone was standing, with the exception of Zachary who watched them, and monitored the confrontation from the safety of his seat. Sam Begay glared at Rita Collins, exuding hostility at her attack on his character. He was getting ready to speak his mind.

"You bit............"

"Sam, relax!" Lemuel Redfeather commanded, attempting to suppress his anger. "There's no need to get hostile here, Miss Collins! We're just doing our job! I know you DNA attorneys take your roll seriously, and I respect that! I mean,............I know you're trying to protect the rights of the individuals!" He said this in an effort to de-escalate a potential confrontation, that could possibly lead to an internal investigation. *It's the last thing the department needs at a time like this!* He thought.

"But I *am* sure that we will have more questions for Zachary, while we continue our investigation. We have two murders to solve, and we'll have to explore every avenue! We just want your client's cooperation. That's all we ask!"

Sam Begay turned his back on Lemuel Redfeather's placating remarks, exasperated, he let out a surly grunt. He slammed the door behind him.

"I'll see you tomorrow, Zachary. Let me know if you need anything. Or if you have any questions, give me a call!" Rita Collins penned her private number on the back of a business card and handed it to him. She patted him on the shoulder as she moved toward the door. Lemuel Redfeather held it open for her. Then he summoned the two guards inside the room to escort Zachary to the holding cell.

The tension had lessened over his presence as a murder suspect, so that the guards, who escorted him back to his cell, did not deem it necessary to handcuff him. He felt his inevitable release at hand.

He paced the hard, cold, tile floor in his cell. It was 4:30 p.m.. *One more day*, he thought. *Just one more day to get back to Daniel with Tracy Baldwin!* And if he didn't? Then what? Zachary couldn't imagine what the consequences would be, but he sensed a heaviness in his chest. Not like a fear for his personal safety, it was more an overwhelming sense of foreboding: a feeling that the future would somehow be altered, irrevocably. That he will have been in some way personally responsible, was a feeling he knew he wouldn't be able to live with!

Zachary lifted the daily newspaper from the cot. He peered at the picture on the front page of a local paper written in Navajo. His own image mirrored back at him, along with the photographs of the two murder victims. The headlines read: Suspect Arrested In Slayings! A subheading read: Police have a local man in custody. It was followed by a statement given by Lemuel Redfeather.

He dropped the newspaper back onto the cot. *They're going to watch me closely!* Zachary told himself, as he fell back onto the thin mattress covering the bare bed springs. *Now everybody will know my face! I won't be able to go anywhere without being noticed. If Tracy Baldwin has heard the news, she's not going to be very receptive to me!* He could only hope that the news from the reservation traveled slowly enough for her not to catch it in Flagstaff, at least until he had time to talk to her.

Rita! Rita Collins! He thought. *She could help if she wanted to! She said to call her if I needed anything! Well, I do need something! She could contact Tracy Baldwin for me. She would have more credibility than myself. But would she do it?* Zachary withdrew the business card from his shirt pocket. The guard would be coming with his dinner very soon. He could ask to make a phone call then.

Lying on the cot with his hand over his forehead, he contemplated his conversation with Rita while he massaged his temples. Then he heard the guard approaching the cell. Zachary quickly sat up on the cot.

"Here's your dinner!" The guard positioned the end of the tray onto the horizontal steel bar that spanned the opening, slightly wider than the tray itself.

Zachary approached the cell door, coming face to face with the guard. "I need to make a phone call! I need to call my attorney. I have some questions that I need answered before tomorrow! Do you think it would be possible?" He inquired of the guard, courteously.

"Take this tray, I'll go ask my supervisor!" The guard replied. Zachary pulled the tray inside the cell, drawing it across the steel bars between them. The guard turned and walked away with a purposeful gait.

When he returned, he brought another guard with him. They escorted Zachary to a small room at the end of the corridor. "You can use the phone in here! Just dial nine to call out. One of us will be waiting outside to take you back. The door will be locked, so knock on the door when you're finished."

The door latched behind him, locking Zachary in the room. A black telephone sat on a bare desk, the only other piece of furniture in the room besides the chair next to it. He pulled the chair out away from the desk and sat down, taking the business card out of his shirt pocket. Then he pressed out the numbers on the phone. Putting the receiver to his ear, he heard four rings before a tired, distracted feminine voice answered. "Hello!"

"Rita, it's Zachary!" There's somethin' I think you can help me with. I have to get in touch with a lady named Tracy Baldwin, before tomorrow! It's really important! She lives right there in Flagstaff, too!" There was a pause over the line for a moment, then Rita responded.

"I know her. Why do you have to get in touch with her, Zachary?" She asked.

"I have an anthropologist friend who has been doing some research that I think would interest her. Who? No, it's not him!" Fortunately for Zachary she couldn't see the sweat break out on his forehead as he fabricated his story. The palm of his hand, that held the receiver, became moist with perspiration as well.

"Yes, I know her. I met her a couple years ago. She was lookin' for someone to guide her to the ruins in remote locations of the reservation. I was with her for several weeks. We became good friends! I don't have her telephone number with me, otherwise I would've called her myself! Do you think you could call her for me?"

Rita was hesitant. "I guess so! I suppose it would be all right! What do you want me to tell her?"

"Ask her to come with you tomorrow. Just tell her that I'll explain more about my anthropologist friend, and his research, when she gets here. Tell her it's regardin' the Ancient Ones, the Anasazi. I'm sure she'll be interested," Zachary said convincingly.

"Okay, I'll call her right now!" Rita agreed.

"Good! Call me back here after you've talked to her! I'm at extension 237. I'll wait here until you call back!" Then another thought possessed him. "Oh yes! My truck! What about my truck? Will I be able to get it back tomorrow?" He asked anxiously. "That's good news! Thank you, Rita! Thank you very much!"

"Okay, bye!"

The door latch snapped. The door swung open into the room. "Are you finished yet?" The guard inquired, peering in at Zachary.

"Not yet! Give me ten more minutes, please! She has to call me back."

"Your dinner's gettin' cold! And we don't warm it up! So you'd better make it quick! Ten minutes, that's all! The guard snapped the door shut.

It rang once and Zachary picked up the receiver immediately. "Yes, Rita! She will? Good! I'm looking forward to seein' her again too! Thanks! What time will you be here? Ten o'clock. I'll be out by eleven? I hope so!"

"Thanks again! Bye!" Zachary hung up the phone. Tossing his head back, he breathed a sigh of relief.

§ § §

The desk sergeant handed Zachary a sealed plastic bag containing his personal belongings. Then he gave him a voucher to sign, and another with which to claim his rifle and hunting knife. Zachary carried the bag over to the counter across the room, on the opposite wall, where he could remove its contents. He scattered the items from the bag onto the counter, taking a mental inventory of what was there.

He opened his wallet first, to see if anything was missing. It appeared to be in order, except that the wallet and its contents had been waterlogged from his dousing in the arroyo. It occurred to him that someone, especially Lemuel Redfeather, could ascertain a great deal from that fact. Zachary hoped it had been overlooked.

Taking note of his comb, some change and his key chain, at first glance everything appeared to be there. Except! Something *was* missing! Zachary ran his fingers through the change lying on the counter. He scanned it with wishful eyes, with expectation that he had overlooked the brilliant gold coin. But he knew he hadn't!

His heart quickened. He turned to look at the desk sergeant with an expression of suspicious query. The man was busy processing some paperwork. Did he dare inquire? If he asked, then what? He chanced opening himself up to further questioning! They were questions he couldn't easily answer: questions that would tend to involve Daniel even more deeply.

The desk sergeant looked up from his work. He caught Zachary's stare. He appeared to read the questioning in the Navajo's expression. Just as he looked ready to respond, Zachary broke eye contact abruptly. Then he turned his attention back to the items on the counter. He hastily scooped the change into his hand and slipped it into his pocket.

A familiar voice echoed from around the corner in the corridor, outside of the open doorway near where Zachary stood. He heard two sets of footsteps as they clacked on the tile floor. Rounding the corner, Rita Collins came through the set of oak veneer double doors. They were propped open into the room, in direct view of the desk sergeant. Without a word he pointed at Zachary, indicating his presence to her. Then his head dropped down in the direction of his work.

Suddenly, he lifted his head again, as another woman entered the room. It was a tall, stately woman. She was one who could not pass without notice. Tracy Baldwin, at five feet and nine inches, summoned up a captivating presence. Zachary's eyes flashed by Rita, who was almost directly in front of him, and came to rest on the tall, slender woman. She was exactly as he had remembered her.

She locked her large, dark — almost black — inquisitive eyes on Zachary. She smiled, a radiant smile. "Hi! How's my favorite guide?" Tracy Baldwin said as she stepped beside Rita Collins. They were a contrasting pair, Zachary noted, when she came to rest next to Rita, and directly in front of him. "Rita told me you've been in some kind of trouble!" She said demurely. "I couldn't believe it! She told me you happened to be in the wrong place at the wrong time! I hope everything is all right?" She glanced over at Rita who smiled reassuringly.

"Everything should be fine! When I talked to the prosecutor, he said that the police investigators had a lot more work to do, if they wanted to build a case! He saw no reason to hold Zachary!" Rita patted Zachary on the upper arm, indicating that he was out of the woods — at least for now. All three of them fell quiet, each of them establishing their own priority for the moment. Then Rita exclaimed, "I'm sure your anxious to get out of here, Zachary! I've got to go! I'll leave you two to your business." She turned away from them, moving slowly toward the door with another thought in mind. Then she paused and looked back over her shoulder. "You know where to find me, if you need me, Zachary! You too Tracy!" Then she exited the room.

Tracy Baldwin looked at Zachary disarmingly. Her graceful poise commanded immediate attention as she spoke. "Rita's wonderful, isn't she!" Her warm sincerity embraced the statement, and made it evident that she held Rita in high esteem.

Nodding in agreement, Zachary said, "Yes, she's a very fine person. She's a good lawyer too! I feel fortunate to have her on my side."

After he had said that, his expression turned to that of a more serious nature. "We've got to get going, Tracy! I have somethin' very important to share with you! Let's go to the impound and claim the rest of my things. I'll explain to you on the way!"

"Sure Zachary!" Tracy agreed. "Let's go! I'm sure whatever it is, it will be interesting! You know how I am when it comes to the Ancient Ones and the study of the Anasazi culture. You had to practically drag me away from some of the ruins last time! Remember?" She laughed good naturedly. She turned energetically, causing her long, chestnut colored hair to sweep across the center of her back.

Following her through the open doors into the hall, Zachary caught up with her rapid gait. Tracy was dressed for trekking the rugged, arduous terrain that lie between them and the ruins. She had obviously anticipated the journey. She had on a pair of sturdy brown hiking boots and, snug, well worn jeans. And the fringed buckskin jacket that she wore, laid open over a soft, red flannel shirt. It was parted from the collar down to the third button, revealing her graceful neck and delicate collar bones, and the soft curve of her upper breasts. Zachary couldn't help but notice when she turned toward him to talk, on their way to the impound area.

It is her demeanor. She could charm and arouse any red blooded male! But who was he to consider such a woman? He wondered. *Besides,* he thought, *she would be better suited for Daniel, if he was interested in such things?*

She stood beside him, silent, studying the cache of hardware stored behind the woven wire cage that housed it. Zachary retrieved the rifle and hunting knife from the uniformed clerk. The clerk handed him a separate envelope with the ammunition clip sealed inside. "Don't load that on the premises sir! Or we'll have you right back in here!" He warned.

He dropped the tagged, truck keys into Zachary's palm. Then he pointed toward an overhead door, that opened to a compound surrounded by a tall cyclone fence with barbed wire around the top of it.

Tracy followed Zachary out through the door, and over to where the truck was parked. As he approached it, he felt elated that it was whole and not in a pile of dismembered metal parts. He recalled the antagonistic comments made by the deputy who rode with him in the squad car. Walking around to the passenger side, he unlocked the door for Tracy. Then he opened it for her, allowing her to be seated before he closed it.

Glancing skyward briefly, Zachary noted the approximate time of day. It was between eleven-fifteen and eleven-thirty. He walked rapidly around the back of the pickup truck to the driver side door. Tracy reached across the seat and unlocked his door as he approached it.

"Thanks," he said, as he bolted in behind the wheel. He slipped the rifle onto the rack behind the seat and secured it. "You've got a watch, what time is it?"

Looking down at her left wrist, Tracy turned it toward her, moving her sleeve away from her watch with her right hand. "It's eleven-twenty!"

The Navajo pumped the gas peddle several times, to get fuel up into the carburetor, turned the ignition, and started the truck, revving the engine. Tracy fastened her seat belt as the truck bolted backward. Zachary turned the truck in the direction of the open gate. He maneuvered quickly through it, and onto Highway 163.

"Are we in a hurry, Zachary?" Tracy inquired, alarmed by the speed at which they traveled through Kayenta. "You certainly don't need to get stopped by the police now! " She cautioned him nervously. "Please slow down!" She implored him with urgency, casting a disconcerted look in his direction.

Realizing that he was causing Tracy distress, Zachary slowed the truck to an acceptable speed. "I'm sorry! It's just that I told someone that we would be there! I mean, at the ruins today!" He struggled to belie her fear over his compulsion to keep his commitment with Daniel.

"Well, I'm sure your friend will understand, Zachary." She told him.

They proceeded south through Kayenta toward the intersection of Highway 160. Zachary checked the gas gauge. "We have to fill up! I'll stop at the gas station on the corner." He glanced over at Tracy who peered at him inquisitively.

"Who's this person that we're meeting? And where exactly are we meeting him?" Tracy asked in a mildly demanding tone. That alone was enough to remind him why an Anglo woman would never suit him.

He knew she was certainly no ones fool. Yet, his answer would have to be somewhat ambiguous. It would have to be such that it would not provoke her distrust, or fear for her own safety. "He's a friend, and a scientist like you! I told him about you! He's very interested in your research. He wants to share some of his findings about the Ancient Ones with you! I told'em I was sure you'd be interested! You are, aren't you?" Zachary spoke with more tact and persuasiveness than he had ever known he had the ability to conjure up.

The truck came to a stop in front of the self-service pumps at the Texaco Service Station, on the southwest corner of the intersection. Zachary looked over at Tracy Baldwin. He looked for a sign that her concerns were alleviated for the time being. Her expression had turned from one of suspicious inquiry to one of excited curiosity. Tracy's ubiquitous eyes glistened with anticipation. The thought of newly discovered information had dispelled any anxious feelings she possessed regarding this journey.

"So, where are we going? What area has he been researching? What's his name, anyway?" She asked excitedly.

Chapter 14

Talk of Witchcraft, Spirits and Dreams

SHE WAS PENSIVE. TRACY BALDWIN CONSIDERED ZACHARY. Eagerly, she awaited any bit of information that he might divulge.

"His name is Daniel! I'll tell you more after I fill up the tank!" The Navajo stepped down from the pickup truck, leaving Tracy Baldwin to speculate on what the new discovery might be. He mused over this Anglo woman. He knew that anything he told her would come under her intense scrutiny. Zachary had seen her analytical mind in action, and he was uncomfortable about being subjected to it. *It is as sharp as the teeth on a steel trap!* He told himself. He didn't want to be caught in it!

When they were back on the highway heading west, her questioning ensued. "Where is this Daniel? What did you say his last name is? Perhaps I've heard of him!" Tracy suggested strongly.

"Do you remember the area near Skeleton Mesa?" Zachary asked, testing her knowledge of the area they had previously explored.

Tracy peered straight ahead, looking beyond the highway. She probed her memory for a mental picture of that place. "Yes! I do remember!" She exclaimed, as though recalling it with keen interest. "It's where the natural bridge is, isn't it? I remember how we had to travel over a rough trail across the open desert to get there. We crossed at least one wash, didn't we? That's the place you told me where your grandfather took you as a boy! Isn't it?"

Her recollection was clear. Tracy's eyes engaged the stalwart Indian, waiting for him to qualify her knowledge of it with a response, perhaps disclosing some revelation about that place. Instead, he was engaged in recall of a kind of which she had no knowledge. His thoughts regarding it encompassed a span of a few days, not years.

She prodded him verbally. "So, what is it about that place that's so significant? What is it that your friend has found there,............that I've overlooked?"

With his hands stretched out over the steering wheel, Zachary leaned forward in an effort to make himself more comfortable: to dispatch some of the tension he was feeling at that moment. He delayed his response, while he checked the rearview mirror for any indication that someone was following them. Zachary squinted in the midday sun as he turned to confront Tracy's questions.

"Lost my damn sunglasses out there! Hurts my eyes to drive like this!" Then he mulled it over in his mind for a another brief moment.

"The best way I know how to put it is,............he's crossed a bridge in time!" He said it in a facetious manner, knowing she wouldn't get the full gist of his meaning. "I mean, he's made some kind a connection between the Ancients and some other advanced civilization. At least that's how I see it! But I think he could explain it a lot better himself!"

Focusing his attention back onto the road ahead, Zachary looked for Indian Route 21, where he would turn north toward Skeleton Mesa and the natural bridge. Approaching the canyon from the west, he hoped to avoid detection by anyone who had the area under surveillance, the police or anyone else who might be watching for them.

A cool wind bellowed through the slit of a partially opened window, above Tracy Baldwin's head. She stared out through it, to the right of the truck, while she pondered Zachary's inference that there was a connection she had missed in her research. Her sense of excitement had turned to self-serving concern. *Is eight years of dedicated research going to be overshadowed by some stranger's clumsy dabbling?* She asked herself soberly. *Some seemingly obscure piece of evidence inadvertently undetected by me?* Who was this novice, this prospector of ancient culture, who threatened to dethrone her hard won position in the hierarchy of her field? She had to know!

"This Doctor Daniel somebody, what did you say his last name is? Maybe I've read some of his research papers!" Tracy blurted, intervening the silence.

Zachary rotated the steering wheel sharply, causing the pickup truck to veer into the right turn lane. Tracy braced herself momentarily. Another twist of the wheel, and the pickup truck was going north on Indian Route 21.

He accelerated steadily. "Sorry! It's hard to see that intersection sometimes!" He cleared his throat. "I don't think you've read any of his papers. He's not from around here. I think he's from back east somewhere! Anyway, I've been guiding him, same as I did for you. Can't tell you much more than that!" None of what Zachary said, did anything to diminish Tracy Baldwin's ardent concern over the transgression of the stranger into her self-designated domain.

"His last name would be helpful, Zachary!" She persisted. "I do know about most of the people in my field!" She told him instructively, trying to seed his memory.

"Sun's out of my eyes now!" He said, obliviously sidestepping any response to her prodding inquiries.

Tracy Baldwin remained silent. She peered straight on, apparently slipping into quiet introspection. She would soon meet this Daniel. If he had unmasked anything of importance, she would recognize its validity. She was sure of it.

As Zachary pondered her intense curiosity, he thought, *She might be privileged to know untold secrets, ancient knowledge lost for centuries! She could have knowledge of another world, maybe even worlds!* This knowledge would change her life forever, as it had his own. A last name would seem so unimportant in the light of it all. He glanced into the rearview mirror, once again inspecting the backroad.

The sun was at their backs, and intense, as they approached the natural bridge from the west. The abandoned trail, once used by ranchers to move livestock to and from a remote grazing area, had been reclaimed by the native vegetation. The pickup truck pushed through the brush and tumbleweed, plowing it from its path. The truck bucked and heaved over ruts and gullies. The ground was dry and hard. A cloud of dust lingered a quarter mile behind them.

Rolling his window all the way down, Zachary remarked, "It's sure gettin' hot out here for this time of year! Hotter than I can ever remember!" He raised his right arm to his forehead, running his forearm across it, wiping the sweat from his brow with his shirt sleeve.

"Can't use the air conditioner. Can't chance it! Wouldn't want to overheat out here, haven't got water with us!" He said soberly, as they traversed a dry wash.

Tracy Baldwin nodded in agreement, although reluctantly, then rolled her window down acknowledging her discomfort. She pulled a kerchief from the pocket of her jacket, that lie beside her on the seat, wiping her forehead with it. Then she pulled her hair away form the back of her neck, dabbing the perspiration from underneath it.

"I don't recall having come this way before, Zachary! Why did you choose it?" She inquired, as she twisted the kerchief into a headband.

He ran the back of his hand over his dry mouth, knocking the crust from the corners of his lips. "Thought I could save some time, instead of comin' in off a Sixteen! Didn't know the trail had gotten this bad!" He said falsely, suppressing his real motivation.

Tracy positioned the headband on her forehead. She wrapped it around the back of her head, then tied it in a small knot. "God I'm thirsty!" She blurted impatiently. "Why didn't we take the time to get some water? It would only have taken a few minutes!"

The Navajo absorbed the brunt of her disapproval, knowing she had depended upon him in the past to tend to the details regarding provisions for their trips. "There just wasn't time! But we'll be there soon. There's water out there! Spring water! He asserted reassuringly. "I left a canteen an' some provisions alongside the arroyo! I left'em for Daniel! But he didn't seem much concerned for needin'em. Just hang on Tracy! We'll be fine, once we get there!" He raised his forearm, sweeping it across his forehead, to avert the sweat that now poured over his brow and into his eyes.

They were traveling along the rim of the Kaibito Plateau that dropped softly into elongated slopes of talus, after millenniums of erosion caused by wind and water. The verdant valleys of the Tsegi Canyon system sprawled immediately beyond, to the east.

The pickup truck crossed over the summit of a rise, then dropped into sight of the natural bridge, or the stone arch as the natives called it. Tracy Baldwin mused over its form. "I've never been able to fully comprehend the magnitude of the forces that shaped this awesome landscape. To me, it conjures up thoughts of a great mover, somewhat like a great architect directing the movements of these forces! If you know what I mean?" She said uneasily, struggling with the idea of a supernatural force, a creator.

Eight years of higher education had dispelled her earlier years of Mormon religious influence. She had learned to deal with anomalies analytically. Reason and logic where her tools as a researcher and a scientist. There was no room for superstition or myths. Her job was to discover and dissect the beliefs of ancient civilizations. She was to ascertain the fears of primitive people, advanced under a veil of ignorance, and explain them.

Yet, she suspected the influence of a higher intelligence on many of the ancient cultures she had studied. The Mayans, the Aztecs, the Incas, all showed signs of outside influences. She thought it to be more like an infusion of knowledge, displaced in the sequence of time. It was the only way that she could define it.

"Zachary, do you believe in witchcraft? I mean, I know that your people are very superstitious! But you've been educated. Do you think there is any merit to it?" Tracy asked with a coyness about her, attempting to delve into Zachary's psyche. "Do you believe that there are supernatural spirits who influence your life?"

"Strange you should ask that! It's been on my mind lately." He replied ponderously. "I went away to school an' learned Christianity. But my grandfather, he taught me the old ways! He and the old men, the singers and the medicine men, they told me much about the spirit world. Lately, I've been wonderin'! I mean these thoughts about it have been swimmin' around in my head." He hesitated to consider it, then he continued. "I've never practiced it! Witchcraft, that is! But, I've been told that spells've been placed on people that I knew, and they believed it! Maybe that's why it effected'em?" He mused briefly. "I don't know for sure! But there's been legends of witchcraft out here on the mesa! And frankly,...........I've experienced some strange things out here myself! But I don't think I'd consider'em witchcraft related. But supernatural spirits are another thing! And I'm inclined to believe in'em," he confessed.

"What kinds of things?" Tracy inquired intently.

He swallowed hard. Zachary's throat was dry and feeling coarse. "Dreams and the like! Since I've been out here regardin' Daniel and his business, I've camped under the stone arch, twice. And I've had a dream each time! Like a vision! Now maybe this sounds strange to you? But if you're askin' me about the influence of spirits, I'd say yes! If you'd asked me a week or so ago,............I'd have said I don't know!"

Entertained by his assertion, Tracy Baldwin inquired further. "These dreams or visions, what were they about?"

Zachary could sense her skeptical analysis. He cleared his throat. "The first one involved the Ancient Ones!" He said nervously. "It was kind of a message from'em! I could see my grandfather in this one. He spoke to me in this dream! He reassured me about a decision regardin' somethin' I'm involved in. So I took his advice!"

She questioned him antagonistically. "You based your decision on this dream?"

"Yes!" He answered, embarrassed by the condescending manner in which she probed his beliefs. "I take it you don't believe in any of this? I mean, you've probably never had any experience with it! I can't blame you, I guess! I suppose we all have to form our own opinions about these things. Mine are based on what I've experienced. You'll just have to decide for yourself!"

"I wasn't trying to criticize you, Zachary!" She said apologetically. "I'm sorry if it appeared that way! It's just never occurred to me to ask you about your beliefs before! I like to know what other people think. It helps me to understand them."

During the ensuing conversation they had lost sight of the natural bridge. The pickup truck crested another hill, near the place where Zachary had been arrested three days earlier. "We're here! The trail's just on the other side!" He stopped the truck in a clearing adjacent the trail that descended into the canyon.

They sat in the truck looking out over the canyon, and beyond to the ruins. The silhouettes of the ledge houses were clearly visible in the afternoon sun, although too distant to make out details.

"You didn't finish!" Tracy Baldwin reminded him. "And the other dream? What about the other dream, Zachary?" She became insistent. She sensed that she lacked a small, but important, detail: a detail necessary to form her hypothesis, much like she did in her work.

Zachary was reluctant. "It was just kind a like a premonition! Like when you think you know somethin' is going to happen! It was like that." He tried to quell her interest. "We've really got to get goin'! It's gonna be late afternoon before we reach the ruins!" He turned away from Tracy Baldwin, reaching for the door handle.

She grabbed his arm. Laughingly, she said, "Promise you'll tell me about your premonition on the way down! I won't let you rest until you tell me!" She taunted him with her large, intensely inquisitive, dark eyes.

They both stepped out of the pickup truck, preparing to descend into the canyon. Tracy fetched a carryall bag, like a large purse, from the seat of the truck. She slipped her arm through the strap, positioning it onto her shoulder. Then she grabbed her buckskin jacket and draped it over her left arm.

"The sun is bright!" Tracy said, reaching into the bag for her sunglasses. "It's hot now, but I know I'll need this jacket later when the sun goes down. As I remember, it can get pretty cold out here at night!" She set the lock and closed the passenger side door.

Nodding in agreement, Zachary reached into the truck, behind the seat, for his jacket. He swiped a book of matches from the dashboard and shoved them into his pocket. Then he took notice of the rifle on the rear window rack. "Guess I won't be needin' it!" He thought aloud, while he latched and closed the truck door, remembering what Daniel had told him the last time they had been together. He withdrew a pouch of tobacco from his jacket pocket, and he commenced to place a plug from it into the side of his mouth, surveying the distant ruins and then glancing at the tall, slender, attractive young woman as he did so.

They followed the switchback, descending rapidly at first. Then the terrain leveled off onto an intermediate plateau, before it dropped away again toward the valley below them.

Tracy Baldwin, thwarted by the omission of details regarding Zachary's second dream, was not content to let it rest. She caught up beside him. "So, what about your premonition? Are you going to tell me or what?" She pressed him.

Seeing that she would not be satisfied until she had the details of the dream, Zachary proceeded with the story. "It wasn't a very pleasant thing!" He balked. How could he tell her of the events without sounding like he had presided over two murders. Saying he had a dream was one thing, but making her believe it was something else. And if he told her, would she turn and run from him, fearing for her own safety? *How much did Rita Collins tell her?* He asked himself. He couldn't be sure. There was only one way to find out.

He continued as Tracy Baldwin walked beside him, listening attentively for his next words. "I was camping under the stone arch, alone! That was four days ago. I was goin' to meet Daniel that next day at the ruins. It was late. I set up camp just before dark. It stormed that night. Rained real hard! Couldn't see a star in the sky! It was pitch black! I turned in soon as the fire died down. I don't know how long I was asleep before I heard the voices!" He paused again.

Tracy listened with the fervor of a girl scout during a campfire story. She stopped. Zachary took two more steps before stopping, then turned to face her. "What is it?" He asked.

"Let's take a break. We can sit over there in the shade. You can finish your story!" She moved in the direction of the shaded place, motioning him to follow.

Tracy sat down on a flat rock, with her back braced against the wall of a cliff. Zachary joined her, finding a niche in the rock across from her. He settled into it. The sandstone alcove offered protection from the heat of the mid-afternoon sunlight.

"This rock is cool! It feels good on my back!" Tracy exclaimed, as she tipped her head back, closing her eyes in a restful manner. The back of her shirt was damp from perspiration. She reached behind her neck with both hands, pulling her long, lustrous hair away from it.

The Indian studied her profile. He admired the fine features of Anglo women, especially this one, since he had spent more time with her than any other. Turning to him, she felt his eyes sampling the details of her silhouette. She was mildly embarrassed. Then she smiled, apparently flattered by his interest. She thought him to be a ruggedly handsome Navajo man. Zachary looked away quickly, in order to avoid contact with her provocative eyes.

"What about the voices?" She said musingly, urging Zachary to continue.

"I dreamt there were three men above on the mesa. They were arguing! Pretty soon one of'em pulls a gun! He points it toward the other two! He was the one with the wide, silver wristband on his right arm! It had large turquoise stones on it!" Suddenly, Zachary was flush. He hesitated for a moment. He had reconstructed a mental picture of his dream that included vivid details. They were details that hadn't surfaced before.

"Go on!" Tracy encouraged him. She saw that he was upset by something he recalled. "What did the man with the gun and the silver wristband do?"

Zachary looked up at her with a sullen expression. He answered with a graveness in his voice that was penetrating. "He shot'em! He shot'em dead! Both of'em! Then he threw their bodies over the side of the mesa! That's where they found'em the next day! In the canyon, near the stone arch." Zachary shook his head in disbelief. He had told Tracy Baldwin far more than he had intended.

"I thought you said this was a dream?" Tracy questioned him

apprehensively. She was overwhelmed by the reality of his telling. Her cool, calm, detached interest turned to fearful anticipation of the answer she was about to receive.

"I did dream it!" He swore to her. "I saw it in my sleep! And it really happened! I know that might be hard for you to believe. But it's true!" Then Zachary inquired nervously, "Did Rita Collins tell you why I was in jail?"

Being shaken by the revelation she had just heard, Tracy Baldwin struggled with the notion that someone could know the details of such an incident without being present. A dreadful crime that she had only caught a few details about on her car radio, listening to the news channel on her way to the university the day before. *Two men were found murdered Wednesday on the Navajo Reservation! The Navajo Police have a suspect in custody, a Navajo Indian man in his late thirties!* The newscaster said. That was all she had heard, and now this!

"She just said you were being held for questioning, regarding an incident that occurred on the reservation! I had no idea it was anything like............I mean,...........I didn't place you with those men!" Tracy said cautiously. Frightened, she chose her words carefully in an effort to avoid antagonizing Zachary.

They sat immobile, assessing one another for a time. Then Zachary spoke. "I didn't kill those men, Tracy! Don't you think Rita would've told you more, if she thought I'd murdered those men? Do you think she'd have let you come out here with me?" He asked her, earnestly addressing her acute sense of reason.

Her tension appeared to ease somewhat, while she considered Zachary's plea. Rita Collins was a friend. And it was certainly true that Rita would not place her in a precarious situation, at least not intentionally. *But what if her trust in the innocence of her client is misplaced?* She asked herself. Certainly, she would have to be careful. She would have to watch Zachary closely, regardless of what he said.

"Rita's a good friend. If she trusts you, I suppose I should too! I'm just overwhelmed by all of this. I'll have to digest it all for a while. But I am surprised that Rita didn't say more about why you were being held!" Tracy added in a reflective tone.

"If she had, would you've come?" Zachary inquired intently. He searched her face for some indication of trust.

"I'm not sure," Tracy answered honestly. She left Zachary with little doubt that he would have to regain her confidence.

"You can leave if you want to! You can just walk away! Take the truck and go back home, if you want! I'll give you the key right now!" Zachary vowed sincerely. "I don't want you to be here if you don't feel safe with me! I would never do anything to hurt you! But if you think so, you should go now!"

Tracy studied him for a moment. She eyed him warily. "I've come this far! And I do want to meet your friend! I feel as though there is something here that I have to know! If I am to accept what you have told me as the truth, Zachary, than that means that some of the things I have believed to be true for years.........are wrong! That there is a supernatural influence in our lives! In my life! I've spent the better part of my adult life trying to dispel myths with logic! Now you're telling me that you have had dreams that have a basis in reality! This is all very confusing! Part of me wants to get up and run, the other part wants to know! Frankly, I couldn't run right now if I wanted to, my legs feel like rubber!" They both laughed.

The Navajo stood, his mass casting a long shadow in front of him. He stepped toward Tracy and put out his hand to help her up. "Let's go! There's someone waiting for us who can help answer your questions! I'm sure you'll find him very informative!" He said, pulling Tracy to her feet. She could feel the strength in his broad, right hand.

As they moved along the trail in the direction of the ruins, Zachary, who followed closely behind Tracy Baldwin, reached into his mouth with his forefinger and ejected the insipid chew he had placed there earlier, allowing it to fall to the ground under foot. Then he spat, clearing his palate.

Chapter 15

The Precipice of Fear

IN THE KAYENTA DISTRICT STATION OF THE NAVAJO POLICE, approximately forty-two miles from where Zachary Thomas and Tracy Baldwin were making their way to the ruins to meet Daniel, Superintendent Lemuel Redfeather sat in his office with Detective Sam Begay and Captain Peter Morgan.

Smoke rose from a burning cigarette on the edge of a butt-filled ashtray at the corner of Redfeather's desk. Morgan and Begay sat opposite him. They poured over information about Jake Garcia and Carl Simmons, that investigators had compiled over the past few days.

Begay took a sip from a half full styrofoam cup of tepid black coffee. He shuffled through the folder he held on his oversized lap. Then he bumped a pack of cigarettes on the edge of the desk, before extracting one from the pack. Tossing the cigarette package aside, he raised a lighter to the cigarette poised on his lips. "God damn! These boys were livin' on borrowed time!" He bellowed, while he scanned the wrap sheet of Jake Garcia.

"This guy was probably the smarter of the two! And that ain't sayin' much for either of'em! These sons-o'bitches were destined to die young!" Taking a heavy breath, he continued. "Says here that Garcia had warrants in four states! He was wanted in Arizona, California, Utah and New Mexico. They both served time in prison! This one had two felony counts, armed robbery and narcotics trafficking! The other one wasn't any choir boy either!" Begay grunted, slamming the file shut on the desk.

Redfeather took a drag from a cigarette burned nearly to the filter, then snuffed it in the ashtray. "What do you think we have here, Morgan?" He asked, as he mulled over the information at hand.

Morgan, a quiet, conservative man with traditional Navajo values, wasn't known to be overly opinionated, or politically motivated. He seemed to be content within his niche. He had ten years experience in his position, and he was comfortable with it. It made him all the more valuable. In addition, he didn't appear to resent it when he was passed over for superintendent in favor of Lemuel Redfeather. This was one of the things that Redfeather liked best about him. And the fact that when asked, he usually had a valid opinion based on the facts.

After a minute of deliberation, Morgan spoke. "Best I can figure is they pissed somebody off! They must've made a bad deal with the wrong guy! This Thomas fella, he's clean as a whistle! Not a want or warrant on him anywhere! Not likely someone just gettin' into it is going to do his suppliers like that! I just didn't see it in'em! These guys were playing hardball! And they struck out big! Frankly Lemuel, we haven't got much to go on here at all! We've come up dry on evidence. There's no murder weapon either! It would help to know if it's an inside job. I mean someone on the reservation, or an outsider! What about this stranger, the one that stayed with Thomas? He could've killed'em without Thomas knowing a thing about it! He could've used Thomas for a dupe!"

Sam Begay snorted at Morgan's last remark. "You sound like that lawyer lady! I think we need to keep on Thomas for a while! He may lead us right to this stranger. I think it was an outsider, and I think he's probably the one! And as far as Thomas goes, he's not cleared completely in my mind, yet! You're forgettin' he has a motive too! He believes these guys busted into his place and shot up his dog! For some guys that's motive enough! Maybe we need to go over the scene again? We could've missed something the first time!" Begay took a deep breath. He coughed, making a meager attempt to cover his mouth with his hand. Then he cleared his throat.

Redfeather leaned back in his chair. He loosened his tie and unbuttoned his collar. Then he raised his arms and laced his hands together behind his head. Stretching, he considered the substance of what both men had offered up to him as possibilities.

"I think you both have something! Morgan, I don't think Zachary Thomas was directly involved in these murders either! But, I think Sam's right about keeping an eye on'em! I believe he's the only connection we have to the stranger! And I think if,..........I mean, when we find the stranger, we'll have our killer! Those tire castings will be comin' back up from the crime lab in Phoenix tomorrow. We know those boys didn't *walk* out there! And we know whoever killed'em, didn't walk away either! There were two sets of tire tracks, theirs and the murderer's! I'm willing to bet good money that they don't match Thomas's truck. The second set of tire tracks indicated heavy lugs, and tread like those used on four-wheel-drive vehicles!" He paused.

Lemuel Redfeather opened the center drawer of his desk and brought out two plastic envelopes. "This is what we have, gentlemen!" He held up one envelope containing a cigarette butt. "We think this belonged to Carl Simmons! This brand was found in his pocket. It doesn't mean that he didn't offer his assailant one, before he was blown away! The lab tests are inconclusive. It rained that night, so there was no saliva present. But our man could be a smoker! That's something we didn't ask Zachary Thomas about his friend, Daniel! It's a good excuse to check in on him!"

He returned the plastic envelope to the drawer. Then he took the other one in his hand, examining the contents for a moment. Redfeather opened the slit on the envelope, letting the object fall into the palm of his hand. "You see this!" He extended his hand to Morgan and Begay, offering them a better look.

"God damn! Look at that! Is that real gold?" Begay blurted, exhausting a deep breath.

"I've never seen a gold coin like that before! What are those mint markings on it? They don't look familiar to me!" Morgan, somewhat of a coin collector, took an immediate interest in the detailing of the coin. Redfeather placed it in his hand for closer examination.

"This was found on the ground at the murder scene atop the mesa! Got a fingerprint off of it too! A pretty damn good one! It's not Zachary Thomas's! That's already been established. And yes! That is real gold, with some alloy mixed in that the lab couldn't identify! We haven't been able to establish its origin yet, but we put out a photocopy to coin dealers around the state dealing in foreign coins! The fingerprint and that coin are going to get us a conviction, when we match'em up with the owner!" Lemuel Redfeather said confidently.

Sam Begay reached across the desk and placed the coin back into Readfeather's hand. "Couldn't be too many of those floating around in circulation! If I was to see one, I'd sure recognize it right off! I reckon I should make some inquiries around! Maybe someone's been showin' it off?"

Redfeather placed the coin back into the envelope. Then he locked it in his desk drawer. "That's a good idea, Sam! Someone may have seen one of these, and the person who had it! Try the folks down at the Highway Cafe in Tuba City first! Talk to the girlfriend of Carl Simmons! Talk to Sue Boggs! And while you're there, talk to the others too! Jeannie and Cal! Then pay a visit to Zachary Thomas! We're bound to shake something loose!"

"Morgan, keep on those lab reports! Let me know as soon as you get those tire castings back! We can match up the make of those tires! Then we'll have the deputies start checking four-wheel-drive vehicles, just in case it's still in the area! I'll pass this information along to the Tuba City District!" Redfeather concluded, pushing his chair back away from the desk. He stood up.

Detective Begay and Captain Morgan rose from their chairs simultaneously. "Let's get on it, boys!" Redfeather brushed by them in a hurry to get out the door. He was on his way to a five o'clock meeting with Jack McCloud in Tuba City.

§ § §

"Tracy, look, you can see the ruins from here! It's only another ten minutes!" Zachary exclaimed, when they reached a clearing within a half-mile of their destination.

"I'm not sure why Daniel didn't come for the supplies I left behind the last time I was out here, but it's lucky for us!" He offered Tracy Baldwin the canteen filled with cold stream water, while they stood in the clearing in sight of the ruins. "Just wet your lips with that! If you must drink now, just take a small sip! The water out of the stream is generally pretty good! But this time of the year you can't be sure! There'll be spring water up by the ruins, you can drink your fill of that!" Tracy pressed the neck of the canteen to her lips, wetting them and moistening the inside of her mouth.

Zachary cupped his right hand against his forehead. He noted the position of the sun. "It's probably around five o'clock about now!" Saying it in such a way that Tracy would qualify it by checking her watch.

"It's ten till! You're pretty good!" She said, genuinely impressed by his observational skills. "I don't see any signs of movement around the ruins! Are you sure your friend is there?"

He fixed his attention on the cliff dwellings. They were immersed in the cool, late afternoon shadow of the sandstone alcove, where they had remained poised in silence for centuries, protecting ageless untold knowledge. Zachary scanned them for a sign of Daniel's presence. "He said he would be there! I believe he's there! He's just keeping out of sight."

Zachary motioned to Tracy to follow him. He started up the path leading to the ruins. Tracy capped the canteen. She clutched it in her hand as she strode to catch up with Zachary.

When they approached the ruins, they traversed the line of daylight into the shadows. "It gives one the illusion of passing from the present into the past." Tracy said, while she moved up close behind Zachary.

"Yes, it does!" Zachary nodded in agreement. He perceived a change in the atmosphere immediately surrounding the ruins.

They continued on the path, ascending the rock ledges that led to the only entrance of the cliff dwellings. They forged through the last section of small trees and brush that formed a secluded barrier across the front of the alcove, emerging into clear view of the ledge houses. Then they stopped, each of them standing motionless in a surdity of silence. The air was permeated with an aged musk that set upon their senses.

Zachary broke the silence. "Daniel!..............Daniel!" He issued the name repeatedly, evoking no response. The name echoed from the grotto, falling flat against the still air. His eyes sought out a lone silhouette among the balconies and darkened openings of the mute ruins.

Tracy Baldwin's discerning eyes panned the ledge houses layer by layer, until her eyes reached the uppermost tier. She exhausted a deep breath with a sigh of disappointment. Turning to Zachary she said, "I can't believe you've brought me all the way out here to meet him, and he's not even here!"

Her thoughts were jerked back to the circumstances surrounding Zachary's arrest. Tracy's comfort level plunged, as she considered that she was completely alone with him, and unsure of his innocence regarding the murders of the two men.

"I'm really sorry!" Zachary said, speaking in an ingenuous tone. "It would be foolish to go back now! It's gettin' late, and clouds are startin' to build in the west! It's gonna storm again tonight. We'd do best to go up and find a place out of the weather!"

He reached out for Tracy's hand to lead her toward the niches and toe holes serving as steps. She declined, stepping back. Seeming unscathed by her reaction, Zachary proceeded to climb the face of the sandstone cliff, leaving Tracy to her own resourcefulness. When he reached the first level of the ruins, near the kiva, where he had met with Daniel, he paused and waited for Tracy.

"I want to take a look around before dark!" She said, as she approached him. It's not often that I get to explore these places, most of my work involves books and research papers!" She also wanted to keep her distance from Zachary for as long as possible: to think, to consider what options were available to her, should she feel the need to affect an escape.

Tracy climbed a crude wooden ladder, left behind by other researchers. It was assembled much the same way as those made by the early inhabitants of the village. Those who studied here had a reverent regard for its preservation, and that of its authenticity, she thought. The level above the central walkway of the village was honeycombed with small apartments. She explored each of the rooms, peering in through the darkened doorways into the obscurely lighted interiors. She touched the soot laden walls, and the earthen floors, searching for some vestige of the previous occupants.

He followed her with his eyes, while he mulled over what Daniel had told him. *"In three days you must bring the anthropologist here to me!" Then why isn't he here?* He asked himself. *But the day is not over yet! And I have done as he asked! Now we can do nothing but wait!*

Throwing his pack through the entrance of the kiva, Zachary entered. He found fresh firewood stacked neatly against the far wall, and also in the fire circle, ready for use. As he laid the remainder of their gear aside, he noticed an eagle feather lying on the stone where Daniel had sat three days earlier. He questioned himself. *Is it a sign from Daniel? Or is it an omen from my grandfather? Either way, someone has been expecting us!*

Taking the feather in his hand, Zachary sat down on the stone. Thunder clapped in the distance, echoing throughout the ruins. The storm was moving in fast. The wind began to rustle the tops of the trees in the valley.

Tracy Baldwin appeared in the entrance of the kiva. "The clouds are moving in! It's getting dark outside!" She ducked through the opening, moving in the direction of the stone opposite Zachary. Sitting down carefully, she crossed her legs in front of her. "The temperature is dropping fast! I thought it best to get inside." Then looking up toward the hole in the roof, she remarked wittingly, "I guess we're not all that much inside!" She laughed, trying to take the edge off the inconvenient circumstances.

"I wish I had my dog, *-Tsoh!* These are the times when havin' him alongside me was comforting! He sensed when somethin' was wrong! And he knew who to trust! I do sometimes! And other times I don't! But *-Tsoh* always knew!" Zachary said, glancing up at Tracy, while he turned the eagle feather in his hand.

The rain began to fall outside. Lightning cracked over the canyon, flashing light intermittently through the hole in the roof of the kiva.

"Where's *-Tsoh* now?" Tracy inquired unknowingly.

"He's dead!" Zachary said soberly. "Somebody shot'em when they were ransacking my place! They shot'em and he crawled into the corner of my workshop and died! He was a big old mutt! But he was a good old boy!"

"How long ago was this?" She asked with a tone of regret.

"You know, it seems like a long time! But it's only been five days! Five days! That's all! So much has happened in so little time! I don't ever remember things changin' so fast before! In one week my house has been vandalized twice, my dog was shot dead, and I've been arrested for suspicion of murder! I'd say that's a lot for one week, wouldn't you? And all I was tryin' to do was help someone, and protect my property!" Zachary put his head down, shaking it in dismay.

It was as dark as night outside the kiva. The large rain drops fell hard. They made a splattering sound on the rock ledge below.

Zachary dug into his pocket for the matches he had placed there earlier. He stooped over the firepit, then struck a match to light the dry grass and leaves tucked under the twigs and branches below the logs. For a moment his face was immersed in an eerie glow that made Tracy Baldwin shiver. It was not in her nature to react so irrationally to that type of stimulus. Yet, she did! Perhaps it was the circumstances that led her here, the things that Zachary told her about his dreams, they were evoking ghosts in her subconscious mind. They were ghosts from a belief system she thought she had left behind, like so many scattered toys, novelties of an adolescent mind.

Her stomach knotted. At that moment she realized what she feared most! It was more than her doubts about Zachary. It was more than being alone there with him. It was more than the egotistical animosity she harbored for anyone who could diminish her status in the face of her peers. It was the thought that she may be forced to pick up those discarded beliefs and, in the light of circumstances over which she had no control, have to re-evaluate them!

Thunder rolled overhead. The lightning cracked and, within a few fractions of a second, a blue-white light flashed outside the entrance to the kiva, expiring with an ear-piercing bang that vibrated the very stone on which the kiva was built.

Tracy shuddered. She peered at the light outside of the entrance, seeing a dark silhouette, of what appeared to be a man, looming at the opening. Zachary caught her startled expression from the corner of his eye. He turned sharply, training his attention upon the hollow form at the entrance. It took shape as it emerged from the shadow of the opening. It was Daniel. He bore an affable smile as he stood, crouched, in the light of the fire.
Tracy's apprehension dissolved as she drank of his presence.

"This is Daniel!" Zachary blurted nervously, while his own sense of alarm scattered. "That's Tracy Baldwin, Daniel!" He said, gesturing with his hand from where he was seated.

Daniel moved deliberately in Tracy's direction, still crouched, so not to come in contact with the low hanging poles that held up the roof. He stopped within an arms reach of her, stooped down, coming to rest on one knee. He extended his hand through the invisible space — her space — the distance at which Daniel sensed that she still felt safe. She took it in hers, offering up a cordial smile, all the while studying the figure poised before her.

He looked the way she had expected. Tracy released his large but tenuous hand, making a mental note of the fact that it was not a hand that had done any manual work recently. It was soft and uncallused. She scanned him rapidly, cataloging his pedigree in her mind.

She looked at the dark brown hat, with the brim turned down slightly in the front, it was water stained, and the heavy, bomber style jacket with zipper pockets, that he wore. Then she took note of the gold, wire rimmed glasses with the spherical lenses, and the placid blue eyes that peered at her through them. Those eyes were in a face that expressed something she hadn't expected. His youthful face exuded a warmth and generosity that compelled her to trust him. She wondered why?

"It's so good to meet you, Miss Baldwin! Zachary has told me so much about you. He says that you're an authority on Indian cultures, particulary the Ancient Ones, the Anasazi!" He said this in an ingratiating tone.

She smiled demurely at his assertion, her attention still trained on his eyes, as he stepped back to take a place against the wall, seating himself between her and Zachary.

"I understand you've made some discoveries of your own, Doctor.........?"

She said, unable to contain her curiousity.

"Oh no! I'm not a doctor! No Phd. I'm afraid! I just have a serious interest in the study of ancient cultures. Please call me Daniel!" He entreated her with an air of humility about him.

Zachary sat quietly, contemplating both of them. Daniel felt Zachary's eyes fix on him. To him there was no discernible difference in Daniel's appearance. His mind's eye saw Daniel the way that he knew him.

"You've done well my friend!" Daniel said, addressing Zachary, while he removed the glasses from his face to wipe away some water spots with a handkerchief, that he had pulled from the back pocket of his khaki pants.

"Did you know what was gonna happen to me? Did you know I was goin' to get arrested? I almost didn't make it back here!" Zachary told him, no longer able to contain his pent up frustration for a more appropriate moment.

Tracy Baldwin sat still, observing them, wondering what kind of situation she had gotten herself into. Uncertain how to react, she eyed them both quietly as their conversation ensued. Although Daniel was fully aware of her scrutiny, he sensed an urgency in Zachary that had to be quenched.

"I knew! But would it have made a difference if I had told you?" Daniel placed the glasses back onto his face. He glanced at Tracy Baldwin long enough to interpret her baffled look. Then he turned back to Zachary.

At once, Zachary understood his logic. *The questions are of no consequence,* he told himself. He was here, and it didn't matter why — or how! It was as Daniel had told him, and that was all that mattered!

The storm moved away from the canyon. The thunder rolled in the distance. And the rain subsided to a light shower that gave way to the night sounds. Smoke rose through the hole in the roof of the kiva, moving in a rippling motion into the heavy, moisture laden air. And the fire's embers glowed, revealing the silhouettes of three single figures, each of their own world. They were assembled for a purpose only one of them knew.

"I told her about the connection you've discovered between the Ancient Ones and the others!" Zachary said, bringing the conversation into the realm of the present, and the purpose for which they were there. "I told her that she best hear it from you!" He still held the eagle feather between his hands as he spoke. "I'd sure like to understand it better myself!" He said, as he slipped the feather between the thumb and forefinger of his left hand. "Maybe you can show her the evidence you spoke of?"

Tracy Baldwin cleared her throat, uneasily. "Yes, I'm anxious to know what you've discovered, that I've overlooked in my research. I've spent years studying these ancient people, and I've traced the history of their trade activity with the South and Central American tribes. All of the information available to date is at my disposal. I've made a number of significant discoveries myself. And I'd like to know what it is that you think you've discovered?" All of which she uttered with a condescending tone in her voice.

Daniel had been gazing into the fire, with his hands folded over his knees, while she spoke. He leaned back against the stone and earthen wall, bracing his back against it, raised his head, and tossed a pebble at the fire with his left hand.

"What you've long suspected, Miss Baldwin!" He said, with an affirming resonance in his voice. "The influence of a higher intelligence upon the ancient peoples. The incongruous knowledge that made them advanced beyond their time and place in history! You've always wondered about it,............haven't you? I sense you would give anything to know for sure,............wouldn't you?"

He wielded his words with cunning. The power of his speech drew Tracy Baldwin closer to her inevitable place among the chosen. His chosen!

She felt a cold chill plunge through her body. *Perhaps it's just the night air,* she told herself.

Tracy Baldwin pondered his words intently. "Yes, I have had suspicions to that affect, as you have suggested! But I've dealt with them rationally, as a scientist. And I also have a suspicion that your approach is less than scientific! Just from the things that Zachary has told me on the way out here, my cognition tells me that you believe there may be some other-worldly phenomenon at work out here! I would hardly stake my professional reputation on such conjecture! Mister whoever you are! However, I am curious about the evidence you have to support your theory!" Even as she spoke with the resolve to remain objective, her fears hung on the periphery of her thoughts. Tracy Baldwin's sense of reality clung to the precipice of her fear.

Daniel assessed her fears, the same as he did for all those he came in contact with. It was the fodder he used to make the chosen ready. He knew that reasoning would be a slow and arduous path and, for what he had to prepare her, it was out of the realm of reason.

"You ask for proof! Very well, you shall have it!" Daniel glared at her. Then you can decide for yourself whether or not to believe it! But remember, once you have the knowledge, it will change your life forever! You will never be able to go back!" He warned her.

Zachary recalled hearing those very same words, the same unmistakable warning. It bit at him sharply, burning like salt on an open wound. *It is true!* He thought. He questioned his judgement in regard to involving the woman. Yet, he realized it hadn't been his decision.

"You make this information sound so ominous! You're not trying to frighten me, are you? I mean, it really can't be all that serious!" Tracy Baldwin retorted, with a glibness intended to mask a chill of apprehension.

"I don't own your fear, Miss Baldwin!" Daniel told her. "Each person has his own monsters to deal with in his way! I'm simply opening a door for you, what you see from it is solely up to you!" Daniel reached for a branch that lie on the ground nearby, he prodded the fire with it. The flames flared up, leaping toward the opening in the roof, then ebbed downward emitting a trail of glowing ash that danced in the smoke stream as it dispersed into the chilled night air.

Zachary strode over to the woodpile to fuel the fire. He listened intently, kneeling at the edge of the firepit, while he fed logs into the ravenous flames.

She pulled her jacket up around her shoulders, while she peered into the fire. She felt his icelike, penetrating eyes fixed on her. "So tell me the secrets of the ages!" Tracy said nervously, in an effort to avert his stare.

"It is no accident that the ancient peoples had knowledge far beyond their technical development! No accident at all!" Daniel said, with a weightiness to his voice. "Of course, you already know that the Incas of South America, and the Toltecs, Mayans and the Aztecs of Mexico, displayed advanced skills in art, architecture, astronomy and the sciences, and in the organization of their societies. Their physicians practiced advanced neurological treatment that has baffled experts in the field. Their dentistry was a marvel for that time as well! You will also recall that they had an advanced calendar, based on very accurate astronomical calculations. Their interest in astronomy went far beyond a primitive curiousity,...........don't you agree, Miss Baldwin?" He paused. She nodded in agreement.

Daniel continued. "Their architectural achievements demonstrated an advanced development in higher mathematics, at a time when there shouldn't have been any! Don't you agree!" He gestured, encouraging her response, while he moved in closer to the fire. He warmed his hands by it.

"I suppose so! I mean, it would appear that way!" She conceded

"In fact, from all indications, Miss Baldwin, these people had an overwhelming fixation on the stars! They built what appeared to be astronomical symbols that could only be observed in their entirety from the air! Yet they had no flying machines that you know of! Correct?"

"Yes, that appears to be true!" She agreed more reluctantly this time.

"Of course, there has been conjecture that the Egyptians traversed the seas. That they accidentally stumbled upon these civilizations, and shared some of their knowledge with them. But, I would say that it is an unlikely supposition,............wouldn't you?"

Tracy Baldwin sat quietly, declining to answer. She anticipated the imminent conclusion.

"You will also note that some the figures depicted in the rock art and sculptures, especially that of the Incas, Toltecs and the Mayans, bear little resemblance to any known life form here on earth! And we mustn't forget the Aztecs. However crude and brutal they were, these once nomadic, barbarian warriors, influenced by scholars from the advanced Toltec Nation, made a rapid transition from a transitory society to a stable centralized government." Daniel paused, taking a deep breath. "Do you recall the story of Moctezuma, the Aztec "Ruler of the World," as he was known, regarding his preoccupation with the prophecy of the return of the half-man, half-god, Quetzalcoatl, and his fixation on the comet that Moctezuma believed signaled the god's return?"

Tracy Baldwin nodded her head, acknowledging her familiarity with the story. If nothing else, she had to consider him well read. "I know that one! He believes that Quetzalcoatl is coming soon to reclaim his dominion of the kingdom over which Moctezuma has been given guardianship, and that if he returned in the year of One Reed, he would strike down kings!" Then she added. "It was because of his superstitious beliefs that he saw Cortez as the returning and enlightened Quetzalcoatl, and welcomed him with open arms, turning his empire over to the Spanish conqueror."

"And so you are wondering what all of this has to do with where we are right now! Aren't you?" Daniel asked, noting her impetuous remark. "Are you familiar with the Navajo emergence story? The one that recounts how the Holy People, the Ancient Ones, travel between four different worlds consecutively, until finally they emerge in the fourth world,..........this one!"

Tracy Baldwin's patience was wearing thin. She was anxious to conclude this dissertation. He would draw on some wild, mystical conclusion, as she had anticipated, and she could dismiss it, she thought. Then she could somehow make it through the rest of the night, and in the morning she would laugh about all of this, and insist that Zachary take her home.

"Yes, yes, yes! She exclaimed harshly, displaying her indifference.

Daniel considered her with an innate calm that disturbed her. His eyes made her feel trapped.

"Their gift was the most advanced!" He continued intoned as though she would have to accept the inevitable, and he was merely laying it all out in front of her. "What if I told you that they could indeed travel between worlds, actually more in the nature of parallel dimensions? If I said that time was irrelevant in the space between them, what would you say?"

"I would say that you are crazed!" She said, disconcerted. "What you're saying is off the wall! It's wild, and it's unscientific! And that's just what I expected!"

"One usually gets what one expects, Miss Baldwin!" He chided her. "If I could prove it to you, would you accept it?" Daniel inquired in earnest, watching her reaction intently.

Tracy Baldwin placed the palms of her hands to her forehead, pressing them against her temples as she slumped forward in disbelief. "How can you possibly prove something like that? Wouldn't you have to witness it? Or be able to do it yourself? I can't believe I'm even saying these things! It's nonsense! Strictly, and utterly nonsense!"

Chapter 16

The Conversion of the Chosen

SHE WAS WEAKENING. HE SENSED IT. DANIEL REACHED INTO HIS shirt pocket and withdrew a gold coin, the same kind he had given to Zachary, and Jack McCloud. He moved toward her with it in the palm of his hand. "Here, look at this! Study it carefully! Then I will show you something else that has been here for hundreds of years!"

She cautiously reached out for the coin. He placed it in her hand. Tracy Baldwin studied it in the light of the fire. "Where is this from? I've never seen anything like it before!"

"It's a gift from a distant world, Miss Baldwin!" He said, as he eased back into his place against the stone wall.

She continued to examine the coin, studying the inscription on it carefully. "This could have been minted anywhere, right here in *this* world! But for the sake of conversation, I'll ask what world? And what does the mathematical formula pertain to?" There was a smugness in her voice, that denoted her determination to cling to her skepticism.

"Turn the coin over and look at the coordinates on it! They indicate a certain star system. Do you recognize it?" Daniel asked.

Tracy Baldwin peered at it intently. "I have a friend at Mount Wilson, an astronomer. I've spent some time with him at the observatory, and he's made me familiar with some of the constellations. This one does look somewhat like one that I've seen before, but I can't quite place it!"

"You would know it as the Pliades! Or the constellation of the Seven Sisters! That's the where, Miss Baldwin! There is a planet there that is very much like Earth. It is also a water planet! The sphere in the center, with the four satellites surrounding it, that's it!" Daniel stated it as though it was a matter of fact.

Tracy Baldwin silently deliberated over her next question. *To ask it,* she thought, *would be an indication that she gave the slightest bit of relevance to any of this!* Again, it was his eyes that calmly peeled away her established sense of reality.

Zachary sat quietly, listening. He wondered what purpose Daniel had in mind for her involvement. Occasionally giving a glance in their direction, he considered his own complicity. It wasn't clear what Daniel had in mind for him. He wasn't able to absolve his blind loyalty to this person, either. *Is it control?* He asked himself. But he never felt controlled. *Destiny?* It was another word that crossed his mind. Until now he hadn't given it much thought, but Daniel brandished it convincingly. *Or was it fate?* He hadn't been in the habit of accepting circumstances in his life as totally predetermined. *Otherwise, what was the purpose of all this talk about change, if it didn't matter anyway? If we didn't have a choice!* He told himself.

Unable to resolve his own feelings for what was happening, he was certain of one thing! He knew where Daniel was leading Tracy Baldwin. He also knew that there would be no solace in the knowledge that she would have the same dull fire of uncertainty smoldering away inside of her, as he did!

"Than how did you come to possess this coin?" The question was out now! She had thought it over, and over again! And she had thought it, until she had thought it aloud! And he knew it, before she thought it the first time!

He stood up in a crouched position. Then Daniel stepped toward the opposite side of the kiva, to a flat, rectangular stone that lie next to the wall adjacent the woodpile. He motioned to her to join him. "Come, look here," he said, "perhaps this will help answer your question!" He motioned to her, again.

Then he gestured to Zachary. "Bring a glowing stick from the fire and hold it over here like a torch!"

Daniel gripped the stone, and he dragged it away from the wall. Tracy stood next to him, peering down at the dark patch on the wall that had been hidden by the stone. Zachary approached them, carrying a branch with one end ablaze. "Hold it here!" Daniel beckoned.

He moved it over the area that Daniel indicated. Then Daniel knelt on the flat stone he had moved away, bent over, and brushed the dust away from the dark spot on the wall. "See this?" He pointed at what appeared to be Indian rock art. Zachary held the torch steady, just above the painting.

Tracy leaned forward, peering over Daniel's shoulder. "Yes! I've seen a good deal of Indian rock art around these ruins!" She replied soberly.

"Look at the coin, Miss Baldwin! Now look at this star map on the wall! Do you see anything familiar?"

Daniel got up from the stone on which he was kneeling, so that she could move in closer. He pressed her on the shoulder with his hand, urging her to move in. Tracy knelt in front of the painting. She ran her fingers over it, lightly brushing away more of the dirt that concealed its clarity. It was there! She glanced down at the coin in her left hand, then again at the painting. Her stomach cramped as she considered the possibility.

"You said you've seen a good deal of this type of painting, Miss Baldwin, does this look authentic to you?" Daniel stood behind her, while she studied the painting further.

Zachary turned to look at Daniel. His querying expression betrayed his thought to ask how Daniel knew the painting was there. But then he thought better of asking. Daniel's eyes smiled at him, knowingly, then came to rest on Tracy Baldwin.

She took a deep breath, then sighed. "Hm! It would appear so! I mean, it doesn't appear to have been painted on here yesterday!" She acknowledged, in answer to his question. "And I am familiar with the dyes the Indians used to prepare their paints. I would have to see it in the daylight to be certain. I can't imagine why it wasn't found before!" She turned to look up at Daniel, peering into his eyes as he loomed over her. There was something absolute about him. His look made her soul feel naked. She shuddered.

"No one was looking for it!" Was his reply. Daniel backed away from her.

Tracy Baldwin clutched the gold coin in her hand, while she knelt there considering him. "How did you know it was here?" She asked, tilting her head back. She closed her eyes, and stiffened in anticipation of the answer she feared he would give! An uncontrollable shiver racked her body.

"I knew of the one who put it here, Miss Baldwin! It has been here nearly a millennium." He replied. His eyes fell away from her as he turned toward the place near the wall where he had been sitting.

A coyote, in the canyon below the ruins, gave a long, shrill cry that filled the voided space about them. It emitted a ghostly affirmation.

Zachary tossed the smoldering stick back into the fire. He stood motionless for a moment, studying the One of Many Faces. Then he stepped slowly around the fire, resuming his place on the stone across from Daniel. He thought that he was beginning to know this man, now there appeared to be another to consider!

"But these ruins are not over seven-hundred and fifty years old! It's not possible! You see?" She said, validating her own conclusion. Her strength welled up into her body more slowly than it had abandoned her. Tracy Baldwin rose from the stone on which she was kneeling, dusted off her pants at the knees, and moved slowly toward the place, near the fire, where she had been sitting. Her eyes never ventured from the stranger, lest, she feared, he would make some transformation in the absence of her attention.

"There is some truth to that!" Daniel agreed, while he considered her. "But the kiva was built long before the present village was erected! This is the third, and final community to be built around it! The Ancient Ones were meticulous in their rebuilding efforts. So much so, that they were able to mask most of the old material that they had recycled into the dwellings. Of course, the stone is something that is almost impossible to date, wouldn't you agree?"

Listening intently, Tracy Baldwin nodded in agreement.

Daniel continued. "The roof beams, on the other hand, are more conducive to dating. And that is where many of the comparisons have caused confusion as to the exact age of the structures!"

"Yes, that is true." Tracy replied in a subdued tone. "Some of the data regarding the exact age of the dwellings is ambiguous at best! But the consensus among my colleagues has been about seven-hundred and fifty years!" She paused. "I must admit that what you have told me sounds plausible. I mean about the age of the kiva!" She hurriedly qualified her remark, so as not to include the painting. Or the conjecture about time travel.

Tracy Baldwin opened the hand that had been clutching the gold coin. She had been squeezing it so tightly that there were indentations in her flesh, where her blood swelled to the surface. "What about the mathematical formula on the opposite side of this coin? What does it represent?" She inquired musingly, while she examined it further.

He considered his reply carefully, choosing his words so that he wouldn't confuse her. "Stated simply, Miss Baldwin, it represents the dark matter, the cohesive force that binds the universe! It is the conduit through which time travel is possible!"

"You say these things as though you have first hand knowledge of them, Daniel. It's all right if I call you Daniel, isn't it?" Tracy Baldwin inquired sheepishly, after considering her previous tactless acknowledgement of the man. Her resistance was failing.

"Yes, certainly!" He replied graciously. And he knew, as he had always known, that she would do his work.

And as for Zachary, he was an observer to the conversion. He could only wonder how many more he would witness.

It was late. Cold encircled her like a pack of lycanthropic beasts, penetrating her weary sinew. Tracy Baldwin tugged at the collar of her jacket, pulling it up around her neck. She leaned in toward the fire. She eyed him scrupulously. He exhibited no signs of fatigue.

"Zachary, is there any food left in that pack? I'm starving!" Her eyes entreated him, while a shallow smile broke softly across her face.

He reached out to the right of him and snatched the backpack up from the ground. Zachary rummaged through it.

"I'm sorry I wasn't better prepared for guests!" Daniel spoke apologetically. "I should have been more aware of your needs! I found some pinion nuts! I can go get them!" He started to get up. "I have a container of spring water, too! I'll go get it!"

She mused at his boyish looks. His face concealed his age well, she thought.

"Here, I have a package of cheese'n crackers! They were wrapped in plastic! They seem to be all right!" Zachary hobbled over to where she sat, his legs being stiff and tired from sitting. "Here's a bag of peanuts, too!"

He stooped beside her. "I'm sorry! I mean, for gettin' you involved!"

"No, no! It's all right!" She said in a surprisingly compassionate tone. She stroked his hand softly, attempting to absolve his guilt. "Please don't worry! I feel fine! Really!" In saying this, whether consciously or not, she was giving absolution to her own feelings, forgiveness for what she considered a weakness in herself. Her monsters were dissolving.

Taking an Indian blanket from under his arm, Zachary draped it over her shoulders.

"Thank you!" Tracy responded, with appreciative eyes, pulling the blanket in around her.

Daniel returned with the meager provisions. "This will have to do until morning!" He offered her the pinion nuts from a clay bowl, it was a vestige of the early inhabitants. In his other hand was a pitcher of spring water. He held it out to her. She took it and tipped it to her mouth, swallowing it in gulps. The cold wetness soothed her parched mouth, and dry throat.

"Thank you!" She said, lowering the pitcher from her moistened lips. Tracy reached out, offering it back to Daniel who had been standing over her. He declined, gesturing for her to keep it. She caught the scent of burning juniper on his clothes, when he turned to face Zachary. The odor permeated the kiva, drowning the otherwise dank, musty smell that pervaded it.

He moved slowly around the firepit, coming to rest in front of Zachary, who looked up to meet his gaze. Daniel lowered the bowl to within his reach. Zachary scooped a handful of pinion nuts from it. All the while, his attention was focused on the eyes that peered at him from behind the glasses.

"I thought you'd explain about the dreams?" Zachary asked, cutting the silence.

Daniel broke eye contact with him, and returned to the place he had been sitting. He sifted through a handful of pinion nuts, chucking several into his mouth. He popped them between his teeth.

Sitting quietly, Tracy wondered about Zachary's dreams as well. If there was an explanation to be had, then she was willing to listen. She had already heard a strangely coherent hypothesis. If this stranger had yet another to add, linking Zachary's dreams to it, she was determined to hear it!

His credibility, as far as Tracy Baldwin was concerned, was not yet enhanced by anything he had revealed. He could be a beguiling alchemist bent on distorting historical fact, and, by planting his own evidence to substaniate his claims, he could create a contiguous part of history with his name on it. She thought, too, that she could discredit him swiftly, and be done with it all. But why had he asked for her? If he wanted notoriety, there were more expeditious ways to achieve it! Unless he wanted someone with credibility to substantiate it all for him?

Musing over the fire, Daniel spoke somewhat tentatively. "Interpreting another man's dream is a difficult thing! I mean by that, that the one who has it holds the picture in his mind. To interpret it, one would have to have had the same picture!" He paused. "And then perhaps the one that was doing the interpreting would understand it differently, because it would not be of his own experience." He paused again.

The only sound to be heard was that of the fire. The flames licked the dry wood, igniting the sap. It popped. The air bred mysticism. And the two others, Zachary and Tracy, sat intently posing no questions. Each of them considered his answer from their own point of reference. Although he thought it vague, Zachary understood his answer in part.

She considered his statement to be dubious at best. Feeling somewhat sleepy, Tracy glanced at her wristwatch. Eleven-fifteen, it read. She yawned.

"I can only tell you of *my* experience regarding dreams!" Daniel said, leaning forward. He pushed his hat back, and off of his forehead, then rested his elbows on his thighs, just above the knee. One hand was tucked under his chin, supporting his head as he spoke.

A coyote bellowed in feral tones. Then another. Their cries reverberated in the night air, seemingly cursing the blackness.

"Once I had a vision!" He told them, with a distant look about him. "It involved four beasts!" He said, with a graveness in his voice. "Each of them was more terrible than the last! And each was given dominion over the earth..........for a time! The first was like a lion with eagles wings! While I watched, its wings were plucked away! Then it raised up from the ground, and screamed, making a terrifying sound!"

Daniel paused for a moment, glancing at one of them and then the other. They viewed him with curious eyes. Zachary took notice of the eagle feather that lie beside him on the dirt floor.

"It had two feet like a man! And a human mind as well!" Daniel continued.

"The second beast was more fierce than the first. It was like a bear! And the teeth in its mouth were like tusks! It was given the order to devour flesh, and cause great pain!"

"Yet another beast rose up like a leopard! It had wings like a bird, and four heads! It was given dominion and established its kingdom."

He spoke in resonant tones. His telling was so effective, that it made Tracy Baldwin shiver under the Indian blanket encompassing her.

"Then I saw it!" Daniel said, suddenly, exhibiting a burst of energy at his recollection and, gesturing with one hand and, pointing upward and away with his forefinger, to the place where his mind was at that moment.

Tracy Baldwin's heart jumped!

"The fourth beast!" He breathed deeply.

"It was the most horrible, terrifying and destructive!" He said with great emphasis. "It had great iron teeth that devoured and crushed with extraordinary strength! What was left, it trampled under foot!"

"I was looking at its ten horns!" He paused for breath. "When suddenly a small horn sprung out from their midst! This horn had a face like a man! And a mouth that uttered foul words to my master!"

Daniel fell silent, again. He stared, distantly, into the fire.

Viewing him gravely, Tracy Baldwin clutched the blanket tightly around her. She held it as though it was shielding her soul.

The Navajo in Zachary anticipated a message in Daniel's telling. He studied the One of Many Faces, intently.

Turning to meet Zachary's inquisitive look, Daniel read the question on his face. "This beast still lives now!" He said in an affirming voice.

Appearing perplexed, Zachary trembled at the idea of the existence of such a creature. "Where is this creature, Daniel? Am I to help you destroy it?"

"This creature is found in the hearts of men! And if it isn't destroyed, man will lose his dominion over the Earth!" Daniel replied. He ignored Zachary's second question as if it was already understood. Zachary hesitated to pursue it further.

"It is all very symbolic, obviously!" Tracy said, in an effort to logically dispel its impact upon her. "And well told, I might add! I take it you've deduced from this dream, or vision as you call it, that the human race is a self-destructive lot! And you, perhaps, think you have a responsibilty to save it?" She stated with impudence.

"Don't you ever question the value of the things that you've believed, without doubt, to be true? Or of the things that you've attached worth to?" Daniel asked, leaving the air blank in dead silence.

She hesitated. "Why, of course I do! And more so lately!" She said, somewhat more thoughtfully, dropping her eyes to the fire. He had made no assertion that Zachary's dream was in any way connected to events of the past, present or future, as she considered it reflectively. But still, there was an eerie implication in his voice. And the story he told, it had a painful familiarity that haunted her!

Something was clawing at her. She wasn't certain if it wanted to get in, or if it wanted to get out! Whatever it was, she grasped the blanket and pulled it ever more tightly around herself.

Zachary had hoped to be alone with Daniel for a while. He wanted to alert him to the fact that the authorities considered him their primary suspect, that they were looking for him in earnest. But he could'nt risk going into detail in Tracy Baldwin's presence.

She fought against her heavy eyelids. They were winning. Tracy struggled to stay awake, for fear she would lose something of herself if she surrendered to it. But the weightiness of it had become more persistent than that of her fear. Tracy could no longer resist sleep.

"I've got to lie down!" She admitted in an exhausted voice, telling no one in particular. She sounded as though she was giving herself permission to succumb to it.

Zachary, who sat in the quiet of his thoughts, without a word, moved to help her find a comfortable place where she could rest. Reaching out to help her up, he guided her to a spot against the inside wall of the kiva, where long grass and leaves lay matted as bedding.

Folding the blanket in half, Zachary laid it down flat over the bedding. He turned the top half open so that Tracy could lie down. She dropped into it, pulling the folded blanket over her. He rolled his jacket and tucked it under her head. She jostled it into place, pulled her long, chestnut colored hair back from the side of her face, then collapsed into a sound sleep. Her hand was still folded firmly around the gold coin.

Raising up, Zachary's eyes addressed Daniel. "I have to talk to you!" Hesitant to chance being overheard, he motioned to Daniel to follow him outside the entrance of the kiva, into the darkness, and out of ear shot of Tracy Baldwin.

Moving out into the cold, dank air, they stood in the naked specter of a mysterious past. There was a hard silence in the heavy air. A gibbous moon highlighted the faces of the ledge houses with a faint surrealism, making the blackened openings appear as the vacant eye sockets of large skulls, that were perched on a shelf in the dark.

"They're lookin' for you!" Zachary said in a guttural tone. With his hands stuffed into his pockets, he gave Daniel a slanted look. "They think you might've murdered the two men they found out here at the bottom of the mesa." He paused, looking down at his feet, as he gathered the words in his mind he would say next.

"They arrested me 'cause they thought I did it!" Zachary raised his eyes to meet Daniel's. "But they're figurin' you had more of a motive!" He scraped the ground with the sole of his boot, shuffling his foot nervously as he spoke. "They're thinkin' you're some kind a drug dealer, and those guys crossed ya some way!" Then he added. "They had that reputation."

Eyeing Zachary with cool concern, Daniel spoke. "I told you someone had a plan, and they're putting it to work!" He breathed the cool air deeply.

"This is part of it!"

Turning the question foremost in his mind, Zachary stumbled over it as it rolled out of his mouth. "Did you...........kill'em? His chest tightened, restricting his breath momentarily. "You knew! You knew they were dead!"

"No, I didn't kill them. It would have served no purpose for me to do so!" He hesitated. "But I could do nothing! It was out of my hands!" There was a hint of regret in Daniel's voice.

Intent on discerning how much Daniel knew about his dream, and the deaths of the two men, Zachary pressed him further. "I saw'em get killed in a dream I had that night! I remember seeing a gun in the hand of the killer! And I remember his hand, and the wristband that he wore!" He asserted in an hoarse, emotional voice. "It was like I was there, watching! Watching those two get killed, and I couldn't do anything about it!" Peering at his cool, steeled, blue eyes in the light that filtered between them from the fire in the kiva, Zachary searched them for a sign of confirmation. "The dream, it was real,...........wasn't it?"

The eyes mirrored the answer back to him.

"What you remember will be important! When the time comes, you will recognize the killer!" Daniel said it in a way that gave it a prophetic tone.

"I don't think anyone followed us out here, but it's only a matter of time before they think about lookin' here!" Zachary warned him. "If you hang around here, they'll find you for sure! You might be better off comin' with us! I could find you another place to hide!" He said, in an effort to convince Daniel that his anonymity was in danger of being broached.

He shook his head in disagreement. "No! That would only put you in more jeopardy. And it would cast suspicion on Miss Baldwin as well. We can't risk it!" Daniel contended in a strong voice. Then realizing that he could have been overheard by her, he continued in more subdued tones.

"Don't worry about me." He said flatly. "It's more important that you return Miss Baldwin with the least amount of attention. She will be embarking on some research that will prove useful to me!"

At that moment, Zachary felt like a pawn. Daniel maneuvered his pieces with great skill. And he was adding to his collection! He wondered if it was for the purpose that Daniel had led him to believe? Or was it for another reason, one that served his own interest?

Realizing that his thoughts were not completely his own, Zachary concluded his self inquiry, abruptly. A chill clutched him as he focused his attention back on Daniel. Facing him blankly, he asked, "What will you do out here by yourself? I mean,..........you have no supplies. I could bring some things back for you tomorrow, but it's risky. How will you get by?"

Reaching out, Daniel placed his hand on Zachary's shoulder. "I'll get by the same way I always have!" He said in a calm, reassuring voice. "Just take care of Miss Baldwin!" A smile perched on his lips.

"Go back inside and look after her tonight! Make sure she rests well. I'll be in touch with both of you again, as soon as it's safe to do so! In the meantime, you should go back to your normal daily routine. Just keep in contact with Miss Baldwin, and give her any assistance she may require!" Daniel said, openly petitioning Zachary's cooperation.

He gave a slight squeeze to the Indian's shoulder, ending the conversation with a nod. Zachary felt that same sensation of energy passing to him from the stranger. It was like a sedative.

Moving his hand away from Zachary's shoulder, the stranger extended it once again. The Indian reached for it, applying a firm grip. He could not help but feel that he had sold his soul to a commitment he could not break. Releasing his hand, Daniel moved slowly into the shadows of the ruins, then out of sight, giving no indication of where he was going or when he would return.

Eyeing the spot where the night had engulfed the receding figure, Zachary slipped back into the kiva. The fire had ebbed to a mass of glowing embers. He posed a somber figure against the subdued light. Studying the obscured form curled against the wall, he lumbered over to the edge of the blanket, and, claiming a flat section of it, he slumped down, then dropped his head onto the blanket in total exhaustion.

In a second of half-sleep, he wished he would not dream............

Chapter 17

The Absolution of Tracy Baldwin

SHE COULD SEE HERSELF VIVIDLY. IT WAS SPRINGTIME. THE AIR was so fresh that she could smell it. The grass in the meadow was a deep green, and sparkled of dew drops that glistened in the late morning sun. It was behind the farm house in Utah, where she grew up with her brother and four sisters. An ethereal haze encompassed her recollection. But it was her, a lanky, budding teenager in the yellow dress, and the matching yellow bow that held her hair in a ponytail.

It was after church. She was running and laughing. There was a warm breeze, and the sun kissed her face giving it a placid glow. She remembered because she had just turned thirteen the week before. The birthday party was held outside on the picnic table behind the house.

She remembered why she was running, too. Her brother, Ethan, was chasing her. He was trying to pull the bow from her hair. Ethan was fifteen, but she could always manage to stay a step ahead of him. She loved Ethan, she loved how he teased her, but he was good to her, protective of her. She knew she could count on him.

Her sisters where older, and more distant. Two of them had gone away to college in Salt Lake City. The other two were in high school; they were busy with chorus, and booster club, and boyfriends. But Ethan still had time for her.

Fredrick was father's hired hand. He had been there, on the farm, since

Tracy could remember. He was like one of the family. He had large callused hands, and a voice that bellowed from his mouth in a guttural roll. His thick, coarse blond hair was bleached almost white, from working outdoors day after day. She could see the deep set, bloodshot, blue eyes in the leathery, brown face that came into hers when he would stoop to greet her and call her *liebchen.*

She remembered, too, his soured breath. This is the part she didn't want to remember. She didn't know why she was remembering. She wasn't supposed to remember. It was a long time ago. Why was this happening?

He would take the cows out to the pasture in the early morning, before she was out of bed. Sometimes, she could hear him singing in the barn. He would sing in German.

Ethan's hand swished by her head in a final attempt to catch the bow. Then she could hear his pounding footsteps subside, dropping off as she distanced herself from his winded laughter.

Tracy ran into the meadow, and down the path toward the pond where the cows would graze and drink. She paused to catch her breath, while she plucked some small pink wildflowers from beside the path. She could hear Fredrick singing in the distance. *He must be bringing in the cows*, she thought.

Clutching a bunch of flowers in her hand, she admired them as she walked along the path. When she approached the pond, the meadow dropped away in a gentle roll toward it. The grass was taller near the pond, taller than her. It obstructed her view of it, until she was almost upon it. The singing became louder. She could hear Fredrick's voice more distinctly. The gurgling, indistinct r's became more audible.

The soft, cotton like, white clouds marching across the sky in blunted shapes, commanded her attention as she descended the path. She was so mesmerized by them, that she failed to regard Fredrick's proximity to her. A rough hand grasped her upper arm, stopping her abruptly. Panic bolted through her. She set herself to scream, until she realized whose hand it was.

"Liebchen! Liebchen!" He beckoned, calling down her fear.

I have to wake up! She struggled with her subconscious mind, fighting the terror it was about to disclose. *Please let me wake up!* She begged herself. She could not stop it this time! This time it *refused* to stop!

"Com vit me, see da new calf! Com, com!" He pulled her by the wrist, leading her down the path and into the tall marsh grass next to the pond. He jerked her into the cover, slipping his hand over her mouth, and took her to the ground.

She screamed for Ethan, but nothing came out. His eyes were cold and empty as he rolled himself on top of her, pinning her down. She could see the red veins in his eyes. And his breath was fetid.

"You be quiet now, or they tink you is a bad girl! You don't tell noting or they tink you is dirty girl!" He wispered to her in a shallow, fouled breath. He pressed himself in on her, fondling her with one hand, while he restrained her with the other. His hands were hard and rough on her flesh. She could still feel them touching her. She writhed with repulsion.

She remembered closing her eyes, hoping he would disappear. Tears streamed from her eyes as he pushed and heaved on her. Then he put his stenchfilled mouth on hers, kissing and sucking. He licked the tears from her face.

"You don't tell, or you vil be punished!" He said, as he finished and raised himself up. She laid there with her eyes closed, not wanting to see him and what he had done.

"Remember, God vil punish you for causing dis sin if you tell!" He scolded, while he tucked in his shirt tail.

She kept her eyes closed, listening to the sound of his footsteps as he walked away. She didn't open them for what seemed like a very long time, telling herself over, and over again in her mind, "When you open your eyes you won't remember."

Bolting awake, Tracy Baldwin startled Zachary. He shook himself, his eyes darting around in the dark for the cause of her alarm. She sat up, sobbing heavily, with her body drenched in a cold sweat. With the top half of the blanket lying across her lap, she wrung it with her hands as she cried. Her face was ashen with fear.

"What happened!" Zachary inquired earnestly, realizing that she had experienced a bad dream.

Struggling to stifle her sobs, she brought them on in deeper, more pronounced agonizing bursts. She tried to speak, but could not. Sitting up next to her, Zachary reached out to embrace her, to offer her comfort. She shuddered violently, shoving him away, and pushing him with such force that he fell over onto his back.

Stunned, he kept his distance. He wondered what, if anything, he may have done to upset her. He sat quietly, observing her for a while. Then feeling the night chill setting in upon them, he made his way to the woodpile and set about rekindling the fire.

It was near dawn when Tracy Baldwin spoke. "I didn't want to remember!" She muttered painfully, keeping her eyes low to avoid looking at Zachary. Still twisting the edge of the blanket, she had been sitting in the same position for hours.

He studied her for a moment. "What is it that you didn't want to remember, Tracy?" He asked carefully, speaking in a subdued tone, so as not to provoke her.

"It's this place!" She said, in a tone destitute of comfort or consolation, finally looking up at Zachary. Her eyelids were red and swollen. "There's something about this place. I didn't want to remember! But I did!" Her voice was quavery and pitched with emotion.

Zachary prodded the fire with a bowed branch. "I thought I might've done somethin' to upset you!"

"No, no," she said, sighing deeply, while rubbing her eyes with the back of her hand. "It has nothing to do with you!" Tracy attempted to force a smile of assurance, but it made the pain in her eyes all the more obvious.

"It was something from the past! Something I thought I would never have to deal with again! It came back to haunt me! And I don't know why it happened here and now! I'm frightened, Zachary! Very fightened! I just want to leave this place!"

Hearing the urgency in her request, he started to throw sand on the fire to suffocate it. "It's almost light now, we can leave soon!" He said as he completed smothering the fire.

There was little said between them on the way back to Kayenta. He took Tracy to where she had parked her jeep the day before. Pulling up alongside of it, he stopped.

"You sure I can't take you into Flagstaff? I really wouldn't mind!" Zachary said, taking her previous emotional state into account, and not knowing to what degree she had actually recovered from it.

Unlatching the door, Tracy turned back to him. "I'll be fine, really! Don't worry about me," she said, managing a smile. "You'll be home if I need to talk to you, won't you?" She inquired with a frightened, uncertain gravity to her voice.

"Should be!" He said, giving a nod. "I won't be doin' too much travelin'! Don't think it would be a good idea right now! If I don't hear from you in a few days, I'll call! If you need anything at all, you let me know!"

She swung the door open and hopped out, grabbing her bag and her jacket off the seat. "I have a lot to do, Zachary. There are some questions that I have to get answers for, regarding our friend! Talk to you later!" She hurried to her jeep, threw her things on the passenger seat, and jumped in behind the wheel.

Zachary watched her drive away, wondering what it was that had caused Tracy Baldwin so much pain.

Later, he sat in the dusk-filled living room of his house. The daylight retreated, leaving a silent emptiness about him. He teased the threadbare ends of the armchair with his fingertips, while he stared into the ensuing darkness. *There is a timelessness about it*, he thought. He had an overwhelming feeling that his life had been on hold: that the things he thought so purposeful, not so many days ago, had no relevance, that he was just passing the time until now.

Perhaps everything up to the time he had met Daniel was a dream, he thought. *And now he was truly alive, that he had awakened to his real life, and this was the beginning of it!* He couldn't help but think this, since he felt whole for the first time. The longing for what he had not known, whatever it was, was gone.

§ § §

"Michael, do you have some time before your next class? I'd really like to talk to you. Let me buy you a cup of coffee!" Before he could answer, Tracy Baldwin had his hand in hers and was leading him down the corridor toward the campus cafeteria.

He looked at her. To Michael, she was a winterish looking woman. Her dark hair and eyes evoked thoughts of a warm, cozy fire on a cold winter night. She was a woman he could easily fall in love with — if he wasn't already?

"Tracy, we haven't spoken in months! What is the urgency about talking today?" The tall, sensitive Michael Severson reproached her with a tone of indignation.

"Michael, I'm sorry!" She said ruefully, avoiding eye contact and hoping to avert any discussion of a personal nature. She dropped his hand as they entered the cafeteria. Tracy still had trepidation regarding the events of two nights past, and the recollection of the past she thought she had buried forever. She was on the edge emotionally, and she knew if anyone could topple her, it would be Michael.

They stopped at the back of a short line of people waiting for service. Tracy, concealing her present state of vulnerability, studied his strong, well defined Scandinavian good looks, and, the deep set, intelligent, blue eyes of the man who she hoped could disparage any credence she may have acquired regarding Daniel's assertions to his origin.

He could not help but be attentive to the large, inquisitive, dark brown eyes that she flashed at him, captivating him as always. "What is it, Tracy? What do you want to talk about?" He asked, unconsciously yielding to her prepossession.

"Something rather strange has happened! And interesting, too!" She paused, then placed two cups on the tray in front of her and slid it down to the large coffee urn on the counter. "I met someone, someone who has an interesting, if not a bit bizzare, theory. I thought perhaps you could provide me with some facts that would confirm my inclination to disregard it completely. Perhaps I'm asking you to validate a foregone conclusion!"

Looking at her somewhat puzzled, while he carried the tray with the two cups of steaming coffee, they walked to a table near the windows overlooking the campus grounds. As long as he had known her, Tracy had never exhibited the slightest degree of self-doubt that he could remember. She had never asked him for advice, or an opinion about anything. He had always viewed her as distantly cool and self-contained.

He placed the tray in the center of a small table, adjacent the window, then pulled out a chair for her. He was intrigued by a glimpse of a side of

Tracy Baldwin he had never witnessed, and was at once absorbed by the specter of it. Taking the seat opposite her, he slipped his athletic frame into the chair and put his elbows at rest on the table. Michael pulled the sleeves of his sweater back on his forearms, adjusting them for comfort.

While he groomed his thick, blond mustache with the thumb and forefinger of his right hand, smoothing it out at the ends, Tracy removed the cups from the tray, then turned to place it on the table behind her. Her long, deep chestnut tresses shimmered in the daylight that radiated through the glass panes. His attention was seized by it, and the waves that rippled across it, from the braiding she'd taken out earlier that morning.

"So what is this theory?" He asked, as he emptied a packet of creamer into one of the cups.

Tracy folded her hands around the warm cup. She peered out through the window with a distant expression. "This is so hard to tell without sounding somewhat ridiculous," she admitted. Her face flushed slightly.

She reached for the pocketbook lying on the table beside her right arm. "Perhaps it would be best if I show you this first," she stated with a hint of reservation. Then Tracy produced the gold coin she had received from the stranger. "Please look at this, and tell me if it means anything to you!" She placed it in his hand. When he brought it toward himself, he appeared startled, as though he had seen it before.

Holding it between his fingers, Michael examined it confirming his suspicion. "I've seen one of these before!" He peered at it, then looked at Tracy inquisitively. "One of my students brought me a coin exactly like this one!" He slipped his hand below the table and into his pocket, then brought up a mate to her coin, placing it on the table in front of her. He placed them side by side.

Appearing dumbstruck, Tracy stared at the two coins for a moment. "Where did your student get this coin? Did they say?" Tracy inquired intently.

"She said that she got it from a stranger, who came into the truck stop where she works as a waitress part-time. She thought it unusual and wanted me to see it. She's one of my first year students, and she was anxious to know if the inscription had an astronomical meaning!" He paused, anticipating Tracy's response.

"Does it?" She interjected anxiously.

Michael gauged her inquiry. He knew from it that she had a great deal more to tell him, than he had surmised himself.

"Yes, Tracy, as a matter of fact, it does! I don't know what the sphere in the center represents, or the four smaller ones appearing to orbit it, but the stars around it, from what I can discern, represent the Pliades or the Seven Sisters in the Taurus constallation. They're young, newborn stars, only some fifty-million years old. Just babies!" He said jokingly, hoping to lighten the mood.

She smiled. Feeling more at ease with the conversation, her tension subsided. "Tell me more, Michael! Like, how far away is this star system? Could there be planets around any of these stars?"

They reached for their coffee cups almost simultaneously, each taking a sip, then returning them to the table. Tracy laughed.

"They are approximately four hundred and ten light years away. Actually they are pretty close by galactic measurements!" He said, kiddingly. He continued. "As for planets, I would say no! These stars are too young and too hot. The largest of them, Alcyone, is a blue giant that emits light a thousand times that of our sun. These guys will burn out long before planets can evolve around them!"

He turned the cup in his hands, while he stared down into it. He looked as though he was searching deep into a black hole for some cosmic secret. Then he raised his eyes to meet Tracy's. "So, what do you know about these coins? Where did you get yours?" He asked flatly, crossing his arms over his chest and leaning back into his chair and considering her with expectant eyes.

Instead, Tracy quizzed him about the opposite side of the coin. "What about the formula, or equation? What did you come up with regarding that?" She asked, delaying her response to his inquiry with one of her own.

He hesitated for a moment. "I'm not a physicist, although today astronomy has more to do with physical data than with pure observation. I haven't been able to determine what it represents, and I haven't had time to make inquiries among my friends in the physics department. However, one could almost establish that it has to do with the composition of matter. But that's just a guess!" He took a deep breath, exhausting it impatiently. "Okay, tell me what you know about this!"

"I got my coin from the same stranger," she said, airing his assumption. Tracy appeared reluctant to proceed.

"Did you meet him at the same truck stop?" Michael inquired, prodding her to continue.

She considered him momentarily. "No, no! I met him through this Navajo friend of mine, Zachary. He had a mutual friend call me, arranging for us to meet in Kayenta. Zachary told me that he knew someone who had information about the Anasazi, that I would be interested in. He had guided me two summers ago, taking me to many of the ruins that only the People know about."

Speaking in a subdued tone, she was able to control the emotion that crept up into her throat. Tracy knew that telling it would be difficult for her, not because of the implication it had in regard to the stranger, but because it had a connection with her dream and the past.

"We went to the ruins below the mesa, next to the natural bridge." She paused long enough to look for some gesture, that he knew the place she was talking about. He stared at her blankly.

She continued. "That's where I met the stranger. It was the night before last. I'm not sure how Zachary came to know him, but he appears to trust him a great deal! Anyway, that's where I got this coin. He told me that there is another world like our own out there." She raised her eyes toward the window, then back to rest on Michael. "He says that's what the sphere on the coin represents, and the four smaller ones are obviously satellites or moons!"

Michael sat motionless, almost mesmerized by what he was hearing. "Tracy, if I didn't know you so well, or as well as I think I do,...........I!" He hesitated to complete his remark. "If it were anyone else, you *know* what I would say!" His tone was adamant.

"There's more," Tracy said somewhat sheepishly. "I'm only telling you the way it happened! He said that the Pliades was the gateway! And that the Anasazi were actually able to travel between worlds. It *is* folklore you know. It's part of the emergence story!"

Hardly able to control himself from bursting into laughter, Michael snickered, a broad smile broke across his face. "Who is this guy? What's his name, Captain Zero?"

"No! Please let me finish! I'm not even sure why I'm telling you this! I just thought you would listen." A note of sincerity rang in her voice that grabbed at him. *If there was ever a time to listen to her, perhaps it is now,* he thought. She was confiding in him. She had never done that before. *It doesn't matter what you think about this story*, he told himself. *Just listen for once!*

"I'm sorry I interrupted! It was rude of me. Please go on!" Michael said, encouraging Tracy to continue.

She appeared to become more anxious as she collected her thoughts. Putting her right hand to her forehead and holding it there, with her elbow poised on the table edge, she continued. "Then he showed me something else. Something really unexpected," she said with her eyes closed momentarily, as though she was recalling a picture of it with her mind's eye.

She looked up at Michael again. "This is the part that makes what he said have even the slightest bit of credibility with me! After showing me the coin, he pulled a stone away from the wall in the kiva, to reveal a rock painting very closely resembling the inscription on the coin. I know what you're thinking, but I'm almost positive that he didn't just put it there; I would have been able to tell. At any rate, it appears to be authentic and would date within the range of the other paintings that have been found in that particular area, approximately seven hundred and fifty to, perhaps, a thousand years old. He, Daniel, says that it's closer to a thousand."

Picking up on the name immediately, Michael wasted no time in pressing her about it. "Daniel, huh? Daniel who? What's his last name? Is he someone in the field of anthropology, or archeology, whose name you recognize?" He raised the cup of coffee to his mouth, then hesitated to drink from it, realizing that it had turned cold while they spoke.

"No. I don't know what his last name is, he never really said. He did say that he had done some independent research. That in itself doesn't surprise me! It's how he found the painting on the wall of the kiva that concerns me. I find it hard to believe that with the hundreds of researchers who have crawled all over that place in the past, that no one has ever stumbled across it other than him." With her hands flat on the table, Tracy Baldwin tipped her head back and let out a sigh of consternation.

Michael glanced at his watch. It was almost time for his class. "Did you ask him how he found it?"

Suddenly, she appeared apprehensive. "He did say," she replied in a subdued tone of voice, as though she was reluctant to share this information. She hesitated.

"Well?" Michael said somewhat impatiently. He glanced at his watch, again. "I'm sorry, Tracy, but I've got to leave in a few minutes."

"These are his exact words!" She replied sharply, placing great emphasis upon them. "I knew of the one who put it here!" Her eyes were like black ice when she trained them on Michael. Tracy watched for his reaction.

Michael stared at her, his expression was one of perplexity. "So in essence, he's saying that he was there, that he had personal knowledge of the one who put it there, more than seven hundred years ago! I hope you don't render any truth to this story? You don't, do you?" He had never seen Tracy like this before.

"I don't know?" She said as she folded her arms in front of her. Feeling a sudden chill, she rubbed her shoulders. "I'm not sure what I believe! But I do remember the conversation we had some time ago! It was the one about the documented sightings, the ones that have been logged for years at the observatory," she said, mindfully jogging his memory. "And what about the ones you saw last summer? Can you be so certain that it's not true, Michael?"

Michael stood up. He had a thought-filled expression. "I've got to go. I'll be late for my class. Can we get together this evening and talk about this over dinner?"

"Not tonight, Michael! Thank you, but I'm just not up to it right now. Soon though, I promise!" Tracy said, offering up a half-hearted smile."Please find out more about this equation for me, will you?" She asked, as she handed back one of the gold coins.

"I'll do more than that!" Michael offered. "I'm going to have an analysis done on this coin. I know a metallurgist who can tell us a great deal about it, perhaps where it originated. I don't believe someone is going around handing out solid gold coins! There has to be some alloys in it, that could shed some light on where your friend is from. Or at the very least, where he's had these made!"

"See ya later!" Michael patted Tracy's hand reassuringly, then he started to turn away.

"Wait! There is something else!" Tracy said with a hint of urgency. "He did say something about the equation. He said that it represented dark matter. He said something about it acting like a conduit through which time travel is possible! I don't know if that will be of any help, but I thought it important to tell you!"

"I'll keep that in mind," he said as he walked away. Halfway across the dinning room, Michael stopped and turned to look at Tracy. She sat alone at the table, staring out through the window, apparently preoccupied with her thoughts regarding the stranger. He couldn't help but notice that she was different, that she had changed in some way.

The window mirrored her past. It was a past she had chosen to forget, a past she had never shared with anyone. How could she ever share that nightmare with Michael? She wondered.

Chapter 18

The Turquoise and Silver Wristband

IT WAS THE RING OF THE GUN SHOTS THAT CAUSED LEMUEL Redfeather to bolt up out of bed.

Awakened by a dream in which he had shot a man, he sat up on the edge of the bed. Switching on the lamp to his right, as his eyes focused, he assessed the room about him, to establish where he actually was at that moment. That he was indeed in his own home, in his own bed, and pulled out of a dream that appeared to be more real than anything he had ever dreamt before.

His heart still pounding, he reached over to the nightstand to grab a half-emptied soft pack of cigarettes. He swiped them off the table into his hand. Lemuel Redfeather sat naked at the edge of the bed. Cool sweat beaded on his forehead as he shook a cigarette loose from the pack. He pursed it in his lips.

Raising his right hand, he pulled the back of it across his forehead to clear the sweat from his brow. Then he dropped the pack of cigarettes back onto the nightstand. He had had dreams before, and nightmares as well, but never any as vivid as this one. He recoginzed everyone in the room with the exception of two men, one of whom he shot. He didn't see the face, just the man's hand coming forward with a gun in a room full of people.

Taking a book of matches from the nightstand, he tore one loose and struck it. While he lit the cigarette, he began to rerun the dream in his mind. He exhaled and blew out the match, then tossed it into the ashtray next to the lamp. Glancing at the alarm clock as he set the matchbook down, he noted that it was 2:05 a.m..

He took a drag from the cigarette, while he reviewed those who were present in his dream. *Sam Begay was standing behind me and to my right,* he thought. *There was another man, a stranger to my left. He was a tall man, slim, with unusual eyes. He noticed that because he had looked to his left before he caught sight of the gun. The room was crowded. It looked like the Kayenta District court room.* Lemuel told himself.

He combed the room again in his mind. *Rita Collins stood next to the stranger*. "Who was he? And why was he in my dream?" He thought aloud, as he rubbed his forehead, and then the back of his neck, bringing his hand down to rest on the top of his bare thigh. *The tall, brunette Anglo woman, yes! The anthropologist, she was there, too! She and Zachary Thomas were standing directly ahead of me. They were in front of the others. There were some tribal members, the old crystal gazer, White Horse, and a road chief, Carl Chee Thatchman.*

Lemuel Redfeather took another drag from the cigarette, then he crushed it in the ashtray filled with discarded butts. A thin line of smoke coursed upward, past the lamp and through the top of the shade, then it swirled and dissolved.

The odor of stale tobacco loomed near the bedside. He patted the pillow on the right side of the double bed, where he slept alone. Propping it up against the headboard, he scooted back onto the bed. He leaned back into it, still pondering the dream.

"Why were those people there?" He grilled himself, while he stared at the shadows that the lamp cast upon the ceiling. Then somewhere between the shadow and the light, he saw the gun coming up between Zachary and the crystal gazer, White Horse. He could see the hand clearly. Someone yelled out! He wasn't sure who it was? *It must have been Dean, the young deputy,* he thought. *He was ahead of me and Sam, and to our right. He saw it just before I did! The man pushed between them. He was aiming at the stranger! I think?*

Glancing at the clock on the nightstand, he saw that it was already 3:15 a.m.. He had been dissecting this dream for over an hour, treating it as though it had relevance. *It was just a dream! Nothing more!* He didn't know why it was so important to him to figure it out? *Instinct*, he thought. *It's in my nature to question: to study people, to anticipate their next move*! That's how he got where he was, by knowing what someone else was going to do so he could be there first!

Reaching over to the lamp, he turned it out. Lemuel Redfeather fell back into bed. He pulled the sheet and the blanket over himself, then he tossed and turned trying to get comfortable. He couldn't quiet his mind. When he closed his eyes the hand came up again. "That's it!" He said aloud, springing up in bed. He peered straight-on into the darkness of the room, his mind still reeling. His mental replay had caught something else! It was a silver wristband with large turquoise stones; it was on the wrist of the hand that held the gun!

"There are plenty of those around," he told himself, lying down on the bed again. "But where have I seen that one before?" He questioned himself, while he lie twisting about. Sleep would not visit him again the remainder of the night.

Weary, Superintendent Lemuel Redfeather sat at his desk. With tired eyes, he addressed Captain Peter Morgan and Detective Sam Begay. "We've gotta find this stranger! I believe he's the one who can resolve all of our questions. I have a feeling he's still around here somewhere. What did you come up with?" He directed his query at Sam Begay.

Turning his head aside, he delivered a raspy cough. His fleshy face and neck shook. Then Begay pulled in another draw from his cigarette, while he appeared to be organizing his thoughts. "Talked to the folks down at the Cafe. Seems some of'em seen this stranger come in with Thomas one time." Smoke rolled out over his thick upper lip while he spoke.

Peter Morgan gave him a slanted look. Begay continued. "The cashier, Genna, says she would recognize him if she saw'em again. Didn't talk to'em other than to say hello. The waitress, Jeannie, says she waited on'em. Thought this guy Daniel was kind a cute!" He chuckled laboriously, then he coughed, and cleared his throat of phlegm.

Lemuel Redfeather managed a meager smile. "Did he talk to her? Did he say anything that would indicate where he's from? Or what he'd be doing around here?"

Morgan was quiet. He considered them both intently.

"Jeannie says he was a quiet sort. Didn't have much to say! She says she knew he wasn't from around here, though. She could tell by the way he talked, kind a distinctive she says! She said Thomas was actin' a little strange that morning. Like, maybe a little nervous. Says he's normally not the edgy type! I couldn't make anything out of it, though." Begay paused, taking a deep breath, he left it there for Redfeather to comment on.

Lemuel Redfeather peered at him appraisingly. "What do you mean by distinctive, Sam? Did she say he had an accent? Like from another part of the country? Southern? Midwestern? Canadian? English? What?" He asked impatiently, appearing somewhat strained.

"None of the above!" Sam Begay blurted with coolness. "She said he talked like he was highly educated!"

"That could be something," Peter Morgan said in a calm, disarming voice. He averted confrontation whenever possible. "Why not check out some of the universities that give grants, or fellowships, for Native American studies? How about the Bureau of Indian Affairs? They could have some professor out in the field doing research. They don't make that much money! Maybe this guy's an opportunist!" Morgan ventured.

Begay's face flashed with a look of resentment. Lemuel Redfeather turned his attention long enough to catch it. "That's why he's a captain," he commented sardonically. Morgan eyed one, then the other, naively. He was neither an arrogant or jealous man.

"Good, Peter! I think that's worth checking out. What about the lab reports? Anything back on that coin?" Redfeather engaged his intellect further, peering at him with a hopeful expression.

Snatching a casefile folder from the corner of the desk, Captain Peter Morgan thumbed through it briefly. "Nothing yet! It's too soon! None of the coin dealers have responded. But with any luck, maybe somebody's tried to sell one. Anyway, I'll put out more inquiries." He paused to clear his throat. The cloud of smoke from Redfeather's and Begay's cigarettes irritated him. He had never acquired the habit, and he found it to be repugnant.

"As far as the cigarette butt goes," he cleared his throat again, "it belonged to one of the deceased. No fingerprints, as we anticipated, but it matched the brand carried by Garcia." Morgan slapped the folder shut on the corner of the desk. "That's it! And it ain't much!" He said, with a tone of disappointment.

"Got a deputy out in a patrol car with the tire tread castings, though! He's making the rounds of the parking lots, here and in Tuba City, matching up any four-wheel-drive trucks he spots. I think it will keep him busy for a few days!" Morgan chuckled, a sight rarely witnessed by anyone who knew him. Redfeather and Begay laughed, too, at the thought of the rooky officer carrying around a plaster casting all day, and setting it down next to the tires of every four-wheel-drive truck he saw on the Nation.

"We're sure to come up with a few matches. Those all-terrain tires are pretty common!" Morgan said, glancing over at Begay who had become stone cold quiet. "What about the site, Sam, did you find anything worth mentioning?" Morgan inquired, soliciting Begay's participation to placate his mood.

Begay snorted like a Bull Mastiff checking the ground. "No signs of a struggle! The sons o' bitches knew'em! We should be checkin' out some of their connections in Page. We might be able to tie'em back in with that stranger." He coughed, then popped a throat lozenge into his mouth.

Redfeather tapped the end of a pen on the desk, nervously, while he half-listened to Begay's discourse. His attention was not fully in the room. It was the dream that kept him preoccupied. It wasn't something he cared to share with anyone. *Besides*, he thought, *dreams don't solve crimes!*

"Carl Simmons' girlfriend ain't sayin' much." Begay persisted. "I have a feelin' she knows more about their dealings than she's sayin'. A man spends enough time in bed with a woman, he's gonna talk about his business! She needs to be kept an eye on!"

Morgan eyed him thoughtfully. "She came in and gave a statement pointing a finger at Thomas! Why do you think she did that, Sam?"

Dropping the pen onto the desk pad, Redfeather's attention re-entered the present and set upon the pertinence of Morgan's question. "Yes, why did she? The statements by the two others, the waitress, Jeannie, and the day cook, Cal, were consistent with Thomas'. Was she emotionally distraught and looking for someone to blame? Or did she have another reason for trying to fuel our suspicions about Thomas? I agree, Sam, that we should spend more time on her!"

Begay squirmed in his chair, causing it to creak loudly. He hated these protracted sessions. They caused his back to get stiff and his neck to ache, either from the tension or the sitting or both. Whatever it was, he could hardly wait until they ended it.

"There's something else missing here," Morgan said in a low voice, thinking out loud, with a distant look to him. "I can't put my finger on it yet, but it's not just the stranger! There's something else?"

Eyeing him with curiousity over his thought, Lemuel Redfeather's expression concurred. "Go out and talk to Zachary Thomas again! Both of you! He may say something he hadn't mentioned before. Check out his place for signs of the stranger." He paused. "And another thing! Watch for a silver wristband inlaid with large turquoise stones, not on Zachary Thomas necessarily." He mused.

Redfeather gave a reprehensive nod at Sam Begay, gesturing with his pen in Sam's direction. "And don't get pushy! You haven't got a search warrant!"

He hated it, too, when Lemuel Redfeather mentioned the obvious. It made him feel stupid. And he resented it! Sam Begay resented them both. But he had resigned himself to the fact that he would never be in their position. For one thing, he knew that he didn't have the education. Another was the right friends. However, he was determined to stick it out. There was a pension in it for him, and it was better than most of the Navajos got that he knew. *It's only seven more years*, he thought, *then they can stick it!*

"What about this wristband?" Morgan asked with a diligent preoccupation. "Where did that come into the picture?"

"Just something I dreamt up!" Redfeather said, only half-jokingly. Then he dismissed it, knowing full well that he had planted it in Morgan's subconscious for another time.

Sam felt an attack of flatulence coming on. "Come on, Morgan, let's get out a here! We'll take my car!" He knew how much Peter Mogan disliked him smoking in the car. He knew he could smoke in his own, and how much it would annoy Morgan. He relished it.

Turning onto the long, gravel driveway, the midmorning sun streaked across the windshield of the squad car. It momentarily obstructed their view of the yard. When they pulled up closer, they could see that the hood was up on the late model pickup truck. It sat directly in front of the opening to the metal storage building. The large sliding doors were pushed open wide.

Peter Morgan and Sam Begay approached slowly, each of them observing every visible angle of the premises for a sign of movement. Begay slipped the squad car in gently behind the pickup truck. They sat for a moment anticipating an acknowledgement of their presence from the house or the storage building, then they cautiously emerged from the vehicle.

Standing next to the open car door, Sam Begay removed his jacket and tossed it in onto the seat of the car. He noted that it was an unseasonably warm day for the first week in November, somewhat balmy. He adjusted his shoulder holster. Then he peered into the shadows of the open storage building.

The sun's projection cast an angular line, extending the width of the opening into the building. As the two men continued to approach it, a pair of boots moved easily across the line from the inside. Zachary Thomas emerged into the daylight, eyes squinting as he focused upon the two men: two men that he immediately recognized, that he had expected.

He sized them up as they came the distance to meet him. He studied Begay's labored movement. *He is a man long past his prime, and long past caring*, Zachary thought.

The other man moved agilely, and with deliberation — he moved like a hunter. There was an apparent integrity about him. "Mister Thomas, how are you this morning," Peter Morgan inquired congenially, coming to rest the distance of a handshake before Zachary Thomas. "We'd like to talk to you. We have a few more questions we thought you could help us with."

Laying back, Begay was mindful of the reproach by Lemuel Redfeather earlier that morning.

"I was just tuning up my truck," Zachary indicated, gesturing with his grease-covered right hand that held a box-end wrench. "I can talk while I'm finishing up, if you don't mind?" He said, addressing both men. Then he turned his head aside and spat on the ground, eliminating a spent wad of chewing tobacco from his mouth.

"No, not at all!" Morgan conceded, while making way for Zachary to move between himself and Begay who stood solidly, still and silent.

Stepping up onto the bumper with one foot, he leaned in under the hood of the truck. "Timing's off!" He commented, as he picked up a wrench and proceeded to adjust the rotor.

Begay stooped in under the hood next to him, regarding Zachary's work attentively for an instant. Then he stepped back and withdrew a pack of cigarettes from his shirt pocket. It was the same brand as the one found at the murder scene. Pulling one from the pack, he caught a sidewise nod from Morgan coaxing him to offer a smoke to Thomas.

"Take a break for a minute, boy! Have a smoke with me!" He offered, extending the pack in clear view of Zachary.

"Your brand, ain't it?"

Zachary Thomas stepped back from under the hood of the truck, engaging eye contact and addressing Begay flatly. "Haven't smoked in years! Don't intend to start up again! It's bad for your health!"

Appearing undisturbed by his furtive admonishment, Begay cupped his hand over the end of the cigarette and lit it. Smoke migrated toward Zachary's face.

"We all gotta die a somethin', don't we, boy?"

Anxious to avert tension that would impede their questioning, Morgan affably converged on the conversation. "Nice place you've got here! I've been thinking about putting up a workshop for myself." He said, skillfully unlocking the stalemate.

Breaking away from Sam Begay, Zachary turned to Peter Morgan. He lifted a rag from atop the radiator of the truck, wiping grease from the wrench and then from his hands. "What is it that you want to know?"

"Did your friend, Daniel, smoke this brand?" Morgan solicited the pack of cigarettes from Begay's hand, extending them toward Zachary for a closer look.

"He didn't smoke," Zachary answered easily. "Why'd you ask?" What have cigarettes got to do with anything?"

"Found one at the scene. We're trying to figure out if the murderer smoked, that's all," Morgan admitted freely. The fact would never be conclusive evidence and he knew it, but it could jog someone's memory and open up another lead.

Begay scrutinzed the house intently, while the other two men where engaged. He could see the back door from his angle of vision. If the stranger was to try to exit, he certainly wouldn't be foolish enough to do so from there. But he could have already slipped out through the front door without being noticed. Without a warrant, he knew he couldn't press the issue of checking the premises. But in his mind, it was also unlikely that the stranger would hide out here. It was to obvious, so Sam Begay dismissed it.

He pressed his attention back on Morgan's questioning. "How well do you know this girl, Sue Boggs?"

"Not at all. I mean other than to say hello and talk about the weather, I never really talked to her." Zachary laid the wrench down on the edge of the truck, just behind the front grill, then he leaned back onto the truck with one foot astride the bumper, and faced Morgan with a relaxed demeanor.

"Wasn't she Carl Simmons' girlfriend?" Zachary asked as though he was jostling his own memory. Meanwhile, he mulled over Morgan's question in his mind, trying to determine in what direction he was headed.

Morgan observed that the question had stirred no reaction from Thomas.

He believed if Thomas had more knowledge or suspicion of her, he'd show it. "Why do you think she was so quick to come in and make a statement regarding your visit to the cafe the evening before the murders?"

"I don't know? Like I told you, I didn't say much of anything to her. She came in when I was almost finished eating. I said hello, and maybe some small talk at the counter before I left, but that was about it!" Zachary said thoughtfully pondering the inquiry.

Taking it a step further, Morgan entreated his memory. "Did you talk to her about the break-ins? Or question her about Carl Simmons and Jake Garcia at all?" He stood pat, anticipating anything that would shed light on her statements.

"I didn't want to tip'em off! I was told that she was seeing one of'em. And I didn't want to say anything that would make her think that I suspected them of the break-ins!" Zachary was beginning to stiffen as the questioning ensued. It was encroaching on an area with which he was uncomfortable. He had to remember quickly what he had told Cal and Jeannie, and how much they had apparently told Sue Boggs.

Morgan was shrewdly persistent. "Who else did you talk to regarding these two men, that you suspected of breaking into your home?" Morgan was confident that if anyone was holding back, he could eventually purge the information from them. He could feel it when someone was lying to him or concealing something. It was an innate talent, one he couldn't explain. It was just there.

Straightening up from his position against the truck, Zachary struggled to abate his discomfort with the question. "I talked some to the other two, Jeannie and Cal! Don't quite remember what I told'em, exactly. I could've mentioned something about it. Can't really be sure!" Zachary hesitated. "Is that all you want to know, or is there something else?"

There was a glint of admiration in Sam Begay's eye as he considered the way Morgan went about his business. Still, he believed that real police work called for more than a little finesse. He trusted his own methods more, and he knew he was a better policeman than Morgan could ever be.

"What about the stranger?" Sam Begay blurted, before Morgan had a chance to address it. "Seen him around lately? Ya know, it would be in your best interest to let us know where he is! We're going to find him anyway!" It wasn't quite the way he would have asked, Peter Morgan thought, but the point was still made.

A slight tic developed in the corner of Zachary Thomas's right eye. "I haven't seen'em since before I went out to Skeleton Mesa, since before those two men were killed! Now if you don't mind, I'd like to finish up here." He said in a bothered voice.

He didn't have a sixth sense, but Sam Begay could detect the obvious. Zachary Thomas was lying! Morgan knew it, too. A look from Begay concurred.

"We'll be going!" Morgan gestured to Sam Begay. "Let's go! We'll let this man get back to his work." The two men started for their car, then Morgan turned back. "You will let us know if you hear from him, won't you?"

Zachary shook his head to affirm it. "Sure!"

Standing firm for a moment, Morgan added, "Do you know if he wears a silver wristband, one with turquoise stones?"

The question stunned Zachary. "Not that I know of," he replied, while a mental picture of the hand with the gun and the wristband flashed in his mind.

"Let me know if you think of someone who does!"

Morgan stepped quickly to the car and got in, joining Sam Begay.

Sure that they would be questioning Jeannie and Cal again, Zachary considered whether it would be wise to talk to them himself. From all indications they hadn't given very much information to the police in their initial statements. Why either one, or both of them, had shared any of the conversation he had with them that night, especially with Sue Boggs, was something that puzzled him.

However he chose to look at it, it certainly couldn't be more incriminating than it already was. And the only thing he could think of, other than the fact that it would only make him look more foolish, was the fact that he had shown them both the coin. The one he had lost!

It was something that bothered Zachary a great deal. He knew he had the coin when he was arrested. It was confiscated with the rest of his personal property. How or why it disappeared was a source of concern to him, since he wasn't certain what harm it could cause in the wrong hands. If someone came across it, and thought it to be a gold piece that they could sell for a few dollars, that in itself wouldn't be significant. Whatever the case, he no longer had it, and he wasn't certain how many others there were?

Taking all of the circumstances of the past two weeks into account, Zachary knew there was one person that he needed to talk to. In his mind, there appeared to be no logical answers for any of the phenomenon that had occurred. There had been enough time to consider it all from the rational, Anglo perspective, given him in his early education away from the reservation. Now it was time to consider it the Navajo way! The way of his grandfather, and his grandfather's grandfather before him.

He would talk to the old man, White Horse, the crystal gazer.

Chapter 19

The Book of Daniel

DAYS HAD PASSED SINCE HER CONVERSATION WITH MICHAEL Severson.

Sharing her thoughts with Michael had somehow eased Tracy Baldwin's quandary over her meeting with the stranger, Daniel. However, it had not eliminated the recurrent nightmare. If it persisted, she intended to consider professional counseling as an alternative. *Perhaps it is time.* She told herself, as she agonized over the nagging memory that she was no longer able to put away, into the remote recesses of her mind.

But the other thing, the details of the dream that Daniel had told, they racked her with chills. She had since established the origin of such a dream, and the reason that it was so familiar. It was a matter that she would have to take up with someone else, someone who would have knowledge of such things. She had already made an appointment for that afternoon at two-thirty, with the Reverend Patrick Tanner. He was a local minister, and the campus chaplain.

Immediately after her early afternoon class, she started across the campus to the small office on the first floor of the largest dormitory. It was centrally located, and easily accessible to the students or faculty from any part of the campus. Reverend Tanner was there every afternoon from 1:00 until 4:30 p.m. on weekdays, and from 9:00 a.m. until noon on saturdays, faithfully, to accommodate anyone who wished to see him. He made his home telephone number available to those who needed to talk to him at any other time. He had done so for over thirty years, since he had been appointed as chaplain of the university.

A chilling November wind cut through the campus. The sun was obscured by broken clouds. Tracy Baldwin walked briskly through the open area that separated the university from the dorms. Placing her hand on the door, she peered through the glass at the slight, pale man who sat behind the old, oak desk. She breathed in deeply.

Occupied with some notations, his eyes raised sharply when Tracy Baldwin turned the latch. She swung the door open easily to enter, standing rigid for a moment with the edge of the door in hand.

"Miss Baldwin, come in. Please have a seat!" He greeted her in an amicable voice, rising briefly from behind his desk to take her hand.

She took a seat in an antique, Queen Ann style chair to his right; it was slanted toward the window, and the dated, floral settee beneath it, at a slight angle to his desk. Another, empty chair, sat next to her askew in the opposite direction. The scent of camomile pervaded the air in the small, tightly arranged office.

"I've just made some herb tea! Can I get you some?" The Reverend Tanner offered in a feeble but gracious tone.

"Yes, please."

Tracy Baldwin unzipped her colorful ski jacket, then reached behind her neck to pull her hair out from underneath it and the back of the chair, tossing it lightly aside.

Stepping in the direction of the antiquated electric hotplate, and porcelain tea kettle on the credenza to his right, Reverend Tanner's footing was, at first, unsteady.

"Do you take honey, or sugar? I have creamer!" He suggested, taking down two exquisitely ornate tea cups from the shelf above.

"No, sir. I'll have it plain, thank you." She replied, as she considered the frail old man, his stoop shoulders and a completely white but full head of hair.

The cups clattered on the saucers. He delivered them to the desk with mildly trembling hands. "Now, what can I do for you, Miss Baldwin?" The Reverend inquired, while he bent at the waist to place the tea in front of her.

Carefully turning the cup of hot tea, so that the ear was toward her right hand, she said, "There's a question I have. It's about scripture. The Old Testament, that is!" She proceeded with a tone of reservation. Taking a sip of tea, she continued."Is the Old Testament to be taken literally? Or meant to have any relevance after the birth of Christ? I mean, in the context of prophecy." She paused, measuring him for a response.

He assessed her with diligent eyes. "Certainly, Tracy,...........it's all right if I call you Tracy?" She nodded cordially, displaying a pale smile. "There is much of the Old Testament, leading up to the birth of Christ, that is only pertinent to those times. But, regarding prophecy, there is some that carries over into the New Testament giving them continuity. Which of the prophets were you refering to? Isaia? Jeremia? Ezechiel? Daniel?"

"Daniel!" She answered haltingly.

"What in particular concerns you about the Book of Daniel?" He addressed her inquiry with encouraging interest.

A knock at the door interrupted her reply. His attention shot to the door. "One moment, please!" He excused himself while maneuvering from behind the desk. The Reverend Tanner surmounted a pile of assorted books, lying on the floor, adjacent the corner of his desk. Moving hastily to the door, he opened it to the courier who held a special-delivery package.

Turning in her chair to observe the transaction, it occurred to Tracy that she didn't know his religious denomination. It was not apparently clear by his traditional clerical dress, the dark grey suit and the black shirt with the full white neckband at the collar. He wasn't a Catholic priest, she knew that. Episcopal? Maybe?

The courier stepped inside only long enough to warm himself, while the Reverend put his signiture on the sheet of paper attached to the courier's clipboard. "Thank you sir," he said, slipping back outside through the half-opened door.

Closing the door behind him, Reverend Tanner cut off the chilling breeze that had infiltrated the room, causing Tracy to shiver for an instant.

"Now, where were we?" He entreated her absentmindedly, while placing the small, book size package on the desk to his left.

"The Book of Daniel," she replied thoughfully, considering whether or not to ask his denomination. Then thinking it irrelevant to her concern, and being slightly embarrassed to ask, she put it aside.

"Oh, yes! Go on, please!"

"The part where he tells of a dream that he has involving four beasts. And the prophecy surrounding them," she said, carefully assessing his expression. She added, "I guess I want to know what it means, and if it has any basis in the present or the future, or if it was only meant for that time?"

Reactively, he turned to the Bible on the shelf behind him. He brought it across to his desk and placed it in front of him. "Now let's see here," he said as he produced a pair of reading glasses from his vest pocket.

Thumbing the index of the large, paraphrased edition, Reverend Tanner broke it open to the Book of Daniel. "Oh, yes! Chapter seven, the Visions of the Four Beasts! Here it is. Very interesting," he commented, engaging it with fervor.

As he scanned the text, Tracy pulled her chair forward. She leaned in for a closer look. "I've read through it several times, trying to discern its pertinence to our time. I could make nothing out of it that made sense to me."

While keeping his place in the text with his right hand, and his left elbow resting on the desk top, he gave her a narrow look from behind his glasses. "Of course, these are considered apocalyptic writings. They are subsequent to the prophetic writings, but still have a basis in the teachings of the prophets. And as follows, the coming of the kingdom of God is the central theme. However, chapter seven itself deals specifically with the second coming of Jesus Christ, and his reign over the Earth. Its theme is congruent with the Book of Revelations."

Sitting back in his chair, he took a long breath and exhaled ponderously. Then he removed the glasses from his face and slipped them back into his vest pocket. The Bible remained open.

"Is Daniel the author of the book? Are these supposedly his actual accounts of that time?" Tracy Baldwin inquired intently, retreating only slightly from the edge of the desk.

"Actually, the author is unknown! But the historical accounts of that time would be as accurate as any, I presume." He mused over her intense interest in this particular scripture. "Why are you so interested in the Book of Daniel, if I may ask?"

Tracy retreated farther back into her chair. "It was a conversation I had with someone, that generated my interest. We were discussing the four beasts. I wondered what they represented? I guess I was overwhelmed by it all," she said, shaking her head. She laughed, making light of it, as though she had been taking it a bit too seriously.

Abandoning his acute curiosity for the time being, the Reverend Tanner addressed her question regarding the four beasts. "The verse is full of symbolism, but the four beasts do represent four kingdoms that arise on Earth and have dominion for a time. It doesn't mean that these are actual creatures, of course!" He produced a smile, causing the aged lines around his eyes to become more distinct.

"But this scripture is very relevant," he conceded in a more somber tone. It warns of the end times. The beasts are a symbolic representation of kingdoms or, as we would call them, governments. The fourth beast is the most significant to me, it represents the final and most powerful, having full dominion over the world. It speaks of the final and absolute destruction of the beast, and the conveyance of dominion to God's holy people, forever! Quite stirring, don't you think?"

Her dark eyes full of thought, she considered his words momentarily. Then she spoke slow and deliberate. "Do you think that any of this prophecy could be associated with things that are happening now?"

Shifting in his chair, the Reverend Tanner turned to the window with a distant look about him. "Yes, I certainly believe so, Tracy! I believe it in my heart," he said, appearing to address her from somewhere else.

Then he turned to face her again. "I've spent my life delivering God's message! After a while it is like any other job. You just do it because it's what you know best. You do it almost automatically, without really thinking about it much anymore. But every so often, something happens to jolt you out of this complacency. It's like a kick in the pants from God, if you will!" He smiled warmly. "At least that's the way it is with me!"

"Then I read the scripture again, and it's as if I'm reading it for the first time! You know what I mean?" His eyes inquired of hers with a soulful expression. "And I see something I hadn't seen before! And it comes through so clearly that it's startling!" He told her in an exuberant voice.

But his tone mellowed. "Anyway, I'm rambling on. But you see what I mean, don't you? It's right there before our very eyes, and sometimes we just can't see it! He sighed. "Yes, I believe we are in those times."

Impressed by his candor, Tracy viewed him softly.

"Is there anything mentioned about a messenger in these scriptures? I mean, like someone who will come to warn us? I know the Bible speaks of angels, but I was thinking in terms of another prophet of some kind." Tracy asked him, now displaying an obvious degree of comfort with the Reverend.

Catching a glimpse of the clock on the wall across the room, Reverend Tanner saw that it was nearly time for him to leave. It was 4:20 p.m.. But he was so intrigued by her keen interest in the subject, that he was inclined to continue the conversation in spite of the hour.

"There is mention of manlike figures in Daniel's dreams, but I think you're probably asking about someone more tangible. The gospels speak of His prophets as being among us, even until the end times. So I would imagine that there are those who could be considered as messengers!"

"But there is no mention of an individual messenger?" She persisted.

"No," he responded firmly. "There is mention of false prophets, of course, and to be wary of them!"

His curiosity was again whetted by her inquiry. "Is there a particular reason why you asked that question?"

There was a reason, obvious only to Tracy Baldwin at that moment. *To mention the stranger at this time, his name, and the fact that he had related a portion of the text in chapter seven of the Book of Daniel as his own, could only be construed as some contrivance to manipulate me in some way*, she cautioned herself.

"It's just that someone I know made the inference that such a person could exist! I questioned the origin of that assertion. I guess I just wanted to clarify it with someone who has a broader knowledge of scripture than myself."

"That's all right! I enjoyed our conversation," Reverend Tanner told her. "I do hope you'll come and see me again? Perhaps you can bring your friend, and the three of us can discuss the scriptures."

"Perhaps," Tracy Baldwin said musingly.

"I do find the prophetic works so fascinating!" He closed the Bible on his desk. He turned in his chair to replace it on the shelf behind him.

Standing up, Tracy Baldwin zipped her jacket. "I've found our conversation very informative, and interesting as well, Reverend Tanner!"

He arose from behind his desk. "Please, let's not be so formal! Call me Patrick, or Pat if you like, all of my friends do," he told her with an affable smile.

"There *is* something else that I'd like to talk about. Perhaps some other time, though," she remarked, thinking he was a good listener, and someone in whom she could confide. "Is there a number where I can reach you? If I have another question,............or to make an appointment for my friend and myself."

"Certainly." He withdrew a card from its holder on his desk, passing it to her. The Reverend Tanner looked at her with a thought-filled expression. "Something else you might find interesting! God gave to Daniel the understanding of visions and dreams! He was well known for his ability. Summoned many times to the courts of the rulers of that day, he interpreted their dreams and the message that they bore." He paused momentarily. "I don't know what made me think of that? But I just thought you might be interested!" He added musingly.

Standing gelid in the doorway, Tracy felt an icy jolt rack her body. She turned toward him again, but averted his gaze. "Thank you, Patrick!"

"Have a good evening, Tracy!"

He considered her while the door closed behind her. *A Fine, intelligent woman, but somewhat troubled!* He thought.

While she walked down the sidewalk, to the faculty parking lot at the east end of the campus, Tracy was numb to the cold air that bit her face. Her mind reeled. *Surely this stranger is an eccentric prankster, or some raving lunatic*, she thought. *But what if he's not?*

I could never discuss this with Michael Severson, she told herself. *He wouldn't sit still for any of it! But, I believe Zachary would find this interesting! Perhaps he would find it as unsettling as I do?*

§ § §

It was decided, Zachary would make the long trip to the camp of the aged White Horse, to seek his counsel.

The old man and his clan lived in the traditional way, off of the land. There was no phone to contact him, but Zachary knew he would be there. And somehow White Horse would know he was coming.

Loading the pickup truck, Zachary readied himself for the drive. The day was young and cold. He checked the tires, while the sun broke upon the horizon behind him. It cast his shadow, elongated, upon the ground. The daylight appeared jaundiced against his skin.

He had taken this trip many times as a boy, visiting the camp of White

Horse, with his father and grandfather. They made the journey on horseback, taking several days. He never knew exactly how long they would be gone. It wasn't important to him then. The duration of their visits were marked only by the passing of the sun. It was a timeless place in his memory. Although the pickup truck had replaced the horse, the men were still the same. They were unfettered in spirit.

This time the trip would take no more than an hour and a half on a semi-improved road. It was about sixty-five miles. But the duration of his stay was unknown, and in his state of mind it was just as well. Zachary had much to understand. He knew that White Horse could help him.

They would probably have a sing, as they did on the visits in the past. The ceremony might last two, or go as many as nine nights. Zachary was prepared. He had assembled a package of goods the night before, required as compensation for the ceremony. *It will probably be a Holy Ways ceremony*, he thought. But he would go along with whatever White Horse recommended.

Anxious to be on his way, but wary, Zachary locked the house. Then he closed and padlocked the large sliding doors of the storage building before leaving. If he was being followed, it was of no concern this time. He would give it no attention. His mind was on other things, and in another time and place.

Taking U.S. Route 160 to 98, Zachary proceeded northwest past the Shonto turn off. Then just south of the Inscription House and east of White Mesa, he turned onto a lesser traveled road. It would take him due north by the Inscription House ruins, and beyond to the sacred Navajo Mountain. The hogan of White Horse rested on a flat near the base of the mountain.

A few things out here had changed, but not all that much. With the exception of some additional hogans and small sheep ranches, the scenery hadn't changed at all. It was still high desert, and primarily remote.

Navajo Mountain was dusted with snow above the eight thousand foot elevation. Its peak was salient against the cold blue pallor of the wintery sky. Patches of opaque, grayish clouds buffeted about the mountain top. It was well within Zachary's range of vision. His journey would end anon.

Soon he would be entering the lodge of a respected friend, a judicious man of ninety-one years, two years older than his grandfather would have been. White Horse was old enough to have heard the stories of the Long Walk, told by those that survived it, and the days of incarceration at Bosque Redondo. They were stories Zachary listened to many times as a boy, told by White Horse, and his grandfather, too. The oral depiction of the hunger and illness, and inhuman treatment of the Navajos was etched clearly into the minds of the young. It caused great bitterness among the Navajos for the Anglos.

These were stories that stirred great sentiment in Zachary. Although he had not been there, he bore great pride in his people. He relished the stories told in the lodge about the notorious Black Horse, and his stand against the tyrannical Bureau of Indian Affairs agent Shipley, in 1892. He stopped agent Shipley from collecting Navajo children to be sent off to the Fort Defiance school. What Navajo history Zachary failed to acquire in the Anglo school, he more than made up for around the fire in the lodge. His rearing was steeped in it.

There were also stories that had to do more with mythology than history. He recalled the name Ba Alilii, the one who was called Supernatural Power. He had the reputation of being a witch. It was said that he cast spells on his enemies. About 1907, he led a small raiding party that antagonized the traders, and the agents of the Bureau in the northern reaches of the reservation. It was not said whether he had ever been apprehended.

Approaching the turnoff, Zachary steered the pickup truck from the coarsely paved road. He veered onto a hard-packed dirt trail, distinguished only by the ruts worn into the native soil. It led him in the direction of White Horse's lodge, yet another three-quarters of a mile from the main road.

Chapter 20

Secret of the Holy Man

IT WAS STILL EARLY WHEN HE CAME UPON THE OCTAGONAL, LOG and earthen structure. The morning sun was in full radiance. Smoke from the fire within the hogan billowed from its center. He came to a stop alongside another, timeworn pickup truck, some twenty-feet from the entrance of the lodge.

Other members of the old man's family lived in the hogans scattered across the flat. It was overshadowed by a range of buttes, that clung to the side of the mountain at sixty-five hundred feet.

There were stirrings about as Zachary climbed down from the truck. There were smells, too, cooking smells that made his mouth salivate. A few small children scurried about. Chickens and goats wandered around haphazardly, looking for a bite wherever one could be found. A woman stood outside the door of the nearest hogan. She propped the door open with the heel of her bare foot, while she shook a blanket. She took notice of him while he walked to the door of White Horse's lodge.

He rapped on the door, solidly, several times. An elderly woman cracked the door open. She was White Horse's daughter-in-law. Her leathery, bronzed face caught the daylight as she peered through the crack. The corners of her eyes wrinkled as she squinted, focusing for a moment on the form standing before her. Then at last recognizing the young man, a smile came upon her face, and a sparkle in her eye.

"Woshdee!" The woman said in a happy voice,"Come in!"

Pulling the door full open, she stepped back allowing Zachary to enter. The old man, White Horse, sat, his legs crossed, on a blanket beside the morning fire. He sat quietly with his eyes closed, and his head bowed. His seventy-three year old son, Raymond Lone Coyote, gave rise from his handmade chair to greet the son of one who was a long time friend.

"Aoo', ya' at' eeh!" He said, "Yes, hello!" Nodding his grayed head stiffly, he raised his right arm, gesticulating shakily in the direction of a small pine table where his wife, Ogin, had set a place for Zachary to take breakfast.

"Kwe'e dah nidaah!" Lone Coyote said, "Sit down right here!" He joined him, taking a place at the table.

"White Horse said we would have a visitor. He did not say who! I am glad that you have come. It is always good to see the son of my old friend! How have you been?" He inquired of Zachary in a quavery voice.

Zachary's eyes took in the primitive austerity of the familiar lodge while he spoke. "I am well! It has been more than twenty years since I visited your hogan with my father and grandfather." Their eyes measured the effects of time on one another.

"The years have been good to you," Lone Coyote said with appraising eyes. "But I am an old man now," he said reminiscently gauging the passage of time. He took up his battered, tin coffee cup and placed it to his lips, musingly. Holding it steady, with both hands, he drank from it.

Then he continued to speak to Zachary in his native Athabascan dialect. "Much has changed in the world around us. I hear and I see what is going on when we are in Kayenta. We hear from the young ones. They have strange ideas! The voice box says crazy things! But mostly I feel it! I feel like many black clouds are near. I don't envy the young ones. I think the Great Spirit is displeased!" He fell silent.

Pondering Lone Coyote's words, Zachary finished his food. "I came to counsel with White Horse. I've had some trouble," he admitted, while placing his knife and fork across the scarred, tin plate.

Lone Coyote contended with a cigarette paper, preparing a smoke with good Indian tabacco. "Then perhaps we will have a sing?" He said, licking the end of the rolled paper. He lit it. The smell of sulfur wafted across the table between them. It stung Zachary's nostrils.

Walking across the dirt floor, the old woman, Ogin, went to arouse White Horse from his blanket.

"Haishjj t'ko!" Tugging at the old man's shoulder, she said, "Someone is here!"

Almost blind from cataracts, he looked up at her through the opacity of his eyes. He acknowledged her by the origin of her name, Wild Rose, saying, *"Shi beehasin,* I know him!"

She helped him to a standing position, then carefully guided him to the able where Lone Coyote and Zachary sat. Seating him, she excused herself o leave. She would go about the camp visiting, and making the announcement hat a sing would take place in their lodge. She left the men to talk.

"Igii atsa' yi nii ni!" Addressing the air before him, his eyes only liscerning shadows, White Horse said, "The eagle brings you! It has been ong since you've come to our camp. I see you brought the spirit of your ather and grandfather with you!" He laughed musingly, adding, "They told ne you were coming! You've come for a message!"

Responding in the Navajo language, Zachary told him, "I've come for ounsel, White Horse. I've come to find out what it is that I should do? I vant to know if the things that have been happening to me are for good or vil?" Zachary spoke in a resolute tone. He surveyed White Horse with an arnest expression.

Lone Coyote had listened intently. "We should have a peyote ceremony. t will dispel the effects of unfriendly spirits!"

A nod from White Horse concurred. "It is decided then! You will stay in our lodge for a ceremony! You are a welcomed guest here, and you will be afe from that which you fear!" He said this with a resonance in his voice hat inspired Zachary's confidence.

But he wasn't sure what it was that he feared. Was it someone? A spirit? Daniel? The changes? Or was it something in himself that he feared? He ealized he would have to contend with it in the days that followed.

"Did you bring the eagle feather?" White Horse inquired knowingly. He xtended his hand, palm open onto the table, waiting for Zachary to produce t. "It is good medicine!" The old crystal gazer told him.

Although he had known the old man all of his life, he was amazed at the bility he possessed. Zachary reached into the box beside him on the floor. He extracted the foot-long eagle feather, the one he had found in the kiva, hen brought it up to the table and placed it across the withered palm of White Horse.

"My eye sight is failing, but I see much! I see even more as the lights grow dim for me in the outside world!" His words related a sense of power hat transcended his condition of mortality. His long, white hair gave him the therial look of a sage. And the opaque milkiness of his eyes appeared to be veil, through which he could see other worlds.

"Then we will visit today, and tomorrow we will prepare ourselves for he ceremony!" Lone Coyote declared. "I must go find the road chief, Carl Chee Thatchman. He must have time to notify the others who will help with he ceremony."

Excusing himself from the table, Lone Coyote hobbled over to the coat pegs beside the door. He took a woolen ranchers jacket from it. Pulling it over himself, he fastened the buttons and tied the belt in front of him. *"Hagoonee'!"* He said,"Goodbye," closing the door behind him.

Offering to stoke the fire, Zachary made a trip to the woodpile against the outside wall. He filled his arms and returned to the fire.

White Horse was silent for a time. Then he spoke, taking advantage of their privacy. "I have had dreams! They are disturbing. I sense supernatural forces at work. There is a good force, a spirit, one who is from the light! There is a dark force, one who comes from the great abyss, who has caused much discord and harm! They are battling even as we speak. These forces are in conflict, and they are choosing their warriors to do their work for them! This is what I know!"

Kneeling still, next to the fire, Zachary could only see the back of White Horse. He could not see the old man's eyes, but he could feel the essence of his words. They engulfed him with an iciness that no fire could avert.

He brought himself up from his knees, saying, "I have had dreams, too! And I've had contact with one who I think is from the spirit world! Is he a messenger? Or is he the dark spirit that you speak of?" Returning to the table, he sat across from White Horse.

White Horse had his crystal on the table. He stroked it with his sinuous fingers. "You have had contact with both," he revealed to him, leaving Zachary more perplexed than ever. "You have to determine the way you will choose for yourself! The ceremony will help you understand what path to take! I think you will choose correctly, though!"

Mesmerized by the words of White Horse, Zachary deliberated over his assertion. "What is this battle over?" He asked with grave concern. "And why wouldn't I choose correctly?"

"You could be fooled! The Dark One is cunning. He would choose someone who is not what he appears! You may think this one is on your side, all the while he will be planning against you,...........*you* and the spirit messenger! He is the *one* who has come to make war against the Dark One!

"But why?" Zachary leaned forward, supporting himself with his forearm, he peered at the old man with the narrow eyes of inquiry.

The old man swallowed hard. He gathered the energy to speak further.

"It is about dominion," he said, forcing the words past his lips. He cleared his throat. "It is to decide whether man will continue to be the caretaker of this earth, or if he has failed in his guardianship and must suffer the consequences!" He paused.

Zachary sat straight up, looking astonished.

The old man went on. "Man was given the land and the water, the animals and the plants. These are all sacred things! The Great Spirit put them in our care. We have not done well! The supernatural powers were in balance in the beginning, but man has thrown everything out of balance! The plants, the animals and the mountains were endowed with this power. Now the balance is greatly disturbed!" White Horse shook his head in dismay.

"Man has not learned to walk the Beauty Way, the way of trust and mutual concern for each other! Men were meant to imitate the gods! To become as Holy Ones! Not to cause all this grief and destruction upon the Earth!" He emphasized this with great sadness. "Now it is up to the Holy Ones to bring the balance back! But the Dark One, he does not want it! He will fight with all of his power to destroy the Earth!"

He assessed Zachary's image through the opaque windows of his eyes. His tone became more subtle. "I believe you are one who is chosen to assist the Holy Ones! There is something I must show you!"

Turning with a feeble motion, White Horse reached for a deerskin sack. It hung on a spike driven into a roof support post, near where he sat. He brought it forth, setting it on the table in front of him. Then he slackened the drawstring, awkwardly spreading the mouth of the sack with his decrepit fingers.

"I received this from a Holy Man that I knew when I was very young." White Horse told him. Then he reached inside, pulling out a gold coin held between his thumb and forefinger. With a trembling hand, he extended it toward Zachary.

"The Holy Man said it was handed down from the Ancient Ones!"

Zachary knew what it was before he had it in his grasp. "I have seen coins like this! The stranger, Daniel, he gave me one like it!" He examined it carefully, taking note that it was indentical.

"Did the Holy Man say who gave it to the Ancient Ones?" Zachary asked.

The old man nodded. "He did! He said it was a gift from a spirit messenger, one from another world!"

If this was true, than everything Daniel had told him was also true. He stared at the coin in amazement, then back at the old man. "Then I have met the Spirit Messenger!" He asserted ardently, placing the coin back in White Horse's hand.

"Then it is so!" The old crystal gazer exclaimed. "But the peyote ritual will help to enlighten your heart and your mind. The Waterbird will guide you!"

Lone Coyote returned later in the afternoon. Ogin had gone to the other hogans organizing a feast to take place that evening.

Through the remainder of the day, and into the night, the men talked about the past, the present, and the future of the tribe. The women brought food. Others joined them, eating and drinking and laughing. They told stories and played games. Tomorrow they would prepare for the ceremony.

It was about 7:15 p.m.. The lodge of White Horse had been prepared for the ceremony. It had been cleaned, and all unnecessary items had been removed. People had begun to gather outside, while the road chief, Carl Chee Thatchman, was inside supervising the preparation of the cresent moon altar.

Blankets had been spread on the ground, around the inside perimeter of the circular structure.

The road chief and his assistants, including Lone Coyote, worked carefully mounding sand and shaping a cresent moon, that faced west to east, with the concave portion facing the door.

Friends of Zachary, and his father and grandfather, and neighbors and relatives of White Horse, waited outside. Each of them had bathed and dressed in good clean clothes, it was the custom.

When the cresent moon altar was completed, the road chief carved a line the length of it. It represented the peyote road. Then he and the fire chief, Lone Coyote, constructed the ash cresent directly in front of it. After that was finished, they laid down four sticks of wood to make a fire.

The fire sticks were laid in the center of the hogan in the shape of an X, with the arms of it facing the altar very short. The long ends splay diagonally away from the altar. Lone Coyote laid a smoke stick, or poker, behind the fire sticks. He proceeded to light the fire, before walking outside.

A brass pot, buckskin drum head, and a rope for tying it were brought in by the drummer chief. He and the road chief bound the drum, completing the final preparations for the ceremony. Then they both went out. Carl Chee Thatchman went outside to make sure everyone was ready, and to bring in his kit and the peyote.

Now it was nearly eight o'clock. The road chief entered the hogan with his kit, and a sack of dried peyote buttons, at least three hundred. He took his place, centered behind the cresent moon altar. He sat on a blanket waiting for the others to come in.

The others entered in the prescribed order. The drummer chief came in and took his place to the right of the road chief. He was followed by the cedar chief, who took his place to the immediate left of the road chief.

Then the one who was considered the patient, he for whom the ceremony was taking place, followed. It was Zachary. He took a place near the cedar chief, to be accessible. The others entered reverently, moving clockwise around the inside. They took places along the outside wall of the hogan, where the blankets had been laid.

Finally, Lone Coyote, the fire chief entered, closing the door behind him, he took his place nearest the door to the north.

It was quiet. The road chief brought out the sacred, chief peyote. It was a special peyote button, decorated with white paint and corn husks. It was the one that the road chief used in all his ceremonies.

He got up from his place and moved toward the fire with the chief peyote and a handful of cedar incense. Sprinking the incense on the fire, it began to smoke. Then he took the chief peyote, and moved it back and forth through the smoke four times. Turning, he brought the chief peyote to the cresent moon altar. He placed it on a circular bed of sage, that had been prepared for it in the center of the altar.

All the people present were sitting erect. They were thinking of good spirits, to make the meeting go well.

Taking a hollow eagle bone whistle from his kit, the road chief, Carl Chee Thatchman, brought it to the cedar smoke. He moved it through the smoke four times. Then he brought it back, and placed it at the base of the moon altar with the mouthpiece up.

Someone coughed. And a few people cleared their throats, but mostly it was quiet.

Producing the eagle feather, the one that Zachary had given to White Horse, the road chief passed it through the cedar smoke just one time. He then handed it to the cedar chief, who passed it clockwise around the room to the fire chief. The fire chief would use it during the ceremony to fan the fire. The cedar smoke was an offering to God. It was believed to bring blessings. And it was used to purify the instruments.

After the fire chief received the eagle feather, the road chief looked about the room seeing that everything was in order. All of the men and women, and the few children who were present, appeared devout.

Beginning with a cigarette for himself, the road chief took the Bull Durham tobacco. He placed it on a cigarette paper and rolled it. He did not light it. Instead, he passed the tobacco to the drummer chief. After he was finished with it, he passed it clockwise around the room until everyone present had a cigarette. Except for the children, they were not allowed to smoke.

Lone Coyote moved from his place to put the end of the fire stick into the fire. He waited until there was a glowing end on it. Bringing it around clockwise, he handed it to the road chief.

Lighting his cigarette first, Carl Chee Thatchman then handed the fire stick to the drummer chief. He passed it back. Then it went hand to hand clockwise around the room. Until everyone's cigarette had been lit.

The road chief blew four puffs of smoke toward the chief peyote, then one puff toward Mother Earth. Then he inhaled again, and bowed his head, blowing several puffs of smoke at his own body. All of the others mimicked his gesture.

Then the road chief prompted Zachary to speak. He was to tell the purpose of the meeting. Everyone, including the children, was silently attentive.

"I have asked for this meeting because I have had contact with spirits." He paused. "And I have had visions," he said haltingly, looking about the room at the faces of those present. "In my visions I saw the Ancient Ones! And my grandfather spoke to me!" Zachary's words became more distinct, and his tone more steady.

"The Ancient Ones wanted me to go with'em, then, in my dream, but I resisted. I told'em that I had much to do!" The people listened attentively, and smoked.

"I pleaded with'em to leave me alone! I told'em that my people needed me! They taunted me with images of my father and mother calling to me!" He paused for a moment, and not a sound could be heard. The people were awestruck at his telling.

Taking a draw from his cigarette, he exhaled. "Then my grandfather appeared and spoke to me! He said I was right not to go, that it was not my time. He said I had something very important do! That I must protect our people from those who would destroy our world!" Zachary took a deep breath. "He said I should listen to The One of Many Faces! To do what he tells me!" He paused again to measure the affect of his story upon the people.

Smoke from the cigarettes and the cedar incense commingled in the room. The flavor of the two together produced an astringent aroma. It created a euphoric atmosphere.

"Then my grandfather took my hand. He pulled me up from where I laid, and took me over to the edge of the canyon wall at the base of the stone arch. Then the image of my grandfather changed form. It turned into an eagle! I watched it glide up over the canyon. Then it flew over the ruins and circled three times, disappearing! I took this as a good omen!"

Almost everyone was finished smoking.

"I also watched my companion, Daniel, disappear. The stranger!" He added. "The one who I think is the Spirit Messenger!" He paused. "I saw him go up into a bright light that came from the canyon floor. I believe it was sent by the Ancient Ones!"

Addressing them further, in a somber tone, he added. "I also had another vision, one that disturbed me greatly! I dreamt that two men were murdered. They argued with a third man up on Skeleton Mesa. I watched as he pulled a gun. Bringing it up from his side, he shot them both. Then he threw their bodies off the edge of the mesa! I couldn't make out who the figure was! But I did see his hand, and a bracelet on his wrist! I know if I see it again, I will recognize it!"

Chapter 21

Peyote Woman Speaks

EVERYONE WAS FINISHED SMOKING NOW.

Zachary put out his cigarette. Then he said, "I would like your help. I would like you to pray with me, so that I can understand what it is that I am supposed to do! So that the spirits will not trouble me further! And that I will know how to deal with them! So that I will find what is true!" He glanced over at the road chief, who considered him with empathetic eyes.

Nodding twice, approvingly in Zachary's direction, to let him know he understood the purpose, it was Carl Chee Thatchman's turn to speak.

Keeping his thick body erect, with his legs crossed, he brought his eyes around to address the meeting. He raised his heavy brows, causing his forehead to crease, while he considered what he would say.

"I am thankful for this meeting," the road chief said in his stately tone. It was his conservative cut that appealed to their sensibility. "Think of me as I pray for our patient, Zachary Thomas. I will help him all that I am able!" He took in a breath. "I'm not sure how, but I think I can help! Let's all pray for the purpose of this meeting," he said bowing his head.

They prayed for about five minutes. Then Lone Coyote passed his cigarette to the man on his right. He got up and moved clockwise around the room, picking up the cigarette butts. He laid them in the palm of his hand, all in the same direction. When he got to the drummer chief he stopped, laying the butts down at the south end of the moon altar.

Moving again in a counter-clockwise direction, he continued around the room, picking up butts, until he was in front of the road chief. He placed the remainder of the butts at the north end of the moon altar. Then he went to pick up his own from the man who sat beside him. On his return from the moon altar, he checked to be sure that everything was in order, and in a straight line from the door to the altar: the chief peyote on the moon, the fire stick to the fire, all centered to the door.

Observing that Lone Coyote had finished, Carl Chee Thatchman started the next segment of the ritual. He got up from his place with the sage and the peyote. Walking clockwise around the north end of the cresent moon altar, he went to the fire to smoke the sage and the peyote, four times in the cedar incense.

Returning to his seat, he first passed the sage to the drummer chief. He took some sage from the bunch, then passed it back to the road chief who handed it off clockwise around the room. When it passed the road chief it became medicine to use in the ceremony.

After the sage had been passed around, it returned to the road chief. Each person rubbed some sage between their hands, then they rubbed it over their head and body. It was a cleansing to prepare themselves for the peyote.

Now it was time for the peyote. Carl Chee Thatchman passed the sack of peyote buttons toward the cedar chief. It went clockwise, each person taking one or two buttons, until it was around the room and back to him.

He scraped the fuzz off a peyote button, put the fuzz under his seat, then he offered it toward the chief peyote. After doing so, he ate the peyote. Then he cupped his hands and spit into them. He rubbed them over his head and his body to get the full effect of the medicine. The others did likewise.

The road chief then prepared to smoke all of the instruments: the cane, the sage, the two-feather fan, and the gourd. He brought them all over to the fire. The drummer chief followed with the drum.

Stepping forward, the cedar chief placed cedar incense on the fire. The road chief took each of the instruments and smoked them. He moved each one back and forth through the smoke four times. Then he smoked the drum and handed it back to the drummer chief. They resumed their places in the correct manner.

Carl Chee Thatchman began to sing. He sang a special song, it was the opening song, and the drummer drummed for him. This song lasted about five minutes. Then he proceeded to sing a series of three more songs, all lasting about the same amount of time. When he was finished, silence returned.

People were still eating peyote, when the road chief passed the cane to the drummer. He passed it between the drum and the altar in the prescribed manner. Then he took the drum from the drummer chief and started drumming, while the drummer chief sang. Everyone listened, while they reflected on the patient, Zachary, and the purpose of the meeting.

The drummer chief chanted and sang four songs. Then the cane was passed between the drum and the altar to the cedar chief. He proceeded to chant and sing, while the road chief drummed for him. Then the drum and cane were passed to the others, going clockwise around the room. Those who wished to, could chant and sing. The cane went on ahead of the drum.

It was 11:10 p.m.. The road chief, Carl Chee Thatchman, began to roll a corn husk cigarette, using Indian tobacco this time. He prepared it, then the fire chief, Lone Coyote, brought him the fire stick to light it. He smoked it twice, then he shared it with the drummer chief.

Beginning a prayer for the chiefs who were present, he said, "This prayer is for the officials here tonight! I pray for our bad conduct in the past." His voice resonated with a tone of contrition. His eyes wandered over the participants. "And I have had some bad dreams, too," he admitted. "Zachary is not alone in this." He paused.

"I don't know if mine are caused from wrong contact with spirits, or bad actions? But they are disturbing, too!" He gave a sigh of dismay. "I don't think God is pleased with the people," he said, lowering his head.

The drumming and singing continued, while everyone prayed with the road chief. This went on for about twenty minutes.

About 11:30 p.m., the road chief started a second prayer for the eagle feathers that would be used in the ceremony. It was for the smoke fans that the people used, and for the instruments.

"I ask God to control this midnight prayer, that it will go correctly!"

Carl Thatchman held his hands outstretched with his palms up. His eyes were raised to the ceiling. Then he looked down toward the corn husks and Indian tobacco that would be part of this prayer. Taking it in hand, he said, "I offer this up as an offering to God for his blessing!"

The drumming and singing stopped. The drum remained where it was. There was a hush.

Rising from his place with the eagle feather in hand, the road chief moved correctly around the the cresent moon altar. He sprinkled cedar in the fire. A puff of smoke rose up. He smoked the eagle feather in it, moving the feather through the smoke in a protracted motion.

Then he motioned to Zachary to join him near the fire. Holding the eagle feather horizontally, the road chief moved it around smoking Zachary off. He brought it up and down on either side of the patient. Then he walked around behind him, moving it up his back and in a full circular motion over his head. Zachary took his place again.

Stillness prevaded the room. The cedar incense was pungent. Moving the eagle feather through the smoke once again, Carl Chee Thatchman smoked himself off with it.

More cedar was added to the fire; smoke billowed from it. Other people brought feathers to smoke. They took turns smoking themselves off, until everyone was finished. Then moving with a hitch toward the fire, Lone Coyote, the fire chief, tended it.

The singing began again while he prepared everything for the midnight ceremony. He lumbered over to the ash cresent. Lone Coyote arranged it in the shape of an eagle, by adding a bird tail of ash below the cresent. He looked up from it to see White Horse acting strangely. Zachary, who sat next to him, noticed, too. He was rocking forward and back, muttering to himself.

It could be he is having a vision! Lone Coyote told himself. He picked up the cigarette butts at each end of the cresent moon altar, then awkwardly, he turned, moving in the direction of the fire again, placing them in the fire: first from the north side, then on the south.

This was significant. The people's sicknesses and shortcomings were contained in the cigarettes, and their prayers went into the cigarettes as well. In burning them, their illnesses and sins were destroyed. The smoke lifted their prayers toward God.

Taking his place again, Lone Coyote pondered over White Horse. He was prone to have visions, and the peyote medicine usually brought them about. It was almost time for the midnight water song, and it could be an important omen regarding Zachary's purpose.

Everyone straightened themselves. The singing had ceased. The drum was passed back to the drummer chief. Carl Chee Thatchman brought himself up, loosing his stiffness, he ambled around the cresent moon altar, clockwise, until he stood facing it. He reverently lowered himself to one knee. He sprinkled cedar over the charcoal. Then he took up the eagle feather and moved it all along the ash bird, smoking it. Then up to the chief peyote, and onto himself. The others smoked themselves, too, while he took his place again. When the road chief was seated they became still and quiet.

It was nearly midnight. Chanting and singing, the road chief sang the midnight water song, while the drummer chief drummed for him. It lasted several minutes. Then he sang two more songs. When he stopped, it was quiet again. He picked up the eagle bone whistle, knelt facing the chief peyote, and blew four times, signaling for the water to be brought in. He set the whistle back in its place, with the mouthpiece up.

The fire chief had gone outside to get the pail of water from the water woman, while the road chief was whistling. He carried it around the room clockwise. Then he put it in line with the poker, the fire, and the chief peyote, kneeling behind it.

Holding the cane, the road chief sang one more song. Lone Coyote took the pail and a cup, he placed it in front of Carl Chee Thatchman, making sure that the handle of the pail was on the east side of the bucket. Then Lone Coyote took Bull Durham, Indian tobacco, and corn husks from the road chief and passed them between the water and the altar. Back in his place, he prepared a cigarette for himself.

Bringing the instruments around the pail from the south, between the bucket and the altar, Carl Chee Thatchman placed the cane, sage, feathers, and rattle facing the north end of the moon. He placed them lying diagonally. Then he returned to his place.

White Horse still muttered, absorbed in prayer, while the drummer chief set the drum between himself and the altar.

Then the cedar chief began to pray. "I want to pray for the holy cedar that takes our prayers up to God," he intoned with great reverence. "I want to thank God for the water, it is needed for all living things! Therefore it is sacred, and..........."

"He must be released! The One of Many Faces! If he is not, the Dark One will win! We will lose our sacred land forever!" He shouted excitedly, his words pouring out over his trembling lips. His speech was stertorous. Everyone was startled, including Zachary who sat beside him. He gave the old man a slanted look.

"Peyote Woman brought me a vision from God!" White Horse persisted. Turning to his right, he rested his right hand on Zachary's shoulder. "You must see that the Spirit Messenger is not harmed! It has fallen upon *you* to do so! I will help you."

Not certain what White Horse had seen, Zachary could only ascertain that Daniel was in some kind of danger. Perhaps he had been apprehended? Whatever the details of his vision, Zachary knew that later, White Horse would counsel him regarding them.

Dissonance riffled the room. Carl Chee Thatchman raised his hands to quiet the people. The sounds trickled off to a murmur. Then there were a few whispers, as the participants regained their attentiveness.

Speaking again, the cedar chief addressed the patient, Zachary. "I believe that the spirits have given you an answer. I believe we were all thinking this way to make it happen. It is good! The medicine is good, and we will continue our prayers in this way!"

Then it was Zachary's turn to speak. "I want to thank all the people for their prayers. I want to thank White Horse for his vision," he said, bowing his head forward from his seated position, with an expression of gratitude.

Sprinkling cedar in the fire, the fire chief prepared to smoke the water. The smoke swelled, creating a wavery stream that ascended toward the hole in the roof of the hogan. Lone Coyote sliced through the smoke with his fan of eagle feathers, breaking the flow momentarily, and drawing it over the water. Now the water could be used for thirst, or curing if anyone chose to use it that way. He then brought the smoke to himself, and fanned himself with it, then everyone followed in the same manner.

Returning to his place, Lone Coyote lit his cigarette and blew smoke toward the water and the chief peyote. He then began to pray. "I have brought this water from the darkness, let it be medicine to cure the patient," he entreated. "I ask God to send blessings on all the chiefs and the people, to help with the purpose of the meeting," he prayed. "Bless Zachary's house and everything that surrounds it! Bless his stock, and his relatives. And bless his work, too," he added. "Bless the People, the Navajo tribe, that is, and Mother Earth, and all those who help."

His cigarette had gone out, he lit it again. Then he passed it down the south side of the room. It went to the road chief, who smoked it toward the chief peyote, then down toward the earth, and then on himself. He passed it to the drummer chief who did the same. Then it went to the cedar chief who smoked in the same manner. He passed it back to the road chief, Carl Chee Thatchman.

"I want to thank you all for coming here tonight." The road chief extended his arms to indicate the entire group. "I believe it is helping. I believe that the medicine is good," he said, folding his hands once more in his lap.

He began to pray. "Water is needed for all living things, bless the water! I ask that God send his blessings on Zachary, who needs his help right now. I also ask that God blesses his home and his land, and everything on it." He continued, saying several short prayers.

Then he moved his cigarette over the chief peyote. He buried it in the ash bird, and covered it with cedar. Picking up the eagle bone whistle, he went north around the instruments and the water. He stopped in the center of the water pail. Kneeling, he proceeded to make the sign of the cross with the whistle in the water. He placed the whistle to his mouth, blowing it in the water, while he moved it from east to west, then from south to north, and back again from west to east and north to south. While he did this, everyone sat straight up. They were reverent, with the exception of some of the younger children who had fallen asleep on their blankets.

The road chief took the whistle back, he placed it with the other instruments. He picked up the eagle feather fan and took it back to the water. Then he made the sign of the cross with it in the water. When he was finished, he stood up with it and sprinkled water in the direction of the four winds. Afterward, he sprinkled himself. Dipping the fan in the water once more, he carried it to the drummer chief who sprinkled himself. Then the cedar chief did likewise.

The cedar chief handed the eagle feather back to Carl Chee Thatchman, who dipped the fan again to sprinkle the patient. Zachary came out from his place to meet the road chief near the water. The road chief walked north past the patient. Then he turned clockwise and sprinkled Zachary. He sprinkled his forehead, then his right side. Then he sprinkled his forehead again, and then his left side. Each of them returned to their places afterward.

Peering to his left, then to his right, he gave the people a sagacious look. "It is time to water the drum. This ceremony is good for the patient and the people," he said, while the drum was passed to him from the drummer chief.

He poured half of a cup of water over the drum, and some over the drum stick. Then he passed it back to the drummer chief.

Taking more water, he drank from the cup. Then the somber road chief poured water out onto his hands. He placed them on his forehead, holding the sacred water there for a moment. Then he moved his hands to the top of his head, holding them there again. Afterward he placed his hands on his ribcage, then slid them down to his legs. He had covered his whole body with spiritual life.

Everyone did the same. The water went to the drummer, then back to the cedar chief, and around the room clockwise. There was some talking going on while the water went around. Not enough to be disruptive, but enough to soften the mood. By this time it was nearly one o' clock in the morning.

The water had returned to the road chief. He then went to pick up his instruments, moving north around the altar. The drummer chief followed him, picking up his own. They returned to their places.

Lone Coyote, the fire chief, got up from his place on the south side of the door, then moved clockwise to pick up the water. He took the pail in hand and went out with it. Then he came back inside without the water and walked around the altar clockwise, returning to his place.

Picking up the cedar, the feather, and the eagle tail fan, the road chief went to the fire. He put cedar on it, and smoked the instruments. Then he went out, just past the woodpile. He stood looking out into the cold darkness of the night sky. Viewing the infinite number of blue-white stars, facing east, he raised the eagle bone whistle to his lips. He blew it four times in that direction. Each time, its shrill sound echoed from the high buttes, returning to him in a diminishing wave that purged the silence.

Still facing that way, he prayed for the south, the west and the north. When he was done praying he turned in each direction, blowing the whistle that way four times, calling down the four kinds of spirits. Those inside the hogan listened intently. For them, the piercing sound was a tenuous thread connected to the spirit world.

An icy wind bolted through the open door, it caused the fire to flicker violently. Then it surged up for an instant. The old man, White Horse, could feel a stirring within his soul.

Walking around the woodpile, the road chief went back inside. Carl Thatchman went to the fire. He smoked the feathers and the whistle. Then he smoked off Zachary with the feathers and the whistle. And then he smoked himself with them. Placing the whistle at the foot of the cresent moon again, he took his place.

Chanting and singing started. The drum and cane were passed to Zachary. He set them down in front of him on the floor. Taking a corn husk, Bull Durham and some Indian tobacco, he rolled a smoke. Lone Coyote came to light it for him, with the white-hot end of a fire stick.

"I want to thank everyone. I want to thank the road chief for the ceremony, and the other chiefs, too," Zachary said, taking a draw from the cornhusk cigarette. He blew smoke toward the chief peyote. With his head bowed, he blew smoke toward the Mother Earth. Then he took another puff and blew it on himself.

"I want to pray for the purpose of the meeting. I want to pray for a full understanding of everything that has happened." As Zachary said this, a tremulous feeling overtook him. "There is something dark, something evil that is stirring. I can feel it!"

Chapter 22

Zachary's Calling

HE SAT ERECT WITH HIS ARMS OUTSTRETCHED, AND HIS HANDS hung loosely over the end of his knees. He tipped his head back, with his eyelids closed, as though he was peering into the spirit world. "I'm not sure what it is that I must do. But I believe I will know when the time comes! I feel I will know soon, who does the work of the Dark One!" Saying this, Zachary could feel a presence, one that was very familiar to him. He sensed that it wouldn't be too long before he would discover who it was.

Then he asked for a blessing on the hogans of his friends, and their livestock and land. Then he prayed for a blessing on the mountains and the waters. When he was finished, he went up to the chief peyote and held his smoke out to it. Then he turned, and handed his smoke to the road chief. The people silently sanctioned his prayer.

Carl Chee Thatchman took a deep draw from the cornhusk cigarette, then he blew the smoke toward the chief peyote. Then he blew smoke down toward the earth, and onto himself. He passed the cigarette to the drummer who did the same. Then it was passed to the cedar chief, and back to the road chief, before the singing started again.

"I ask God to bless Zachary's prayers. To let him see with the understanding of his heart, and his mind!" When this was said, Carl Chee Thatchman took the cornhusk cigarette and a handful of cedar incense. He went around the cresent moon, and the chief peyote, to the fire. He put the cigarette into the fire, then he sprinkled it with cedar. The smoke was fragrant.

Calling Zachary from his place, the road chief directed him to sit next to the cresent moon altar facing the chief peyote. Then with a placid motion, he fanned him with the smoke from the fire. While the road chief did this, he chewed some peyote to fix it for the patient. As he prepared the medicine for the patient, he thought of the purpose of the meeting, the chief peyote, the universe, and God. The road chief himself became medicine.

Then Zachary raised himself up. He turned, clockwise, full circle in front of the altar and sat down again. In doing so, his sins were now gone, and only good spirits occupied the space around him.

After preparing the medicine, the road chief put more cedar on the fire. Then he walked past Zachary, turned clockwise, and put the peyote in his right hand. Zachary swallowed it without chewing it. The road chief took the eagle feather fan and smoked Zachary with it on his chest, head, arms and legs, to get the medicine throughout his body. Then the road chief put more cedar on the fire and went back to his place.

While Zachary drew smoke to himself from the fire, increasing the effect of the medicine, some people started to go outside. It was time for them to stretch their legs, and go to the toilet if necessary.

Zachary went back to his place. Several people took turns offering prayers. More peyote was eaten. By now it was nearly four o'clock in the morning.

Lone Coyote, the fire chief, got up from his place near the door and came foward to fix the charcoal. He added live coals over it. Then he put more wood on the fire. Afterward, he straightened the charcoal on the south side, sweeping there. Then he went around to the north side, doing the same. When he was finished, he went out to find the dawn lady to bring in the morning water.

Blowing the eagle bone whistle, the road chief signaled the morning water song. A new ceremony began. He put more cedar on the fire, and smoked himself. Others followed. Facing the altar, he knelt. He brought the whistle to his mouth again, and blew it four times. Then he laid it next to the altar, facing it north and south, with the mouthpiece to the north. He sang the water song.

The dawn lady brought the water pail inside, placing it as before. She set it down in line with the fire and the chief peyote. Then she knelt behind it.

Shaking the gourd rattle, the road chief, Carl Chee Thatchman, sang three more songs. The drummer chief beat the drum in cadence with the gourd rattle and the road chief's singing.

After he had sung, the road chief laid down the cane, sage, feather, gourd, and fan in the proper order. He placed them slanting north-northeast, with the butt of them to the southwest. He carefully arranged them in this order: next to him he put the cane, then came the sage, then the feathers across the sage, then the rattle across the sage the same way, and then the eagle tail fan slightly separated from them. When this was done, he beckoned to the dawn lady. Giving her a parrot feather, with it in hand, she returned to her place at the head of the water pail.

The cedar chief began to pray. "The bad things are behind us! We have cleared the surroundings of bad medicine through the process of this ceremony. It is time to reflect on only good things, and how to best live our lives." He paused, taking stock of the people, and he looked to his left at Zachary.

"We must support our friend and brother, Zachary, on his pathway. We should do all that we can to preserve the future of the People." He looked about solemnly. Cautioning those present, he added. "It has been decided by the Holy Ones, in ages past, that we would be the caretakers of the land in return for the blessings we have received from it!" Saying all that he wished, he then placed more cedar on the fire.

While she knelt behind the pail of water facing the altar, the dawn lady took the parrot feather and drew smoke over the water. She passed the feather over the water four times. Other people approached the fire to smoke themselves, drawing it to them with their hands or their feather fans. Except for a few murmurs, it was fairly quiet. A few people prayed under their breath.

The road chief took up a cornhusk, and the tobacco. He passed it around to the dawn lady. It was handed to her from someone nearest to her right side. She rolled a smoke. Then she passed the cigarette materials back, it went clockwise. Receiving a light from the fire chief, Lone Coyote, she puffed on the cornhusk cigarette until the end glowed with an amber ash. Then she drew on the cigarette and blew toward the chief peyote and over the water, twice. The smoke flowed in a gentle stream, rising in a diffused cloud several feet away.

"I pray for a blessing on this morning water," the dawn lady said fervently, as she knelt with her hands folded in front of her, her head lowered. "I pray that the patient, Zachary, will take this water for his benefit! That it will bring him peace and well being in the future. That it will bring him a long life, too!"

The fire chief came to relight her cigarette when she had finished talking. She gave the cigarette to the drummer chief who approached her from the south side. He turned and made a gesture toward the chief peyote with it. Then he returned to the side of the road chief, Carl Chee Thatchman, offering him the smoke.

After the road chief blew smoke over the chief peyote, he passed the cigarette to the drummer chief who did the same. While the cedar chief took his turn smoking, the road chief started the last prayer.

"Many prayers have been offered here for the intentions of Zachary." Carl Chee Thatchman reflected in earnest. "The medicine has brought visions to some! This may help. I'm sure many blessings have been brought about for his purpose." He nodded assuredly. "I ask for a blessing on the morning water, that it brings us health and prosperity! And a bright future for the People!" Leaning forward, he extended the cigarette over the chief peyote and placed it in the fire.

Seeing this, the dawn lady poured water on the Mother Earth. Then she straightened her blanket. She picked up the cup, and raised the handle of the pail without turning it. Taking them around the cresent moon altar, she set them before the road chief. Then she returned on the south side of the altar.

The road chief took up the instruments. He carried them around the south side, between the cresent moon altar and the pail, placing them in order at the north side of the altar. Sprinkling cedar in the fire on the north side, he watched for a moment while the smoke rolled toward him. Then he stooped to pick up the eagle bone whistle, returning with it to his place.

Taking the eagle bone whistle, the road chief made the sign of the cross in the pail of water, while he blew gently into it. When he was finished, he placed the whistle with the other instruments to the north. Then he took up the feather and dipped the end of it into the water. He turned to his right, and with a light snap of the wrist, he sprinkled water on the drummer chief. Then he turned to his left, sprinkling water on the cedar chief.

Now it was time to sprinkle the patient, Zachary. The road chief, Carl Chee Thatchman, dipped the end of the feather into the water, again. He leaned over toward Zachary, who sat to the north between the cedar chief and White Horse. After sprinkling the patient, he returned the eagle feather to its place with the other instruments.

The road chief moved the water pail in front of the drummer chief. Taking a half-cup of water, the drummer poured it over the drum and the drumstick. When he had done this, everyone who had been sitting, assumed a kneeling position. The water was passed back to the road chief.

Drinking first, Carl Chee Thatchman took a sip from the cup. He then handed the cup to the drummer who sipped from it. The drummer passed the cup back to the road chief. He handed it to the cedar chief. After the cedar chief was finished drinking, the cup and pail were passed around clockwise so that everyone could drink.

Each person drank, then sprinkled some water from the cup onto their body. When the water got around to the drummer again, the dawn lady came around from the south to take up the water. She picked up the pail and went clockwise with it, taking it outside. Then she returned to her place for the remainder of the ceremony.

Singing resumed. It was time to prepare for breakfast. The fire chief Lone Coyote, fixed the charcoal again. Outside, women were bringing the food and placing it near the door of the hogan. It was almost 6:00 a.m..

When the singing was over, the fire chief went out to get the food. First he brought some fresh water to drink. Then he went out to get the dishes o corn, fruit and meat, and placed them in the center of the hogan. While he was doing this, the drummer chief rolled another cornhusk cigarette.

After bringing in the food, Lone Coyote took a fire stick, he walked between the water pail and the fire. He went around the south side of the cresent moon altar to light the drummer chief's cigarette. When it was lit, he returned to his place going back the same way.

Everyone was singing now, while the drummer chief smoked for the chief peyote, the water and the food. Then the road chief, Carl Chee Thatchman, smoked, while the drummer prayed over the food.

"We receive this food as a blessing from God," the portly drummer said, wholeheartedly. Then he added, "We give thanks for it! And we are thankful for the success of this meeting, too! I believe Zachary will understand and know his purpose," he said, turning in Zachary's direction with a affable smile.

Zachary viewed him and the others kindly. It had been many years since he had been with them in this way. He felt relieved somehow, as though part of his burden had been taken up by them. He was grateful for this feeling, and his expression showed it.

The drummer chief took the cornhusk cigarette over the chief peyote. He placed it in the fire. Then the cedar chief came and placed more cedar in the fire, while singing continued.

Calling the drum and staff back to him, the road chief started singing one of three songs. He sang for about fifteen minutes, singing all three songs, while the people were reverent. They considered the purpose of the meeting, and asked for blessings of their own. They also prayed for the food. Carl Chee Thatchman sang the closing song. It lasted about five minutes, by this time it was six-thirty in the morning and the meeting was ended.

A medley of conversations erupted. Some people went out to stretch their legs. Others brought in more dishes of food. Zachary followed White Horse outside to look at the dawn.

The old man stood facing the east, staring into the rising sun. His diluted sight could only capture a glimmer of it. Zachary stood by him, away from the others.

"I've seen many suns come and go!" He reflected, while the sun's ochre rays illuminated his face. "Maybe more than my share. But I'm sure glad to see this one, too! And maybe 'cause of you, our people will have many more good days to appreciate." He smiled, still looking ahead into the daystar perched upon the horizon, with its coronal nimbus. Zachary stood pondering the face of White Horse, and his words.

"It still looks the same to me," the old man quipped. "Better'an ever! She's like a good woman, you get used to havin' her around!"

He turned toward Zachary. "You figured it all out yet? I mean your purpose and all?"

"Not all of it!" Zachary responded with a riddled expression. "Maybe I'll never fully understand it! I know now there's more to it than helpin' the stranger, Daniel. It's got to do with me, too. I got involved in something,............something I don't fully understand! And I'm learning things about myself that I never knew before. I kind a feel like I didn't have a choice in the matter, though."

White Horse mused. "You had a choice! But you chose the way someone knew you would. It's destiny's way I guess. It's the way we learn. I think you've been given an opportunity to test your real strength! To know what kind of metal your made of!"

He reached out with his trembling hand. Grasping, he took hold of Zachary's thick forearm. "You know that vision I had during the ceremony?"

"Yes," Zachary said, considering the old man with intensity.

"There's a man with a silver bracelet, with turquoise stones. He's a wealthy man, well groomed. I couldn't make out his face, the image wasn't clear enough. But he's the one who's working for the Dark One. He's the one you'll have to watch out for! I feel he's someone you know and trust!"

White Horse shook his head with a distressed look, still bracing himself on Zachary's arm. "They're going to find your friend,..........this Daniel. You can't let them harm him!" He said in a tremulous voice. "You've gotta make sure that he's freed! Even after they figure out who killed the two Anglos, he won't be safe!" He paused for an instant to capture his breath. "I'll help you best I can!"

§ § §

Back in his Kayenta office, Superintendent Lemuel Redfeather sat at his desk reviewing the evidence. On the desk before him, he had the transparent plastic bag containing the cigarette butt. He flipped the sealed end with the forefinger of his right hand, while he poured over the casefile folder containing the ballistics report on the bullet fragments, that were found during the autopsies on the victims bodies.

The report indicated that the deceased men had been shot with a .45 caliber handgun at close range. Each man had been shot more than once. Jake Garcia had been shot twice in the upper chest. The other man, Carl Simmons, had been shot three times: once in the left side, in the upper shoulder just below the collar bone, and in the lower back.

Lifting his eyes from the report, Redfeather considered the significance of the placement of the wounds on each victim. *Garcia must have been shot first,* he thought. *He died within minutes. Simmons must have turned away trying to escape. He didn't die immediately. So he was still alive when the assailant threw his body over the edge of the mesa. They knew him. There were no signs of a struggle. Apparently there was no physical contact between them. They may even have been expecting whoever it was!*

He flipped a page and continued reading. One bullet lodged in Garcia's chest cavity. The other went on through some soft tissue and exited his back, splintering one of his ribs. He paused to consider why his team of investigators hadn't found the bullet on the ground atop the mesa. *Except,* he thought, *we don't know which way they were standing. They could have been facing the gunman with their backs to the cliff.*

Stretching back in his chair, Lemuel Redfeather rubbed the back of his neck. He produced a gaping yawn, an indication of several recent somewhat sleepless nights. He had to make something out of this case. And he had to do it soon! If he didn't, the state boys would be nosing around hot and heavy!

At one point he had considered more than one assailant, which could have implicated Thomas and his companion, the stranger named Daniel. But the few footprints that were found the next day, after the rain had washed most of them away, left no indication that there were more than three people present on the mesa. *But what if someone else was waiting in the four-wheel-drive vehicle?* He asked himself. *Suppose there was a witness to the murders?* Something no one had considered until this moment!

Loosening his tie, he unbuttoned the collar of his shirt. He reached for a pack of filtered cigarettes that lay on the desk to his right. While he mulled over the prospect of a witness, he shook one loose from the pack. Lighting up, and taking a hit from the cigarette, he scanned the report further. The report was conclusive in that it indicated only one murder weapon. Both men were shot with the same handgun.

The report also stated that the wound Carl Simmons sustained in his left side caused most of the damage. It ricocheted around in his chest cavity, damaging several major organs. The wound to his shoulder was clean. The bullet passed through the flesh. The one in his lower back hit close to his spine, glancing off a rib and tearing one of his kidneys nearly in half. *Lowlife or not, this one suffered,* he told himself.

Snuffing out the cigarette in an overfilled ashtray, Redfeather's thoughts went back to the idea of a witness. *What if the girlfriend, this Sue Boggs, had been waiting there in the truck for whoever it was to knock these guys off? Maybe she had a motive? She might not be grieving as much as everyone thinks? Especially if there's some money involved, perhaps lots of it!*

Thumbing through a few more pages, he found little more of interest in the coroners report. Lemuel Redfeather picked up the bag with the cigarette butt. He held it up between his thumb and forefinger. It was a worthless piece of evidence, and he knew it. For a moment he considered dumping into the ashtray with his own. Then he tossed the bag back down onto the desk, letting out a sigh of exasperation.

Only a few coin dealers had responded so far, none of them favorably. They had neither heard of, nor had they seen anything like it before. One and all suggested having an analysis done on it to determine its elemental composition. Thereby, perhaps they would be able to determine its origin.

Redfeather thought of a metallurgist he knew in Flagstaff, a professor at the university. He flipped through his desktop directory. Stopping at the name of the metallurgist, he jotted it down on a note pad along with the telephone number. *I'll make the call today!* He told himself.

Snapping up another file folder from the desk, Lemuel Redfeather began to review the M.O.'s of the vehicle owners whose tire tread pattern matched that of the casting. There were five.

Looking at the first one in the folder, he recognized the name of that man. "Charlie Waterman, he's a local," he thought aloud. "No arrests........no DUI's........no traffic violations! Age 52........married...........three children................not likely!"

Licking his forefinger, he turned the top sheet. "This one's out a state, Reno, Nevada." His eyes scanned the sheet with promise. Divorced.......age 35.........two children........pays child support. "The ex-wife lives in Phoenix," he mused. "Wife had'em arrested over a domestic dispute more than two years ago! DUI.........license was suspended for a year. Sounds like a winner!" He muttered. "Works construction............"

Maybe he's a gambler? He thought.*Could be involved in drugs? He could've known the dead men, those boys got around! What was he doing in this neck of the woods, anyway? This is no short cut from Reno to Phoenix,.........if he was visiting his kids? Too far out of the way, unless he was sightseeing! Maybe? Maybe he brought the stranger with'em? There's a thought!* He set that one aside for Sam Begay to follow up.

"Hm," he said aloud, after thumbing to the next page. What he saw startled him at first. For an instant, it left a sunken feeling in his abdomen. *Jack McCloud?* Then he laughed to himself. *That crazy kid even went over to the tribal council office in Tuba City. Imagine the balls on him, checking Jack McCloud's fourby!* He chuckled, but with a glint of apprehension. Putting it aside, he checked the two remaining reports. Two more locals. Nothing about them stirred his interest.

"What else?" He asked himself aloud. "What is it that we're missing?" He scratched the back of his head. Then he reached for another smoke. *We've got no murder weapon! No Witnesses! We don't know the motive! And we've got a coin of unknown origin!*

"We don't have a damn thing," he moaned. *And there's a stranger out there somewhere, by the name of Daniel, who may be able to answer all of our questions! But we don't have him either!*

He sank back into his chair. Drawing on his cigarette, he pondered the notion that Zachary Thomas must know the whereabouts of the stranger. That if they gave him a chance, he'd lead them right to him.

Why is he protecting this man? Lemuel Redfeather wondered. *There's nothing in his background to indicate criminal behavior. He keeps to himself. He's never been in trouble with the law. He comes from a decent family. What's the connection here?*

Chapter 23

Lemuel's Plan

REELING IN HIS CHAIR, LEMUEL REDFEATHER TURNED TO FACE THE windows and the open blinds that had been to his back. He peered through a slit in the blinds, contemplating the day. He wondered if it would always be like this for him. Would there always be some impending tragedy that would soil his perspective on life? When he looked out the window, he saw a stark but beautiful land he hadn't had time to appreciate in years.

Appreciate? He mused, as watched a young woman who was coming up the front walk of the courthouse with two young children in tow. Remembering his own family, the wife he once had, and the two children who had grown away from him, he considered whether he had appreciated them as much as he could have. But that was the past! And it was gone! And nothing he could do *now* would ever bring them back! But the vagrant thoughts and the guilt persisted.

Still, he sat reflecting on the past. A car turned into the parking lot. The windshield and the chrome bumper flashed the sun's reflection into his eyes, causing him to squint and turn away to another matter.

Apparitions of a stranger skulked in his subconscious mind, stealing over his thoughts. *There has to be a plan. Some way to systematically smoke out this stranger!* His cigarette had long since burned to the filter, leaving a precarious ash that he carefully guided over to the ashtray, with his hand cupped underneath it.

Maybe by making Zachary Thomas think that the stranger was in some sort of jeopardy, and that he needed our protection, we could lure him in! Convincing him that it would be in his friend's best interest won't be easy! I've got to think of someone who has some influence over him, someone whose opinion he respects. It has to be someone who he trusts and admires!

He deliberated for a moment. *McCloud! Of course! He was a long time friend of the Thomas family. Thomas even went to him with the stranger! And about the trouble he had with those two men! Jack McCloud doesn't know it yet, but he may be our ticket to the stranger, Daniel.*

Except,..........why didn't anyone know his sir name? Surely Thomas asked? But he could be holding back. What about Jack McCloud,..........he's pretty wily? He would have asked!

Lemuel Redfeather straightened his tie. He hadn't seen Jack in several weeks. Perhaps this was a good time to talk to him again, something new may have come to mind about the stranger. He could also recruit Jack's assistance over lunch, regarding his plan to convince Thomas to give up the whereabouts of the stranger. Pressing the intercom button on his phone, he summoned the front desk receptionist.

"Vera! Call Jack McCloud's office. See if he has any plans for lunch today."

"Yes, Mister Redfeather," a young voice crackled over the intercom.

He glanced at his watch, it was 11:15 a.m.. Taking hold of the files spread across his desk, he straightened them into a neat pile. Then he stood up, taking the light gray, herringbone sport jacket from the back of his chair. He was pulling it over his arm when the receptionist called him.

"Anita says he has nothing on his calendar from noon until one, sir! And she said that he says he'll look forward to seeing you!" Then she giggled at the manner in which she had relayed the message.

Pressing the button to reply, he said, "Thank you, hon!"

The ride from Kayenta to Tuba City was always a welcome diversion for Lemuel Redfeather. Unless, of course, Sam Begay intruded upon his interlude from the demands of his position, with a call on the radio in his raucous voice.

It was usually when Sam was bored. He'd babble about some trivial detail, perhaps regarding an auto theft he was working on. Or someone who had called about her cousin who was being abused by her husband, who was a drunken s.o.b., and left her and her two kids sitting in the back of the pickup truck all night, while the bastard went into a bar to drink somewhere off of the reservation.

He'd ask whether or not he should follow up on it, when he knew the answer was an overt one. That no one ever pressed charges in these cases, they just liked to call and complain. And it was so prevalent that it was given very little attention. But the little toad would call anyway, right after he gave Peter Morgan an ear full of the same crap, to make a federal case out of it!

Sometimes he thought Sam Begay was worse than having a nagging wife. But something else was nagging him at the moment. That dream! The details of it were still fresh in his mind. He had never remembered one for quite this long a time, except for dreams involving more personal matters.

Like the one he had after his wife died. He had it over and over again for more than two years. That's when he was taking his own therapy, whiskey and barbiturates, to sleep through the night. Then the drinking extended into the day. Until he had almost lost his job and Jack McCloud intervened on his behalf. It was either get counseling or lose all that he had left. He took the counseling, and put himself back together. It had been almost three years ago.

But this dream was different. Why did the stranger in it match, so closely, the description of the one that they were seeking? He had read the descriptions from the statements given by Zachary Thomas, that of Jack McCloud and the people at the Highway Cafe. Was that enough to form a picture in his mind, one so lifelike it seemed uncanny? And people that he knew, but had not seen in quite some time, White Horse, the crystal gazer, and Carl Chee Thatchman, the peyote road chief, why were they part of this dream? But all of that spiritual mumbo-jumbo was not an intrinsic part of Lemuel Redfeather's thought processes. At least that's what he believed.

He was just four miles away from Tuba City when it happened.

"Lemuel! Are you there? Come in!" His radio barked. "This is Sam!"

Withdrawing the mike from its holder on the dash, he responded in a tone of perturbance, "Yes, Sam! What is it?"

He sounded close. That worried Lemuel.

"I called the station. Vera told me you were headed toward Tuba City. She wouldn't give me your destination. Jist said it was business! I'm goin' over to the Highway Cafe ta have lunch, and talk ta that Boggs woman, again. Thought ya might wanna come along!" Then he did what he usually does, he cleared his throat over the radio. It never failed to raise Lemuel Redfeather's ire.

"Thanks Sam! Sounds like a good idea, but I don't know if I can make it! I'm meeting Jack McCloud." While he was talking, Lemuel Redfeather was computing the advantages of meeting some of the potential witnesses. He was thinking it might not be a bad idea to get a handle on who these people were. If there was something Sam was missing, he might be able to pick up on it! That idea in itself was a good one, having lunch with Sam Begay was not!

"Tell you what. You go ahead and have lunch, and I'll get there as soon as I can! Over!"

"See you there!" Sam Begay belched before he released the send button on his radio. Afterward, he chuckled to himself.

It was nearly 12:15 p.m. when Lemuel Redfeather pulled in alongside Jack McCloud's four-by-four truck. Peering through the window of his car, the tread design on the front wheel of the truck caught his attention. That hint of apprehension surfaced again. He shrugged it off, as he had done earlier.

Once inside the Tuba City Tribal Council Office, Anita, Jack McCloud's secretary and receptionist, announced him.

"Mister McCloud," the attractive young Navajo woman said over the intercom, with a schooled enunciation to each word. "Mister Redfeather has arrived for your luncheon appointment. Shall I send him in?"

"Yes, please send him in, Anita!" The reply came back. She escorted Lemuel Redfeather into Jack McCloud's office.

"Where've you been, stranger?" Jack McCloud said in his charismatic voice. He stepped out from behind his desk to meet Lemuel Redfeather, nearly halfway across the room, as though he was greeting a brother.

"Thank you, Anita. You can go ahead and leave for lunch now if you'd like," he said, dismissing her.

"Come,..........sit down!" He took Lemuel's right hand in his, with a firm grip, he pulled him forward to embraced him around the shoulders. He patted him on the back. Then he wended his way back to his desk, while Lemuel Redfeather took one of the two ostentatious, black leather, high back chairs in front of him. They were obviously custom made, as was the ornate, arrogantly sized oak desk and Jack McCloud's own regal seating.

For as long as Lemuel Redfeather had known Jack McCloud, he had never failed to be impressed by his august manner. And his raconteur of a good story was renowned in the tribal political arena.

Perceptive as he was, Jack McCloud sensed that Lemuel had something on his mind. "Is there some business you want to discuss before we go to lunch?"

"There is," Lemuel admitted. Slipping back comfortably into the leather chair, his arms resting astride the thickly rolled and padded arms of it, he said, "It's that murder case, the one involving the two men from Page. It's been almost a month now, and we're nowhere near solving it!" The Superintendent conceded. "I've been considering a way to draw in that stranger, the one Zachary Thomas introduced you to!"

Jack McCloud assessed Lemuel with thought-filled eyes. "Do you still think that Thomas had something to do with the murders?"

"Well,...........he's certainly still a suspect. I've been trying to figure out the connection between Thomas and this stranger named Daniel. Is there anything more you can tell me about this man? Something you may have remembered since we last talked?"

Looking down at his desk for an instant, with his hands resting upon it and folded in front of him, he appeared to be searching his memory. Then he raised his eyes to meet those of Redfeather, and his probing expression.

"It's like I told you before! This guy was strange! He spoke like we were adversaries,............like he was delivering a message to me,............personally! Frankly, I didn't like the way this guy looked at me!"

"How's that?" Lemuel Redfeather queried.

"Just made me feel uncomfortable. He had those cold, killer eyes! That's what made me think he was on drugs,..........or maybe part of a cult. Maybe both?"

Reaching for his cigarettes, Redfeather asked, "do you mind?"

"No. Go ahead." Jack McCloud nodded, gesturing toward the ashtray at the corner of his desk.

"Refresh my memory on this message, Jack. What made you feel like it was directed at you personally."

"Oh,..........you know. It was just the way he said it," he said, somberly recalling the meeting. "The stranger said something about two forces meeting, and that it would be decisive. As if I was supposed to know what he was getting at! Kind of spooky, actually! It was some stuff about the convergence of worlds, and that only one of them would survive extinction." Jack McCloud paused for a moment, capturing a thought. "Oh, yes! There was something else he said. He mentioned that he had been around long enough to have witnessed this battle before! That's when I almost laughed in his face, but I didn't want to provoke him. I figured he might be hallucinating!"

"What kind of battle was he talking about? Did he elaborate?" Lemuel asked.

Jack shook his head. He breathed in deep. "No. Not really! He talked like he might've belonged to some environmental organization. You know how militant they are these days! So I asked him, trying to get a handle on where he was coming from. He just continued to glare at me!"

"So how did Thomas react to all of this?" Redfeather asked, inviting an opinion.

Along with his forceful personality, Jack McCloud was highly opinionated. Sometimes controversially so. And he seldom hesitated to render it when asked.

"Well, you know that I knew his family and him for quite some time. They were almost like my own family. But Zachary was always somewhat of a loner. You can ask his brother, Marvin! Anyway, I could never get very close to him, although I tried!"

Jack McCloud balked. "Now, I'm not saying that I thought he was the type to get into trouble! I just think that he's the type to be susceptible to someone like this stranger,...........and his strange ideas. I think this guy just sucked him in! I think he was just as astonished as I was at what this guy was saying. But he didn't say much! He acted as though this guy had some kind of power over him."

Releasing a sigh, Jack said, "I don't think Zachary's a murderer. I don't think he would kill anyone,..........unless, of course, it was in self-defense!"

Lemuel ruminated. "What do you think the connection is,..........between Thomas and the stranger?" Leaning forward, he buried his cigarette in the ashtray.

"It's like I said! I think this stranger has a hold on him! Zachary is, obviously, easily led and he's fallen for some spiritual contrivance!"

Taking pause at that last remark, Lemuel Redfeather measured its substance. "What makes you think it's some spiritual connection?"

"Well I,.........I just assumed if it was some type of a cult thing, that it would be that!" Jack McCloud implied haltingly.

"Say, if we're going to have lunch, we had better get going!" He said, glancing at the Rolex on his left wrist.

Lemuel Redfeather reached into the pocket of his sport coat. "There is something else I wanted to show you before we go!" He brought out the gold coin. "This was found on Skeleton Mesa where the two men were murdered," he said, handing the coin to Jack McCloud. "Have you ever seen anything like it?"

Holding it flat in his palm, Jack McCloud said in a non-reflexive tone, and with a controlled expression. "This is a very unusual coin." He turned it in his hand to view the opposite side. "I can't say that I've ever seen anything like it. Who do you think it belonged to?" He passed it back to Lemuel Redfeather with his palm moist, and beads of sweat forming above his upper lip.

"Got a fingerprint off of it! A pretty damn good one! But we haven't been able to match it up with anyone, yet! We're sure it's not Zachary Thomas's print. Didn't match the victims either! Must've belonged to their assailant." Redfeather turned it in his palm, considering it while he spoke. "Can't be sure! But we're trying to determine its origin. When we do, we may be able to pin down who it belonged to. There couldn't be too many of these around!"

Jack McCloud's expression concurred. "No. I suppose not. Have you got any leads on where it came from?"

Slipping it back into his pocket, Lemuel Redfeather replied, "Not yet! But I'm going to have an analysis done on it. Hopefully, that will shed some light on where it came from. As far as the stranger goes, I have a plan that I think might flush him out! I'll need your help! We can talk about it over lunch."

Standing, Jack McCloud said, "Sure, anything I can do, Lemuel. I'll be glad to help out!"

At the Highway Cafe, after gluttonously consuming two helpings of the luncheon special, the odious Sam Begay sat with the plain but busty Sue

Boggs in a booth opposite the lunch counter. With a toothpick that he kept rolling around one side of his mouth, he plyed his dubious investigative techniques.

He coyly alluded to her knowledge concerning the business dealings of her deceased boyfriend, Carl Simmons, of which she claimed total ignorance. Her gasp of astonishment, and a glimpse of her natural endowment, as she leaned forward stressing her complete surprise, was enough to convince Sam Begay that perhaps this fullfigured young woman, with a ruddy complexion and frizzy, brown hair, was a misled victim of circumstance.

That, coupled with her doleful, brown eyes, and the fact that Sam's brain cells had been invaded by his testosterone, had obliterated what little objectivity he may have possessed, while he sat listening to her expository concerning her tumultuous relationship with the now deceased Carl Simmons. Until Lemuel Redfeather and Jack McCloud strolled over and disturbed his intense concentration, causing him to break the death grip that his eyes had on her cleavage.

"Sam, are you making any progress here?" Lemuel Redfeather quipped, scooting onto the seat next to him.

"A,.........yeah! Miss Boggs, this is a.............Police Superintendent Lemuel Redfeather, and a..........Jack McCloud!"

"Nice to meet you, ma'am!" Lemuel Redfeather said, nodding cordially in her direction with a smile.

She got up from the table. Avoiding eye contact with Jack McCloud, she allowed him to slip into the booth. "I've really got to get back to work at the counter! As you can see we're still fairly busy, so if you will excuse me?" Appearing a bit distressed, she moved brusquely away from the table.

"What did you say to her to make her so jumpy, Sam?" Lemuel chided him in jest.

"Is that the girlfriend of one of the men that was murdered?" Jack McCloud asked casually.

"Yeah, that's her!" Sam Begay answered, pensively measuring Jack McCloud.

They had only been acquainted through Lemuel Redfeather, who had managed to keep distance between them, keeping their contact as brief as possible. He did that for two very good reasons that were obvious, if only to him. The first was that he knew how obnoxious Sam Begay could be, given the opportunity. And he was cognizant enough to know that if Sam said too much of the wrong thing, which he was prone to do, Jack McCloud had enough influence to, at the very least, make Sam's life with the department miserable. Or if he chose to, apply enough pressure to have him severed from the department. The other reason was that he knew how obtrusive Jack McCloud's opinions could be, solicited or not. Summing up the situation, Lemuel Redfeather knew it could be a volatile mixture of pesonalities that would cause him a great deal of unpleasantness from either side.

"You remember Sergeant Sam Begay?" Lemuel Redfeather asked, while he dug into his pack of cigarettes, coaxing one of the last few from the pack with his finger. He offered one to Sam. "He's working on the murder investigation, under the direction of Captain Peter Morgan."

Reaching across the table, Jack McCloud extended his neatly manicured hand to the surly Sam Begay. "Nice to see you again, Sam!" He said, smiling tolerantly, while Sam clutched his hand like the jaws of a vise. Sam's grip squeezed the large silver ring he wore, the one with the turquoise inlay, hard enough to inflict some pain. He held it long enough to get a good look at the silver wristband under the cuff of Jack McCloud's shirt sleeve. Lemuel Redfeather noticed it, too.........

The awkwardness of the moment was deferred, when Jeannie Parsons came over to take their orders. "Hi, fellas! It's not often I'm honored to serve three gentlemen of such prominence at one time!" She said, facetiously, in a summery, southern tone. Smiling, she asked, "Can I take your orders?"

"Sure, I'll just have the chef salad," Jack McCloud said, without deliberating over the menu. "And bring me a cup of coffee and a glass of water, please."

Lemuel Redfeather's attention was still riveted to the wristband.

"Lemuel, are you having anything? I'm buying today!" Jack McCloud quipped.

"Yeah, sure!" He replied, exhaling a cloud of smoke. He turned to Jeannie. "What's the special, hon?"

"Ask your friend there! He's had two of'em!" Jeannie said, chuckling sardonically. Sam Begay's eyes cast a peevish look from under his heavy brow.

"It's chicken fried steak today." She blurted, after observing Sam's humorless expression.

"Okay, that sounds good! And a cup of coffee too, please!"

"I'll take a refill, too!" Sam Begay bellowed hoarsely.

"By the way, Miss Parsons. You are Jeannie Parsons?"

"Yes, sir!"

"I'm Lemuel Redfeather of the Navajo Police Department," he said, extending his hand.

"I thought so!" She said musingly.

"I know that you've already given a statement, and Detective Begay here has questioned you regarding Zachary Thomas, and the stranger named Daniel. But I was wondering if there's anything you may have remembered since then? Something that might be of help to us in finding the stranger. Some small detail that may have come to mind? Maybe something that he said?"

"Well........." Her eyes glanced between Sam Begay and Jack McCloud

"Nothing really! I've told Detective Begay everything I know."

Lemuel Redfeather took a business card from the inside pocket of his sport coat. "Take this! And if you should think of anything at all, call me!" He paused. "It could even help clear up matters for Zachary Thomas,............he's still under suspicion you know? Anyway, we're just trying to get at the truth! If the stranger is innocent, than he has nothing to lose by coming forward!"

"You'll let them know *that* if you see either one of them, won't you Miss Parsons?" Lemuel Redfeather viewed her curiously, sensing she had more to tell. He also sensed a smoldering pain behind her gentian blue eyes, a pain likened to his own. He found it interesting how people with a similar experience could sense it in one another.

"I suppose so. That is, if I see either one of them!" She said, peering at him mindfully with unspoken words. Then she left the table.

"Do you think she knows where the stranger is, Lemuel?" Jack McCloud queried.

"Don't know!" Lemuel mused, still looking in her direction.

"I still think the girlfriend knows more'n she's tellin'!" Sam Begay growled. "I'll jist keep after her!" Begay coughed recklessly.

"You do that, Sam!" Lemuel retorted.

Jack McCloud considered them both impatiently. "So what's this plan you have, for smoking out this stranger?"

Looking at him in earnest, Lemuel said, "I think I've just implemented the first phase of it, Jack! The second phase concerns you and Zachary Thomas. I want you to call on him and let him know that you empathize with him. Let him know that he can trust you all the way! Talk about his family. Tell him you thought the stranger appeared to be a decent fellow, just a bit misguided maybe. Make him believe you're on his side! He's bound to confide in you, eventually!"

"Then you let me know how things are going. When you've got something, like the stranger's location, we'll take over! But don't put yourself in jeopardy! No sense in taking any chances on your own! You'll promise me that, won't you Jack?"

Chapter 24

A Startling Hypothesis

FOR SIX DAYS TRACY BALDWIN HAD TRIED, UNSUCCESSFULLY, TO contact Zachary Thomas at his home near Kayenta. When she was finally able to reach him, he was vague about what he had been doing. His reluctance to discuss anything regarding the stranger, Daniel, over the telephone, prompted her to suggest that they meet to share their findings. Moreover, she was curious to know if he had heard from Daniel. So she agreed to make the trip from Flagstaff to Kayenta the following day.

It was nearly ten o'clock in the morning when Tracy Baldwin arrived at the back door of Zachary Thomas's home. The sun shone brightly, but the air had a frigid bite. She knocked several times. Then she cupped her hands and raised them close to her face. She breathed on them, warming them while she stood waiting, rubbing them together vigorously to ward off the chill.

The door latch snapped. Zachary stood before her. His muscular frame occupied the opening.

"Come in," he said, while he buttoned the front of the red and white plaid, flannel shirt that he was wearing. He stepped back from the doorway. A swell of warm air enveloped her, dispatching her chill as she entered. The air was fragrant with the smell of burnt juniper logs from the wood stove.

"It's good to see you, Zachary," she said, removing her jacket.

"I've got a pot of coffee on! Have a seat at the table. I'll be with you in a minute." He walked over to the kitchen sink to wash out two cups.

"Have you heard from Daniel?" She inquired, as she took the chair nearest the sunlit dining room window.

Drying the cups with a ragged towel, he turned to face her. "No,..........I haven't!"

"Well, do you think he's still around?" Tracy Baldwin posed anxiously, her mood one of intensity.

He brought the cups to the table. "I *know* he's still around! But I'm not sure where he is!" Zachary poured the coffee. He took a chair at the corner of the table nearest her. "But I don't think we're going to haf'ta find him! I think he's going to find us!" Taking a careful sip of the hot coffee, he added, "Or someone's going to find him for us!" Then pausing, with a mindful expression, he said, "They're still lookin' for'em ya know! The police detectives were out here askin' more questions! They were wantin' to know if I've heard from'em!"

She warmed her hands delicately on the sides of the cup. Her pale fingers contrasted the rich burgundy color that adorned her long nails. "What did you tell them?" She inquired, with a pensive gaze from her dark eyes.

"Nothing. I told them nothing!" He was adamant in tone. His stoic face revealed little of his mood, although he looked at her appraisingly, taking notice of the hot pink sweater that accented the blush tint of her complexion.

Pulling streams of her long, chestnut brown hair away from her face, Tracy Baldwin said, "I've talked to some people that I know, regarding Daniel. And I've heard some interesting things! I thought perhaps you'd want to know about them!"

Pouring their cups full again with fresh coffee, Zachary asked, "What kind of things?"

She took a sip. "Well, I talked to my friend, Michael Severson, the one that's the astronomer. I showed him this coin," she said, producing it from her handbag that lie on the floor beside her chair. "I kept it in my hand the night that Daniel gave it to me," she added, placing it on the table between them.

Zachary pondered it. "He gave me one like it, too! But I seemed to have lost it! I know that I had it in my pocket the day I was arrested. But when I went to claim my belongings after they released me, it was gone! I think someone at the police station took it!"

"We're not the only ones that have them, Zachary. Our friend has *obviously* been around," she said in an imformative tone. "My friend, Michael Severson, had already seen one! He got it from one of his first year students, who was curious about the inscription on it. She wanted to know if it meant anything."

"Where did she get it?" He asked her flatly.

"She works part-time as a waitress at a truckstop restaurant in Flagstaff. Apparently she got it from one of her customers."

"I know!" He said. "We were there the same day I met him. He left a tip for the waitress. I couldn't believe it when he told me! I thought he wanted to go pretty much unnoticed, then he did that!"

Tracy gauged Zachary with an evaluating expression. "Do you think that he did it purposely? I just find it ironic, that the very person I went to about it just happened to have seen one! Don't you think that's a strong coincidence, Zachary?"

"Since I've been out to see an old friend named White Horse, I believe more than ever that he's intended for some of these things to happen all along."

The bright gold piece, lying on the table between them, caught the Indian's eye again. "What did your friend tell you about that coin?"

"He told me that this configuration of stars, on what would be the face of it, represents the Pliades or Seven Sisters in the Taurus constellation." Tracy picked it up to show him the side that she was referring to. "The sphere in the center, with its four satellites, had no particular significance to him."

"But it does represent a part of the heavens?" The Indian asked, wishing her to validate his conclusion. "And the other side, what does it say?"

She viewed him somewhat amused, but without showing it. It was his sometime childlike conception of things that intrigued her. She found it endearing. His abstract view of the world in its connectedness, always appeared to be at the forefront of his thoughts.

"Michael says it has to do with the composition of matter, the stuff that the universe is made of!" She told him.

To Zachary it made perfect sense that the stranger would know this. He took this as further assurance that Daniel was indeed the one who the Ancient Ones knew as the Spirit Messenger. Zachary's eyes were distant with his thoughts.

"He's going to have it analyzed!" Tracy said, moving her cup aside. The coffee had gone cold.

He grew more attentive. "Can I heat more coffee for you?"

"No, thank you, I've had enough. But there is more I have to tell you," she said, with a pause of consideration. Her eyes beamed with intellect. "Remember the dream that Daniel related to us? The one that he said *he* had,..........involving the four beasts?" Tracy asked.

"Yes, I remember it!" Zachary replied.

"Did you know that it corresponds to some verse from the Book of Daniel in the Bible?" Tracy inquired of him, uncertain of his religious education.

"No. I mean,............it's been a long time since I've read the Bible. When I was in elementary school, we studied it as part of the requirements for attending the Mormon boarding school, that and the Book of Mormon. But that was many years ago. And after I started high school, here on the reservation, I never picked it up again."

For an instant, Tracy considered what the best way would be to make her point. "Do you have a Bible in the house?"

"Yes. My mother always kept one, but............."

"Could you go get it for me?" Tracy asked.

"Sure, let me go find it! I think I know where it is!"

Zachary got up and went into the living room. He returned in a few minutes with a well used family Bible. "My mother read the Bible often. My father was more traditional. He believed in the old ways, like my grandfather did. Not that he didn't believe in Jesus Christ and all! But he thought our traditional ways were a better way to worship the Great Spirit!"

As she thumbed through the yellowed pages of the old Bible, Tracy considered what Zachary had just said. She realized that his integrated belief system allowed him to have a more comprehensive view of his spirituality. That he did not have to choose from one source, saying *it* was right, therefore everything else was wrong, but that he could draw from more than one place to construct a belief system that best served his needs.

"Here it is!" She said, pointing to chapter seven in the Book of Daniel. Tracy turned the Bible toward Zachary, so that he could read the verses for himself. "Read this Zachary. Tell me what you think!"

Reading it to himself, his eyes encompassed the page. *Visions of the Four Beasts* was the subtitle. His deep set eyes moved with discernment as he took in the words. An expression of recognition came upon his face, when he reached the verses describing the appearance of the four beasts. He shook his head in amazement.

He lifted his eyes from the page. "Why do you think he uses the name Daniel? And why do you think he would talk about this dream like it was his own?" Zachary assessed her for an opinion.

"Those are the questions that I pose to you, Zachary Thomas!" Tracy Baldwin asserted. "Tell me what *you* think, first! Then I'll give you my opinion."

"I must tell you that I believe he is *more* than what he appears. He is more than just a mortal man. I have come to this conclusion after my visit to the camp of my friend, White Horse, the crystal gazer," Zachary said, convinced of what he was about to tell her.

"The old man has visions. He is a seer! I have known him since I was a child, when my father and grandfather took me to visit his lodge. His words are to be trusted!" Addressing her with deeply expressive eyes, he said, "So I believed him when he told me that I have had contact with one from the spirit world! He said that, that one is the Spirit Messenger, he is The One of Many Faces! He is the one who comes from the light!" He paused. "That one I am sure is Daniel!"

Reaching for the coin on the table, he took it in hand. "White Horse had one of these!"

Tracy Baldwin appeared surprised. "Where did he get it? Has he seen Daniel?"

"No. It was given to White Horse by a Holy Man, who said it was passed down to him from the Ancient Ones. He said it was a gift from a spirit messenger! One from another world!" He considered her for a moment, with a thought-filled expression. Then Zachary continued. "But he also said that I have had contact with one from the dark side. One who is the messenger of the Dark One! White Horse told me that he is someone I know and trust! He said that these two forces are here to oppose each other. And that I am one who has been chosen to help the Spirit Messenger."

"And you believe this?" Tracy queried skeptically.

He assessed her doubt-filled eyes. "Yes, I believe this." He answered in a subdued tone. "And there is more! I also believe that he has chosen others!"

"All right! Who else do you think he's chosen to help him?" She asked more receptively.

"I think you've been chosen, too!"

"Now wait a minute............"

"Think about everything that's happened so far, Tracy! Do you think it's a coincidence that you're involved? He asked for you! He told me when I contacted you that you wouldn't refuse! Somehow he *knew* you would come."

Tracy viewed him with the analytical expression that was familiar to him. "Zachary, you have to understand that I am a scientist. I have to look for a rational explanation for things, based on fact. Don't think that I haven't considered the possibility that he is more than just an ordinary being! I have!" She took a long breath. "The things that Daniel said to me have raised some disturbing questions in my mind, questions that have caused me to reassess my own spiritual beliefs!"

Looking at him soulfully, she added, "I've even gone to a minister at the university, asking him questions about biblical prophecy! There is a part of me that can't dismiss the implications here! And that troubles me! That, and the fact that the night we were out at the ruins I had a dream, call it a nightmare, about something from the past I had chosen to forget."

Zachary gave her an understanding look. "I knew there was somethin' else! Somethin' more than just what Daniel said that disturbed you."

"It was something that happened a long time ago. I thought it was forgotten! I mean, I chose not to remember it! But the dream was so vivid. It was almost like it was happening again!" Tracy's voice cracked. "I don't understand why I had to recall it that night? Maybe it was due to the fact that I was so tired, and stressed out!"

Stifling her emotions, she said, "I think there is more here than just a spiritual connotation! If I am to consider any of this as valid at all, I would have to base my conclusions on a more scientific hypothesis."

"Meaning?" Zachary mused.

"Meaning," Tracy declared, "that you have formulated your conception of who this stranger is, based upon how *you* perceive the world. You see him as a spiritual messenger." She smiled mischievously. "I've taken it a step further!"

"Based on what he,............Daniel, has indicated regarding his knowledge of the Ancient Ones and other ancient civilizations,............these are *ifs* now! Remember, I'm merely making suppositions here! And trust me, I wouldn't discuss this with anyone else but you! At least at this point in time."

Smiling almost inperceptibly, Zachary laughed inwardly. He wondered if what she had just said should be taken as a compliment? Was she saying that she trusted him enough to confide in him, or that he was someone whose opinion of her mattered very little, therefore she was willing to risk appearing foolish. Could he and the Anglo woman really be friends? Could they be more than that? Regardless, he was intent on hearing her theory.

"Okay, how do *you* see this stranger?" He asked her, recalling what Daniel had told him in regard to the way that others would see him, their mind's eye perceiving him the way that they wanted to.

"Well, like I said." Tracy continued, looking astute. "Taking into consideration his knowledge of past civilizations. And the fact that he knew the location of that wall painting. Then giving him credit for having firsthand knowledge of its origin, and assuming that his assertion regarding the time frame in which it was placed there is accurate, one could say it is plausible that his claim in reference to time travel is correct."

She paused, measuring Zachary for a response. He was silent, viewing her curiously. "Then there's the coin! Or coins! I hadn't considered them very significant at first. But when they started showing up in the hands of other people, like my friend, Michael Severson, the astronomer, and now your friend, White Horse, it makes me wonder if the Ancient Ones had a visitor over seven hundred years ago! It would fill some gaps," she persisted.

"It would explain how some of the mythology evolved, regarding the migration of the Ancient Ones between worlds. It might also explain how other civilizations had some advanced knowledge that appeared to be otherwise out of the realm of their capabilities for that time." Tracy mused. "What if it were possible?"

Zachary had listened attentively. But her suppositions posed more questions in his mind. "So you're saying that Daniel is not a spirit messenger? That he's some other kind of being? If that's true, than what about the dreams?"

His comments gave rise to contention regarding her own dream. Yet Tracy Baldwin saw it as a separate matter, not to be confused with anything having to do with the stranger.

"I'm not saying that he may not be a messenger! I'm questioning whether or not he is a spirit messenger! Don't you think that the Ancients could have misinterpreted the stranger's identity? Because of their lack of understanding of the world, they could only perceive him as a god or a deity!"

"Yes, but what about the dreams?" Zachary reiterated. "How do you explain them?"

"What makes you believe that Daniel is responsible for your dreams? Did he tell you that he was?" Tracy asked.

"No. But they appeared to be connected to my involvement with Daniel, and the circumstances surrounding the murders of the two men on the mesa. Anyway, I haven't told you *all* of what I know about him! I've seen him do some things! He has these powers!"

Her dark eyes searching him with intensity, Tracy's face posed an inquisitive expression. "What kind of powers?"

"Telepathic powers! He can tell what you're thinking! It happened a couple times while I was with him! He knew what I was thinking about," Zachary insisted.

"Are you sure he wasn't just guessing?" She asked.

With a resolute expression, he said, "Not about the things that he knew! And there were other things, too. He saved my life in Flagstaff! He has this way with animals! And some kind of healing power! I'm not sure what it is, but when he touches you, you get this tingling sensation! Then it feels like some warm energy is moving through your body! I know I didn't imagine it!"

"All right! Suppose he can do these things..............."

"No. Not suppose!" Zachary protested rigidly.

"All right! All right!" Tracy relented. "Even from my point of view, a more advanced being might possess extraordinarily well developed senses, or powers! But that doesn't make him a spiritual being! After all, the mind can be a very powerful tool, and at best, we only use ten percent of its capacity."

Considering her premise, Zachary added, "He can move objects, too! We were out at the stone arch when I asked him to bring me the ice chest, while I was preparin' our dinner. I expected him to get up from where he sat to bring it to me. Instead, he just stared at it! Until it started slidin' across the dirt! By itself!"

Giving her a perplexed look, he said, "I think he's a spirit messenger! White Horse *says* he's a spirit messenger! Now you're tellin' me that you think he's an extraterrestrial being of some kind, that visited the Ancient Ones over seven hundred years ago! That would make him well over seven hundred years old!"

"Remember what he said about knowing *of* the one who put the painting on the wall?" Tracy said, jogging his memory. "I'm not saying that he necessarily *is* the one who visited them seven hundered and fifty years ago! But he could be part of a race that did!" She breathed deeply.

"As you can see, I've been giving this a great deal of thought. And I've even asked my friend, Michael Severson, to do some research for me. I've asked him to try to establish the origin of the metal, or metals, in the coin. I've also asked him to try to decipher the equation on the back of the coin! But I've told him very little of what we already know! He's very objective. As well he should be!" Tracy shook her head in consternation. "I seem to have lost some of mine! Objectivity, that is!"

Zachary deliberated. All of her conjecture caused him to query further. "What about the biblical context of Daniel's account involving his dream? How does this all tie together?"

Laughing, Tracy said, "I was hoping you wouldn't ask! But, like I told you, I've been doing a lot of thinking! And, of course, I've come up with a theory about that, too!"

"Which is?" Zachary asked.

"I hope you're ready for this! If what I think is true, it could shatter the foundation of organized religion!" Tracy hesitated.

"Go ahead! *I'm* not going to chastise you for heresy!"

"Well, what if! What if all of the religious mythology, and doctrine on which we as societies have established our beliefs and value systems, was a product of our ancient ancestors contact with an advanced race that has monitored our evolution?" She paused. "What if all the great teachers were, in fact, transplanted at critical times in our history to, say, bring us along our evolutionary path? Maybe even to a point where we would be ready to make contact with such beings? Imagine that!"

"And you're saying that this is that point in time?" Zachary asked.

Tracy mused. "I sincerely doubt it! I mean, I think we, as a world society, are hardly ready. Unfortunately, I think we have a long way to go! But maybe because we're getting closer, we're up for some sort of evaluation of some kind?"

Pondering her thoughts momentarily, Zachary asked, "What about him using the name Daniel? Why did he relate the dream to his own experience?"

"Why not?" Tracy offered. "If you were making contact with a somewhat primitive race of sentient beings, and you had knowledge of the thoughts and ideas on which they based their belief system, wouldn't you use something that you thought was a mutual basis for communication? Besides, I'm not totally convinced, based on what you've told me of his powers, that he couldn't have influenced thought patterns to create a dream sequence in our minds!"

"Then he could be an extraterrestrial," Zachary conceded. "And if he is capable of traveling in time, than he could be bringing us a message about the future! To warn us! Maybe that's what he's been trying to tell me all along?" He hesitated thoughfully for a moment. "Than White Horse could still be right about what he saw in his vision!"

"Perhaps," Tracy admitted.

"And what about the Dark One that White Horse spoke of? Who would he be?" Zachary asked her with inquisitive eyes.

Peering out through the dining room window, Tracy gathered her thoughts. "There is duality in everything," she mused. "It is the natural order of things throughout the universe, I suppose! For every force there is an opposite force. What kind of a world would it be, if we didn't have anything to which we could make comparisons? If everything was only one way, than how would we recognize what is best? Where would our choices be?"

She Laughed. "I've gone off on a tangent here, but to answer your question,...........maybe it's us! Maybe it's the darker side of our nature, that someone is trying to save us from? Or maybe it's another life form? The universe must be full of them! Perhaps not all of them are benevolent beings, Zachary! I don't know!"

"But why did he choose us?" Zachary inquired. "Do you think it was a matter of chance?"

"I don't think it would have been left to chance!" Tracy asserted. "Perhaps because we are familiar with the point of contact, the ruins! I'm not sure! Maybe we'll get a chance to ask him?"

Zachary viewed her with a ponderous expression. "Not maybe, Tracy! I'm sure we will be seeing him again. I can feel it!"

"Then what do we do in the meantime?" She asked.

"Wait," he answered, as he looked speculatively beyond her, through the window into the distance.

Chapter 25

The Guiltless Eyes of Passion

AN ICY, WAXEN MOON DOMINATED A COLD STYGIAN FIRMAMENT. It was filled with myriad shimmering celestial lights.

Perched on a ledge above the ruins, huddled against a crag of stone, he stood vigil over the tableau bathed in the lunar glow. His acute aural sense monitored what his keen nocturnal vision could not. Every feral sound, and every stealthy movement assailed his superior perception.

With a woolen blanket wrapped taut to his body, his now bearded face was immersed in a dim aura of light and shadows. His disciplined eyes charted the heavens like an ancient mariner. Peering steadily into the night sky, he searched the heavens for a glimmer from the distant beacon that had hailed his arrival. Now he sought its cue for his departure.

He looked wily, as he considered what he had come for. Stroking his beard, he knew it was time for him to move. He had studied his adversary, and he knew how to rout the beast from his lair. They were venerable foes, he and this one. Each of them had taken their turn at being the hunter and the hunted! The One of Many Faces had won and lost equally as many times. And again, the outcome was uncertain!

Smoke drifted without course, from the smoldering fire in the center of the kiva. The aroma of it beckoned to him, arousing his sense of primitive comfort. He would take shelter for the night, and in the morning he would commence the final leg of his arduous journey.

Tossing the blanket from his shoulders, he arose. He retrieved it from about his boots, shaking it, as he pulled it up from the ground. Bundling the blanket under his arm, he wended down the cliffs to the kiva.

Once inside, he stoked the fire. The flickering yellowish light cast his animated silhouette on the aged walls of the kiva, as he spread the blanket on the earthen floor beside the fire. He sunk down onto it, warming his hands by the flames that hungrily licked the dry juniper suckers he had fed into it.

Gazing into the busy flames, he watched as the sap boiled out of the wood, then caught fire and sizzled, while burning droplets fell to the ground leaving a charred black crust in its wake. He contemplated where he would go first, and who he would encounter in his path. He knew all of them. He knew every detail about them, and what they feared!

He drew his pack near to him, taking from it the pemmican that he had prepared for himself. Unwrapping one of the dry meat cakes, he took a bite. In his mind, he acknowledged gratefully that what the Ancient Ones had taught him had served him well. He reminisced about the seasons he had spent with them in this place: about the times that they counseled in this kiva, and about how they had grown to revere one another. Then he remembered the medicine man with affection, and the last words they had spoken..

§ § §

"I'm glad you could make it this evening," Lemuel Redfeather said.

Jeannie Parsons sat down on the bar stool next to him. He was sipping a diet cola. "Can I buy you a drink?" He asked, glancing over at her.

"Sure," she said passively, placing her purse on the bar next to her. Her flaxen hair was let down. It cascaded luxuriantly below her shoulders.

Lemuel Redfeather hailed the bartender. He was at the opposite end of the bar attempting to wake up an Indian, whose head was lying atop his folded arms in a drunken stooper. The man had been drinking all day. He had cashed his government check before he arrived with a pocket full of cash. Now his pockets were empty and his friends had left him.

It was a Thursday evening, and business was unusually slow for this time of day. A few Indians sat together in a booth across the dimly lit barroom. There were two Anglo men who sat next to each other at the bar, several stools down from Lemuel Redfeather. They took notice when Jeannie Parsons arrived. Then they resumed their conversation.

"What can I getcha', ma'am?" The burly, thick-bearded bartender asked with a snaggletoothed smile. His black eyes leered at her, with beads of perspiration looming over his brow. The sleeves of his western style shirt were rolled over his flabby forearms. And his bright red suspenders clashed with the green and white, sweat stained plaid shirt.

She averted his gaze while answering, "A gin and tonic please. Lots of ice and a twist of lime."

"Comin' right up, ma'am!" The bartender lumbered away to the backbar, his stout buttocks strained the seams of his pants, and his unkempt, long, curly black hair jutted wildly, giving him the appearance of a cannibalistic troglodyte. It was a sufficient deterrent for most of his routy customers.

"Sorry to bring you all the way out here, Miss Parsons. I just didn't want to meet anywhere on the reservation. Gray Mountain's the only place I could think of close enough to where you live," Lemuel Redfeather said apologetically, while he considered her soft blue eyes. The tone of her creamy complexion was lucid, even in the subdued light from the neon beer signs over the backbar. The same light caused her long, dangling silver earings to shimmer contrastingly against her pale skin. He noticed.

"That's all right," she told him, taking a pack of filtered cigarettes from her purse. She withdrew one from the pack, then raised it to her mouth, laying the pack down on the bar. Lemuel lit it for her. Then he lit one of his own.

"Here's yur drink, ma'am! That'll be two fifty," the bartender said, wiping his brow with the same towel that he had used to wipe down the bar. Lemuel Redfeather patted the stack of bills in front of him to indicate that he was paying. The bartender took two bills and some change, then he sauntered to the other end of the bar to resume his efforts to eject the Indian.

"Didn't know women from Texas drank gin and tonic!" Lemuel quipped. He took a long hit from his cigarette.

"Texas ain't the only place I've ever been!" Jeannie retorted. She smiled at him, revealing her full, blush lips.

He took a sip of cola. "Where else have you been?" He asked casually.

"I use to live in Vegas! I left Brownfield, Texas, for the big city lights when I was nineteen. Wanted to be a dancer!"

Lemuel mused over the ice in the bottom of his glass. "So, how did you end up out here?"

Jeannie took a long draw from her cigarette. She exhaled. Then she said, "I got real tired of the fast life! I wanted to get as far from it as possible!" She raised the sweating tumbler to her lips and took a lengthy sip.

Pondering what she had said, Lemuel asked, "Why didn't you go back to Brownfield?"

"You sure ask a lot of questions!" She said, uncomfortably.

"It comes with the job. I guess I get carried away sometime!" Lemuel admitted. "What I really asked you out here for, was to tell me what you know about this stranger, Daniel. And about Zachary Thomas! I had a feeling that you had more to say the other day, but you were hesitant!"

"I see!" Jeannie nodded, lending credence to his observation. He thoughtfully studied her expression.

"I've really told your detective all I know about the stranger." She insisted. "I only met him the one time! He struck me as someone who wasn't from around here! But he didn't seem to be the criminal type. I mean, into drugs or anything like that!"

"You said that Thomas was acting somewhat peculiar! Do you know him well?" Lemuel asked pointedly.

"I just know him from the cafe." Jeannie offered flatly. "He comes in a lot! And we talk sometime,.............that's all! That morning when he came in with this Daniel, he seemed kind of tense. Otherwise, he's usually pretty easy going! Do you think they murdered Jake and Carl?" Her eyes inquired of him intently.

He deliberated over her question for a moment, while he took another cigarette from the pack, then Lemuel offered her one. He lit hers, then his own. "We don't have any other suspects! Thomas's background leaves no indication that he would be involved in anything illegal, but he, and maybe this missing stranger, whoever *he* is, were out around the mesa the night that the two men were murdered!" He paused to take a hit from his cigarette. "Unless *you* have something more to offer that would help clear them?" He posed to her, with a furtive curiosity.

Jeannie peered into the bottom of her empty glass. "You mind if I have another?" She asked in an edgy voice.

Lemuel caught the attention of the bartender. He ordered another drink for both of them.

"Did you see either one of them in the cafe after that morning?" He asked.

"Well.........." She was reluctant. "Zachary did come in for lunch, late one afternoon!"

The bartender returned with their drinks. "Thanks," Lemuel said, pushing some bills toward him. He was quiet until the bartender walked away.

"Did you talk to Thomas when he came in?"

That same look of concealment, the one that Lemuel Redfeather so readily recognized from years of experience, crossed her face. She was suddenly feeling cornered. Jeannie took a heavy sip from her drink, while she considere how what she knew could effect the stranger, Zachary Thomas, and hersel as well. Yet, she believed in their innocence. And she knew she was here fo that reason. But that wasn't the only reason she had agreed to meet Lemue Redfeather here, in this place, at this hour.

Turning to him, she parted her lips slightly, then hesitated. "Yes, w talked," she admitted. "He was worried about the break-in at his home! H thought that Carl and Jake had followed him and Daniel. He said he though they were looking for something! I knew that Sue,............Sue Boggs, wa seeing Carl. They came into the cafe from time to time. I told him that the were *bad* boys! And that it wouldn't surprise me if they *had* broken into hi place."

"What did he think they were looking for? Did he say?" Lemuel wa pensive.

"He showed me a coin. It was a gold coin! I haven't seen very mar gold coins, but this one was unusual. It kind a reminded me of one of tho special addition type of coins, that you see advertised in the magazines. You know! Those commemorative kind!" Jeannie implied, moving her hands expressively as she spoke.

Lemuel Redfeather maintained his remoteness. He lit another cigarette. Absentmindedly, he forgot to offer one to Jeannie Parsons. She took one of her own. He lit it for her.

"Did he say where he got it?" He asked.

She was hesitant. Taking a hit from her cigarette, she considered him for a moment with mindful eyes. "He said he got it from Daniel. He called it a token."

"A token of what?" Lemuel queried persistently.

"I don't know. He didn't say. Friendship, I guess!" Jeannie supposed.

"Did he say if the stranger had more of those coins?"

"He didn't."

Fidgeting with the cardboard coaster on the bar in front of him, he asked, "If this Daniel wasn't there with him, did he say where he might have been?"

"Well,...........first he said that Daniel was out at his house, keeping an eye on it while he was in town. But later he said that Daniel had disappeared while they were out near Skeleton Mesa," she admitted more freely than ever. The second drink had loosened her tongue.

"Disappeared?"

"Yeah. He said they were camping under the stone arch that night. Daniel had walked off during the night while Zachary was sleeping, he said! He was going back out the following night to find him!" Jeannie swirled the ice cubes in her glass, then she downed the remainder of her drink.

Lemuel mused confidently. If his hunch was correct, before too long he would be finding the stranger. His instincts had signaled him correctly about Jeannie Parsons as well. Although he remained expressionless, his adrenal glands were secreting at an accelerated rate. It was at times like this that he felt the primitive blood of his ancestors pulsing through his arteries. He likened it to the culmination of a successful hunt. *After all*, he thought,*we aren't far removed from the animals. There are only the hunters and the hunted! It's the scent of the kill that sometimes drives us!*

"So they were *both* out there that night!" He thought aloud.

"I guess so!" Jeannie replied. "I mean, if he was lost out there somewhere? At first, when he told me that Daniel disappeared, I thought maybe Jake and Carl kidnapped him to get more of those coins! But Zachary said there was no evidence of it!" She contemplated the melting cubes in the bottom of her glass.

"There is something else I forgot to tell Detective Begay," she added. "Carl and Jake were in the day before I saw Zachary that last time. They knew about the coins, because they asked me if Daniel had given me anything special! I just remembered it!"

Lemuel was pleased with all that he had heard. It was starting to come together in his mind. "Did it ever come up during the conversation, as to where this Daniel was from?"

"Yes," Jeannie recalled, "now that I think of it! That's the strange part! Zachary said that he didn't belong here. It was the part of our conversation that kind of scared me. Zachary seemed convinced that Daniel was from another world! I had never heard him talk so *strangely* before! He just seemed *so* convinced," she said emphatically. "It was like Daniel had some kind of hold on him. He worried me!"

Jeannie searched the inside of her cigarette pack with the forefinger of her right hand, it was empty. "I'm out!" She said, looking around the room for a cigarette machine.

"I have some!" Lemuel offered.

Looking at her watch, Jeannie said, "It's getting late. It's already eleven thirty. You have a long drive ahead of you,............unless you'd prefer to spend the night at my place? I mean, it is much closer. And I hate to see you drive so far at this hour! We could finish our conversation there. I'll put on some coffee, if you like!"

He saw no reason to decline. It was part of that painful recognition that drew them. He knew that. Admittedly, at least to himself, he was curious about her pain. It was those unspoken words that caused him to ask her here under the guise of business. But she knew, as well as he did, where this was leading. Neither one seemed resistant to it.

"Perhaps that's a good idea. Are you sure it won't be an inconvenience?" Lemuel asked as a matter of propriety.

"Not at all! I wouldn't have offered!" Jeannie asserted. "Just follow me! I live about thirty minutes away!"

Leaving Highway 89, eighteen miles north of Flagstaff, they turned onto a secluded gravel drive that meandered through a ponderosa pine forest, along the edge of a small pond, then it emerged beside a meadow. A gibbous moon in a midnight sky effused a delicate aureole of light that enchanted the surroundings.

A whitetail doe stood frozen, blinded by the headlight beams, its slender legs set rigid. Its large, brown, guiltless eyes absorbed the light, reflecting it back at them. Then with a single skiddish leap, it cleared the brush alongside the road and dissappeared.

They arrived at the rented alpine bungalow shortly after 12:00 a.m.. It was nestled in a thicket of spindly aspin, on the edge of the meadow, overshadowed by the snow capped San Francisco Peaks. Several small cabins skirted the edge of the woods. A few solitary lamps dotted the windows of each. The coachlamp at the door of the A-frame cottage emitted an amber light. Jeannie turned her key in the door as Lemuel ascended the steps to the edwood deck behind her.

Entering, she asked, "Can I take your jacket?" Jeannie turned fluidly to ne guest closet. She slipped out of her coat and hung them both up. "Have a eat. I'll make some coffee," she said. Then she dashed off to the kitchen.

Lemuel sat down on a wood-frame maple sofa with quilted cushions. He urveyed the interior of the cottage. Its oblique walls were covered with orizontal knotty pine boards that met at an apex above the second story loft. 'he loft was skirted with a pine rail, it served as a bedroom. A red, tubular piral staircase jutted up from a polished, pine floor to meet an opening in ne rail. The large, open room where he sat, was furnished with two maple hairs, laden with overstuffed cushions and throw pillows of earthy hues, nd two round maple lamp tables, with early American milkglass lamps atop elicate white doilies: one placed in the corner to his right, between the sofa nd one chair that was set in front of a large window. The other sat across the oom beside another chair, next to a tall, field stone fire place that was built nto the wall.

It's neat and comfortable, Lemuel mused, reaching for a magazine from ne coffee table in front of him. He noted the name on the address label, then e placed it back as Jeannie entered the room. He wondered what she was unning away from? Suspicion was an innate habit with Lemuel Redfeather.

Placing herself beside him on the sofa, at a distance she felt comfortable or the moment, she said, "The coffee will be ready in a few minutes." Jeannie miled demurely.

With his arms outstretched on the back of the sofa, Lemuel considered er. Then he said, "Somehow, I don't see you this way, out here, isolated rom everything like this! It seems out of place for you."

"There may have been a time when that was true," she said, "but I've hanged. And the things that I want have changed, too." Her tone was ngenuous. She got up from the sofa. "I'll go get the coffee!"

"Can I help?" Lemuel asked.

"Sure! Do you take cream or sugar?" Jeannie inquired as he followed er into the kitchen.

"No, thank you. Just black." He replied, with a politeness to his voice hat intoned more than a casual regard.

When she reached the counter where the coffee pot and two cups rested, emuel came up behind her. He pressed up against her, placing his arms round her waist. He held her there. She closed her eyes. She tensed. He nelled her hair. Then he kissed her neck. He moved his hands up slowly ondling her compliant breasts. She turned in his arms and opened her eyes, eering deep into his. She moistened her full lips, leaving them parted. Then e held her tightly, kissing her with years of pent up passion.

After hours of exhaustive love making, they lie naked in her bed fondling nd caressing one another. And saying those unspoken words. The scent of sex lingered between them.

Lemuel rolled over on his back. He put his hands behind his head and stared up at the ceiling with grief-filled eyes.

"What's wrong, Lemuel?" Jeannie asked in a tone of deep concern, as she leaned over him and gently stroked the side of his face with a supple hand.

Emitting a deep sigh, he answered, "It's been so long. I guess I knew this would happen. I guess I wanted it to!" He took a hollow breath.

She kissed his forehead. "What is it that's hurting you?"

Reluctantly, he said, "I lost my wife five years ago. I guess I've just been afraid." He hesitated. "When I saw you, I knew I wanted you. But I just didn't think it would happen this quickly!"

"How did you lose her?" Jeannie asked.

"She commited suicide."

"That's awful. I'm sorry," she said, with solace in her voice.

With a reflective look, Lemuel said, "I blame myself. I should've seen it coming! But I didn't! I was so involved in my work." He swallowed hard. "My children hold me responsible. They blame me because I wasn't there when she died. They're right! If I had been there, I could've prevented it!"

Looking away from his face, with an anguished expression, she said, "We can't always know these things! We don't know when something is going to happen. We just do the best we know how at the time!" Jeannie's eyes swelled with tears. "I guess we just have to go on. We can't blame ourselves forever. It doesn't bring them back." She said, baring her conscience. She started to sob. Then she laid her head down on his chest.

He put his arms around her and held her close for a time, massaging her back tenderly with his hand. The sentience of her velvet-like skin was soothing to him.

Then, stroking her hair, he asked, "What is it that you're running away from?"

Jeannie remained silent.

"I could see it in your eyes when I met you. It was that same persistent pain that I recognized," Lemuel told her.

At last she spoke, "I lost my son when he was nine years old," she admitted, controlling the sentiment in her voice. "It was six years ago in September. It's been hard. I've blamed myself, too! It doesn't seem possible that it's been that long already. Sometimes it feels like it just happened yesterday. There's not a day that goes by, that I don't think about it! I wonder what I could have done differently. I don't think you can ever put it completely out of your mind, you just become more comfortable with the pain!" She sighed deeply.

While he caressed her, Lemuel asked thoughtfully, "What happened?"

"I was raising Matthew by myself! I had gotten pregnant in my senior year of high school. That's why I left Brownfield! I knew who Matts father was, but I couldn't tell my daddy! He would have killed him! So I left! I wanted to get as far away from there as possible, and get a fresh start! I thought I could get a job in Vegas and make some real good money, so I could support Matt and myself," Jeannie said all of this with a ponderous expression, appearing to relive every detail of that past.

Lemuel listened in silence. He listened attentively. He looked upon her with empathetic eyes, that welled up with painful recollections of his own. And with too many, lonely, tiring hours of reflection over a past that he could not alter.

She went on in a torrent of soulful reckoning. "I waited tables in a coffee shop for a while, until Matt was a year old. An elderly woman, who lived in the apartment next door to mine, sat with him during the day. Later I found a woman who cared for children in the evenings. She babysat for the girls who had kids and worked in the casinos at night. That's when I got a job as a cocktail waitress. The money was good. Some weeks I made almost a thousand dollars in tips. We were able to get a decent apartment, and I was able to give Matt all of the things that he needed." She added, "With my hours, I was able to get him ready for school in the morning, and be with him for a while when he got home. Things were really going well!" Then Jeannie paused, casting her eyes downward in regret.

"Until I met this guy! I had a few male friends, that I saw occasionally, but nobody serious. It was just me and Matt. I didn't have a lot of time for a social life, working most nights! I got hit on a lot at work, mostly drunks. There was never anyone that I would've trusted or cared to go out with! Then I met a man who didn't work in the casinos. He had a daytime job, working construction. I met him in a supermarket one Saturday morning, when Matt and I were shopping. He seemed really nice! Matt didn't have a male figure around, and he really took a liking to this guy! We started seeing each other when I was off, and he'd come into the casino now and then and visit with me on my breaks. Well, one thing led to another, and pretty soon he was living with us. He would stay with Matt while I was at work. Sometimes they would go to ball games, or he would take Matt to the arcade to play video games. I thought he was the answer for both of us! I thought he was just what we both needed." Jeannie paused reflectively. "It just seemed so right!"

With reluctance, she added. "I guess I didn't know enough about him! I began to get suspicious when I started getting strange phone calls during the day. They would ask for Greg. When I asked for their names, so I could have him return their calls, they would hang up! When I asked him about it, he said that they were just people he had worked with on construction jobs. That they were just trying to reach him about work, and that they would call back at night when I wasn't there! I had no reason not to believe him."

She emitted a deep, remorseful sigh. "But that wasn't it at all! He was selling drugs at night! And he was taking Matt along with him to make his connections. He lied to Matt, so Matt wouldn't tell me. I didn't find out until it was too late! One night, apparently something went wrong with one of his deals. Someone opened fire on the car with a semi-automatic weapon," she said tearfully. "Greg was struck in the head by a bullet, while he was driving away. He was killed instantly. Matthew was sitting beside him in the front seat. He was shot, too! But it was the crash that killed him. The car swerved into the path of a large truck. Matthew's body was thrown through the windshield and................" Jeannie sobbed convulsively.

Gasping, she said, "I didn't even know about it until I finished my shift. There was a message on my answering machine,............from the police! When I called, a sergeant asked me to come down and identify the bodies. I was alone. I didn't even know if I could make it! So they sent a squad car to pick me up. Afterward, the sergeant called my best girlfriend to come and get me!"

It was almost daybreak when Jeannie, who was spent of emotion, said in a piteous voice, "I thought it was a horrible nightmare,...............but I could never wake up from it!"

Chapter 26

The Day of the Hunters

BY DAWN, THE STRANGER HAD ALREADY PUT SEVERAL MILES between himself and the ruins.

Parking his four-wheel-drive truck on the ridge below the stone arch, he stepped down onto the crust-hard ground. It crunched beneath his feet. The dank essence of winter had set upon the primordial landscape. He braced himself against the frigid wind, drawing the collar of his coat snug to his neck. The ocherous rays of a young sun were puny against the biting cold.

Withdrawing a pair of binoculars from the interior of the truck, he set them on the hood. He brought out a backpack, and then a rifle with a scope mounted to it. He placed them atop the truck next to the binoculars.

He was a seasoned hunter.

Moving adroitly, the stranger scudded along the arroyo that carved its way through the canyon. He knew the hunter had come. With cunning, he left the crumbs of evidence that marked his trail.

The heavy footed Sam Begay burst into Lemuel Redfeather's office. Throwing the door open without caution, it caused the glass pane in the door to rattle as it bounced off the wall. He bounded across the floor and landed with a thud into a chair in front Lemuel, who was shaken from a somnolent state.

"Lemuel............," he bellowed, "the Reno P. D. picked up that fella you M.O.'d from the M.V.R.!"

"DON'T EVER DO THAT!!!" Lemuel growled, catching Sam by surprise. He rubbed his eyes, trying to focus on the hulking caricature seated before him.

Assessing the frazzled specter, and stifling his exuberance, Sam Begay said in a much subdued tone, "Jeez, Lemuel, you look like shit! You ain't looked that bad since............. Must a had a bad night, huh?"

With his hand supporting the side of his face and his elbow planted firmly on the desk, Lemuel peered at him with redened, intolerant eyes, asking, "What's up Sam?"

"Well,...........it's like I was sayin'! The Reno P.D. picked up the guy from your M.O.. They questioned him regardin' his whereabouts for the last six weeks. Looks like he has an alibi! He was workin' for a contractor in Reno at the time of the murders. Didn't miss any work either!"

"So what was he doing around here within the last two weeks?" Lemuel retorted.

"Says he was pickin' up his kids from his ex in Phoenix, and they did a little sight seein' on the way back. Says he wanted to show them real Indian ruins!" Sam Begay grunted. "Checked it out myself with his ex! She confirms it. Says he told her he was comin' up here, before returning to Reno with the kids for Thanksgiving! Looks like a dead end!"

"Yeah!" Lemuel concurred. "But we're getting closer to the stranger! I got a bit of information that makes him look like he's our man! Seems Zachary Thomas has one of those coins, too! He got it from the stranger. At least that's what he told Jeannie Parsons, when he showed it to her! Her description of it matches the one we found up on Skeleton Mesa," he said, adding, "And that's not all!

Slumping back into his chair, Sam Begay raised a suspicious brow.

"The stranger wasn't at Thomas's house the day that Thomas came into town, to pay a visit to Jack McCLoud, like he told us! Seems he had disappeared out at the mesa sometime the night before, according to what Zachary Thomas told Jeannie,.............I mean Miss Parsons," Lemuel added nervously. "That means he was already there, when Zachary Thomas returned that night!" Lemuel nodded assuredly. "He's got to be our man!"

Sam Begay mused, "When'd you talk to the Parsons woman?"

"I told her to call me if she remembered anything! Well, she did! She called me yesterday morning. Wanted to meet me to discuss it," Lemuel remarked casually.

"Ahuh!" Sam quipped, raising both brows. "So you think Thomas is his accomplice or his patsy?"

"I'm just not sure, yet!" Lemuel replied.

"What about the tire tracks? They don't match up with Thomas's truck!"

Begay groused.

Lemuel raised a mindful eye. "It could've been a hunter! May've been up there a day or two before! A coincidence!"

Acquiescing, Sam Begay shook his head. "Yeah, why not!" Then he thought further. "What about the coin? Do we know where it was made? Maybe we can track this stranger that way?"

"I meant to take it to a metallurgist in Flagstaff yesterday, but something else came up!" Lemuel stated in his own defense, against Sam Begay's accusing eyes.

"Yeah, I know!" Sam quipped.

Opening the top drawer of his desk, Lemuel reached inside for the bag containing the coin. He had returned it after his meeting with Jack McCloud. To his bewilderment, it was not where he had put it.

"It's not here! I know I put it here the other day!" His hand scrambled over the contents of the drawer, searching frantically for the coin. "Jesis! What could I have done with it?"

"You a...........sure you didn't leave it somewhere?" Sam grumbled. "Maybe...........a, never mind!"

Pulling the drawer out of the desk, Lemuel dumped its contents onto the desktop, causing Sam Begay to view him in amazement. "It's just not here!"

"Vera," he shouted over the intercom. "Get Peter Morgan in here!" Then he took a swipe at the articles on his desk, whisking them back into the empty drawer he held at the edge of the desk. Replacing it, he dropped back into his chair, rubbing his forehead in disbelief. When Lemuel Redfeather realized how he looked to the befuddled Sam Begay, he quickly regained his composure.

Captain Peter Morgan stepped halfway through the door opening with a puzzled look about him. "Vera said you wanted to see me!" He stood there momentarily, awaiting a response.

"Come in and close the door!" Lemuel Redfeather commanded. "Take a seat!" Sam Begay considered him with big eyes .

"Is there a problem, Lemuel?" Peter Morgan inquired politely. Sam just covered his eyes with his hand and shook his head, contemplating a long and agonizing session.

"Yes, there is a problem. A piece of evidence is missing." He retorted in a more moderate tone. "The coin is missing from my desk drawer. I want to know if you've seen it?"

Peter Morgan gave Lemuel an appraising look. "No, I haven't seen it since the last time you brought it out, and said that you were going to have it analyzed. Maybe you left it somewhere, Lemuel," he said, absent of guile. He mused over Lemuel Redfeather's haggard look.

"I know it was here yesterday!" Lemuel insisted. "If you don't have it! And Sam doesn't have it! And you two are the only ones who knew where it was beside myself, than where is it?"

Each of them glared at the other, waiting for a response. None was forthcoming.

"Vera, come in here please!" Lemuel mustered politely over the intercom. He snatched a nearly empty pack of cigarettes from his desk. He lit one. Then he straightened his tie, and sat back in his chair, taking a long draw from his cigarette.

Before him were all those who had access to his office. Everyone else, including the few deputies who worked out of the Kayenta District Station, had no reason to come into his office. And nobody could get in without going by the desk of his receptionist, Vera Yazzi.

Peter Morgan offered his chair to the young woman.

"Vera, has anyone been in my office recently, other than Sergeant Begay, Captain Morgan, or yourself?" Lemuel Redfeather asked her.

She looked at him sheepishly. "Well, I'm not sure. I mean, no one has been in here while I was up front, but................"

"But what, Vera?" Lemuel coaxed her.

"But yesterday afternoon after you left, Mister McCloud was here to see you! He asked if you were here, and I told him you weren't! But I had to go to the ladies room, and there was no one else here, so I asked him if he could watch the office for just a minute! I know I wasn't gone for more than five minutes at the very most! Honest!" She confessed.

"I thought it would be all right because of who he is, since you know him and all," she said with apprehension in her voice. "That was okay, wasn't it?" Vera asked. She looked over her shoulder at Peter Morgan, then to her side at Sam Begay, and then back to Lemuel Redfeather, searching each of their faces for approval.

Lemuel nodded approvingly, letting the young woman off the hook. He exhausted a stream of smoke through his nostrils. "Yes, Vera, that was all right! You can return to your desk now! Thank you!"

Before she had cleared the door, he picked up the phone. He punched out a number that he didn't have to look up on his desktop directory. Sam Begay and Peter Morgan eyed him knowingly.

"Hello, Anita! This is Lemuel Redfeather, can I talk to Jack please? Oh,............ he's where? Hunting? Where is he hunting?" His tone changed perceptibly, from that of socially polite, to that of serious inquiry. "He didn't? No, everything's all right! Just tell him I called when he comes back. Thanks. Bye!"

"Jack's gone hunting!" Lemuel peered at the two men with a worried expression. "I have this feeling in my gut! I think we'd better go hunting, too!"

The two of them had known Lemuel long enough to read his mood. They knew when he had a hunch that he felt strongly about, it was worth acting upon!

"Get two fourby units, four or five deputies and a couple dogs! Gear up for tracking and get out to Skeleton Mesa! I think we're going to find our stranger real soon!" He moved hastily from his chair, pointing them toward the door. "I'm going to call the state for a copter, just in case! When you get there, you'll probably be able to determine where he's going without too much trouble. My guess is the canyon!"

Moving swiftly down the hallway, he added, "I'll be there as soon as I can get things squared away around here!"

§ § §

Zachary paced the floor in his kitchen. Tucking in his shirt tail, he waited for Tracy Baldwin to return his call. Before the phone on the wall rang the second time, he had the receiver in hand.

"Yes, Tracy! It is important! Something is up! Jack McCloud was by here last night. He said he wanted to stop by and let me know that he was on my side! That he didn't believe I had anything to do with the murders. He told me he would help me clear myself completely, if I would help him find the stranger! He said he felt an obligation to me, because he knew my family so well."

"I don't know what's motivating him! But he's different somehow! He was asking me a lot of questions about the night of the murders. About where Daniel and I were! He seemed to know more than he was asking, though!"

"Well, he wanted to know if we had been out to the ruins. I think he's gone looking for Daniel! I just don't think that he drove back to Tuba City last night! I've changed my mind, I don't think we should wait any longer! I want to go find him myself! How soon can you get here? Good! I'll be ready," he told her. Then he hung up the phone.

§ § §

He had moved from the protection of the forest of twisted pin oak, gnarled juniper, stands of fir, and spindly aspen, into the open of the sandy arroyo basin, that snaked its way westward toward a maze of buttes, mesas and staggering gorges.

Trekking even ground, he intended to increase the distance between himself and the hunter. He knew that he could be seen from higher ground by the acute eye of his insidious stalker. But his knowledge of the terrain was far more advanced. It sprang forth from its origin dated in antiquity. With craft, he baited his snare.

Standing at the crest of a bluff, about midway to the canyon floor, the hunter removed his sunglasses and folded them away into his vest pocket. He raised the binoculars that hung from a strap around his neck. Placing them to his hawkish eyes, he focused on the ruins in the grotto on the canyon wall to the north. He panned them for a sign of movement. Then he stole a sweeping glance down the canyon floor to his left, and westward along the arroyo basin, until his eyes seized upon a lone figure.

Miles ahead, but easy to track, he thought. Adjusting the magnification of his lenses, he assessed the movement of the stranger. He appeared to carry no weapon or provisions. *He shouldn't be to difficult to overtake,* the hunter told himself. *He'll be hungry and tired in a few hours! No telling how long he's been out here?"*

He capped the lenses on the binoculars. Then pondering his prey, he took an apple from his pack. He bit into its pulp with fervor. Relishing the hunt, he devoured it. Then he pitched the core, took up his rifle and proceeded down the switchback with an agile stride, descending it rapidly.

"It's McCloud's all right!" Sam Begay shouted to Peter Morgan and the team of deputies bailing out of the two, four-wheel-drive police vehicles. The dust was still settling behind them. He felt the hood. "It's cooled down! He's been out here for more'n an hour! He's got a jump start on us!"

The deputies swung the tailgates open, unloading the nervous dobermans. The muzzles kept them from snapping at the men in their excitement. Their handler took charge of the tense canines, while the deputies gathered their gear and weapons with rapid efficiency.

Morgan stood next to Begay, with his hand shading his eyes from the advancing sun. "We'll set up a command center right here," he said with a calm directness. "Let's divide the men into two teams! We'll have'em work each side of the canyon!" The stout Sam Begay grunted, nodding in agreement. Then he snorted and spat freely on the ground.

Donning his aviator styled sunglasses, Peter Morgan, in his dark brown departmental issue jacket, navy blue dress pants and his polished black boots, moved forward to the top of the ridge overlooking the canyon floor below, and the ruins in the distance to the north. He stood, a mature, trim silhouette against the rugged backdrop with a contrasting finesse to his partner and the surroundings. He appeared more of a diplomat than a policeman. But he had the dignity of a commanding officer. His ten years as a non-commissioned officer in the U.S. Army had left its influence upon his demeanor.

Removing his sunglasses, Morgan placed the field glasses to his eyes. He traversed the switchback with them, hoping for a glimpse of Jack McCloud. In its descent, the trail came into view only sporadically. It was otherwise obscured by scrub pine and foliage. "He may not be down in the basin yet, Sam. More than likely, he's still working his way down on this side of canyon!"

Then he focused on the arroyo and followed it with a perceptive eye. His head turned slowly with the range of his view. Halting, he said, "There is someone out there, Sam! But it's not Jack McCloud!" He passed the field glasses to Sam Begay, then he put on his sunglasses. "Odds are, it's our stranger!"

Focusing in the same direction, Sam picked up on the same figure moving across the basin. "Whoever it is, he's damn near to the other end!" Sam noted. "And he'll be out of sight before long!" Sam lowered the glasses from his face. "He'll be under cover again when he reaches the neck of the canyon, then he has several choices!"

Peter Morgan considered him knowingly. "Yes, but only one will get him out of the canyon system and onto a highway. Once he gets back up on the flats, he'll be easy enough to pick up!" He folded a stick of gum and placed it between his teeth. He offered Sam a piece. Then he chewed it with a slow deliberate expression. "Let's get McCloud first. Lemuel's going to be real interested in what he has to say about all of this!"

They gathered the team on the ridge, studied a map of the canyon, and assigned sectors to the two respective units. "You team leaders will keep in contact with Sam here. Radio him at regular intervals! About every ten minutes after you get down into the canyon," Morgan said. "I'm going to stay with the unit, and keep in touch with the station!"

Guarding the flame of his lighter from the wind with his cupped hands, Sam Begay lit a cigarette. He watched the team of deputies descend, musing, "It's kind a like shootin' fish in a barrel, ain't it," as he stood contemplating the depth of the canyon below. He sported a flagitious smile.

Peter Morgan retorted, "It seems too easy!"

Morgan returned to one of the vehicles, calling in to Lemuel Redfeather, he reported on the status of the search. He confirmed Lemuel's hunch regarding the purpose of Jack McCloud's hunting trip. He also confirmed the fact that the stranger, as best he could determine, was retreating from the canyon.

Then he asked for the state police helicopter to spot the location of the fleeing suspect, only to receive some distressing news. The nearest available helicopter in Flagstaff, was socked in by a winter storm that was dumping heavy snow and ice on the airport. Wind gusts were up to fifty miles an hour and the storm was moving rapidly to the east. It would be on top of them by late afternoon.

They would have to cordon off the stranger's only escape route, soon, or risk losing him. Peter Morgan knew they would have to act quickly. But there were no more available deputies in the Kayenta District. He asked Redfeather to have a team dispatched from the Tuba City District. They hoped that they would arrive in time to subdue the elusive stranger.

But Lemuel Redfeather would do more than that. He would not leave it to chance. Being determined not to lose the stranger, he would take charge of that operation personally.

Chapter 27

The Raging Heart of the Hunter

MENACING, HEAVY GRAY CLOUDS ROLLED OVERHEAD. THEY buried the sun in an obscured veil of portent. The temperature plummeted in the wake of the impending storm. It promised to be a harsh and bitter awakening of winter.

Entering the neck of the canyon, and once again in the cover of a sparse but buffering forest of rockbound conifers, and spires of stratified sandstone, he took refuge in the lee of a large slanted slab of stone that formed a leanto. It was high, and fronted by a clump of juniper, affording a concealed vantage point from where the stranger could observe the approaching hunter.

He huddled against the rock, shivering in the unrelenting assault of the bone biting cold that permeated the air, in the onslaught of a cruel storm that he was illprepared to withstand. He considered that he had already been too long in this place, longer than he had anticipated. The extended duration of his sojourn had begun to diminish his powers. His resistance to the elements of this terrestrial environment was waning at an accelerated rate, causing cellular decay.

Unwrapping the last of the pemmican cakes, he took notice of his quivering hand. His deterioration was now physically evident. His skin was turning a tawny hue and losing its flexibility. What he could not see, but was piercingly aware of, was the aging of his face. The flesh around his eyes and mouth had begun to wrinkle. And his hair and beard had turned ashen.

As he finished the final morsel of food, his thoughts turned to Zachary Thomas. He was dependant on Zachary to know when it was time for him to act. He had planted the seed of discernment in his mind. Now it was time for Zachary, and his other chosen, to do what it was that he had instilled in their subconscious.

His ability to focus on the thoughts of others had been effected, but he was still capable of receiving strong thought generations regarding himself. He believed that Zachary Thomas had knowledge of his peril. Knowing he would have to move again soon, he plotted the course in his mind. If he could make the climb to the flats before the storm's full fury set upon him, he felt assured that his rescue would be imminent. He clenched the coin in his hand, the token by which he could still be recognized.

Looking down the narrow gorge at his backtrail, he concentrated on the approaching hunter. He could not be seen, but his presence could be felt. *The stalker,* he thought, *has still to be reckoned with!* He had not lost his shrewd perception regarding him.

§ § §

Tracy Baldwin pulled up alongside Zachary's pickup truck in her jeep. Beside her sat Michael Severson, the astronomer.

The rugged Indian bolted from the back door of his house in a heavy woolen coat, with the collar up against his neck. The determined black eyes of the stalwart Navajo shone fiercely, as he approached the jeep with some provisions in his substantial hands. The rifle that was safely tucked under his arm, augured obtrusively of possible danger.

"I thought you were coming alone," Zachary barked tersely. "Who is he?" He asked before an introduction could be made by Tracy Baldwin.

Apparently flustered by his tone of rebuke, she said in a ruffled voice, "This is Michael Severson! I told you about him! He's the one who was checking on the coin for me! Don't you remember?"

Assessing the blond, fair skinned stranger with hard eyes, Zachary asked, "Why did you bring him?" He stood steeled against the side of the jeep, peering into the bewildered blue eyes of the scientist.

"He can help us!" Tracy said, giving Zachary a perturbed look. "Michael has had the coin analyzed! He's discovered some very interesting facts about it! I'm sure you'll want to hear about it on the way to the canyon!"

Michael extended his hand. "I really do want to help!" He intoned with sincerity.

Wringing his hand firmly, Zachary said, "Alright! We've got to move fast! This storm is going to get a lot worse! Your jeep will serve us better in the snow!" He told Tracy. "You drive, and I'll direct you to the back road that we took the last time!"

He slung his gear into the rear of the jeep, slid the rifle in behind the seat, and catapulted himself into the back seat behind Michael Severson.

"Let's step on it! We haven't got much time!" He commanded from the back seat, as Tracy slammed the jeep into gear and spun it in a sliding u-turn that headed them in the direction of the main road.

The wind carried the snow in a horizontal plane. It was wet and heavy, making travel hazardous. They proceeded south on Highway 163, through Kayenta to Highway 160 that would take them southwest to the Shonto turnoff. From there they would go north to the Inscription House Road, where they would turn onto a rough trail leading to the flats west of the Betatakin Canyon.

Meanwhile, Lemuel Redfeather awaited the arrival of the deputies from Tuba City. They would converge on the same location in approximately forty-five minutes. He paced the floor in his office, anticipating a call from them when they reached the Shonto turnoff. Then he walked to the window. He stood looking out at the rapidly building storm. He wondered how a day that started out with relative calm, could turn so tumultuous in only a few hours.

As he monitored the progress of the team in the canyon, his mood steadily migrated from that of confident control, to one of fearful embitterment. They had reached the arroyo basin without encountering Jack McCloud. He apparently had had a formidable head start, and was well ahead of Morgan's team. The dogs had picked up the trail early on, but the heavy snow was impeding their progress.

Lemuel was fearful that he would have to call back his men. He didn't know what was driving Jack McCloud, but he desperately wanted to find out! And he didn't want to risk losing him. He wasn't sure if Jack had anticipated the storm and prepared accordingly. He pondered his dilemma. It was either jeopardize his men, or possibly lose a friend, and an influential tribal council member. And, perhaps the only explanation he would ever have for Jack's strange behavior regarding the stranger and the murdered men.

And the stranger? Perhaps he will be more easily apprehended by the team of deputies from Tuba City, he thought. He needed them both. Lemuel Redfeather couldn't afford to lose either one of them at this point.

"Lemuel!" A voice cracked over the radio transmitter. It roused him from his meditation at the window. It was Peter Morgan's voice. "My men are having a rough time of it down there! We weren't prepared for this storm! If we don't call'em back, they might get snowbound. I don't want to chance it!"

He sat down at the radio. "Keep'em down there for a little while longer!" He said unwaveringly. "If they don't spot Jack McCloud soon, we'll call'em back! But I hate to give up on Jack! Over!" He awaited a response with a peaked look about him.

"I hear you Lemuel. I agree. We'll stick it out for a while longer. Maybe another thirty minutes! But I think that's all we dare risk!" Then Morgan added. "I'll tell Sam! Over!"

They had less than a thirty minute lead on the Tuba City deputies as they went north on the Inscription House Road.

"Michael, tell Zachary what you've discovered about the coin! You can explain it better than I can," Tracy insisted, keeping her eyes trained on the rapidly diminishing roadway ahead.

With an intellectual expression, the Nordic looking Michael Severson turned in his seat to address Zachary. "I must admit," he stated, "when Tracy came to me with her inquiries regarding the gibberish that this person named Daniel had expounded, I was extremely amused. However, the existence of the coin did give me cause to wonder what this person was up to! And, of course, the fact that the coin bore a symbol of some astronomical siginificance, prompted me to have it examined as Tracy requested."

Producing the coin that he had brought with him, he handed it to Zachary. "I understand that you've already seen one of these. I brought this one in case it would serve as a greeting between myself and your friend, since Tracy believes that I was intended to become the recipient of it!"

He pondered the coin with the intense eyes under his judicious brow. "And what is it that you've discovered?" Zachary said, raising his eyes to meet those of Michael Severson.

"It's extremely interesting." Michael said.

At that moment Zachary realized that Tracy had gone past their turnoff. "Turn around here, and go back to the other side of that wash we just crossed! Then turn left! You'll be able to follow the trail. The wind will be driving the snow from behind us!"

Swerving to the shoulder of the road, the jeep bounced off the ruts in the frozen soil, that only hours before had been soft mud. Then Tracy turned around, fishtailing in the middle of the road. She straightened the jeep and went back to the turnoff.

"I don't think we'll need to lock the hubs for a while, the snow isn't deep enough yet," Zachary told her. "But we've got to keep moving fast! I know he's out there! And I know he's waiting for us!"

Zachary nudged Michael Severson. "The coin! What about it?"

"Oh, yes!" Michael continued. "It would take a nuclear explosion to melt it!" He said quite academically. "It's difficult to analyze something that can't be broken down under normal processes! The metallurgist was competely baffled by it! He said it is definitely not solid gold! But he had no clue as to what it consists of!" He mused. "The man was very inquisitive about where I acquired it!"

Michael added. "Of course, he wanted to keep it for a while longer, but I thought it best that I get it back until I've had an opportunity to talk to Daniel myself!"

Tracy interjected. "Remember the conversation we had regarding my theory about who he is?" She asked Zachary.

"Yes, I remember!"

"Well. I feel more strongly about that hypothesis! If he is who I think he s, and what he said about time travel is correct, it could change the way we ive on this earth! The way we view religion!" She said excitedly. Grasping he steering wheel with resolve, she added, "It could rewrite the history of nan!"

Zachary considered the intent with which she spoke. "Then he may not e a spirit messenger at all?"

"Not in the sense that you anticipated, Zachary!" Tracy asserted. "But till a messenger of spirit! A spirit of a different kind! Perhaps the spirit of a ace far more advanced, and beyond the common prejudices that plague us!" She added, "Maybe he's here to absolve us of our past, and raise us to a new evel of thought about our place within the universe?"

Michael had listened intently. "That brings me to another point! The nscription on the coin. You see, I had a physicist look at the equation on the ack of the coin. He concurred with me! It does have something to do with he composition of matter! But the physicist was uncertain about its exact elationship. He said that he believed it was only part of an equation. That here was more! He said that it definitely fit in with quantum mechanics! But t would take some time to resolve it!" He paused. "Unless, of course, your riend can resolve it for us!"

§ § §

Cursing the blizzard that pelted his face with ice crystals, and stung his lesh with a burning cold sensation, he raised his hand to avert the battering now. He peered ahead through the horizontal flow of white that changed irections erratically, straining to recognize the terrain, to get a fix on the ntrance to the narrow passage through which the stranger had disappeared.

The bleak storm had buried the canyon in an eerie isolation, that devoided t of a sense of time and relative location. Jack McCloud plodded ahead against he force of it, struggling to maintain a steady footing. He was driven by nother force, that compelled him to seek out the one person who could be he instrument of his demise. He was the only person that Jack McCloud new with certainty, had knowledge of the black secret he guarded with uthless ardor.

Finding the partially concealed entrance to the gorge, he moved urreptitiously, looking about for signs of passage by his adversary. Upon ntering, his ears were relieved from the blustering cries of the savage wind. A deadening stillness overtook him in the shelter of this crevasse of steep, igh walls, and scattered crags of fallen rock.

He listened cautiously for the sounds of movement. There were none orthcoming. It troubled him that between himself and the opposite end of ne gorge, that ascended to the flats in broadening steps of talus, there was a naze of concealment.

Coming nearer to the oblique flatsided stone that jutted from the rock wall, he considered the first of many obvious hiding places. He relieved the safety on the triggerguard of his rifle, making an audible snap. He moved guardedly through the clump of juniper that buffeted the opening under the rock. Emerging from the brush, he stiffened with a rush of panic when a chunk of ice crashed on the rocks above him. Then searching further, he detected the evidence of someone's recent presence. He thought he sensed him near. Like a hungry animal, his greedy eyes paced to and fro. With distorted eagerness, he lunged from cover to cover, gasping apprehensively with each exertion. The weight of his own fear staggered him. It was the fear that he would have to kill again! And perhaps again after that! His heart exploded time after time, with increasing compulsion. He could hear the concussions ringing in his head. It was causing a painful restriction in his chest.

Crashing to the ground on his knees, Jack McCloud's soul was drowning in his own desperation. He slumped forward, bracing himself on the butt of his rifle. It was the dark side of himself that he hunted and wished to destroy, after all. It was that side of himself of which he could no longer bear the weight. The revelation that he had already lost it all, had brought him down. The splintered bones of his own evil lodged in his throat.

§ § §

"Look!" Tracy shouted. "Right over there! I think that's him!" She drove in the direction of the muted figure, obscured by the wind driven snow.

They came upon him, wavering. "If that's him, he's not in very good shape," Michael Severson said.

He fell to the ground in front of them. Stopping the jeep several feet before the body that lie in the drifting snow, they rushed to the man's aid. Zachary turned him over to confirm his identity. He was bewildered to look upon the aging, haggard face. "It has to be him! But look what's happened to him!" Daniel was unconscious.

"His hair!" Tracy noted. "It's all gray, now!"

"Grab hold of his feet!" Zachary directed Michael Severson. "Let's get him to the jeep, quickly! He's nearly frozen!"

Tracy Baldwin ran ahead to open the back flap on the canvas cover of the jeep. The two men carried Daniel around to the rear of it. Tracy Baldwin pulled him up inside, laying him on the blanket that she had spread onto the floor.

"We've got to get him warm," she said. She covered him with another blanket. "Where can we take him where he'll be safe?" Tracy asked Zachary.

"Stay in back with him!" Zachary told her. "I'll drive! I know where we can take him!"

Michael Severson dropped the flap, zipping it shut. Then he darted to the front of the jeep. Working swiftly, he and Zachary locked the hubs on the front wheels to engage the four-wheel-drive. The furious blizzard peppered their exposed flesh, while they struggled to clear the packed snow from the front of the jeep. Clearing it hastily, they got back inside.

They turned in the direction of Navajo Mountain. Zachary avoided the trail that they had come in on. He knew they would have been followed. If they could make it back to the partially improved road, they stood a chance of making it the twenty-four miles, to the hogan of White Horse, before the road was drifted closed.

Advancing on the location where the stranger had fallen, the Tuba City Police fourby unit plowed ahead steadily. Inside the unit with two deputies was Lemuel Redfeather. He was determined that the stranger would not escape him. They followed the now partially covered tire tracks. Blowing snow sifted across the trail, filling the ruts made by the jeep.

Lemuel deliberated over who he thought would chance coming out there in this storm. *Who else could have known where the stranger would be?* He asked himself. He knew that Jack McCloud was still somewhere in the canyon. That was obvious. But who else, outside of himself and his men, had any idea what was going on out here in this storm?

Zachary Thomas? He mused. *How could he have possibly known?* It just didn't make sense. But nothing was making too much sense these days.

The storm hindered the radio transmissions from the canyon. A garbled message came across. It was indistinguishable at first. Then he heard the name Jack McCloud. Lemuel Redfeather tuned the radio, trying to bring it in more clearly. Again, he heard the name and part of the message. It was more audible this time.

"We found him, Lemuel," he heard a voice say. It was Peter Morgan's voice. "The team found him! They're bringing him up! I'm afraid It'll be a while before we get out of here, though! Over!"

One down, he thought. *And only one more to go!* He attempted to reply, "That's great Peter. Good work!" He wasn't sure if his message had gotten through. But it was good news.

Now he had to concentrate on the stranger. The trail had ended. The tire tracks were filled in. And the police unit's tracks were being erased by the drifting snow.

Alarmed, the deputy said,"Sir! There's just nothing out here! We've lost'em! I can't even tell where we're going now! We'd better turn back!"

He was right! Lemuel Redfeather knew he was right. "Damn!" He swore. "We can't just leave him out here! What if he's out there somewhere? God, man! What if he's out there somewhere?!!" He pounded on the dash with his fist.

The deputies stared at him waiting for his decision. Lemuel calmed himself. "Turn around! You're right! Just turn around!" He breathed a heavy sigh. "If he's out here, there's nothing we can do for him now!"

"Maybe someone picked him up!" The deputy offered.

Lemuel reflected. "Maybe."

The fourby bucked the drifting snow. Lemuel Redfeather peered through the windshield into the headlight beams, they penetrated the hypnotic flow of white. The windshield wipers thrashed frantically, continually falling behind the onslaught of icy scale. His face bore a cataleptic expression. He had become obsessed with the stranger.

Chapter 28

The Brutal Storm

T APPEARED DUSK. THE SKY WAS TUMULT WITH DUN CLOUDS. 'he storm had shrouded the land in a white mantle that cloaked its aboriginal :arkness.

Tracy Baldwin huddled Daniel. His head lie in her lap. She attempted to 'ard off the cold that had sapped his strength, by stroking the chilled flesh of is face with her warm hand. His unconscious face bore little resemblance to ie man she had met in the kiva.

She pulled the woolen blanket snug around his upper body. Then she eached for his curled hand, attempting to warm it. Working his stubbornly losed fingers, she felt a cool, metal object drop against her palm. It was a oin, a coin like the one that she, Zachary and Michael possessed.

"It *is* him!" She cried out. "Here," she said, handing the coin over the eat to Michael Severson. Zachary could barely take a glimpse. His eyes 'ere fast on the fading roadway. But it was enough to encourage his spirit.

Although the storm was now subsiding, the gale winds kept the white aze aloft. Visibility was poor, but Zachary's familiarity with the terrain kept im apprised of their location.

Driving in low gear, the jeep buffeted the snow drifts that had wafted cross the road. It groaned as it lunged forward, crawling laboriously.

"It can't be more than five or six miles ahead," Zachary said with a efinitive expression. A bitter night was rapidly swallowing up the landscape into darkness. He pulled out the knob that turned on the headlights. An effused light spread itself across the reflective snow. It aided them little in recognizing the boundries of the road they traveled.

Without warning, the jeep sputtered and died. Zachary quickly turned out the headlights to preserve the battery. Then he tried to restart it by turning the ignition and pumping the gas. He tried over and over again. Each time it became more evident that the battery was weakening. The starter turned the engine ever more slowly with a crankish growl. Until it moaned irretrievably.

"We may have run out of gas!" Tracy ventured. "I had only about a half of a tank! I hadn't even thought to fill it! I didn't know we were going to end up out here!" She exclaimed.

"What do we do now?" Michael Severson posed to Zachary.

Zachary looked at him ponderously. He took a brief moment to answer. "We don't have much choice! The temperature is dropping outside by the minute! Soon It'll be freezing in here! We've got to move! We'll have to try and make it on foot!" He stated this decisively.

"How can we make it with Daniel? We'll have to carry him!" Tracy said anxiously, considering their options.

"I'll carry him!" Zachary told them. "You just help me as much as you can! Just keep moving! If you keep moving we can make it. It's the only chance we've got out here!"

"Can't we wait for a while? Can't we wait until someone else comes along? Maybe someone will come by here soon and find us!" Tracy proposed, while she held onto Daniel ever so tightly. The fear in her trembled in her voice. She was already starting to feel the cold infiltrate the flimsy covering of the jeep. She began to shiver.

Michael Severson could see the futility of it. He could sense her apprehension. "Tracy, there isn't anyone coming! We haven't seen another vehicle since we picked up Daniel! We have to do as Zachary says. We can't wait any longer!"

"Wrap him in the blanket before we open the jeep!" Zachary said. "Cover his head with it, too! I'll carry him over my shoulder."

After they wrapped Daniel in the blanket, each of them readied themselves. They pulled up their coat collars tightly around their necks, to keep the wind from penetrating their upper body. They donned the hoods of their coats, drawing the strings and pulling them in tightly around their faces. Tracy wrapped a scarf over her head and tucked it in under her hood, leaving only a small opening from which to see and breathe. Then they slipped on their gloves and got out of the jeep. The punishing wind assailed them.

They trode arduously through the deep snow that had drifted around the stalled jeep. Zachary reached the rear of the jeep before the others. He unzipped the rear window flap and pulled down the tailgate. Then he leaned inside, pulling Daniel toward him, until he could bring him up to a seated position on the back of the jeep. Doing so, he leaned his shoulder into the midsection of the weak, perhaps dying semblance of a man. He brought him up over his broad, muscular shoulder, and poised him there.

Michael Severson reached inside to retrieve the rifle, and the pack that Zachary had prepared. Inside the pack was a flashlight. He brought it out, then switched it on, giving them a light to guide their steps.

Abandoning the jeep, the imperiled party strode off into the darkness, with only Zachary's cognition to guide them. They turned their faces from the seizing wind that captured their breath, plodding through waist high drifts of snow.

With a blanketed torso drapped over the girth of his substantial back, Zachary strode vigorously. The Navajo had tenacious mettle. Michael Severson trudged in his wake, carrying the rifle and the pack. He held the flashlight, waveringly, trying to anticipate what was ahead.

Tracy Baldwin guarded her eyes with the back of her hand, while she strained to keep up with Zachary and Michael. She clung to the back of Michael's coat, trailing in the parted snow.

§ § §

Creating a new priority, the unprecedented, early winter storm had dumped almost two feet of snow on the Navajo Nation. Traffic had ceased to move along Highway 160, that was the Nation's only major link with the adjoining Four Corners region. Trucks were snowbound in drifts that formed in tall obtuse waves across the highway. Working through the night, it would be late morning before the state highway crews could begin to make a dent in the unfathomable tons of snow that blocked the roadway.

In the meantime, ambulances and emergency rescue units were detained at their stations, unable to answer calls for assistance, while local road crews began the night-long task of clearing the critical arteries that separated them from stranded victims of the storm. Air lifts would be in progress by morning, bringing assistance to snowbound travelers and the sick in the outer reaches of the reservation. Food supplies would be dropped to those that lived in the most remote areas of the Nation, who would be unable to travel for days, perhaps even weeks.

It had put a snag in Lemuel Redfeather's search, but it had not averted his preoccupation with the elusive stranger. His men had been fortunate. They had been able to escape the devastating fury of the storm without tragedy. Peter Morgan, Sam Begay and the deputies made their way back to Kayenta at dusk, in the final ravaging hour of the storm, with little more than minutes before the roads would have been impassable.

They were successful in another way as well. They appeared to have rescued Jack McCloud from his impending death.

"Will he pull through?" Lemuel Redfeather asked the doctor, with grave concern about Jack McCloud.

"He's had a heart attack! Frankly, I'm surprised he survived it! Your men did a marvelous job of keeping him alive! Only time will tell, Mister Redfeather! Right now he's in intensive care. We can only hope for the best!" The doctor cautioned him. "You're looking somewhat tired, Mister Redfeather, perhaps you should go home and get some rest. There's nothing you can do here! We'll call you if anything changes!" Then he walked away.

With the exception of a lone Navajo woman, who sat patiently awaiting news of her pregnant daughters delivery, Lemuel Redfeather stood alone in the waiting room of the hospital. He sipped a cup of coffee. And he assessed the the prospects of his investigation. As before, he was no closer to solving the crime, or resolving the issues that plagued him concerning Jack McCloud. The coin found among Jack McCloud's belongings, added another note of irony to the already entangled web of suspicion. It had all taken an uncanny twist. If Jack died, he was certain that important information would die with him.

The stranger, he mused.*What if he's buried under the snow somewhere? How will I ever know what part he played in all of this? Two men die, and it remains a mystery, forever! Then no one is the victor, and the hunt goes unrewarded!*

§ § §

Michael Severson felt her slip away. He turned with the flashlight to look for her. Tracy Baldwin knelt, tottering in the furrowed snow. He hastened back to pull her up.

"Come on Tracy! don't give up now!" Michael implored her, taking her arm to bring her to her feet. He took hold of her arm and placed it over his shoulder, bracing her, with his arm around her waist, they trudged forward again.

He shined the light ahead of them to locate Zachary. The Indian had stopped about fifty yards beyond them. When he could no longer hear the snow crunch under their feet, with the staggering weight of Daniel across his shoulders, he turned around to wait for them. Then he rearranged the weight on his back and went on.

It had been two hours since they left the jeep. Battered by the severe cold and the fierce wind, their strength was waning to varying degrees. Zachary could feel his legs burning under the labor of each step. Inside his heavy coat, sweat was exuding from his pores, brought out by the torturous burden placed upon his body. But his face, hands and feet stung from the bite of the bitter cold.

Tracy's extremities were now numb with cold. She was nearing exhaustion. Only the emboldened strength of Michael Severson could keep her upright. Michael brought her along with sheer will. He was determined that neither one of them would perish.

Then, off in the distance, a faint glimmer of light caught Zachary's keen eye. He measured the distance of it by its luminosity, determining it to be no more than a mile. Standing solid, he waited for Michael and Tracy to catch up. He dared not set down his burden to rest his aching joints, for fear he would be unable to raise it back up. And judging by the way that the other two lagged behind, he detemined that they would be unable to assist him.

When they reached him, he pointed out the light in the distance, hoping to give them the encouragement to endure a while longer.

"Look!" Zachary said with gasps. "That's it! I know that's it! Come on, let's keep moving!"

It was a steady uphill climb, that tortured, even more, their already ravaged bodies. They gulped the air that froze their lungs with each breath. Zachary lurched, moving slowly forward time after time, nearly succumbing to the pressure that compressed his shoulders more every minute.

Michael Severson trode mechanically in Zachary's trail, inching forward with Tracy Baldwin in tow. His hand was like a vise around her upper arm, refusing to release her from her obligation to survive. The flashlight that he carried had long since expired, and been discarded without deliberation. The pack remained strapped to his back, although he had become wholly unaware of it. And he dragged the rifle alongside himself with his free hand.

Each grueling step brought them ever closer to the heralding beacon of light that they ardently coveted. They were now close enough to distinguish the scent of the smoke from the fires in the hogans. It was a gas lamp that hung by the door on one of the lodges that guided them. The dark, snow capped mounds protruding from the vast field of white, appeared to grow larger with every step. Until at last, they stood before the lodge with the lamp by the door. It was the lodge of White Horse.

Staggering, Zachary moved toward the door, until he was near enough to fall against it with a thud. Then he slid to the ground, driven down by the unyielding weight of his friend. Not more than twenty feet away, Michael Severson had dropped to his knees in exhaustion. He still held onto Tracy Baldwin's arm. She laid on her side in the snow, semi-conscious.

A voice came from within. *"Hai t'aash?"* The voice inquired, "Who is that?"

Zachary strained to speak. *"Bi- shi, Zachary!"* He muttered. "It's me, Zachary!"

The door swung open to faces filled with compassionate temperament, that had been enhanced by a veil of years: and to the welcomed glow of warm embers from the evening fire.

Chapter 29

At the Brink of Truth

THEY TOOK THE SHROUDED BODY FROM ZACHARY'S shoulder, dragging it inside to the warmth of the fire. Then Zachary pulled himself to his feet in the doorway, and lumbered painfully to help Michael Severson and Tracy Baldwin. Taking up winter robes, the elderly couple came out to assist as best they could.

Seeing that Tracy lie in the snow without movement, Zachary struggled to lift her up, bearing her weight as he carried her inside. Lone Coyote and Ogin grabbed hold of Michael Severson's arms and brought him up from his knees, supporting him while they guided him into their lodge.

White Horse had already awakened to the commotion, and he had surmised the identity of the late visitors. Indeed, he had experienced a premonition that told the old sage to anticipate their arrival. So confident was he, that he had instructed Lone Coyote to set out the gas lamp. He had begun to tend to The One of Many Faces. He recognized him not through his eyes, but through his hands. White Horse could sense the vibrant powers of the one whose visit he had long awaited.

Looking gravely concerned, Zachary's expression betrayed his fear as he inquired of White Horse. "Is he alive?"

"Aoo'bi t'hinishna'!" White Horse said, "Yes, he is alive!" His quavery hand stroked the forehead of the stranger, who lie on the blanket before him. "We must help him and the others regain their strength!" He told his son and

daughter-in-law, who were already feeding warm broth to the two Anglo people, Tracy and Michael.

It was nearly ten o'clock. They had been trudging in the snow and cold for almost four hours. Zachary sat on a blanket, peering into the fire. His thoughts were distant as he carefully thawed his extremities. Gradually, the throbbing pain was subsiding in his legs. He rubbed his hands together, massaging the feeling back into them. Then he picked up a cup of hot broth and, shakily, put it to his lips, sipping as he mused.

The old woman, Ogin, sat on the edge of a cot where Tracy Baldwin nursed a cup of broth. She massaged the nearly frostbitten feet of the young woman with her callused old hands. Tracy's redened face and chafing nose bore the signs of a nearly fatal adventure. She was too weary to speak of it.

Michael Severson sat in a chair beside the fire, next to Lone Coyote whose eyes considered the flaxen haired young man. "How do they call you?" He inquired in his gracious but tremulous voice.

"Michael! Michael Severson," he responded with strained effort. He barely lifted his eyes from the fire when he spoke. Then he added, "I didn't think we were going to make it!"

"You must rest now!" Lone Coyote told the young man. "There will be plenty of time to talk!" He helped him to his feet, then over to a cot alongside the wall of the sparsely furnished hogan.

Putting Tracy and Michael to rest, Ogin and Lone Coyote assisted White Horse in tending to the stranger. Each of them stood vigil throughout the night, bathing him in heated water and coating his frostbitten flesh with unction.

Ignoring the urgings of the others for him to rest, Zachary remained awake as long as he could, keeping watch over his friend along with them. Until his overwhelming fatigue overtook him and he collapsed on the blanket in a deadened sleep.

Ogin, Lone Coyote and White Horse took turns attending the stranger into the early morning. When the former two had expired into much needed sleep, White Horse sat attentively waiting for the stranger to rouse. He had waited all these years, holding the Ancients' coin in safe keeping. In his youth, White Horse had been given the coin, and the legacy of the message that the Spirit Messenger would someday return as he had promised the Ancient Ones. It had been given to him by the Holy Man who taught him, passing on the gift to him.

Now lying before him in his lodge was the promise of a prophecy fulfilled. White Horse pondered the figure of the man, as much as he could see with his decrepit eyes. He loomed anxiously, deliberating over whether this form was man or spirit, or both. Both, he concluded, as he knew all men were. *Why would even a spirit messenger be different?* He asked himself.

The bearded, white haired stranger stirred, letting out a groan and giving

White Horse a start. Then the old man smiled a toothless smile, encouraged by this show of life. The stranger's eyelids parted slightly, indicating that he was near consciousness. His breathing became more pronounced. His head rolled from side to side. And White Horse felt the long spent excitement of youth return to his tired old body. He was anxious to counsel with The One of Many Faces as the Ancient Ones did.

It was still very early morning, and the others slept soundly. White Horse remained quiet, not wishing to disturb them. Then the stranger's eyes opened, revealing the azure lucidity of them. The old man could only distinguish that they were open, and that they were light of color. His failing vision would not allow him the luxury of detail. Taking the hand of the stranger, he felt that the pulse of the man had quickened. Then the stranger gave his hand a squeeze, gripping it firmly for a moment.

"You are better now?" White Horse asked softly.

"I am better," the stranger said, parting a frail smile. He took notice of the cloudiness in the old man's eyes, and passed on his gratitude through another gentle squeeze of his hand.

"Ha'zho''o iyaago nitah ya''a'hoot'e'e'h doo!" White Horse told him. "When you eat well, you will be healthy!" The stranger understood him. He nodded in agreement.

Raucous snores from Zachary brought amusement to them. They both chuckled lightly. "We have much to discuss, but there is time," White Horse told him. "Now you must have nourishment!" Walking with a hitch, the old man left the side of the stranger and went to the hearth to prepare some coffee. Soon the others would be aroused.

Afterward, he lumbered to the cot where Ogin slept, to wake her. He bent protractedly at the hip to nudge her blanketed shoulder with his feeble hand, waking here gently from her respite. "Ogin," he wispered, "the stranger is awake and hungry!"

She turned over in her bed to greet the old man with patient eyes. "That's good, White Horse," she told him with a gritty morning voice and a cheerful smile. She shared his elation over the stranger's recovery. "Wake Lone Coyote to tend the fire, and I will prepare a meal!" She said this throwing the covers aside, and rising up slowly to seat herself at the edge of the cot. Then she waited a long moment for the resurgence of circulation to her limbs, massaging the sleepy tingle from her arms, before slipping her feet into the soft moccasins that lie beneath her dangling feet.

Ruminating with the thought that her aging body responded more slowly than it had when she was a young woman, her high-spirited nature was still intact, as she pulled a winter robe about her shoulders to ward of the chill, until the morning fire was ablaze. Then she went about her work with a vigorous good humor.

Lone Coyote stoked the embers with dry juniper logs that caught fire quickly, giving off a welcomed rush of warmth. The sweet scent of the burning juniper, and the essence of fresh coffee mingled in the dawn air of the cozy lodge. The pleasant emanations, along with the busy clatter of Ogin and Lone Coyote, aroused Zachary from his profound sleep. The others followed shortly afterward, stretching sore muscles and recounting the trials of the grueling trek in the merciless cold, each of them savoring the hospitality and the warmth of the lodge.

Ogin had taken it upon herself to feed the stranger, while the others ate from the morning table. She was curious about this one that had attracted so much attention. "Do you have a name?" She asked him, while she raised his head to tuck a rolled blanket underneath it. She supported his head and neck with it, so that she could feed him some mush.

"Yes, my name is Daniel," he told her in a weak but pleasant voice.

"It is a name from the Christian Bible," she mused aloud. "How do you come by it?" When he was hesitant to answer, she filled his mouth with mush, displaying a coy expression, acting as though it was an idle question. Then she looked at him with the stealthy eyes of a fox.

When he had finished the bowl of mush, Ogin wiped his chin with a damp cloth and gave him another furtive look. "You will be well, soon," she told him. When the old woman got up from the floor, Zachary came over to speak to his friend. The others had finished eating. They were lingering over coffee at the table. And Ogin was preparing a place for herself.

"It is good to see you alive!" Zachary said, standing over him. He came down on one knee, close to Daniel, and leaned over him to make their conversation more personal. "I wasn't sure you were going to make it! You looked very bad last night! But you're looking much better now!" He studied the invasive, blue eyes of the stranger. "I wasn't even sure it was you, at first! What happened to you out there? You look much older now!"

Daniel's face yielded a pensive expression. "I'm not able to endure the rigors of your environment for too long a time. My aging process catches up with me. It becomes accelerated. "I'll have to leave very soon, or I will die here."

Zachary was taken back by the word "die." *Spirit messengers don't die,* he told himself. "Than you're not a spirit messenger?" He asked.

"Not the way you perceived me, Zachary! But a messenger all the same," Daniel said.

"Than Tracy is right!" Zachary said this in a tone of bewilderment. "She knows who you are!"

"I have much to explain to all of you before I leave!" Daniel vowed.

White Horse joined them with an object clenched in his fist. He came down near the face of the stranger, next to Zachary. "Do you recognize this?" He asked, opening his gnarled hand to expose the coin he had guarded diligently all of his life.

Daniel nodded. "Yes. How did you come by it?"

"It was given to me by a Holy Man. He told me it was passed down through generations from the Ancient Ones. He told me that some day the Spirit Messenger would return! That I would know him! Although I cannot see you well, I feel that you are the one!" White Horse said with assurance.

Then he added. "The Holy Man told me the story of the one who dwelt for a time with the Ancient Ones, teaching them the secrets of the stars and of other worlds. When this messenger was ready to leave, he gave this gift to the Holy Man of that council. That Holy Man revered the gift and its secrets, and passed it along so that each of his successors would protect it!"

"I knew that you would come!" The sagacious old man exclaimed. "And I have so many questions for you about the Ancients!"

Daniel mused at the old man's ardor. He was pleased that the medicine man had taken such assiduity in protecting the coin, and the secret that it represented. Looking upon the serene face of White Horse, he was fondly reminded of the one he had given it to. And now he had come full circle. He had returned to the place he had visited once before, where he had initiated the mission that he was now bound to complete. Then he would return to his place of origin, until another time, or perhaps a successor would take his place.

§ § §

Lying in a bed in the intensive care ward of the hospital, in a private room that reeked with the odor of astringents, Jack McCloud lingered in a sedate, semiconscious state, with catheters and I.V.'s protruding from his body. Electrodes were taped to his chest and arms to monitor his vital signs, and he was connected to state-of-the-art cardio-pulmonary life support equipment.

The sickly pallor of his complexion emphasized his critical condition. He lie covered to the shoulders by a white sheet, with his raven black hair buried against a moderately stuffed, firm hospital grade pillow that provided only the necessary support of his head. His eyelids were swollen puffs of skin, but with a now detectable split, and the whites of his eyes showed through and were contrasted by the dark lashes that lined the separation.

Clutching his hand firmly, with her fingers tucked under his cool palm, Tessa McCloud sat, in the subdued light of the quiet room, vigilantly next to her husband's sick bed, waiting. The pulsating beep of the monitor was the only sound in the room. It was a room that appeared devoid of any connection with the normal everyday world, that was part of their lives together for the last thirty years. She considered intently, the flamboyant and articulate man who was unable to communicate with her at that moment.

In the hallway, just outside the door, Lemuel Redfeather sat impatiently awaiting signs of Jack McCloud's recovery and return to consciousness. He craved a cigarette, but he was reluctant to go outside to smoke. He craved the answers to his questions more, more than the satisfaction of his addiction. His addictions included his job as well. This case in particular, was too close to his personal connections and adjurations. He was bound by it intimately, to resolve it.

Jack McCloud's eyelids began to twitch perceptibly in the subdued light of the room. His pupils crossed the slit in his eyelids as they moved erratically. Tessa McCloud felt a light tremor in his hand. Then she felt it again. Still holding his hand, she arose from the chair to peer at his face. The muscles in his face began to twitch. Then his dry lips parted slightly. With stifled elation, she reached for the nurse call button. The light came on the monitor at the nurses station, and a light came on above the door to the room. Lemuel Redfeather was roused from his preoccupations by the nurse that moved brusquely toward him and the open door of the room. Then the doctor rounded the corner of the hallway with a hurried gait, converging on the room along with the intensive care nurse.

Lemuel Redfeather sprang to his feet, as they swept by him through the door. Thinking the worst, his face produced a morose expression as he peered through the opening. Then he stepped quietly into the room, just beyond the door. From his vantage point, he noted the relieved, calm look on the face of Tessa McCloud. The doctor pulled back one of Jack McCloud's eyelids. Holding his pen light over it, he studied the dilation of the pupil. He looked at the other eye as well, while the nurse checked his vital signs.

Standing there, his view obscured by the doctor, who leaned across Jack McCloud, Lemuel Redfeather heard an audible groan. A smile broke across his weary face. He walked pensively to the side of Tessa McCloud, placing his arm around her shoulder. She glanced up at him momentarily, with an appreciative expression, then she quickly turned her attention back to her ailing husband, who appeared to be in the twilight of consciousness.

The doctor stepped back. "It looks like he's going to make it," he said, addressing both Tessa McCloud and Lemuel Redfeather.

"When will he be able to talk?" Lemuel asked tersely. He dropped his arm from Tessa McCloud's shoulder.

"He's really just coming around! I just want him to remain quiet for now!" The doctor asserted strongly, viewing Lemuel Redfeather with stern eyes. "Perhaps in a few days you'll be able to talk to him. I'll let you know!" His hand came across between Lemuel Redfeather and Tessa McCloud, touching her comfortingly on the shoulder, he drew between them and focused his attention on her concerns.

Lemuel sustained the brunt of the doctor's icy rebuke. He remained impassive. No one could understand how much hinged on the words of Jack McCloud. Certainly not this doctor, and not even Jack's wife could know the gravity of the thing in which he may be involved. And this was not the time or place to discuss it with her, at least not without being able to talk to Jack st.

So he would absorb the shun, and walk away for today, but he would be ck as soon as Jack was able to speak. And nothing would stop him from tting the information he so desperately sought. Nothing!

Chapter 30

Untold Knowledge

THROUGHOUT THE DAY HIS STRENGTH RETURNED, UNTIL HE could walk about unassisted. Inwardly, he knew that he could only sustain himself a short period of perhaps a week, no longer. Any more time than that, and the degenerative process would be too far advanced for him to survive. It went unexpressed, because it would be to complicated for the others to understand fully, yet his appearance revealed the obvious onset of a deteriorating condition.

The sun shone brightly in the western sky as the day advanced toward evening. Zachary and Michael Severson had cleared away the snowdrift that blocked the entrance to the hogan. The snow had been piled halfway up the door opening. The day was calm and clear. So much so, that the sun's reflection on the snow made it difficult to look upon it for too long a time, without squinting or becoming snowblind. They worked, assisting the others in the camp to clear away the snow and make paths between the lodges. Everyone was out clearing the snow from the pickup trucks. The children plunged into snowbanks and threw snowballs at one another. The men of the camp tended the livestock.

About midday, a two engine Air National Guard cargo plane had rumbled overhead. It dropped a bundle of supplies to the isolated camp. The onlookers watched, with their hands shielding their eyes from the sun, as the floating bundle glided toward the earth, attached to a billowing, white parachute that hovered gently against a cloudless blue sky. In a land of loess earth, red rock, sandstone, and scattered, robust desert flora, it appeared a peculiar sight to see the ground blanketed by the frozen white ice crystals that would otherwise be associated with more north temperate regions. Yet, in a matter of days, it would all disappear under the warming rays of the Southwestern sun.

It would be two or three days before the road to the camp was passable. Tracy Baldwin expressed concern over the safety of her jeep. Zachary assured her, that when the tribe cleared the road, they would take care to move it aside without damaging it. But there was a greater concern that each of them shared regarding the jeep. It was that anyone who found it would know their approx- imate location. And until they had time to determine why it was that Jack McCloud had come after Daniel, and who else, if anyone, was looking for him, they needed to keep the knowledge of their whereabouts limited to those in the camp.

Another concern was that it wouldn't be too long before Tracy Baldwin and Michael Severson were missed. There was no way to call out of the camp to let anyone know where they were; there were no phones. There was no means to communicate with the outside world, whatsoever. Even if there were, they weren't sure who they could trust not to notify the authorities. Neither one of them knew anyone who they could explain the circumstances to, without sounding like they had lost their minds.

They were stranded, and pressed for precious time to learn what they could about the stranger, before they were either found or he would have to leave them to save himself.

Ogin was preparing the evening meal. The fragrance of the steaming food filled the lodge. She refused Tracy's help to prepare the food, but she allowed her to set places for the seven people. Insisting that the men be served first, she went about taking the food to the table for them. Tracy acquiesced and helped her, otherwise feeling awkward to sit down while Ogin continued to work. The meal was plain but copius. There was a platter of roasted potatoes, and one of corn and beans. The meat was that of a young lamb, roasted over the fire since early in the day. No one hesitated to eat their fill.

Lone Coyote and White Horse took turns telling stories of the past, and about the times that Zachary and his family had come to visit their hogan. They were amusing stories, and everyone enjoyed the meal and the good hospitality. Michael Severson enjoyed the stories, too, except that he was preoccupied with the stranger and anxious to ask some questions. He took occasional glimpses of him with inquisitive eyes. Daniel noticed.

Everyone had finished eating, and Michael viewed the white haired stranger pensively. He could no longer contain his curiosity. He looked at the bearded face across the table from him and connected with the eyes that had evaded him during dinner.

"Who are you really?" Michael Severson asked boldly. "What are you doing here?"

The lucid, blue eyes of the stranger considered him for a long moment, while the others peered at him with equal curiosity. Michael Severson had flatly asked the question that was foremost in the minds of all of them. Now perhaps each of them would have an opportunity to know why they were here. They would now know why they were chosen.

"I am a messenger! That part is true. I have traveled thousands of lightyears!" He looked at them all with an earnest expression, speaking concisely and with deliberation. "But I am also a hunter! I have been hunting the same enemy for almost a thousand years! On world after world! Each time it is the same, we are adversaries. We both have won and lost equally as many times. But the prize for the victor is not the annihilation of the loser. Rather, it is the annihilation of the planet on which the battle has taken place. And the battle does not take place with weapons, we use the resources available to us of the world that we are on. That includes the inhabitants! I came here because *he* is here!" He said this with detectable ire in his voice.

The others viewed Daniel and his words with astonishment, but Michael Severson was not so convinced. "How can you prove this?" He asked. Then he produced the coin that he had carried in his pocket. "What does this coin have to do with any of it?"

"It is a gift! The coin itself has no monetary value! It is just a token, as I have told Zachary. But it has a significant meaning! And the Dark One does not want that meaning to be known! The information would ruin his plan. It would give your kind incredible knowledge that would liberate you from the boundries of this Earth, and make you children of the stars! You would no longer be his captive prey! And I will have won this battle!" Daniel said with a tone of certainty.

Ogin wished to speak, her mind was unsettled regarding the question she had asked him that morning. He had not answered. "Your name? If you are of some other world, than what would your name be?"

Tracy interjected. "Yes. I want to know as well. Why do you use a Biblical name? Why did you speak of the dreams of prophecy by Daniel in the Bible as your own?"

The others listened with profound interest, waiting to hear.

"Did you think that prophets and prophecy were limited to your own world? What do you think is out there, in this galaxy, beyond the boundries of your solar system, where your planet is only a speck of dust orbiting an average star in the midst of a spiral arm, containing millions of such average stars? Did you think life was limited to your tiny world?" He paused to assess them. "And did you think that the one God, was only the God and the Power for your world, and not that of everything that exists beyond it?"

"On another world you would not be able to say my name, yet it would mean the same! And the prophecy remains the same! It is the same prophecy for all worlds! Why would the same God make it different somewhere else?" Daniel had made the implication well enough for all of them to understand. There was no doubt among them concerning his meaning.

"Intelligent beings of all worlds have been given the right to choose, and to learn from their choices! And to either grow, or perish! And so it is with your kind! It is a critical time in your history! That is to say whether or not there will be a history written among the stars for a race of beings called humans!" The stranger spoke with a strong, resonant voice, that emphasized the meaning of his words. There was not one present who was not affected by them. But Michael Severson was intent on asking the questions that were most prevalent in *his* mind.

"What is the proof?" Michael asked again.

"Proof?" Daniel said musingly. "The proof that I am sitting here? That all of you are here with me? That each of you have a coin?" He paused, a glint of irony pervaded his speech. "Consider what each of you has gone through to be here. Consider that you have been driven by your own quest for something more, something beyond the limits of your own knowledge. It is your belief in reaching beyond your own limitations that makes you the chosen, each of you in his own way!" Taking a deep breath, he added. "If it is further proof that you need Mister Severson, the message on the coin will be proof enough, after I have gone!"

"Then what is the meaning of the information that the coin will give us? What is this information that will release us from the boundries of this world? Can you tell me that now?" Michael insisted.

"That all knowledge exists. It has been there from the Great Beginning! If it is not known, than it has simply not been discerned! I have given you the key to that knowledge. It is on that coin! I will tell you something from a scientific point of view that you *will* understand! Once you realize that all particles are linked and have an effect on one another, even unto the far reaches of the universe, then you will know how I have been able to travel! And you will be able to project yourself as well, through space and time, by using that connection."

Michael Severson pondered the coin he held in his hand. "All that is right here?" He asked.

"It is," Daniel told him. "It is the link that will take you beyond the stars, but not until you are ready!"

"Than you have been here before?" White Horse asked.

"Yes. I came to monitor the progress on this planet. That's when I was greeted by the Ancient Ones, as you call them. They were a kind and gentle people. They treated me well, so I left them this gift. I taught them how to use it to travel between worlds. And I also knew that someday I would return. I hoped it would be kept in the right hands until that time! It was!"

"How did you live so long?" The old man asked him in a trembling voice, with an inquisitive expression.

Viewing them with mindful consideration, Daniel said, "I come from the oldest civilization known to exist in this galaxy! We are not many now, but we live long! We have evolved through all the periods that younger civilizations, such as your own, are now experiencing. And we have gone far beyond our cradle of life, our mother planet. We reached out for greater knowledge and perfection. We have made the ascent from the physical existence, to that of an integrated consciousness. It gives us great strength! Someday your own kind will join us, *if* you are able to make the transition to a universal society. Even races that are only a few thousand years older than your own have done so!" There was a symbiotic overtone to his speech. He addressed them from a place of eons of evolution, far beyond the beginning of his own kind.

Zachary had listened intently, and one question kept cropping up in his mind. "Will you die?"

"This body is borrowed matter, it is deteriorating, and I will have to abandon it, but my intelligence will never die! It is that energy that you consider spirit! As an entity, of course, we are always connected to a higher intelligence. I will just become part of the Greater Consciousness, no longer able to transform myself on a physical level! But than, I'm tiring of it anyway! I have no desire to repeat this transformation again! There will be another who will take my place!" Daniel told them.

Lone Coyote had not spoken, he had listened attentively. "Where is your enemy, this Dark One that you speak of? How will you know how to find him?" He asked.

"He is looking for me!" Daniel told them. "And he will find me! But not before I've completed my task,...........then I will leave!" His face took on a distant expression, as if he had projected himself into the future. Then he added. "He's not someone you would suspect! Someone here has already spoken to him! He disguises himself very well!"

Some of them took on puzzled expressions. They looked at one another, pondering who it could have been. Then Zachary said, "That could mean any one of us! Do you know in particular who has spoken to him?"

"It is difficult for me to know. I'm tired, and my energy is waning. But I know someone has had contact with him. I can sense his essence!"

Deliberating over the question, Zachary placed a hand to his forehead, he rubbed it thoughtfully. He looked as though he had a notion regarding the identity of the Dark One. "Could it be Jack McCloud?" He asked Daniel. "He was looking for you! I know he was, because he came to my house night before last askin' me to take him to you!"

"His motivation was a selfish one!" Daniel responded. "But he's not the one! The one that the Dark One controls is well protected!"

Tracy Baldwin had another thought concerning the outcome of this confrontation. "What if *he* wins? What will happen then?"

White Horse knew the answer all too well. He understood the two forces on a spiritual level. These were the same forces he had discussed with Zachary, and the possible outcome, too! But now, he was anxious to hear the details of it himself. More than anything, he wanted to know how this dark force could be defeated. He valued the ways of his people. Although they were changing, they still held on to their traditional beliefs, and it had made the Navajo Nation strong. He wanted his people to survive and prosper, and he would do anything to see that their future was assured.

"Yes," White Horse asked, what will happen?"

From the end of the table, he peered at them earnestly with the penetrating blue eyes that commanded their attention. He had a cold, factual look about him and he spoke in sonorous tones. "If the Dark One is allowed to take control, the history of your planet will be written as an epitaph, much like that of my own!" Daniel took the coffee pot from the side of the table and filled his cup, then he offered it to White Horse who sat on his right.

"This is a long story, but an important one!" He told them. "So listen carefully! I'll tell you the history of another civilization like your own! Then you can decide what you want to do about it!"

"It is a story about my own planet of origin! It was similar to yours in some ways, so I've been told! I'm far removed from the generations that inhabited the planet, by thousands of years! So I can only tell you what I know of its history!"

"They say it was a beautiful water planet, rare among worlds throughout the galaxy. It had lush vegetation, and clean air and water. It was said to have been a virtual paradise, a glimmering oasis in its solar system! There were many bright stars visible in the night sky! And we had seven moons, although not all of them were visible at one time, four could be seen in various stages! They say it was magnificent!" Daniel spoke as though he had a picture of it implanted firmly in his mind

Michael Severson interrupted. "Than that is what the picture represents on the coin! It's your planet of origin, isn't it!"

"That's correct!" Daniel told him. "It is there so that we will never forget where we came from, and where we are going!"

"But to return to the story! Over thousands of years our society grew from bands and tribes, into more complex social groups. Along the way we had wars and power struggles, much like your own kind. It was mainly over resources, very much like what is happening here on your Earth now! It didn't impair the ecosystem of our planet while our weapons were primitive, and our consumption of resources remained at a moderate level. But as our technological capability grew, we started to poison our own environment!"

"After only two hundred of your Earth years, we had done irreversible damage! But it didn't stop there! Our people seemed determined to squeeze every ounce of life out of our planet. Even after we were warned by our finest scientific minds about our impending doom, we went on with the rape of our planet. We contaminated our fresh water supplies, and our air became polluted. Voices cried out for change, but were silenced in the clamor of greed and destruction. War after war broke out. Vast regions of our planet suffered in poverty and sickness, while others prospered from their misery. Greater weapons of destruction were unleashed on large populations, to keep them from rising up! Our atmosphere started to change! Our vast agricultural areas turned into dust bowls. Through overuse of irrigation, we depleted the last of our subterranean fresh water supply, until mud and silt was the only thing we could pump from the bowels of the planet! Winters were shorter, and summers became hot and unbearable. The global winds carried black rain around the planet, coating everything with the foul emissions we had dumped into the atmosphere!"

"There was growing discontent in our areas of large population. Crime and violence ran rampant. Our governments were losing control of the masses! So they formed coalitions to deal with the rising unrest. There was an inequitable distribution of goods. Our technologies were changing so rapidly, that our average citizens weren't able to keep up! Soon the skills of the majority of our population were obsolete! We had built so many machines to do our work, that great numbers of our population were unemployed."

"We had an enormous overpopulation that drained our dwindling resources! Our water was polluted with toxins, and our air was full of harmful pollutants and trace metals. New wars broke out over the remaining resources! Biological weapons were unleashed on the planet, rendering entire continents lifeless!"

"While all of this was occurring, a group of our scientists, who had warned of the coming catastrophe, were preparing to leave the planet. They had used our technology for a more beneficial purpose. Their plan was to colonize some of our moons, from which the best of our race would be able to reach out toward the distant stars and planets. They were the visionaries! The dreamers!"

"Shuttles were built to take technicians and equipment to sites on the moons, where colonies would be established! While the general population digressed in apathy, new civilizations were started for a selected segment of our society! It wasn't the wealthy or the powerful, but those who believed in a higher purpose for our kind! While our planet became increasingly unfit for habitation, they gathered many of the great minds on the planet together to populate the colonies."

"In the days before the Great Holocaust, there were power struggles among the remaining leaders of government. One great powermonger emerged from among them to take control of the entire planet! Finally, all the stores of horrible, destructive power were unleashed on the planet! A thermonuclear holocaust of indescribable proportions had taken place! All that was left were the dead and the dying! Burned out shells of cities stood smoldering, while roving bands of pathetic mutations wandered the wastelands, living off of the remains. The planet had been reduced to a burning cinder, unfit for habitation!"

The mood among them was somber. They sat quiet and reflective as Daniel continued to speak. "I heard it said once, that my mother planet was a pearl in a sea of stars! I never got to see her! It has been five millenniums since the Great Holocaust! And my kind have colonized their way across the galaxy, but we have never forgotten where we came from! We have told our story so that generations will never forget! We have traveled hundreds of thousands of lightyears, and had never found anything like it, until we came upon your planet Earth! Another pearl in a sea of stars!"

With a look of assurance, he said, "You are not alone! The universe is not a stagnant, dead pool! It is an ocean, teeming with life! And the same dualities exist throughout it!"

White Horse could see that the Ancients, and his own people, were much closer to the Great Truth in their understanding of the universe, and their place within it. That they were indeed brothers and sisters of the stars, and all that exists! It gave him a great sense of peace to know that his own people walked the Beauty Way.

They talked for hours further, asking questions about his race and all that they had encountered throughout the centuries of exploration. He amazed them with accounts of young and old civilizations. And his encounter with the dark force that plagued each of these worlds. They also talked about the *one* that he had dedicated his energy to oppose, the Dark One!

Daniel made it clear to them that he was leaving them with this information, and that it was up to them to use it in the best way. They would have to take what they knew, and the information on the coin, and use it with their influence to promote changes. He assured Michael Severson that the equation on the coin would be applied to the known physical laws of subatomic particles, and that it would provide a revelation to the scientific world regarding them.

"Why us?" Michael Severson asked. "Why not make contact with world leaders? With the U.N.? Why a handful of people in a remote corner of a sparsely populated, desolate country? Couldn't you have made your point more dramatically, another way?"

Daniel was amused, he smiled. "Did you want a fleet of spaceships to land on the lawn of your nation's Capitol? We are not an intrusive race! A show of force has never been our intent! It's what your kind might expect, though! Our only intention is to offer knowledge! To assist your kind in making a transition. We would never force anything upon you!" He paused. "I know that you are a scientist, Michael, an astronomer. You have been looking to the heavens, hoping to learn from them! And that is good! But now you must also look into the faces of strangers! You never know who they might be!"

"I have no doubt that I will do that, after today!" Michael assured him.

In the late hours, before midnight, they discussed how they would help Daniel get back to where he needed to be in order to leave, before he was found by the soldier of the one that he so vehemently opposed. It meant that they would have to go out in the morning to recover the jeep, take some gas to get it started, then take Daniel back to the canyon where he would be able to make his departure. They understood that it was imperative that he leave soon.

"We'll need the battery from your truck, Lone Coyote," Zachary told him. "I doubt that the road will be cleared by morning, so we won't be able to drive to the location of the jeep! We're going to have to walk! We'll have to carry the battery and some gas! Once we get to the jeep, we'll know whether the road has been cleared up to that point! If it hasn't, we'll have to decide then whether to risk traveling or wait! It will be up to Daniel to decide."

A sudden thought had racked Tracy Baldwin with a feeling of apprehension. "Someone from the university has probably tried to reach me today, when I failed to call in! If they don't hear from me tomorrow, I know someone is going to get suspicious! And I know Michael has the same problem! If only there was a phone here! We could at least call and make up some sort of an excuse because of the storm! But the roads around Flagstaff will have been cleared by now!"

"Yes," Michael said. "She's right! Something else crossed my mind, too! The plane that flew over today! You don't suppose that they would report a stranded vehicle, do you?"

He had left it open for anyone to comment on, but Zachary confirmed his reason for concern. "If they spotted it, they definitely will report it! They would report anything that looked like someone was stranded. There could even be an air search by tomorrow!"

Chapter 31

Of Life, Death and Truth

AT THE HOSPITAL, LATE THE FOLLOWING MORNING, LEMUEL Redfeather confronted the doctor concerning Jack McCloud's upgraded condition.

"If you insist, Mister Redfeather!" The doctor told him. "But please don't agitate him! He's still in serious condition! I don't want him to be put under any stress right now!"

Lemuel considered the doctor impatiently. "I've known Jack McCloud for many years, Doctor! We've been friends since childhood. I certainly wouldn't do anything to upset him! I just want to know what happened out there! It's my job!" He insisted.

"And taking care of my patient is mine!" The doctor said peevishly. "I'm also concerned about the well being of Misses McCloud! She's been under an enormous amount of stress! I certainly wouldn't want to see her upset in any way!"

"I can understand that, too, Doctor! Believe me, that's the last thing I would want to do!" Lemuel started to relax his aggressive posture. "I was the best man at their wedding! I've known both of them for years! Please don't worry! I only want to ask Jack a few questions. That's all! I'll ask Tessa to leave the room for a few minutes,............to get some coffee, while I talk to Jack, so she won't be involved or upset by it!"

"Please make it brief!" The doctor relented, still displaying the furrowed brow of annoyance. The gray-headed, distinguished looking cardiologist stepped around Lemuel Redfeather in the hallway. "I've got to see some other patients!" He said in a curt tone, with a quick glance over his shoulder as he strode away down the hall.

Lemuel was left standing in the middle of the corridor, outside the closed door of the room where Jack McCloud lie convalescing from an almost fatal heart attack. He hesitated for a moment, straightening his tie before he started for the door. He poised himself to meet Tessa McCloud in an unobtrusive manner, before he knocked lightly. She had been friends with his late wife. He didn't want to cause her any discomfort, if it was at all possible.

"Tessa!" He said in a shallow voice. He parted the door slightly. "It's Lemuel! Can I come in?" He swallowed hard, awaiting her reply. He was anxious.

Reaching the door, she pulled it open slowly and quietly. She answered in a near whisper, "Come in Lemuel. Jack's been in and out of sleep all morning, but he's awake now. I'm sure he'd be glad to see you!"

The same rhythmic beep emanated from the heart monitor. Each synchronized cycle represented another second of life. It meant that a life continued for that particular epoch of time. Until the next one! Somehow it had always been taken for granted that the next one would come, at least by those who heard its continuous audible blip, until their aural perception ignored its mundane consistency. But if it stopped, they would notice!

Tessa moved back from the door, allowing Lemuel to enter. He stepped into the room. Then he reached for her to give her a hug. "How's that sturdy bull doing?" He asked her, holding her close for a brief moment. He patted her back.

"He's been able to talk. Just a little, of course! He told me he was cold, so I asked the nurse to get him another blanket," Tessa said, looking over at the pale specter that was her husband.

The window shades were drawn, immersing the room in a frail light. The room bore an aura of limbo, a place between finite life and infinite death. Jack lie there, quietly breathing on his own. His eyes were open, and they appeared recalcitrant. It looked to Lemuel as though Jack was staring at him, as he stood at the foot of the bed with Tessa, who held his arm.

"Tessa, I'd like to talk to Jack alone," Lemuel said. "Do you think you could leave us for a few minutes? I'll take good care of him while you're getting yourself some coffee!"

"Sure. I suppose it would be all right." She was reluctant. "I really haven't eaten very much in the last few days! I think I'll go have a bite to eat. I'm sure I'll feel better!" She turned toward the door, then hesitated. "I won't be gone long!"

Lemuel's eyes were fixed on those of his long-time friend. He saw something there that he hadn't seen before, his own mortality. He stood there for a long moment. Then he walked around the end of the bed to Jack's side, and stood over him.

"Jack,...........how are you doing?" Lemuel asked him in a solicitous tone.

He replied in a weak but audible voice. "Not too well..............my friend,............not too well." Jack McCloud looked up at Lemuel Redfeather with knowing eyes. They were eyes that revealed the truth. It was the truth that Lemuel had suspected, and the truth that Jack McCloud knew for certain would finish him.

"Why Jack? Why were you out there? I have to know!"

Jack McCloud began to take laboriously deep breaths. "He was the only one who knew,............I wanted to silence him! He would have ruined everything, ...everything that I've built!" He paused. His eyes began to water.

"Why did you do it, Jack?" Lemuel asked him, already regreting that he had to ask. A bitterness welled up in his throat. "Why did you kill them? What was worth it, Jack?" Lemuel felt angry, bitter, and sad all at once.

Tears were streaming down the side of Jack McCloud's face. He looked away from his friend. He stared straight ahead. "We had a good thing going for almost three years. I kept my back turned, while they did business! I knew who they were dealing to! I thought nobody was getting hurt! The people they were supplying would have gone off the reservation for it anyway! When the heat was on them in California or Nevada, they would come around here for protection and,.............and I got a piece of there business from out of state." He coughed. His breathing was becoming noticeably more strenuous. If I needed a favor, they would take care of it for me!"

Lemuel could hardly believe what he was hearing. They had known one another for almost fifty years. They had been best friends. Their wives and children had been friends, and he had never really known Jack McCloud at all! He had never known the extent of his ambition and greed. To hear this now — in this way — was as devastating to him as when he was told that his wife had committed suicide. Yet, he had to listen to it. It was part of his job.

"They promised they wouldn't deal to kids!" Jack McCloud muttered, choking on his emotion. "Then I found out that my son, Jamie, was buying from somebody in his high school. When I confronted Jamie, he told me who it was. So I checked it out myself. I stopped the kid outside of the school one day,.............and I threatened to turn him in, if he didn't tell me who was supplying him with drugs! That's when I found out! Those rotten bastards were supplying my own kid!"

His chest was rising and falling at an accelerated rate, but Lemuel Redfeather didn't notice. He was too engulfed in the tragedy that had unfolded before him. He knew the rest of the story.

"So when the stranger came to town, you saw an opportunity to get rid of them. To get them out of your life! And you could make it look like an outsider did it!" Lemuel paused. He looked away from the pitiful sight that lie in front of him. He shook his head grudgingly.

"Yes,.............that's it! That's it, Lemuel! That stranger,.............I thought he would just go away! But you were so determined to find him. I knew it wouldn't be over,............unless he was gone, too! But than it never would've been over,...............would it, Lemuel?" His voice had swelled with remorse, and his eyes were contrite. "I can't tell Tessa,.............I can't,...............I"

Jack McCloud began to gasp. He was struggling to breathe. Lemuel finally noticed. He peered at Jack with an empty expression, devoid of compassion. Jack McCloud reached out to Lemuel, desperately trying to grasp onto him, to cling to perhaps, who was once, his only real friend. The heart monitor was beeping erratically. The blips on the small screen became increasingly shorter strokes. Until there was only a flat line, and the beeps had become an incessant blur of noise.

"Code blue! Code blue!" Came over the intercom. Lemuel stood there. He looked at Jack. Jack McCloud's eyes were open, but void of perception. His eyelids twitched perceptibly, but he was otherwise motionless. He had stopped breathing. His hand had fallen to the side of the bed. It hung limp. The room filled with nurses and intensive care staff. Lemuel was pushed aside, but he still stood there, looking. Thinking.

The cardiologist had been called. The staff physician and the critical care nurses worked frantically, straining to revive him. Their efforts were becoming more and more futile, as they injected him and shocked his chest over and over again. Then the physician shook his head, somberly yielding to the inevitable. Without uttering more than two words, his staff had understood the prognosis. He peered at his watch, writing down the time on the chart at the bedside. It was 12:35 p.m.. CAUSE OF DEATH: CARDIAC ARREST.

Lemuel Redfeather strode sullenly down the hall. He brushed by Tessa McCloud, who was returning to her husband's bedside. She stopped, peering at him in bewilderment, as he walked on by her dejectedly, with his eyes distant and empty. She watched him disappear around the corner, and she wondered what he and Jack could have talked about, that would make him act that way? Suddenly, she was filled with apprehension. She hurried toward the hospital personnel, that were gathered outside of the room.

Walking outside, through the automatic, glass door at the lobby entrance to the hospital, Lemuel Redfeather pulled on his overcoat. He left it unbuttoned. He paused on the concrete approach to the main entrance. The air was crisp. The sun shone bright in his eyes. He squinted. Taking his sunglasses from his vest pocket, he placed them carefully upon his face. He looked out over the parking lot, and the midday. Then he took a pack of cigarettes from his pocket. He drew one out and lit it.

It's better this way, he told himself. *I couldn't tell her anyway! Now, I'm the only one that knows for sure. There's no proof! There's no evidence! Maybe no one ever has to know? But,..............there's still the stranger!* He took a long hit from his cigarette, then he started walking toward his car.

When he returned to his office, Lemuel Redfeather received a message from Peter Morgan, who had already gone out with Sam Begay and two deputies to check on an abandoned vehicle, that was reported to have been seen some forty-five miles away, near Navajo Mountain, on the Inscription House road. It had been seen by the Air National Guard pilot and his crew as they flew over the area, checking, with field glasses, for signs of anyone who might be stranded. They reported that there was no one near the vehicle, but they had spotted a blond, young man, standing with a group of Indians in a camp where they had dropped some supplies. They assumed it must have been his vehicle, but they thought it should be checked out.

Another report had come in earlier that morning, concerning two missing people from Flagstaff, whom where thought to be in the area. A Miss Tracy Baldwin, an anthropologist who taught at the university, and an astronomer from the Lowell Observatory, Michael Severson, who also taught at the university, were reported missing. They had been last seen leaving the university parking lot together on Wednesday morning. A detailed description of them, and the vehicle that they were driving, was faxed over from the Flagstaff Police Department.

Lemuel sat at his desk, pondering the report. Slowly, pieces of information ell together in his mind. Until a phantom thought possessed him. The roublesome, unresolved dream emerged. He played out the characters in his nind. Then the scenario presented itself more clearly. Except for the man vith the gun! The one that he couldn't recognize. It was that hand that came p from between Zachary Thomas and the old crystal gazer, White Horse, hat had caused him to wonder. It was the one that bore the silver wristband vith the large turquoise stones. *"It isn't Jack McCloud,"* he thought. *At least ot now!*

But he *had* made the association between the missing anthropologist, e astronomer, Zachary Thomas and the stranger. He gave the total picture rther consideration, while he sat with his elbows poised on his desk. He rew smoke from a cigarette, deep into his lungs. It caused a warm, burning nsation inside his chest. Then he exhaled forcefully.

Peering intently over his desk, beyond the closed door of his office, with rk, thought-filled eyes, he recalled the location of the stranded jeep, and at of the lodge of White Horse.

If dreams can predict future events, than this one is well on its way to coming a reality, he told himself. *That is,.............if I believed in such nsense! But there is no one left to hold the gun! And I'm about to bag the anger! And Jack's absolution!*

He went to the radio. "Morgan,..............Begay! This is Lemuel!"

Amidst the static, came a response. "Yes, Lemuel, this is Peter Morgan! Go ahead! I hear you!"

"How's the road where you're at? Has it been cleared?"

Morgan responded. "Yes, Lemuel, as far as I can see ahead! It's hardly more than one lane, though!"

Pressing the button on the transmitter, Lemuel said, "The people you're searching for! They're harboring a fugitive!" He paused. There was silence on the other end. "When you locate them, you'll find the stranger! And Zachary Thomas!" He paused again. "Be careful! We don't want to lose him this time! Do you know where the old crystal gazer, White Horse's lodge is located?" Lemuel asked.

There was a long moment of silence, then a reply. "Yes, Lemuel, I do! What makes you think that they're out there?" Peter Morgan asked.

"It's just a hunch! But I think the old man is a friend of Zachary Thomas! It would be probable that he would try to hide the stranger out there! If the jeep is still there, proceed to the lodge of White Horse!" Lemuel told him. "Let me know as soon as you see anything! Over."

"Okay, Lemuel! Over." The radio went silent.

They had gotten a late start by the time that Zachary had removed the battery from Lone Coyote's old pickup truck, and siphoned gas to fill a five gallon gas can, that they would carry with them to the jeep. Lone Coyote had assembled a small complement of tools for Zachary to carry with him, in the event that they would need to make repairs. Ogin had prepared some food for them to take along. She packed it in Zachary's backpack.

White Horse desperately wanted to go with them. He kept insisting tha he needed to be there. The frail old man said that he sensed a bad omen "Something is waiting for you out there," he told them. His clouded eye appeared fearful. The urgency in his voice gave them cause for apprehension but they were determined to leave. They convinced him that the trek woul be too arduous for him to make, and that it would only slow them down. H agreed — although reluctantly.

Their load was cumbersome, and Michael and Zachary shared the burde of the heavy five gallon gas can, and the battery, by exchanging one for th other, to give each of them an equal opportunity to conserve energy as the trudged through the snow. Tracy Baldwin and Daniel trailed closely behin them. She toted the backpack and a container of water. Daniel had s weakened, that he was only able to sustain himself, and unable to assist b sharing the burden with them. Occasionally he would stop, resting on Tracy shoulder for moments at a time, catching his breath.

It was much warmer than the day before, and the snow was beginning melt, leaving it wet and heavy. This time it wasn't the devastating cold th impeded them, but the warmth of the midday sun, that caused them to fe the exertion beneath the burden of every step. Each of them were stifled in the heavy clothing, that they had worn three days earlier to ward off the extreme cold.

They had reached the main road, and found that it had been cleared beyond the camp. It gave them encouragement.

"The road has to be clear to the south! That's were the snowplow would've come from!" Zachary told them confidently. "We'll follow the road now. It will be easier to walk, and to carry the gas can and the battery!"

Patches of glistening, black asphalt shone through the packed, white snow where the plow had passed, baring the pavement. It had mounded large, crusted chunks of milky ice on either side of the path, that it had carved down the center of the roadway. It would reach the state line of Utah, then it would turn around and widen the swath it had made the entire length of the road, nearly fifty miles in length.

Zachary knew that. He also knew that if the snowplow returned before they had an opportunity to recover the jeep, they could be spotted by the drivers. There was usually more than one driver along on these long, mundane routes. The drivers took turns, so that each of them could take a nap to keep from dozing at the wheel. They also had a radio aboard so that they could report their progress, or any difficulty they might encounter. They were in regular contact with the highway department, and monitored by the state police for road conditions. It was very likely that they had also reported the stranded jeep.

Mulling this over in his mind, Zachary became more troubled about the prospects of them successfully returning Daniel to the stone arch. It puzzled him, though, that Daniel appeared somewhat reconciled to his fate — whatever it might be? It was almost as though he knew something was going to happen. White Horse seemed to know as well. Now Zachary, himself, could feel it!

What were his words regarding his adversary? Zachary mused. *"He's looking for me,..............and he will find me!" Out here?* He questioned himself. *Where? Another time and place? And who really is his adversary, anyway?*

They needed an hour and a half at most, and they could be well on their way. That is, if the jeep would start. Zachary looked back over his shoulder at Daniel. Michael Severson, who was walking beside him, noticed. Considering Zachary's expression, he turned his head to take a look for himself. He thought something might be wrong. Tracy and Daniel lagged almost fifty feet behind them, talking as they plodded along the roadway. The unlikely messenger from another world, appeared to be striding along steadily. Michael trained his attention back on the road ahead, silently endeavoring to carry the bulk of the lead-acid battery.

Zachary peered at the tall, lean figure he had first encountered on that cool, crisp October morning, alongside the highway some six weeks earlier. He realized that in that brief time, he had grown to consider him a good friend. *A strange friend at that!* He mused. But he had developed an unexplainable affection for what he perceived at first to be just a man, and now something more, from a distant place he knew nothing about, but could only imagine.

The jeep was in sight. "There it is, half-buried in a snowdrift!" Sam Begay bellowed hoarsely. He coughed. "Snowplow went right around it! It ain't goin' nowhere for a while!" He chuckled laboriously.

"Let's stop and take a look," Peter Morgan told Dean, the deputy who was driving. Morgan motioned toward the jeep, squinting as he caught the sun's reflection off the snowbank.

They pulled up alongside the stranded vehicle, then stopped. All four men got out of the police unit, including the deputy that rode with Sam Begay in the back seat. He was more than willing to get out and distance himself from Sam Begay, however briefly it might be, after the long arduous ride from the Kayenta station with the noisome detective.

"We oughtta get the registration, to see if it belongs to one of the two missing professors!" Sam Begay blurted. Getting out from behind the front seat, he tumbled onto the icy pavement. "Damn, slippery shit!" He cursed, bringing himself up off the road with the assistance of the young deputy, who immediately volunteered to climb over the snowdrift and crawl inside the jeep to look for the registration.

Peter Morgan stood on the road, next to the jeep, peering over the embankment of snow. Sam Begay and Dean stood next to him, awaiting a response from Carl regarding the identity of the owner.

"Look around in there, for anything else that might give us an idea o what they were doing out here!" Morgan suggested, while the deput rummaged through the glove box.

"I found it!" He shouted. "It belongs to a Miss Tracy Baldwin with a Flagstaff address. Do you want me to bring it out so you can see it?" H asked, yelling out through the open window of the jeep. He could ony see wall of snow beside him.

Peter Morgan shouted back at him. "No. That's all right!" Leave it there That's all we needed to know. The highway department will need th registration, if they have to tow it to storage until the owner can pick it up!

Sam Begay quipped. "Assuming they're not laying out there frozen unde the snow somewhere!"

"Do you see anything else?" Morgan inquired of the young man.

He rifled through the jeep, searching under the seats. Then he climbe over the seat to the back cargo area. The canvas window flap fluttered in th afternoon breeze. The tailgate had been left open. His eyes probed the corner and the crevices of the floorboards, until he observed the glint of a shiny, gold object protruding from a crack in the floor. He pried it out with his pocket knife.

"I found something else!" He yelled out from the opening in the rear of the jeep. Then he crawled out over the top of the piled snow, and slid down to his feet to meet the earnest face of Peter Morgan, who peered at him through his aviator sunglasses.

"What is it, deputy?" Morgan asked.

"This, sir!" Carl opened his clenched fist to expose a gold coin. It was the kind Peter Morgan and Sam Begay had seen before.

Taking the coin from the deputy, Morgan turned to Sam Begay. "Lemuel was right!" He tossed the coin in the palm of his hand in plain view of Begay.

Sam Begay mused heavily. He brought his thick hand across his mouth, pulling on the flaccid flesh of his jowls. "Now we have three, possibly frozen under the snow out here somewhere!"

"Possibly!" Morgan said. "Maybe four! According to Lemuel, they could've made it to the camp! If someone led them there? Even in that storm!" He ventured. "Let's go check it out!" He squeezed the coin in his hand.

"Zachary Thomas?" Begay asked.

Morgan nodded. "Yeah."

Sam Begay appeared perplexed. "I'd like to know what these coins are all about?"

Chapter 32

Judgement Day

THREE MILES FROM THE ABANDONED JEEP, THEY CRESTED A small rise in the road. They were at a disadvantage to the sun as they strode westward. But the glimmer of a reflection from the windshield glass of an oncoming vehicle was apparent. It shimmered in the waves of convection that ascended from the road, causing it to dance ominously in their sight.

Zachary halted abruptly, causing the others to stop and take notice with alarm. Only moments were available to them to make a decision. Their options were few. They could walk calmly, and hope that the vehicle would pass by without concern. Or they could stay on the road, and flag it down for assistance, thereby making it easier to get the gasoline and the battery to the jeep, and Daniel to the canyon. But Zachary thought swiftly. *It would be too risky!*

"Move quickly," he told them. "Get over that ridge of snow, and lay down flat in the ditch next to the road!"

They clambered over the crusted ridge of ice and snow. Zachary set the gas can on its side, partially burying the red container in a snowdrift. Michael dropped the battery on the lee side of the ridge of snow as he crossed over, letting it sink below the surface. Then they prostrated themselves in the swale beside the highway — waiting — waiting to hear the sound of the passing vehicle.

The high-profile tread of its tires sang on the wet pavement and slush as it came nearer. Zachary hoped that their silhouettes would be buried in the snow, and indistinguishable to the approaching car. The whir of the engine became more audible as it came closer and closer. Until a perceptible zing could be heard upon the point of its recession. And the trail of its exhaust could be seen over the top of the ridge as it disappeared.

Its sound diminished in volume to the point that Zachary felt safe enough to emerge from the snowfield. He scurried up the embankment to see that he had made the right decision. The red and blue emergency lights atop the vehicle were still within his field of vision. And the black lettering on the white van stood out boldly — Navajo Police.

Knowing the distance yet to be traveled to the jeep, he questioned in his mind whether they stood a chance of recovering the vehicle before the police van returned. He motioned to the others to join him at the top of the ridge.

"That was the police!" Zachary told them to their alarm. "I think they know where we've been! Someone must have spotted the jeep." He assessed each of them. His dark eyes flashed a deep concern. "What do you want to do? Do you want to continue?"

He looked at Daniel, who appeared weary. "Maybe we can explain enough to them, so that they might understand! Maybe they'll help us to get you where you need to be! We could just wait for them to come back!" The staunch Navajo suggested.

"They're not going to let me go, Zachary! There's more to it than that! They're not going to believe you!" Daniel said, convincingly. "It has something to do with the killing of those two men!"

Tracy and Michael looked at him with grave concern.

"It can't end this way!" Tracy declared. "Daniel is giving us a gift! An opportunity! We can be more than we had ever hoped! The future of our race may depend upon it! We just can't let him die!" She said passionately. "We owe it to him to get him back to where he came from!"

Zachary and Michael agreed.

"Let's not waste any more time!" Michael said. He picked up the gas can, and started walking in the direction of the jeep.

"Okay," Zachary said, "then we'll do it!" He took up the battery and followed.

The hood was still open on the rusted, roadweary pickup truck, when the police van pulled up alongside of it.

"Is this the hogan?" Sam Begay asked brusquely. His stomach was growling noticeably. He hadn't eaten since early that morning. It was already two o'clock in the afternoon, and he was becoming ravenous. He had already gone through a pack of gum — Peter Morgan's — and he was getting nervous and irritable.

"I think so," Peter Morgan replied.

"Damn it! I hope they're here!" Begay groused from the back seat of the van.

Peter Morgan got out of the van and started toward the door of the lodge, when an old man came out to meet him. It was Lone Coyote. "What do you want here?" His quavery voice inquired. The slight, aged Indian met the police captain with dauntless eyes.

He removed his sunglasses to meet the old man's steady gaze, with an unyielding expression. "I understand you have some guests here," Peter Morgan stated, cunningly.

"We've had many guests in our lodge! Which ones do you speak of?" Lone Coyote asked him coyly.

Ogin, the wily old Navajo woman, peeked from behind the door. She was watching the other men who stood outside of the truck, behind Peter Morgan and Lone Coyote. To her eyes, they were a surly looking lot of young Navajos. She thought them too damn pompous looking to be respectable Indians. *But the fat one,* she thought, *he's just too disrespectful looking!* She would have just as soon taken a broomstick to him!

"There are some Anglo people who were lost in the snow storm several days ago. We're just trying to find them! We hope that they are still alive? Do you know where they are?" Peter Morgan asked him.

"We haven't seen anyone like that out here!" Lone Coyote told him. "It's just me and my wife, Ogin, over there!" He said, nodding toward the old woman in the doorway. "And my father, White Horse! That's all! You can see for yourself, if you want! You're welcome to come inside!"

"What about Zachary Thomas? Has he been out here to visit you recently?" Morgan asked.

Lone Coyote measured him for a brief moment. Squinting slightly, he replied, "Not for a couple weeks. He was out here for a sing! But that was a while ago!"

Turning to his men, Peter Morgan gestured to them to get back into the van. "Sorry we bothered you, sir!" He told the old man. He put his sunglasses back over his eyes. Then he looked over at the pickup truck. "Something wrong with your truck?" He asked Lone Coyote.

"Oh,............it needs a new battery! It wouldn't start this morning!" The tempered old man told him.

"I see," Morgan said flatly.

He strode back to the police van. Getting inside, Peter Morgan said to the others, "They were here! My guess is they took the battery out of that truck, hoping to start the jeep with it! But we didn't pass them on the way! They could be traveling off of the main road to avoid observation!"

"That'd be doin' it the hard way!" Sam Begay bellowed hoarsely. "They'd hav'ta be carryin' that lead battery! Damn things are heavy! And they're not going ta get that jeep freed up real soon! Even if they got to it right after we left it!" He asserted in his raucous voice. Then he coughed. "I don't know about you, but I'm gettin' hungry!"

"We're all hungry, Sam!" Morgan told him. "But there are no restaurants within fifty miles of here! We're just going to have to wait until we've taken care of our business. We'd better get back to that jeep!"

When they were near enough, they saw that the jeep was buried in a snowdrift. They stopped within a hundred yards of it, to look upon it in desperation.

"Even if we can get it started, we'll never dig it out in time!" Michael Severson said in a tone of severe frustration. Lowering the gas can to the pavement, it smacked loudly when the weight of it met the hard surface. He gulped large breaths of air, trying to recover from the arduous trek.

"Look!" Zachary told them impatiently. "This battery is getting heavier by the minute! And I'm not going to put it down here! So let's get down there, and we'll take our chances. We can dig out the jeep!"

They began to move decisively. Zachary opened the hood of the jeep, and with the few tools he had, he removed the dead battery and replaced it with the one from Lone Coyote's truck. Michael emptied the contents of the five gallon gas can into the gas tank, saving a small amount to prime the carburetor. With a small shovel that she carried in the back of the jeep, Tracy dug frantically, tossing snow away from the side of the jeep nearest the pavement. Daniel helped her, straining to move the large chunks of snow with his hands, and trying to gauge his energy at the same time.

Michael Severson poured from the gas can, what seemed to be less than an ounce of gasoline, into the bowl of the carburetor. Turning the ignition key, Zachary pumped the gas pedal vigorously. The engine gave out a long, loud groan. Then it cranked over in several rapid bursts, until it backfired and chugged plaintively. It began a rough idle. Zachary pumped the gas lightly again, clearing the rough combustion to a smooth reverberation.

Tracy smiled a large smile of relief, as the black smoke cleared away from the rear of the jeep. "We *can* make it! We just have to get a little more of this snow cleared away!"

While the engine of the jeep roared to a warm, steady idle, each of them dug, carving snow away with both hands, until an uneven path was cleared away from the front of the jeep to the pavement. It appeared that their escape was imminent, as Zachary rocked the jeep loose from its icy bedding, freeing it with the four-wheel-drive. It crawled onto the highway in low gear. After unlocking the hubs, to disengage the four-wheel-drive, the others got in quickly. They sped southward.

"We have less than five gallons of gasoline! It will get us there, if we don't have to use the four-wheel-drive again!" Zachary informed them. "That means we can't go back into the canyon the same way! We've got to follow the Inscription House road back to the Shonto turnoff, to get back into the Betatakin Canyon!"

The road had been cleared to two full lanes as they neared the Shonto turn off. Michael and Tracy kept a vigilant eye to the backroad in watch for the police van. It appeared possible that they had gotten a significant lead on the police. They could only attribute this to, perhaps, some diversion by Lone Coyote that may have led the police astray. At least this is what they wished to believe, whether it was true or not.

But as they reached the tee in the road at the Shonto turn off, it became apparent that they had only delayed the inevitable. Flashing lights, a police barricade, and Lemuel Redfeather awaited them. And in pursuit was the police van with Peter Morgan and Sam Begay, who had called ahead to alert Lemuel Redfeather. The stranger was within his grasp, and he wasn't about to let go!

"It's over!" Zachary relented as he slowed the jeep, approaching the blockade with apprehension. "Now we'll have to do it their way!"

They came to a stop, about one hundred feet from the two police cruisers that blocked the road diagonally, with armed deputies pointing the barrels of shotguns over the hoods of the vehicles, directly at the windshield of the jeep.

One portentous figure augured perceptibly from the rest. He raised a bullhorn, and with it, he commanded in a tone of obtrusive ire, "GET OUT OF THE VEHICLE WITH YOUR HANDS OVER YOUR HEADS! NOW!!! OR WE'LL OPEN FIRE!" There was no capacity for doubt regarding the sincerity of his threat. He had been strung out to the limits of his ability to cope, and he made it audible. There was also no reason to believe that his deputies would do otherwise than to carry out his command.

They did it! They got out of the jeep, carefully, so as not to give the slightest indication that they would possibly resist. Zachary stood alone on the driver's side of the jeep in the bright sun, squinting at the sight of flashing chrome badges, and shiny, blued gun muzzles, with his hands planted firmly on top of his head. It reminded him of the last time he had been arrested by a deputy who held a shotgun to his midsection. But this time there were more than a dozen.

Tracy, Michael, and the tall, bearded, white haired stranger with steeled blue eyes, who stood in front of them, stood in dire trepidation over the scene that played out before them. The air was deadly silent with the tension that balanced precariously, and irretrievably, on the edge of a violent chain reaction, that could be initiated by the slightest precipitated movement.

The police van pulled up behind them. Its brakes screeched a long, drawn, unnerving shrill sound. Footsteps crunched starkly, cautiously, behind them, until they could feel the hot breath of contempt pouring down their necks. And in front of them, a man with a seriously grudging face, who approached them with deliberate steps, and a .38 caliber pistol drawn on The One of

Many Faces who, at long last, stood before him.

Until they were face to face, and the eyes of each met in a frenzy of muted inquiry. And the right hand of the man that held the gun, twitched perceptibly with the unraveled nerves that ensued him upon the culmination of the hunt! That, and a disheveled temperament were threatening to unload six rounds into the figure who promised to eradicate the memories of a lifelong relationship — the way he had wished it to remain! And for that alone, he held contempt for this intrusive figure. At least he considered it for a quick moment!

"Who the hell are you, anyway?" His voice cracked with tension, and roiled of anguish, as he leered at the improbable nemesis that loomed before him.

Daniel answered with a calming resonance, indicative of his manner. "I'm just a stranger, a visitor."

"I think you're more than that!" Lemuel said flatly. "I think you're responsible for the deaths of three people! One who I knew very well! And I don't think that you'll ever leave this reservation! At least not alive anyway!" He breathed deeply, and exhaustedly. "Cuff them and bring them down to the Kayenta Station!" Lemuel Redfeather told his deputies.

Daniel looked upon him with the quiet eyes of assessment, as one would measure an adversary.

Another pickup truck converged on the scene from the north. It contained Carl Chee Thatchman, who had visited the lodge of White Horse shortly after the Navajo Police had been there. When Lone Coyote told him about the circumstances surrounding the stranger, Daniel, and the plight of Zachary and the two Anglos, who had brought him to their lodge, he agreed to take both Lone Coyote and White Horse to find them. They knew that Zachary and the others would have difficulty convincing the police of their story concerning Daniel, and they were willing to intercede in whatever way possible.

White Horse had gone as far as to bring along the coin he had guarded for so many years. *He would tell the story of the coin's origin,* he thought. *It would certainly have to convince them that he, The One of Many Faces, was not an ordinary man, that he must be released so as not to interfere with powers much greater than their own.*

They had arrived in time to watch from a distance, while the four were taken into custody by the Navajo Police. Lone Coyote recognized the one with the dark glasses, who had peered at him with cool, unrelenting eyes. He mused to himself over the true nature of that man. Most he could unravel with little difficulty. But there was a miry depth to this one's inner self, that would not surface so easily.

In Kayenta, at the District Station, the four of them had been booked: one for murder, and the other three for aiding and abetting a criminal, and for obstruction of justice. At this point the prosecuting attorney was more than willing to make a motion to hold them over for arraignment, pending trial. He wished to dispose of the case promptly, as much so as Lemuel Redfeather. The longer it went unresolved, the more opportunity there would be for a jurisdictional dispute. However, Lemuel Redfeather already knew that it was inevitable. And the arrest of the Anglo professors was enough to stir up too much unwanted publicity, the kind that would ultimately evoke an investigation by outside agencies. He also knew that it could focus attention on the stranger, and the circumstances surrounding the death of Jack McCloud. He would avoid this controversy at all cost! Even if it meant creating a fortuitous ending for the stranger. He was convinced that he was prepared to do that!

Tracy Baldwin made two phone calls: one to Rita Collins, her long time friend and attorney, and the other she made to someone else, someone she had counseled with in the past. It was Reverend Tanner. She briefly explained the circumstances that had gotten her involved in this situation, and she expressed her belief that the stranger was innocent. She told him that the stranger was the man she had been talking about when she visited his office. He was quiet and reserved over the phone, but he indicated his concern for her and the fate of such a prominent extraterrestrial visitor. Regardless of his reservations involving her story about the stranger, he told her he felt compelled to support her in any way he could. He agreed to be present at the arraignment proceedings the following morning.

The news of the arrests had spread across the Navajo Nation with a swift breath. The Kayenta District Courtroom was full by nine o'clock the following morning. A throng of people waited outside, anxious to hear whether a Navajo man would be held over for the murders. Or, if only the stranger and the Anglos would be held for the murders. Members of the news media represented more than a third of the people present in the courtroom. Local, as well as national news syndications had received word of the arrests. The presiding judge was expected to arrive at any moment, to hear charges against the accused.

They were all present that morning. Michael Severson, Tracy Baldwin, Zachary Thomas and Daniel were seated in the front row with the attorney, Rita Collins. They were under heavy guard. Lone Coyote, White Horse, and Carl Chee Thatchman sat together, several rows behind them. At the back of the room stood Sam Begay, Lemuel Redfeather and Peter Morgan, and two deputies at the door to turn away the overflow of curiosity seekers, who tried to enter the already packed courtroom. One of the deputies was Dean, the one who had arrested Zachary Thomas the first time, at the stone arch.

There was someone else, Lemuel Redfeather noted as he scanned the crowded room. Sitting in the third row, directly behind Tracy Baldwin, was an Anglo man he had not seen before. He peered curiously at the back of the man's grayed head, and his stiff white collar protruding from a blue-gray, pinstriped suit jacket. He wished that the man would turn around so that he could see his face. Lemuel surmised, by the stiffness of his collar, and also his posture, that he was a clergyman. And he supposed further that the man was there to give moral support to one of the accused. He wondered which one?

The Navajo judge entered the courtroom. The room was tumult with scattered conversations and murmurs. Announcing the judge, the bailiff requested quiet in the courtroom. Gradually, the sounds subsided into an attentive silence. Until only the sporadic coughs, cleared throats, and clicking pens, could be heard. A reporter near the back of the room attempted to get up and snap a picture of the proceedings, but was subdued by one of the deputies. Heads turned to view the disruption, then quickly turned their attention to the judge who pounded his gavel strenuously, bringing order back to the courtroom.

"Court is in session," he said. "This is a preliminary hearing to decide whether those accused should be held over for criminal prosecution! Each charge will be adjudicated as to its legality on the basis of the evidence set before this court," he said in an authoritative manner. Then he added. "The prosecutor will please present the formal charges brought against each of the individuals named in this motion," the judge stated, expeditiously.

Rita Collins knew the case well. She knew that regardless of the obscure circumstances surrounding the presence of the stranger, Daniel, there was no evidence that actually linked him to the murders. Sensing that the prosecution was grasping at straws in order to hastily dispatch the case, she was determined to have it dismissed. When it was her turn to present her arguments regarding the disposition of the motion, she motioned for a dismissal on the grounds of insufficient evidence.

And as expeditiously as he had presided over the hearing, the Navajo judge concluded that there *was not* sufficient evidence to hold the stranger on the charge of murder. He further concluded, "There was no intent on the part of the other parties to harbor or abet a criminal, or to obstruct justice." Lemuel Redfeather and the prosecutor had failed to make a case on the tendrils of evidence that they had presented.

The courtroom erupted into hysteria upon the motion of the judge to dismiss. Lemuel Redfeather, who had been sitting in the last row on the isle, brought himself up from his seat in a languid motion, with a long measure of all that this decision implied for him in the months ahead. He was sullen. Vagrant thoughts crowded his mind, as he stood listless, and oblivious to the scene that was taking place before him.

Then the apparitions of a dream began to assemble in his mind, as the crowd dispersed. It left him with a clear view of the the people who stood at the front of the room. He moved toward them, with an overwhelming feeling of fatalism, and a deeply hightened sensation of being sucked through a funnel of time in suspended animation. An unwilling participant being swept along in a tide of convergence that would reconcile the requirements of this time and place, he would fill a void in history, that would otherwise go unoccupied for eternity. And there was nothing he could do to stop it!

Behind him, and following him to his right, was Sam Begay. The tall, slim stranger, with the unusual eyes that troubled him, was standing at the head of the isle to his left. The room was still somewhat crowded, but he could make out the others. Rita Collins was standing beside the stranger. They were watching him come down the isle. Directly ahead of him stood Zachary Thomas and the Anglo woman, Tracy Baldwin. They were peering at the stranger as their lips mimicked words that were inaudible to him. The astronomer, Michael Severson, stood to the right of Zachary Thomas, just behind White Horse, the crystal gazer. Slightly out of range of his peripheral vision, to the far right, was Carl Chee Thatchman and Lone Coyote.

When he was within ten feet of the stranger, whose eyes drew his attention again, something happened. It was a cue. He knew what was going to happen next, and he could only participate. There was no going back now! His hand was inside his vest, reaching for his revolver, as he heard someone call out.

"Look out! Look out!" The young deputy cried out. It was Dean, off to his right and a few feet ahead of him, who drew his attention to the man who pushed between Zachary Thomas and White Horse, raising a gun and pointing it in the direction of the stranger.

In what appeared to be fractions of a second, the man was in clear view. Reflexively, Lemuel Redfeather slipped the revolver from the vest holster under his coat. And before the man was able to take aim, Lemuel Redfeather bore down on him with three decisive shots that rang throughout the courtroom in resounding reverberations. Until the sound dissipated at precisely the moment that the gunman collapsed to the floor.

It had happened just the way he had dreamt it! Lemuel Redfeather stood gelid, with his gun still in his hand. It hung limp, pointed at the floor, over the body of the man who wore the blue-gray, pinstriped suit with the black vest and the white clerical collar.

"Who is he?" Someone asked. Another voice said, "I think he's a priest!"

The others were beginning to thaw from their terrified amazement, at what they had just witnessed. Detective Sam Begay and the deputy, Dean, stooped to assess the condition of the wounded man, that lay face down on the floor in front of them. Dean quickly recovered the revolver that was on the floor, only a few inches away from the man's hand. Sam Begay rolled him over, carefully, taking his pulse. And noticing the silver wristband with the large turquoise stones, he looked up at Lemuel Redfeather with a substantiating expression, and somber eyes of inquiry.

"He's still alive! Does anybody know him?" Sam queried, as his eyes searched the crowd gathered around him.

Until Tracy Baldwin, who was gasping with astonishment, was able to articulate. "It's Reverend Tanner! I know him! He............. I thought he was a friend!" Her voice trembled. Tears streamed down her face as she leaned over to take a closer look at the man who she had regarded as a symbol of trust.

Peter Morgan walked up behind Lemuel Redfeather. He placed his left hand on Lemuel's right shoulder. Keeping it there firmly, and supportively, with his right hand he grabbed hold of the revolver that dangled precariously from Lemuel's right hand.

"Someone better call an ambulance," Lemuel muttered.

"It's already taken care of!" Peter Morgan told him reassuringly, from over his shoulder.

With a handkerchief, Sam Begay applied pressure to the abdominal wound that was bleeding the most profusely. He looked again at Lemuel Redfeather with an empathetic expression, while they waited for the paramedics to arrive. Lemuel stood lithe; he peered back introspectively.

Supporting the Reverend Tanner's head and shoulders in his lap, to help him breath more easily, and to keep the blood from filling up his lungs, Dean said, "He's conscious!"

His eyes were open. He looked up at the faces that hovered over him. "He was going to change everything!" He muttered. "Nothing would be the same anymore!" He coughed. Blood trickled down the side of his mouth, as he strained to speak. "Don't you see..............?"

Daniel stood over him, opposite Tracy Baldwin. The Reverend Tanner's eyes found him. For an instant they were filled with detectable malice! Then his body went limp, and his head fell to one side, his eyes still open and strangely filled with malediction, as though cursing the stranger.

"Why him?" Tracy asked Daniel with a bewildered expression, and a voice pitched with emotion. "Why would *he* be the one?"

Daniel considered her thoughtfully. Then he said, "Even the most well intentioned are sometimes blinded by the obsession of their cause, Tracy! And the highest mind is as capable of treachery as the most depraved. Perhaps more so! Because he is so confident that he is right! So confident, that he opposes anything that threatens to overthrow the position that he guards most vehemently." He peered at the figure lying at his feet. "Change is feared by most! To some it is their greatest adversary!" He said, letting out a deep sigh of regret.

"Who can we trust?" Tracy asked him.

"Yourself! Trust yourself!" Daniel told her.

Epilogue

A MULTITUDE OF ONLOOKERS HAD GATHERED OUTSIDE THE courtroom. The clamor of intense speculation regarding the fallen clergyman resonated through the crowd as they stood waiting, hoping to catch a glimpse of the bloodied results of a violent act with their own eyes, to assimilate the reality of the event that had just taken place.

While the deputies were occupied with controlling the crowd outside of the courthouse, the paramedics pushed through them and into the courtroom. They moved swiftly and efficiently. But they were too late.

Detective Sam Begay and Captain Peter Morgan attended to the details of an investigation, while Superintendent Lemuel Redfeather, who was still in shock, was seated near the isle where the incident had occurred. One of the paramedics was administering to him, and inquiring as to whether or not he felt he needed medical attention for his trauma.

Except for the remaining witnesses, everyone else had been cleared from the room. Tracy Baldwin and Michael Severson stood back, away from the center of the activity where the tragic event had unfolded. Michael embraced her. He held her close, with his arm around her shoulder, while they watched the paramedics move the body onto a stretcher, after Begay and Morgan had outlined the body on the floor and taken pictures of the deceased.

Amidst the commotion, White Horse hobbled the short distance to where Daniel was standing. He moved slow and deliberate with a hitch to his gait, until he stood before The One of Many Faces.

"You'd better go now, while you have the chance!" The old crystal gazer urged him. He reached out for the stranger with his leathery, gnarled hands and, taking hold of Daniel's hand with both of his, trembling, he said, "I'm sorry to see you go! I feel like you are one of us!" The old man told him in a quavery voice, with watery eyes obscured by a veil of years. "I'm sure that you have much more to teach us!" He mused. "Perhaps another time, though!" White Horse pressed the coin that he had kept into Daniel's palm.

"Perhaps," Daniel said, with distant eyes, remembering with fondness his friends and their parting in the remote past. Then he viewed the old crystal gazer as he had once viewed the old medicine man with whom he had counseled.

Gesturing shakily, White Horse summoned Zachary. "Take him away safely!" He told him.

Carl Chee Thatchman, who had been standing nearby, tossed his keys to Zachary. "Go! Hurry! Take my pickup truck!"

They moved with discretion toward a side entrance, so as not to have their departure noticed by the others. Hastening out the door and down the side steps of the courthouse, they proceeded with stealth across the parking lot, avoiding observation by the crowd that had gathered around the main entrance. They found Carl Chee Thatchman's pickup truck. Within minutes they were out of the parking lot and onto the highway.

"Will you make it?" Zachary asked Daniel. He was concerned for the weakened condition of this specter of man, who he had seen do some extraordinary things some six weeks earlier.

"Yes. I believe I will be all right! If you get me back to the stone arch, I can leave from there! They're expecting me."

As they sped along the highway that was now only wet and covered with occasional slush, but otherwise back to two lanes, the sound of the tires running on the wet pavement emitted a soporific sound, and the warm rays of the sun intruded into the cab through the windshield of the truck. It caused a lethargy to settle upon Zachary, as he peered at the road ahead with a thoughtful look.

"Will there be others?" He asked in a sedate manner.

"There always have been!" Daniel told him with certainty.

"Is it over? Will everything be all right now?" Zachary questioned him. "Will things work out well for us, now that he's dead?"

Daniel wished that he could tell him *that* with certainty. But the answer was yet to be determined, somewhere in the future, beyond their time.

"It's never over, Zachary! There will always be others! Someone will come to replace him! And someone will come to replace me, too! The *hunt* will continue! And the war will go on!"

His brow became furrowed. "But I thought you won?" Zachary asked im with a confused expression.

"Only this time! The rest will depend upon what you and the others do ith what I have given you! How your kind uses that knowledge will etermine whether or not you will survive!" Daniel told him in earnest.

As they scudded along the road to the stone arch, the daystar was in idheaven. The snow remained in scattered patches upon the landscape, parated by dun swaths of loess soil. Red rock protruded from under white ıps of melting ice, and Kayenta sandstone buttes swelled boldly from the esert floor against the backdrop of a vivid blue sky, with scattered, fragile ouds, that drifted like delicate lace in an ethereal firmament. The sides of ıe mesas were streaked with white strips of residual snow, that spread into road skirts at the base of them. They looked like great mammoths awakening om a brief nap, from under a puny cover of white dust.

A feeling of well being pervaded them, as though things had been made ght again — at least for now. And destiny's hunger had received gratification - for the moment.

It is a world of unique qualities, the stranger mused to himself. *A world ithout comparison, to be treasured for sure! And these are unique beings ıat inhabit it! They are capable of attaining unfathomable heights of chievement, and of the highest good! Yet they are capable of the most espicable and selfish and destructive acts!*

When they reached the stone arch near the canyon, Zachary stopped the uck and they sat silent for a long moment. Each of them searched their eart and mind for the right words to express the bond that had been created etween them. They found it difficult to say farewell in a manner that was cceptable to each of them. But in the end, the unspoken words were those at said most boldly those feelings that could not be expressed in words.

"You've told us about the world that you came from, and something out the worlds that you've seen! But what is really out there, far beyond ır solar system? Beyond the stars that we take for granted in the night sky?" achary asked Daniel with an indomitable curiosity.

The star traveler looked at him with a soulful expression, and with eyes at glistened with memories of distant places, and of worlds so remote that could never hope to visit them again, but could only visualize their splendor his mind. He wished Zachary could see it, too — if only through his mind's ye.

"I'll tell you this," the star traveler said, *"There is world upon magnificent orld! And beyond that, the most beautiful music you've ever heard!"* Then raised his left hand, placing his palm over Zachary's right temple. "Close our eyes for a moment, I can give you a glimpse of it! And listen as well! ou will see and hear things that no one of your kind has ever experienced!" e told Zachary. "Or ever imagined!" He closed his eyes and concentrated the places he had been, and on the things he had seen and heard.

Zachary gasped in amazement. “Is this what we have to look forward to?”

“I hope so!” Daniel said. “I hope so!”

He got out of the truck. He held the door open and peered back at Zachary. “Remember, you’re not alone!” The star traveler told him. Then he closed the door and walked away toward the stone arch. As he climbed the stone steps and entered the arch, a wave of light subdued him. It shimmered for an instant, until he disappeared.

Dare to dream...............